# A
# POISONER'S
# TALE

# A POISONER'S TALE

CATHRYN KEMP

**UNION SQUARE & CO.**

**NEW YORK**

**UNION SQUARE & CO.**

**NEW YORK**

First published in Great Britain in 2024 by Bantam, an imprint of Penguin Random House UK.

This 2025 paperback edition published by Union Square & Co., LLC.

ISBN 978-1-4549-5746-1 (paperback)
ISBN 978-1-4549-5747-8 (e-book)

For information about custom editions, special sales, and premium purchases, please contact specialsales@unionsquareandco.com.

Printed in Canada

2 4 6 8 10 9 7 5 3 1

unionsquareandco.com

Image credits: Arcangel: ©Malgorzata Maj (woman); Shutterstock.com: AcantStudio (flourish); Lukasz Szwaj (texture) Cover design by Elizabeth Mihaltse Lindy Interior design by Rich Hazelton

For Leonardo

# PROLOGUE

## Rome, July 5, 1659

It ends with the scaffold. Five women: blindfolded, shorn, dressed in sacking, trembling before the gallows. All of us wearing our own noose, now slack, now heavy around our necks.

*The Foul Sorceress Giovanna.*
*The Treacherous Witch Graziosa.*
*The Most Wicked Temptress Maria.*
*The Devil's Whore Girolama.*

Then me, *the Poisoner of Palermo*. The woman who started it all. My ending written by the *avvisi*, the gallows pamphlets, though I am still alive, still breathing, still waiting.

For years, no man in Rome has been safe. For years, I have brewed my potion, dispensing it to the city's wives and whores. I have kept to the shadows, avoiding the Inquisition and its hawklike gaze; the guards like talons reaching into the stews and brothels of the back streets. For years, I have kept my daughter safe, my circle of poisoners too. And now, finally, our uneasy luck has run out.

Crooked from the work of the strappado we stand like five black crows, flinching. A hush descends over the crowds. I imagine stepping onto the stage, the audience awaiting my first line, the heat from the flames in their sconces making my greasepaint run. I might be Arlecchino, hunched and mute before the words tumble out of me like acrobats.

But this is no play. This is where my story finishes, amid the stench of the baying, unwashed bodies crammed into Campo de' Fiori to watch our sisterhood die in the full glare of the midday sun. Those men who scribble their salacious glee within the pamphlets do so without mention of my life or my heart. They do not know me. They do not know us. They write my tale without my consent, without my voice.

We stand, silenced. Our voices are not heard above the din of the city, the scratching of the scribes, the peal of the bells. Men who have never met us will tell our tale to those who come after. They will forget that we are flesh-and-blood women who have lived, and who now die, at the mercy of those who judge us. We are women with no future, who grasped at life on our own terms—and will now die for it.

Our secrets lie within these pages, and yet no true words will be written about us, or none by our hand. Time has run out. The crowd sways. The sun bleaches the square. The seconds die away, as the final moment approaches.

The drumbeat begins again. The prayers I am instructed to say fall silent on my lips. The rope tightens.

# PART ONE

*Extremis malis, extrema remedia*
(Extreme ills, extreme remedies)

—Latin Proverb

# 1

Palermo, Sicily, 1632

Footsteps echo across the marble floor. They come closer until the doors to my bedchamber open, revealing my mother. She seems to hesitate; then, resolved in some way, she steps forward, closing the doors behind her.

"Mamma," I say, grateful for the interruption.

My sampler lies knotted in my lap, its feeble stitches already unraveling. A lone fly buzzes in the stifling heat of late summer, taps against one of the windows.

My mother says nothing at first. I watch as she paces, waiting as her heels clack and her skirts rustle. I yawn, bored to death by the tyranny of embroidery.

"I have a secret," she says, eventually. She stops moving, turns to me, her hands folded in front of her stomacher.

There is a pause.

This I already know—or have guessed.

When the household is sleeping, I often walk the dark corridors and chambers of our villa—restless, fidgety, unable to settle into the night. Though my evening milk is warmed with lavender, I resist its soporific balm. Yawning, I rise from my bed, leaving behind the canopies, bolster, and fine linen sheets to walk in silk slippers. Sometimes, I wander into the gardens, making for the plants that are grown for their medicinal use. The sage, fennel, basil, and lemons—their scent brings me comfort. Their wild nature, hidden in plain sight in our villa, when all else is cultured or arranged, is soothing to me.

It is during many nights such as these that I have hidden in the shadows and watched Mamma leave by the servants' door. She sidles out, alone, into the Palermo night. I wait until she returns, not long before dawn, before I return to my chamber and ponder what has passed, where she has gone, what it may mean.

At Mass, I have seen her pass small glass vials of something that resembles water to women who whispered their worries so I would not hear, who exchanged knowing glances. These same women never again acknowledged us, and though I asked Mamma who they were, and what business she had with them, I was never given an answer. When I was younger, I was distracted by a sugared plum, my questions forgotten instantly. Now? Now, at the age of thirteen summers, I have stopped asking. I have other things to concern me.

Why then is she here like this?

I pull at a tangle of rose-colored yarn as I wait. For what? As the seconds pass, I am unsure if I want to find out.

"*Amore mio*, you've asked many times about a particular cure I make. I've never answered your questions, but you're old enough now to know the truth."

My heart begins to thud. My body, as if awakened from a dream, shudders to life. Suddenly, I want to be somewhere, anywhere, else but here. I think perhaps I already know my mother Teofania's secret. Suddenly, I do not want this knowledge. I half stumble to my feet, my ruined sampler peeling off my robe and tangling to the floor.

Mamma is quick. She comes to me. Holds my hands in her own. Looks up at me from where she is now kneeling while I sit back down. Our eyes meet. They are so alike. As green as the River Oreto that meanders from the mountains to the sea.

Perhaps I have known this secret for a long time. It cannot escape my notice that the women my mother helps wear widow's weeds thereafter.

"You already know, Giulia. I can see you've guessed the work I do for women who can't help themselves any other way."

"You give something bad to those women," I say. These are the first real words I have uttered since she walked in. My voice croaks. My throat feels dry when I try to swallow.

"You'll know everything tonight, my love."

The words hover over us like mosquitoes above stagnant water. Mamma's *trinzale* glows gold in the sunshine that slants through the windows. A single lock of wheat-colored hair has spilled from its delicate sheath, and I have an urge to push it, curling, behind her ear, just as she does for me. I concentrate on an unruly thread. I pull it as if that would solve things, and it breaks. Two frayed ends.

As Mamma looks up at me, I feel a strange disconnect. It is as if the room shrinks, and I start to hear a high-pitched, undulating sound. I look down to steady myself, and instead of my fine leather boots peeking out from under my skirts, I see my feet, bare and bloodied. The stench of dank water, of rot and decay, fills my nostrils and I fear I may faint. Then, the sensation of creeping cold moves through me. I want to run, to bolt like a startled horse. Just as quickly, it vanishes. My feet are once again shod in fine leather. The room is once again as it was, smelling sweetly of warm frangipani blooms and dust from the courtyard.

My mother continues to watch me.

"What have you seen?" she asks. "Is it the Sight?"

She is referring to that which we cannot grasp. A knowing without understanding. A foreboding of what may be to come. It is something she says I was born with. I cannot be sure of it. The future sighs just out of reach. Sometimes, I catch faint traces and murmurs, but they are merely that. The clarity of this latest tremor catches my breath. It is unusual, yet still I do not trust it. It may mean something or nothing at all.

"Nothing, Mamma. I'm tired," I lie through cold lips.

She drops her gaze. She stands up, placing a hand on the patterned upholstery of the chair I still sit upon. She nods, though I see she does not believe me. The spell is broken. We are as we were—mother and daughter, wife and stepdaughter—and the day must resume with useful tasks suitable for a rich merchant's household.

"When you have finished your . . . work . . . please join me in the kitchens. Valentina will need you to harvest herbs for tonight's supper. And, Giulia?"

"Yes, Mamma?" I say, wishing now that I had shared what the Sight showed me. I can feel the space between us, and it stretches out to the edges of the room where painted vases sit on walnut tables.

The silence returns. I keep my eyes downcast. I feel bereft, as if I carry a double burden. I have seen a vision, a tremulous thing, a yawning of something to come, and it frightens me.

"We must tell no one about this conversation. And tonight . . ." At this point, Mamma looks doubtful, as if she wishes to turn back and begin this scene again. Perhaps in the theater, the players may withdraw from the stage, may go back on their words, and strut and laugh at their error. This, we cannot do. We are stuck now in a story that will play out as the audience hollers, as the players snap their fingers and the characters fight and tussle.

"Tonight, I will show you how it's done."

# 2

It is late when Mamma rouses me from sleep.

Rubbing my eyes against the light from the candle, I am pale faced, caught in the place between sleep and waking. It must be close to Vigil. There is no sound anywhere, except the settling noise of the house. This velvet silence stretches only as far as the high walls that run the full length of the villa complex, from the kitchens at the far end, past the herb garden, through the empty chambers that lead off the central courtyard—all still, all hushed, all silent.

"Get up, my love. We must leave. There is work to do." Mamma's voice is barely audible.

I fumble for my robe, not thinking to disobey. With clumsy hands, I drag the heavy material over the crumpled linen of my *camicia*, pushing my arms into the slashed satin sleeves. Mamma is waiting with a cloak. She drops it onto my coverlet to turn and lace my bodice, pulling it tight in a haphazard fashion.

"Come, there's little time," she breathes.

I follow her out of my chamber. We creep down the stairs, watched only by the portraits that hang from the walls. Francesco, my stepfather, is a man without family or status to boast of, and so many of the portraits are in his likeness. His painted eyes seem to know us; each brushstroke, each daubing of thinned and mixed pigment and oil seems to follow us downward until we stop.

We pause for a moment, and I hold my breath as I see movement, a streak of ginger—the silent lope of the villa cat. He stops. Turns to stare at us with wide, unblinking amber eyes. Then, he turns his feline head and lopes his feline body off again to hunt for his supper.

I exhale.

"Where are we going?" I ask.

"Hush. You'll know soon enough but stay close to me," Mamma hisses.

We skirt the courtyard, reaching the servants' entrance, which I have never used. Without a candle, I trip. Mamma reaches for my hand as the handle turns and we are—inexplicably—outside, standing in the narrow alleyway where the great doors of the villa sit. I have never before been *outside* after dark. I have never before set foot on these hexagonal flagstones without protection from guards armed with halberds. Usually, I step straight into a carriage, one that regularly gets stuck, the alley being only just wider than its berth. These cramped streets are a mystery to me.

Sensing my disquiet, my mother nudges me forward, and we walk, every inch of me trembling.

It is black as charcoal as we make our way through deserted pathways and alleys. Here and there, we hear noises: coughing, laughing, arguing, then silence. We disturb an old woman sleeping in a doorway. She pokes her head out of a pile of rags, grumbling as we pass. Now and then, I stumble on uneven pathways.

Soon, we are standing outside a church. It is Sant'Agostino, deep in the twisting lanes of the city. I know this place. We come here by day, and by carriage, to help the lay sisters supplement their income. We come as healers and herbalists, with my stepfather's approval. The skills I have been taught by Mamma have been passed down from all our mothers—the wisdom of simple plants and simple remedies, or so I thought.

By day, Mamma and I enter through the main portal, the stone rosette above our heads. We help the nuns make tinctures and ointments to sell for income, grinding herbs and spices to make drafts and potions for common ailments: toothache, fevers, pains of the joints, and of teething babies. We make creams to soften the skin and unguents to heal bruises.

There is a side door off Via Sant'Agostina, one close by the entrance, which I have paid little heed to before. It is this entrance where a young woman stands, her head covered by her cloak. I am confused, wary. My head spins as my mother, with a silent gesture, greets this person who is a stranger to me. I scuttle behind her, wondering if they can hear the pounding of my heart.

My mother makes three gentle scratching sounds on the wood with her nails. No louder than a mouse. I cannot imagine who would hear this, but in seconds, the door opens. Inside, there is darkness. It is absolute. Then, a face appears, covered by the long black veil of a nun. The woman beckons us, and I recognize Sister Clara, who has always been kind to me. She starts when she sees me.

"Yes, Giulia is here tonight," my mother says. "Come, we must make haste before the bells for Vigil sound."

The nun, who has a plain face and is closer in years to my mother than myself, looks over my shoulder.

"Did anyone see you?" she asks as she shuts the door. It creaks on its metal hinges, then is still.

Mamma takes off her hood.

"No one followed us, Don't be alarmed, Clara. We thank you for your help. We would do nothing to endanger you further."

The cloaked woman from outside pulls off her hood, revealing her face.

"Faustina!" I cried.

My mother's assistant nods but says nothing.

"Quiet! The nuns are abed, but many do not sleep well. You must be silent," the nun says in a low voice.

We are now being ushered into the dark recesses of
Sant'Agostino convent. There is no sound except for our tread
on the stone floor. I know instantly where Clara is taking us.

In a room that leads off from the arched cloister, planted
with palm trees to give shade in the fierce heat of summer, lies
the still room. The place where medicines are made. So this is
where my mother goes when her husband lies dreaming. Suddenly, I want to stall like a horse that senses a snake coiled in the
reeds of a riverbed.

This moment is the crucible. It is the place I will return to
in my mind for the rest of my life, where all melts into alchemy,
where the tides of fate lap at my feet, and my destiny begins to
unfold. Could it have been different? Even now, I do not know.

The flagstones are cool underfoot. Apothecary jars line the
wall, containing resins, bark, plants, and spices. Recipe books,
their edges curling, sit in a pile. Then, our equipment. Glass vials,
the *alambicco* with its gourd and long neck, terracotta bowls, a
large pestle and mortar; the stuff of distillation and preparation.
Jars of vinegars, oils, and alcohol line the wooden tables.

I hang back, watch as Mamma decants water into an earthenware cauldron. Then, she takes a length of linen and winds
it around my face, covering my nose and mouth. She does not
look directly into my eyes as she works. My heart beats like the
drums on a saint's feast day.

Mamma pours small gray pellets into the water, then stop-
pers the cauldron with a lid of copper. Faustina lights the fire
underneath it, and they step back. Both turn to me.

"It's time you learned our real work, Giulia," Mamma says.

Faustina nods.

"What I'm about to tell you would see us hanged, yet it is a
risk we willingly undertake."

I swallow.

"We make something that frees women from bad marriages, or from men who hurt them," Faustina says.

"Giulia, we make poison."

As Mamma speaks, the flames leap up, orange and bright. The candle bobs, casting shadows that dance and sway. Demons, grotesque and leering, hover at the edge of the room. The devil himself slides into a corner, grimacing. Here, our business lies outside of common physick, as the shadows creep, as the bells toll, as the feral cats arch and spit. I look between my mother and her assistant, and cannot find words to reply. Soon, the metallic vapor of the lead shot fills the room. Still I have said nothing. I wonder if I will faint. The airless apothecary room, the warmth of the city night, the hellish visions: all combine to render me dizzy, unsteady; intoxicated. Head swimming, I shiver, though there is no breeze. Faustina glances over at me and smiles as I watch from a distance. She is busy with another preparation now, tendrils of birthwort to help the pains of birthing.

"Come, Giulia. Come closer," my mother says, glancing over at me.

Breathing is difficult. I see she needs my assistance, yet I cannot move. I am struck dumb with terror. Like my blood, it runs hot and liquid through my veins. And yet, there is fascination here too.

"Giulia, this is the most important of our remedies. It's the one I use only when it's absolutely required. It is a medicine to be used sparingly, and with full knowledge of the consequences."

I look over at my mother—her face bound by her own coverings, her rich skirts cloaked with a faded, stained apron, her eyes dark in the gloom. They stare at me as if they would bore into my heart and see what is written there: my failing courage, my burgeoning curiosity, my utter confusion of feelings.

"Are you afraid, daughter?"

Unsure what to say, I stall again, my throat dry, unable to pluck words from the air.

"Giulia, you should be. When my mother showed me how to make her *acqua*, I didn't want to learn. I was scared. I didn't want to face the danger, and it was only her utter conviction that we did good work—women's work—that made me learn for myself and carry on. This is why I'm teaching it to you. This is your destiny as much as it was mine."

I stare back at my mother as she turns away from me while I digest this news. We are a family of poison-makers. I hardly knew my grandmother—she died when I was young—but, of course, I knew of her skills with herbs. I did not know this was her legacy too. But is this one I want to be a part of? I could run back to the villa. I could pretend I know nothing of this. I could tell my stepfather and end this tonight. Yet I know I will not.

"But why make it, Mamma? Why do this if it's so dangerous?" I ask.

For a brief moment, she says nothing. From outside come the sounds of the night streets. A goat bleats. A baby cries. A dog barks, then falls silent.

"I have to help them, Giulia. I can't walk away from them. You, of all the young women in this city, should know this."

Me.

Of all the young women in Palermo.

"I understand, Mamma," I say. I mean to sound defiant. Instead, fear makes me sullen.

Mamma exchanges a glance with Faustina. I catch sight of her olive eyes above her face covering, her thick brown tresses swathed under the linens, the single faint line that shows when she creases her brow. I have known her for two years now. Why did she say nothing of this to me? Faustina turns back to her preparation before I can ask her. I notice a sore feeling. An injustice. Faustina knew and I did not. My mother makes something that endangers us all, and I did not know. Yet, they have brought me into their enterprise, and I am considered woman enough now to know this secret. I also recognize a strange sensation: a well of desire inside me, a thrill of something I do not yet understand.

"We have a duty to our sex, Giulia. I don't know why this is our fate, to help the abused women of this city, but it has fallen to us. Yes, it's dangerous. What else would you have us do? Nothing?"

Perhaps I should shout yes to that. Instead, I step forward, shaking.

Mamma nods. She points to the cabinet where the special ingredients are kept, its contents locked away. I am amazed when Mamma produces the key, turns it in the lock, opens the small door. She takes out a ceramic jar. Upon it is a sign, a cipher I do not recognize.

"We boil the antimony like this," she instructs, turning back to the roiling liquid. She places the jar on the table beside me.

"It seeps into the water. Careful, don't touch it. It won't kill you that way, but it's dangerous nonetheless."

As I watch her, something unfurls inside me. This is the stuff of death itself. This will be a liquid with the power to decide if a person lives or dies, a power only God can wield. I am in turn entranced, repulsed, eager. I see Mamma with new eyes. I had thought her submissive, meek even, in the presence of her husband. She is the epitome of an elegant merchant's wife. She demonstrates in everything she does that she knows her place—and yet, this. This rebellion is a secret we now share, the act that now defines us: mother and daughter, poisoner and apprentice.

It is intoxicating to me, a girl whose life is constrained by our status, a position we were not born to. When we are not required at the convent, my days are spent deciphering Latin texts, learning psalms by heart, embroidering samplers, or following my dance maestro's instruction. It is a far cry from the freedoms I enjoyed as a child, but it is a position many with empty bellies may envy.

The steam rises. The temperature, already stifling, grows suffocating. For a moment, the room swims in front of my eyes and I feel a sense of familiarity, as if I have done this before, as if I know it all already. Mamma's voice interrupts the enchantment.

"Pass me the arsenic. Don't open it. Step away from me when you've done what I ask of you."

Mamma commands me as if I am a servant girl.

As I reach for the jar of crystalline white powder, something strange happens. The thudding in my chest calms, and the panic begins to clear.

"How much do we need?" I ask. I cannot explain why I do not pass the jar to my mother.

"We need half a pound," she says. She looks at me as if seeing me anew.

I nod. I decant the powder, taking care not to spill it, into the nesting scales that sit on the scarred wooden table stained with tinctures and distillations. My hands do not tremble. Through the thick masking, I can taste the bitter metal tang as the heat does its work. I approach the seething alchemy, shaking a little now as I carry the bowl containing the powder. The candle sputters. I realize my arm is steady as I nod to Mamma to lift off the lid.

I pour the arsenic into the cauldron, as I am told to do. I watch it all dissolve, the deadly contents merging together, a potent, silent fusion.

Then my ears detect a sound so light it barely registers.

"Do you hear that, Mamma?" I ask, curious about the humming sound that seems to intensify now, reverberating around my body—a low vibration, as delicate as a hummingbird's wing.

My mother watches me like a bird about to release its young from the nest, wondering whether it will spread its fledgling wings and fly or plummet to the ground.

It is her turn to shrug.

"I hear nothing, daughter."

Blinking, I realize she is telling the truth. It appears only I can hear the voice of the poison as it forms itself, as it boils and seeps and infuses together. I return my gaze to the elixir, the bringer of death.

"What do I do now? Is it ready?" I say, reluctant to turn away from it.

A moment's pause.

"You add the essence of nightshade, the belladonna. Just a few drops will do." Mamma reaches for a jar containing the juice of the berries that grow only in darkness. But I am too quick for her. I snatch the jar before she can take it. This, I am used to handling. Young girls, desperate to attract a lover, come to us seeking this most beguiling—and dangerous—plant. We hand out small vials, advising one drop only in each pupil, to be used sparingly and never ingested, for to do so would bring on fevers and pains.

I stand over the mixture. One drop. Two drops. Three, then Mamma murmurs to stop. The drops swirl and then vanish into the liquid. Stepping back, I am aware of the low note of the liquid changing. The hum becomes higher, its frequency shifting—and by this, I know as instinctively as how to blink or breathe, that the remedy is ready.

"It's done," I say, turning to Mamma who stands beside me. Again, she looks at me quizzically.

"Yes, daughter, it's done." A strange silence settles between us. Something is different. The balance of power between us has shifted.

Together, we decant the solution, its bitter, choking aroma filling the stone-walled space. I hold each small glass vial in my hand, which shakes only a little, until each is full and stoppered with dough. All are secreted inside the same cupboard as the jars of arsenic and juice of nightshade. This time, as I reach up, I notice the large leather-bound book that sits on a shelf.

"Take it. Bring it to the table. This is the last of your lessons tonight," Mamma says. I can tell by her voice she is weary, and I wonder at the difference between us. I have never felt more alive, as if each vein throbs and pulses with a new intensity.

The book is heavy. I lay it on the wooden surface that is mapped with knife marks and scratches. I brush off the remaining strands of birthwort.

"Open it."

The pages are thick vellum, and more than half of them are written upon in my mother's hand. I squint. The light is poor, and at first I think this is a book of cooking, of recipes, but then I see the ingredients, the names of customers, the cost of these services.

"This is my ledger, my love. I call it my book of secrets, as it contains every woman I've helped, every remedy I've given them, for their health or for their situation, and the price of my help. You'll see many of my services are free."

"But, Mamma, why write all this down? What if it falls into the wrong hands?" I ask, turning the pages. "There have been so many—"

"Because this is my work. It is the work of a lifetime, since I was old enough to understand herb lore. These women have no name, no recollection of their lives, the injustice, the unfairness.

They may never have their names recorded anywhere except perhaps at birth, marriage, and death. Nothing is ever writ of their lives, their ailments, their sufferings—except in here. Yes, it's dangerous to write them down but I wouldn't deny them the dignity of being inked onto a page. For many, it may be the only proof they existed at all."

It is then I notice another hand at the very front of the book. It is scratchier, shakier, the words less legible.

"Who wrote this?" I ask.

There is a moment where nothing is said. Then Mamma replies but her voice has changed its timbre, has dropped somehow.

"It is your grandmother's. I took her ledger when I left. It was the only part of her I could carry with me."

The night coils around us like smoke from a dying flame. I run my finger over the words that I see now are faded, the pages yellowing.

"It's late. Giulia, we must leave," Mamma says in a whisper. I close the ledger. I hold it tightly as I carry it back to the cupboard to be locked away, safe and hidden, just as we wish to be.

Later, once I am alone in my chamber, I draw the *tarocchi*—gilded, fraying tarot cards, a gift from one of my mother's sisterhood of harlots in the land we left behind.

The villa cat, an excellent mouser and my only friend, purrs and rubs against my hand as it moves over the cards. Gattino stretches and settles himself, licking his paws as he does. He must have eaten well this night. His purr is deep, throaty, sated.

As ever, I fancy I feel the *tarocchi* pulsate with their own secret potency. I pull the first one at the top of the deck: *La Fortuna*, the Wheel of Fortune. It lies in my hand, reversed; the crawling, crushed unfortunate is pivoted to the top of *la rota*, casting the king-like figure to the bottom. Those heading down now head upward. Those heading up, now head downward.

I feel a shiver of something, a knowing that is as yet indistinct, like mist curling over the sea.

# 3

The next night, Mamma comes to wake me again, but I am already waiting.

We creep, furtive as foxes, through the sighing villa. As Francesco snores. As Valentina, our cook, dreams. As the servant boy rolls over on his straw pallet, scratching his ass, we leave. This time, Mamma turns toward the port.

"This way," she says.

We walk quickly, avoiding the main streets, choosing instead the crumbling *vicoli*, the alleys that criss-cross the city. Here and there, a candle, a flame in a sconce, but mostly, it is darkness, the kind that wraps itself around you. The kind that hides those who wish to stay hidden.

I recognize the name of a street I have only ever heard of from our cook and her gossip. We are close to the port side, a place notorious for its brothels and taverns. The fresh scent of the sea, the salt and briny tang of it, overpowers the animal stench of the streets.

Men, mostly sailors, mostly drunk, wander past. They gesture crudely to us, though we are covered by our cloaks. Two Arab men swathed in pale-colored robes stop and stare. They click their tongues and mutter something I do not understand. The scent of orange and lemon trees, warmed by the sun, lingers.

My mother turns suddenly into a tiny, pitch-black alley. My heart beats so fiercely I fear someone will hear it.

Then, she hesitates.

"What is it, Mamma?" I whisper, looking around, seeing no one.

Before she replies, a door opens, throwing a shaft of candle-light onto the adjacent wall.

"Come, quickly," a voice says.

I follow, almost tripping on my mother's skirts.

Inside, women in various stages of undress stare back from the edges of the small chamber, observing us. Some return to their whispered conversations. Others keep looking. Their faces are painted with crimson slashes for lips, their eyes blackened with kohl. Some wear what look like togas, and I realize, belatedly, that we are in the back room of a brothel.

I am instantly comforted.

I grew up in a place such as this, though our rooms were gilded chambers in Philip of Spain's palaces in Madrid, and our makeshift family of outcasts were courtesans plying their trade with strutting noblemen. My mother was one of those courtesans. As she lifted her skirts for coin, I was left to roam free among the courtiers and servants, the harlots who fussed me and fed me comfits, the court gentlemen who bought me ribbons, the cooks who swiped at me, laughing, when I crept into their kitchens and stole warm bread from the ovens.

If I close my eyes and concentrate hard, I can still taste the chewy, steaming bread. It tastes of childhood, of freedom.

Sitting by the empty hearth is a woman, perhaps the same age as Mamma, who looks away as if she has not heard our arrival. The air is tinged with sweat and perfume. She has hair that reaches to her waist, and high cheekbones, giving her an almost regal air.

"Caterina?" Mamma says.

The woman turns her head, and I cannot help it. I gasp.

Where the curve of her cheek once ran now lies a jagged cut. It runs down from her dark eyes to her chin. The wound is fresh. Even in the low light, I can see it is seeping blood that appears black. She is—*she was*—beautiful.

"You came," she says.

My mother walks to her, puts down her basket of remedies. The woman sits so quietly, so elegantly in this hovel with slanting low ceilings and the skittering sound of mice from its corners.

"Of course we came," Mamma says.

She takes Caterina's hand, and I kneel beside her. A single tear forms in Caterina's unharmed eye, runs down her cheek.

"He says he'll kill me," she says. I can barely hear her.

One of the girls spits on the floor.

"Whoreson," the girl says. She cannot be much older than I, but her expression is bitter, her face burdened. I catch my reflection in a looking glass propped up on the mantelpiece. My eyes are wide as Gattino's, my face pale. Looking back at the girl, I fancy something passes between us: a recognition perhaps of all that is different between us and our lives. The urge to explain who I am rears up inside me, but I say nothing.

There is a murmur of agreement in the room.

"What happened?" Mamma asks, taking fresh linen from her basket.

Inside are our remedies: salves, soothing draughts, moss to staunch bleeding.

Caterina winces as Mamma dabs her face.

"He says next time, he'll cut off my head and hang me from the rafters," she begins. All eyes are upon her. All hearts beating faster. Her voice is quiet. How has her life come to this?

"He kicked my belly and killed the baby. Then he gave me this so I don't forget." The woman turns her face back to the empty fireplace. "As if I could ever forget . . ."

She places a hand on her stomach.

A door opens somewhere inside the building and there is a sudden roar of noise; people laughing, a viola da gamba being plucked, carousing, and debating. The door is shut just as quickly, and the room returns to its expectant hush. A single candle flares, the draft making the flame dance.

"He objects to your living, Caterina."

There is a moment's pause.

As if as one person, we all lean in.

Mamma takes out a jar containing a thick salve. I recognize the calendula and marigold mixture I made up only the day before. The woman nods. Another tear follows its slow course down the ravine of her face while Mamma dabs the cream onto the wound.

"He says no man will ever pay me again now I have this, so I say to him, 'How will we eat? How will we survive if I can't work?' There's never an answer. When he has drunk away all my money, he disappears, sometimes for days or even weeks, but he always returns, and when he does . . ."

She stops. She draws breath.

"He says if I work again then I'll pay with my head. He says I'm his and only his . . ." Caterina's voice trails off now.

The candle burns out, leaving the animal odor of melting tallow. The room is cast into darkness. There is movement, then a long sliver of orange light as a door is opened, the same sudden sounds, and a woman steps out. In seconds, she returns. Before her bobs the flame of a new candle, held in her hand. She places it next to Caterina and sits back down. Mamma nods.

There is a stillness to the room.

"Giulia, pass me the linen clout, thank you," Mamma says.

I do not hesitate. Grateful to be given a task, I dig into the basket and retrieve the fresh pads. My hand touches something small, cool, and solid, a glass vial perhaps, and, in that touch, I know why we are here, surrounded by whores, in a place forgotten by God. I should feel frightened. I should cross myself, step away and leave this unholy business, but I do not. More than that, I feel calm and at peace, like a river flowing onward to the sea. I see for myself why my mother dispenses her poison. I look around and see it in their shocked faces. In the puckering skin of Caterina's face. In her eyes that glitter. I understand all.

I may be young, but I can guess how this story ends: a butchered corpse, her skirts floating around her as she floats in the waters of the Papireto, where they once grew papyrus—now the place where fortune-seekers fish out the bloated corpses of women like her and those unfortunates killed for their purses. Perhaps the city's officials will drag her out, her weighted skirts sodden, her face blue and mottled, and try to find her family to give her the dignity of a funeral. Highly unlikely. Dead harlots are not worth a single scudo. Better Palermo is rid of her kind, they say.

Then, strangely, one woman, who has until now stayed silent, turns her head to Mamma.

"Are you a sorceress? Can you magic away this man?" she asks. Her chest rises and falls as she speaks. I feel her fear as if it is mine.

I glance at my mother in alarm. This is a perilous word—a question wise women recoil from. We sit, caught between breaths. The woman's face is shrouded by darkness at the edge of the room. My mother shakes her head, but it is I who find the words. Even among prostitutes, we cannot be known as witches.

"We have no spells. We cast no curses," I say, my voice trembling.

All eyes gravitate to me. They did not expect me to answer.

"Any medicine my mother brings for you is made from material given to us by God, and God alone." I do not know if I believe my own words. Our kind have our own pagan gods, deities of the land and sea, not a father high in the sky. Yet, I find I invoke His protection anyway.

"But, still, you have medicine that can cure our friend's predicament? That can rid her of this devil?" The woman sits forward, and I see her now. She is thin, her long hair lank around her neck. There is a fierce quality to her gaze. I feel Mamma shift beside me. I cannot tell if she wishes we were able to bewitch this man, or not.

"We heard that you go out with the outside women, the fairies . . ." The girl with the bitter expression speaks. Now, she looks hopeful, shy but inquisitive. I see her as she is beneath the whore's satins and her painted face: she is a child at heart, fanciful, thinking us touched by the supernatural. I shrink back from her gaze, fearful again.

"We're not sorceresses." It is my mother who speaks now, with authority this time. She raises her voice. "We're here to help right the wrongs you suffer. We administer only what's good and natural. Don't say those words. They have a power of their own and will bring holy terror down upon us all. And who else will help you but us?"

There is a rustling, a muttering, as this too is acknowledged.

Caterina grasps my mother's hands. "She speaks the truth. Only they can give us freedom, and freedom from this is all I want."

I notice she includes me alongside my mother in this pronouncement.

"You never saw us. We never came. Promise us," my mother says, looking around the small space.

"I promise, we all promise," the scarred woman says to Mamma.

Without prompting, I reach back into the woven basket. I discover there are two small vials. They clink as I draw out one of them, wrapped in one of the linen clouts. I pass it to my mother, my hand shaking only a little. We share a brief look, one of grim understanding. I am no longer an observer, no longer just a pupil; I am complicit. But I realize that any fear has vanished, any doubt has fled. Her plight has made this moment as clear as the sun on a winter morning. It is sharp, bright, absolute.

"One drop of the remedy in his ale tonight, then wait," my mother says, taking the vial from me. "He'll start to sicken, to vomit. Hold off until it settles. Call the doctor. Do everything a wife would do. Wait a week, then do the same again, in his broth, in his water with lemon.

"Follow this advice and the end will be quick, but he'll have time to make his peace with God. He'll have a good death, and you'll be free of your tormentor."

There is a watchful silence, an exhalation.

Then, a shudder passes through the room like a wave, rippling across the sea. The girl whose glance I shared looks back at me.

"Will he know? If he guesses, he'll kill me."

I can barely hear Caterina. Somewhere, a cat pounces, a rat scurries, a dog barks. Somewhere, her lover turns over in his sleep, pats the sheet, looking for her shape next to his, then falls back into his dreams, emitting a snore and a sigh.

"It's tasteless. Like water, just like water," Mamma says. She stands up, as do I. This time, I pick up the basket.

"Just a few drops and your problem will be solved. Stay with him. Care for him. He'll be dead within a month."

Caterina reaches into the folds of her robe. She takes a small velvet pouch, holds it out to me. My mother shakes her head, and so I push her hand away. I have much to learn of the way of these exchanges. This is a trade but, as I will discover, it is more often an exchange of secrets over coin. This is not new to me. I live in a house of secrets—and I have learned how to keep them.

"There's no charge for one friend helping another," Mamma says as we smooth down our skirts and make ready to leave.

It is close to dawn. Outside the sky is streaked orange. We walk in silence: Mamma to the villa chapel to begin the day's devotions as commanded by her husband, me to my chamber to rest before the bells ring for prayer. Inside the door, there lies a scattering of tiny bones. A bird's torn wing, its claws, the whiteness of its entrails, are all that remain of Gattino's feast. Curled on the bed, his tail twitches as I enter. He does not look around, but his ears remain pricked. He is watchful, as I must be. I slide under the cover, feeling the warmth of his fur, the languid weight of his body, and I know I will not sleep.

Each night now, we brew the elixir in the still room, watched by a wooden figure of Santa Rita, the patron saint of the impossible, of boundless miracles. Word spreads out from the convent through the square, the marketplace, the washrooms, the chambers of the city. It moves like a breeze, alighting here and there; upon the women scrubbing linens, upon the women tanning hide, upon the cook, the seamstress, the woman gutting fish. Whispers seep like smoke, drifting into the ornate places, the scented gardens. They reach beyond the high walls of the wealthy houses and villas to the ears of those women of Palermo who, though clad in finery and rubies, are just as trapped in the marriages arranged by their fathers and brothers as the woman spinning cloth or wed to an alehouse brute in her hovel. No woman can ever be granted a divorce—that privilege is bestowed only upon a discontented husband. Therefore, she must take other measures to end an unhappy union, make other arrangements to gain the freedom she desires, if she can bear the risk.

Word of our poison travels and is unstoppable; Faustina makes sure of it. At Mass when the priest is chanting, she speaks of it. When buying bread, oil, tomatoes, she nods to the sellers. They know without asking. She whispers in the alleys, the taverns, the squares and even as she scrubs laundry. Her words fly through Palermo like a flock, a treachery of ravens, blocking out the sun as they beat their wings and caw. Then, they come. Each night, a scratch at the door, a cloaked figure, sometimes an exchange of coins.

Each night a vial dispensed, or perhaps two—every transaction recorded in Mamma's book of secrets, her ledger containing every name, every remedy dispensed.

Each night, a man of the city should sleep less soundly in his bed, though who can tell? He continues to grunt and snore, to scratch and mutter, to dream of his mistress, his money or debt, his hardship and sorrow. He will roll over and fling out an arm, or a leg. He will pull the sheet, entangled in his solid limbs. He will sigh and stretch, then when the cock crows, will rise from his slumber, piss into his pot, and look around for his meal, to break his fast before starting the day. She will watch him go, her eyes alighting on the glass vial that sits on her ornate dresser or the dirt floor. Perhaps she still has it stowed in her skirts. Perhaps it sits on her dressing table if she is a woman of means, innocuous among the skin creams, perfumes, and ointments. Once dispensed and placed in others' hands, our potion is unstoppable, its power—and its reach—unknowable. Who can tell who the next victim might be? Who could guess whose ale or broth may contain those few drops? Coin rarely changes hands. Most have nothing to give in return.

*September 1632 (by Teofania's hand)*

*Caterina, buttana, salve of calendula
and marigold for wound-healing,
one vial of acqua (Teofania)*      *No payment*

*Alba, weaver, salve of borage for
bruising of the skin,
one vial of acqua (Teofania)*      *No payment*

*Hortensa, buttana,
two vials of acqua for her father
and brother (Teofania)*      *No payment*

# 4

They say we were born under a black moon—a sign of malfortune—or so our cook Valentina tells me when she is feeling vengeful.

"Oh, it's a potent sign of powerful evil when the moon disappears and leaves the sky dark as the Devil's dick," Valentina says, delighted by her malice. "Only bad can come of it," she adds and flicks her eyes to me, daring me to repeat it to my mother.

I do not repeat words spoken by the cook's restless tongue, the inconsistent snippets of gossip that flow from Mass to the marketplace and into our kitchen like flies to a carcass. I would not give our cook the satisfaction.

It is Sunday today, and we are due to leave for Mass shortly. The first cool air of autumn has brought me down to Valentina's kitchen to sit by the fire. The cook scowled as I arrived, but I ignored her and foraged for a *cannolo* and fresh milk to drink. Her usual grumbles must not be enough to sate her, because she turns her attention to baiting me. She wipes the crumbs from her mouth and casts me a strange look.

"What?" I say, between mouthfuls. Valentina's *cannoli* stuffed with almonds, ricotta, and honey are worth the trip to her hearth—and her inevitable bad humor. She raises her eyebrows.

"There are rumors . . ." she begins.

I shrug. "There are always rumors," I say, biting into the pastry shell.

"Not like these, pretty one. These are the kind of things that women like you, like your mother, should heed."

Women like me.

Women like my mother.

As Valentina speaks, her chin trembles. Is it indignation or glee? Hard to say at this point, and so I wait.

Whatever is coming must be salacious indeed.

In the meantime, I will not give her the satisfaction of asking what she knows. No good can come of this knowledge, that at least is plain.

The silence is broken by the servant boy, or Whipping Boy as I call him, who is slouching in the corner. He coughs and grins over at me. He stares too long and so I scowl back, making him blush and look away.

Eventually, I sigh. I can see what it is costing Valentina to hold on to this information. She is like a dam overflowing with storm water. She must speak or burst. Taking pity on her, I put down my pastry (reluctantly).

"Pray tell me, what should we heed?"

Valentina has surprisingly small eyes in her large head, made bigger by the shawl she wears wrapped around her hair. She is a woman built for the savage work of the kitchen: the kneading of dough, the whipping of thick milk, the heaving of grain sacks, the boning of beef ribs, the snap of a chicken's neck. She has arms like a sailor's and a girth so wide, she turns slightly sideways when she enters a room. Her eyes dart everywhere with keen intelligence, taking in everything she sees. Her ears are sharper than a hawk's. She knows things about people they are barely aware of themselves.

"The rumors are that you and your mother are devil's whores and no decent mistress will ever place a dainty foot inside these walls."

Valentina's voice is rushed, giddy. So it was glee.

I sigh again. "This is nothing new," I say. "We're outsiders. I'm the daughter of a courtesan made respectable by marriage to my stepfather. Everyone knows this. What is it to us?"

Valentina looks disappointed. Then, almost as an after-thought, she speaks again.

"There's talk of witchcraft in the city. A slow poison that can kill a healthy man in a few doses."

This time her words hit their target. The impact is swift, lacerating.

She makes the sign of the *corna*, her first and last digits extended as the others fold together, to ward against *il malocchio*. She could be dismissed on the spot for repeating gossip gleaned from Vucciria marketplace. I swallow, wipe my mouth.

She watches me, and there is something new in her gaze. Perhaps she wonders if, at last, she has gone too far. We have lived in Palermo for two years. We would be deaf and blind indeed if we did not know what the city wives think of us: a king's whore and her fatherless bastard raised into society. We would be fools to think we could ever be accepted here, but these words go further. They bring suspicion to our hearth. They bring fear. For Valentina to say all this . . . her boldness in voicing these rumors is what scares me.

I do not show this to our cook. Suddenly, her *cannolo* sticks in my throat and I feel queasy. I throw the uneaten mess into the fire. Scowling now at Valentina, I say, "Perhaps you should watch your broth, then!" giving her the pleasure of a sharp retort. I stalk out, her words trailing after me like hornets to their nest, stinging.

A black moon. A cursed life.

At Mass, we alight from our carriage onto the flagstones in front of Cattedrale di Santa Maria Nuova di Monreale. The air is cool and fresh as we are elevated on the hillside above the stink of the city.

The whispers start before we have set foot inside the great cathedral. We three stand at the entrance: Mamma, Francesco the trader, and me, parting the sea of worshippers just as if we were Moses at the Sea of Reeds. I hold my head high, my back straight, while the wives and daughters of the city's great men turn their veiled faces away from us, while their husbands and fathers cough and shuffle their feet. It was not always so. I have wilted in front of their scorn many times before, but today I feel different. Over the few short weeks I have helped Mamma, I have discovered a new sense of becoming: a feeling of being entrusted, of being part of something. It is a fledgling thing, this feeling, and despite Valentina's warning—if that is what it was—I am emboldened.

There is silence, broken only by the tread of our heeled boots on the marble floor. My stepfather Francesco moves to place his hand on the small of my back, but I swerve away from his touch as we walk to the pews that run down the central aisle. The noise echoes into the golden ceiling, upward to the angels depicted above our heads. Skirts rustling, eyes scanning the congregation that is so horrified by this notorious family of ours, consisting as it does of a famously pious man, his courtesan bride and her bastard child.

You would think they would be used to us by now.

We stepped off the boat—gulls keening over our heads, wind whipping our faces—more than two years ago. But memories are long here. They will never welcome us into society. My mother is too beautiful, too scandalous, for these women to accept her, while their husbands eye us both like hunting dogs on the leash. I have learned to shrug while they sneer. I know already from their sour glances that I have inherited my mother's fair looks, enhanced by the sheen of youth. I know I have hair the color of sunshine that ripples like a field of wheat, skin that blushes soft pink, and a red rosebud mouth to pout with. I have all this, and I am learning to live with its blessing—and its curse. What I do understand is that we have fallen into the viper's nest of Palermo society, and as they writhe and bite, we must face the serpents, and hiss and fork our own tongues.

I catch the eye of a wealthy merchant's daughter. She turns away, as haughty as her mother, and I feel the weight of our exclusion, our difference. Yet today it makes me defiant. Look this way, if you dare! Throw your curses at us! We have secrets that would shock you far more than my ignoble birth by my harlot mother.

We slip into our seats. Mamma takes hold of the Bible placed there, and it sits between her gloved hands. I look around at the richly dressed women, their jewels glinting, the lace at their throats delicate, fine, rising up and falling down with their breath. The high altar sits at the far end, gilded and bedecked with finery, consisting of a large ornate cross and six candles, three on either side of it. Mary, the Virgin, and her child are pictured in mosaic, surrounded by archangels Michael and Gabriel. Above them all is the face of Christ. He looks like he is frowning.

I glance at Mamma and see she is staring at someone. Following her gaze, I recognize Caterina, though she has hidden the wounded part of her face with a dark lace veil. She is standing away from the crowds in the shadowy reaches of the nave, half a head taller in her *chopines*, her dark hair formed into two peaks on her head in the Venetian style known everywhere as the symbol of prostitution. She is staring back at Mamma, and she is smiling.

A shiver runs down my spine.

This smile can surely mean only one thing. The deed must be done: the drops administered, the medicine dispensed. It is then

I realize she is wearing black. She is wearing mourning dress. It is the first time I have seen a woman who has used our potion. Yes, I have helped Mamma dispense it, but there is a world of difference between handing a tiny vial to a bruised woman and seeing her weeks later, dressed as a widow.

The candlelight seems to blur. I feel faint. I clutch the pew to steady myself. Mamma seems to notice. She mutters something to me, but I do not hear. She takes hold of my hand, and in that small gesture, I remember we are being watched, we are in public. I cannot sink to the ground. I cannot show anything but the mute deference expected at Mass. At the same time, I feel the strength of her grip, and in turn, it strengthens me. I remind myself of Caterina's wound. I force myself to picture it, each tear, each slash, the blood congealing. Though I am nauseous now, and scared, the horror of Caterina's face, of the man who did that to her, leaves me strangely numb. I should feel remorse or guilt, and in this moment, as thick plumes of incense fill the air, I discover I feel neither.

As my shock recedes, I feel a jolt of something like excitement, a thrill perhaps. Justice has been served, albeit in the shadows. The power of this leaves me breathless, and though the service is under way and the muttering and shuffling, the sniggering and sly looks have ceased, I am distracted by these new feelings, this strange elation, while a ripple of silence fans across the congregation.

Heads bow, like plants wilting in the shade. I bow mine, knowing I am smiling.

A large bejeweled cross, embellished with gold and gemstones, sways over the heads of the faithful, carried down the aisle. The priest follows, swinging an incense carrier, as do the other men of God behind him.

As my arm moves in line with all the others, making the sign of the cross, I catch sight of Francesco staring at me, as he always does, from the tail of my eye. He looks at me as if he would devour me. This brings me sharply back from my thoughts. Mamma stands between us. Perhaps she is aware of his gaze because she shifts as she sits, turning to whisper something to him. I see him drag away his eyes, move them to his wife, leaving behind something tainted by them. He watches the way I cross myself, to see if I move just as he would wish me to, in the correct way, the holy way. He watches as if he would see under my skin. As if he would rip it open and, amid the bloody, pulsing innards, would make sure, inside, my heart is pure.

I look down at my hands. I see them shake but only a little. In my head, I draw inward, away from his study of me, leaving only my shell, my carcass on the outside to deflect his attentions. I think of Gattino, how he curls around himself while sleeping on a warmed stone bench in the ornamental garden, disappearing inside his soft fur. Now and then, he peeps up, checking who is there, sniffing the air, his ears moving back, then forward, before he settles down again, wary, waiting. Like him, I am adept at scenting the breeze, guessing which way things may blow. This is my only safety—that, and Mamma's love. I put my hands in my skirts and find the small pouch I take with me wherever I go. Inside it are the trinkets, the talismans, I carry. None are worth anything except to me. A blackbird's feather, oily and black; a deck of *tarocchi*; a shell given to me as a child by the oil seller in Madrid; a sprig of rosemary, known to ward off *il malocchio*, the evil eye. Pagan treasures. Banned treasures, says the Church, though they are harmless enough. In my heart, they represent a freedom I can barely remember from my days growing up at court in Spain, skipping through opulent corridors, passing regal portraits painted in oils and framed with gold, down hallways lined with great gilded mirrors.

Later, once the service is finished and even we are sent away with God's blessing, I catch sight of Caterina again. As she leaves, the veil slips. The livid red line that runs down her face is still puckered, but the marigold cream has long since soothed the redness, closing the wound. Her throat is bare of any adornment, her cheeks and eyes painted. She catches sight of me and smiles again before wrapping her shawl around her. A boy, an African who must be her servant, waits for her. He holds out his arm, and the pair, Caterina towering above him, make their unsteady way to her small carriage to head back toward the port.

"Mamma, Mamma, it's her," I say, snatching this moment away from Francesco's relentless, unswerving scrutiny as we await our carriage. He has walked over to join the merchants and noblemen who stand outside the cathedral doors, strutting like ravens. No one dares come over to us in Francesco's absence. Noblewomen and merchant wives, their servants hovering close by, stand in small, richly colored groups, watching.

"Yes, it is," she replies.

"Mamma . . ." I begin again, then stop as I am unsure now what to say.

My mother glances around us, and in that gesture, I catch myself and the beginnings of my questions. I realize this is no child's game, and I would be a fool indeed to say any more. Instead, I stare back at the scornful glances until each gaze falls away. Perhaps it is a sin to bear both beauty and pride, though both were surely a gift from God. The gifts are not well received by Palermo society. That, at least, is certain.

Back at the villa, Whipping Boy leads off the horses. We dismount from the carriage, but not before I catch him glancing back at me. Valentina is already cross. There is venison charring. Francesco waits behind me, his wiry frame, as ever, too close. As I grip the handle and step out, my stomach turns. "Valentina, I'm coming. What's the problem?" Mamma sighs, following the truculent cook as she lumbers toward the kitchens. My mother's voice grows fainter. "I'll tell the boy, leave it all to me . . ."

It is clear there has been an altercation between Whipping Boy and Valentina—again. They cannot live in peace together, just as we cannot. This is a house of discord, of uneasy silences and sharp words. It is a house where we are forced to be blind to one another, to be deaf and mute as well. Francesco places his palm on my back. As I step out of the carriage, his hand lingers.

# 5

I was twelve years old when my stepfather took my maidenhead. Within a few months of arriving in Palermo, I finally understood why his gaze followed me, his thin lips slick with saliva. His infatuation with my mother seemed to wane almost as soon as we set foot on Sicilian soil, and it was then he turned his attention to me. I already knew something of men's desires. You do not grow up in a circle of harlots and remain blind to what goes on between a man and a woman. I had seen erect members and their noble Spanish owners in the act of copulation as I peeped out from behind the curtains around Mamma's bed. I watched in fascination while Mamma made a show of cooing and moaning as gentlemen, in various states of inebriation or lust, lunged at her, her legs apart, her face hidden from view as she entertained them on an elaborately patterned chaise longue.

The first time I became aware of her nocturnal activities, I was convinced she was being wounded. Woken abruptly from the deep waters of a child's sleep, disoriented and half-dreaming still, I heard groaning. Someone was in great pain! Someone was so frightened they panted and grunted! Mamma was normally next to me as I slept, her warm body holding mine. Where was she? Why was I alone and so scared?

Dazed, rubbing my eyes and clutching at my nightdress, I gathered all my courage and scrabbled through the curtain to find her. I cannot imagine how I must have looked, coming out from my hidden sleeping area. My face was screwed up against the light of the candles. My heart was pounding as I rushed at the man who was attacking my mother, now her defender, small and fierce. Fear had replaced—or perhaps was driven by—pure rage at him harming her. The shock on the face of this man who dared paw at Mamma stays with me still. Shock, which quickly turned to mirth.

"She growls! Tame your daughter, señorita," the lordling drawled, one eyebrow raised, his manhood still purple and swollen in his hand.

"Giulia, *amore mio*, you must sleep now. This is Mamma's work. I'm safe. No one's trying to harm me," she whispered as she turned and swept me into her arms, carrying me back to the tangle of sheets I had left so abruptly. "How lucky I am to have you to fight for me, my daughter, but you must stay behind the curtain, just as I've always told you to." Mamma drew the drapes back around us, and, holding me in her arms, began to stroke my hair.

I was not so easily soothed.

"Mamma, I'll fight him!" I wriggled, wrenching open a sliver of the curtain and growling in truth now at the man who grinned, slouching back on the daybed. I may even have bared my teeth. Eventually, once I was sure my mother was not in danger, I settled down.

The grunting increased until, suddenly, it ended. The chink of coin and sluice of water told me Mamma was finished for the night. When the same sequence of events—the sighing, grunting, exclaiming, chinking, sluicing—happened the next night, and the one after that, I soon learned how it played out between women such as Mamma and the men who bought her.

So, many years later, when I awoke with a start one black night in my new home, Francesco's large hand clasped over my mouth, the other grappling in the darkness with his breeches, I knew instantly.

I sank my teeth into his hand, and he screamed like a pig bound for slaughter.

"*Buttana!* Stay still!" he cursed, as I tried to grapple a man used to hard riding across foreign lands.

"No! Get off me!" I shouted, breathless from the fight already. My small limbs kicked out at him. I writhed and yelled, spat in his face, and cursed him for a devil, but it was no use. He was a man, and I was a child. I still am.

"Get off me . . ."

My sobs strangled in my throat as he grabbed my night shift and pulled me down the bed toward him. His breath was sour with wine, and with a single sharp slap, he overpowered me. I cowered now underneath him as his knee pinned down my thigh and he did what he had come to do. I screamed, partly from the pain—it felt like he was tearing me—partly from outrage. How dare he do this! But that thought soon vanished as I struggled, which only excited him more. Of course, he could dare. He was—*is*—master of his house, and of his wife, and of me. He could do whatever he wanted, and I was utterly powerless to stop him.

I recall the absolute knowledge I held that *someone* would come and stop this onslaught. That someone would hear and would rescue me.

There were footsteps. Then, the sound of the door being pummeled. Then came my mother's voice, angry at first, then beseeching.

"Stop it! Take me, husband," she cried. "Take me and leave my daughter. She's still a child."

Francesco ignored her. He muttered something indistinct, then lunged again. I was crying now, the tears of a frightened girl, all fight having left me. Everything hurt: my leg where his weight held me down; my private parts, which felt split apart;

and my wrist, which he held in his grip. A few more thrusts and he was finished. Rolling off me with a grunt, he said not a word as he began to re-form himself: his disheveled breeches, his crumpled linen shirt, his hair slick with sweat. I curled away from him, trying to make myself as small as possible, and waited for him to leave. I listened as his breathing slowed. Not bothering to rush, he dressed himself back into being Francesco, the trader. Francesco, the wealthy citizen. Francesco, the God-fearing Christian. The bed surrendered his weight. Footsteps. Then a key inserted back into the lock. The scraping of metal against metal. So, he had locked us in. Deep in slumber, I had not heard. Then the door closing on the latch and, at last, he was gone.

Mamma's voice came now as the door opened, then was muffled behind the walls when it closed. I did not stir. I lay, beyond weeping, beyond pain, just listening now. She raged. She wept. Perhaps she lunged at him, her fists beating his chest, her nails clawing his face. I like to think she did.

The sounds ended. I pulled my body in tighter. I could not hear Mamma anymore. I did not wonder how he silenced her. Perhaps I already knew. The yellowing, livid bruises that marked her skin the next day mirrored my own, and I realized that my childhood, such as it was, had come to an abrupt and brutal end.

I follow Mamma to the kitchen, uneasy at being left in Francesco's company after Mass.

Valentina is still banging pans. Whipping Boy is hiding somewhere in the yard outside, probably in the outbuilding used for brewing. Inside, the kitchen is warm. The fire spits; meat juices spill from the roasting carcass. My mother is tying a linen apron over her church finery, her hands already white with flour.

Whipping Boy reappears at the doorway, sheepish now. Valentina throws a curse, and he scuttles away, grinning. I catch Mamma's eye and we smile. Valentina returns to the dough that lies in a sagging round ball on the kitchen table. With her reddened hands, she picks it up, reaches down into the grain sack and retrieves a handful of flour, scattering it liberally across the wooden table, which is a mess of pots, a slab of butter, melting, and a platter of fresh eggs, tufts of feathers still stuck to them. She wipes the same hand across her forehead, leaving a streak of powder. She is still mumbling as she begins to knead. Soon, the sound of Valentina's grunts as she pulls at the dough, pummeling it into submission, is replaced by her humming a country melody. Mamma is cracking the eggs into a bowl, while Whipping Boy, his back arriving before his front, drags a new sack of flour across the flagstone floor.

Something akin to harmony is restored.

My mother pushes the bowl toward the cook, wipes her hands, and removes the linen from her skirts. She gestures for me to follow her to the herb garden where we will gather thyme and wild garlic. Shooing a stray chicken out of her way, Mamma walks ahead of me into the daylight.

"Mamma," I say as I follow her out.

"What is it, my love?" My mother sits on a bench under the loggia. The sun is hot even as summer has already slipped into autumn. From the kitchen, there are still the sounds of everyday life: Valentina's song, Whipping Boy's whistling, the metal crank of the spit as it turns. Francesco must be in his chamber. There is no one here except us.

This idea of mine didn't just form during the church service. It has been prowling the far reaches of my mind since that first night in the convent, when I learned how to make my mother's poison. It has reached out to me since, with increasing urgency, and so the words come out in a rush.

"We could use your *acqua*, Mamma. We could give it to my stepfather, and he will never again come to my bedchamber."

The air in the garden seems to still as if waiting. The olive trees are silent. The trickle of water from a nearby fountain seems to slow. I realize my breath has stopped.

In a voice I can barely hear, my mother replies. "Don't think I haven't thought of this, *figlia mia*. Many nights have I wanted to . . . administer . . . the cure for his unnatural desires."

She looks as if she would say more but stops.

"But why don't you?" I say, turning to her, clasping her hands. "It would be a simple thing. We do it for other women, why not for us . . . for me?"

My mother turns to me. Her beauty never fails to surprise me, to catch me unawares, as it does now. Her eyes are perfect green, the color of water. Her skin is cream clotted by the dairy, her mouth and lips are red and full. She holds herself like a queen, her back straight, her bearing as noble as any of the she-devils who turn from us at Mass. It takes me a moment to realize she is looking at me with pity. Her hand, released from my grip, smooths my cheek.

"Giulia, our situation is different. My husband is close to the Church. He may be one of the *Inquisitori*. Indeed, I suspect this is so. If anything happened to him . . ." She pauses. "There would be investigations. There would be inquisitors asking questions. He isn't a tanner, an innkeeper, a laborer. He has high status, and we'd place ourselves—and our friends—in extreme peril. It would bring death to us, and I wouldn't be able to save you. This is why we must submit. This is why I can do nothing. If there was any other way—"

"There must be a way, Mamma?" I say.

Here, my mother draws me to her side with gentle care. She cradles me as she tells me the truth of our lives.

"We can't escape, daughter. We're bound to my husband as his chattels. If we left, he'd hunt us for the rest of our days."

I imagine Francesco and his men as hunting dogs, their teeth bared, salivating.

"We'd be destitute, Giulia. I never want to feel the emptiness of a hungry belly again, and neither would you if you knew."

I listen, quiet now, unable to truly understand her logic, a tear making its slow journey down the contours of my face. Mamma has told me a little of her past, before her life as a courtesan at Philip of Spain's court. Originally from Rome, she married a Spanish soldier, leaving her mother behind and traveling to Madrid. It was the usual story of hardship, hard choices, hard living. When he died in a tavern brawl, she became a whore to survive. Here, the story changes. A chance meeting with a nobleman and she was ascended into the life of a palace harlot. There is so much I do not know about her, that I can only guess at. A swell of emotion, like a surge of the tide, washes over and into me—a confusion of anger and helplessness, and something else. Something hard, something that fractures the light like a diamond.

I see my mother's distress. I understand what it costs her to know what her husband does to her only child. This must be unendurable, and yet she endures. I see in a moment of sharp, bitter clarity, I must do the same.

# 6

I am changing.

For weeks, my body has told me it is different. I have felt a yearning for something I could not name. A new sense of the physical world around me. When I wash each morning, I draw the soaked linens against my skin, feeling every touch, every sensation: the warmth of the water, the slight rough pull of the material, the cold of the winter air. When I walk through the gardens, I feel as if for the first time the crunch of the gravel beneath my boots, the gentle sunlight against the back of my neck. The world and all its offerings seem suddenly heightened, more alive to me. I brush my hands over the lemons that grow in the garden, the oranges too. Their scent, sharp, uplifting, is a kind of sensory exploration. At the same time, the urge to escape my constrictions has only grown.

The walls of our villa feel like a prison now I have tasted the sweetness of our forbidden excursions. I long to climb them, to straddle the cooling stone, to jump down the other side into the streets that teem with life. Perhaps the stench and bustle would send me running back into my gilded cage. Perhaps.

My stomach has begun to cramp with pain, and I know what is to come. I know my transition from child to woman is under way. I will soon become a girl of fourteen, and I already know this is my courses starting. I am not coy nor alarmed like the young girls from good homes who are told nothing of how their bodies work. I know where babies come from, and how they get there in the first place. I know that each month, my harlot mother refrained from entertaining the gentlemen of the court for a week while she bled as the moon glowed silver. My time as a changeling—from my child state to that of a woman—has ended.

My mother has sensed it too. She would be a poor wise woman if she had not. We are grinding together spices in the still room when I feel suddenly faint. Francesco has been away for a month traveling the spice routes and is not due back for weeks. We have lived by our own rules again, at ease together, Mamma and I.

"Sit, Giulia. I should be preparing a tonic for you. You'll need fennel, valerian, and chaste tree to ease your stomach. It will pass and soon, but rest awhile. Take some rags from the basket. You'll need them when the blood comes."

I smile over at her.

She adds: "You're a woman now."

At this, I blush. Faustina, who is carrying a basket filled with pouches of dried, crushed herbs on her hip, stops, smooths my hair with her free hand.

"You'll be a beautiful woman. You'll have many suitors, and so you must choose wisely." Smiling, she moves away. My mother and I exchange a long look, one of understanding, and trepidation. Suddenly, life feels like a thread that is slowly unraveling, casting its length behind us. Where will it stop?

A week later, and there is no sign of Faustina.

"Is her mother worse?" I say to Mamma as we prepare for the work ahead. It is late. The nuns are sleeping, all except for Sister Clara. It is the first time we have been back to the convent since that day when my courses started. Clara sent word that the convent was to have an important church visitor and we could not risk exposure.

My mother shakes her head.

"I sent the physick but had no reply. It's unlike her to say nothing but maybe she has been busy and forgot to send word back. She has many brothers and sisters to care for, as well as her mother."

This sounds reasonable, yet when I return to my work, there is a buzzing noise in my ears. It hums in the background as I measure out the white powder. I shake my head and it recedes, pulling back like the tide from the shoreline. We make the remedies in silence tonight. If we think any thoughts, they remain unspoken.

Two days later, Valentina stands at one end of the yard, hands on hips, frowning. She glares at Whipping Boy, who seems frozen to the spot. My footsteps make both of them turn around. A stray cockerel pecks across my path, and I shoo it away. Gattino eyes the scrawny creature but decides to trot past, his tail in the air.

"Mamma says I must help you." I glower at her, squinting into the winter sunlight.

"The mistress needs to send me better. What can I do with a useless boy like this one?" she says, gesturing with one arm toward the boy who eyes us warily. "My eyes weep when I see him dropping the wood for the stove, leaving the milk to curdle. Holy Mother of God, why am I cursed with such a fool?" Valentina raises her weeping eyes heavenward.

Inwardly, I sigh. "Let me churn the butter. Go and fetch the rest of the fuel," I say to Whipping Boy.

He slouches off, but not before he throws me a look of pure devilry.

"One day, you'll see. I'll return to Piana, to the mountains. I'll live with my sister. She's always inviting me. One day, I'll go . . ."

The cook addresses no one in particular as she complains and grouches while we walk into the warm interior of the kitchens. There is a fog of cooking smells: suckling pig on the spit, almonds toasting in the pan, broth simmering.

From the other side of the walls come the street sounds that frame our lives: the oil seller, the herbalist, the farmers up from the countryside, the lowing cattle, the clang of bells. There was once a time when I could wander a city freely with Mamma, through Madrid's wide boulevards, past its cathedrals and taverns, markets, and shops, browsing for fabric or lace, seeking the scented perfumes the ladies of our circle preferred. Now, I am as caged as one of the little sparrows in the marketplace, behind the high stone walls of our villa. Sometimes, I yearn for what lies beyond. I know Mamma sees my frustration; perhaps she feels it too. Sometimes, when no one is looking, she catches me in her arms with sudden fierceness, as if she would squeeze these dangerous urges out of me with her love.

The curds lie sodden and milky, already reeking of the cheese they will become. I take hold of the handle and begin to turn it, churning the barrel's contents, looking round at the kitchen to see what else needs to be done. Valentina is muttering to herself about the fish having spoiled already, slapping fresh dough onto the large wooden table. Flour puffs into the air like a wild mushroom spitting out spores, and she proceeds to knead it, violently. Whipping Boy has escaped to the wood store. The ashes lie black under the spit.

Suddenly, I stop what I am doing. The air arranges itself around me, and I realize he is back. There is no noise, no bustle to announce him—yet. It is as if the gods are whispering into my ear; I know in my belly he is come back, though he is not expected. Then, there is the sound of a man's voice, hollering for attention.

I am never ready to hear Francesco. I drop the handle and step back, almost knocking over a large terracotta urn filled with grain. The voice shouts again, authoritative, inescapably male. He is demanding his horse be watered and rubbed down with hay. And where is his wine? Where are his servants? His wife? Why are they not greeting him?

Valentina's muttering ceases. She leaves the dough, wipes her hands on her apron and hurries out. I stay where I am, blinking. He is back early. His business trip must have been a failure. What will this mean for us? Will there be beatings for the servants? For Mamma? Or will he restrain himself just to the sneers and sighs, the pointed looks?

I try to swallow but my throat resists. I try to move but my body is stuck. The ripe yeasty smell of the milk is suddenly over-powering. Then, Mamma's voice, as if from a great distance. She appears a few moments later, calling for bread, wine, salt. She casts me a look. One that says: stay still, don't move, stay hidden—for now. And, as if she hasn't seen me, she carries on, her expression neutral as she claps her hands to summon her master's servants to do their lord's bidding.

Many times, I have wondered how my mother was so mistaken in her suitor. If she had any idea of Francesco's real intentions, she would never have agreed to the marriage. Of this, at least, I am sure, as I stand in the kitchen, as still as a hare caught in the fox's sight. Perhaps his whispered words of affection had deafened her to the truth, his protestations of love rendering her instincts mute. Perhaps it had been her arrogance, parading his proposal like a gemstone, flashing and winking in the Spanish sunlight. She had scored a great victory among her kind, and against every respectable, ignored wife, by marrying above her station, against all codes of religion and society. How had she not noticed when his eyes followed me? How had she not seen how he licked his lips like a wolf about to devour its prey?

# 7

At dinner, Francesco chews slowly.

Mamma sits as still as a woman carved from white stone. Valentina hovers behind her master, shifting from one awkward foot to another. I drop my eyes to my platter. I cannot bring myself to eat in his presence. Silence fills the space, stretches around us, broken only by the methodical motion of my stepfather's jaw as it works, grinding meat.

On the table there is a suckling pig, still tender and steaming on the bone. The afternoon was spent in a flurry of activity, the cook anxious to prepare food fit for his return. Platters of grapes and olives sit beside it. A pale jellied pudding quivers.

Francesco looks up as if he has forgotten we are there. He pauses, drains his goblet.

"Bring more wine," he commands. His voice echoes, though the chamber is not large. He makes a gesture with his hand, waving Valentina out.

Without a word, the cook moves her bulk out of the room, away from the strained, expectant hush that surrounds the table with its heaving plates, its chairs and their incumbents, the yellowing wax of the candles, their wicks blackened.

We wait in silence. Francesco swallows.

We watch as he fidgets on his seat, his ass sore from the day's ride, his boots still dusty from the road.

Eventually, he grunts. His gaze slides from his plate to his wife, then onward across the table to me.

I flick my eyes down again, but not quickly enough. I catch a gleam of something, a small delight in my discomfort, perhaps. A metallic sound as Mamma's fork scrapes against her platter.

Long seconds pass before Valentina huffs in with a carafe, the slide of the liquid within it mimicking her movement. Wine slops on the table as she pours but Francesco waves her away, apparently unconcerned. Sitting back now in his carved wooden chair, he wipes grease off his long, slender fingers. Slowly, his legs ease out in front of him, the goblet held by his now-clean fingertips.

"How was your trip? Did your business conclude as you wished?" Mamma breaks the silence. Her voice is smooth, lyrical. I do not know how she can talk to him as if he is like us, as if he is not *him*.

At first her husband appears not to have heard. Then, an impatient movement with his head.

"It was satisfactory." He shrugs, taking another sip.

I glance up and catch sight of the liquid as it stains the corners of his lips, black in the gloom against a flash of white teeth. Nothing more is said and for a moment I think the matter is dropped. I almost breathe but Mamma speaks again.

"Forgive me, husband. You're back earlier than we expected. Can we know why we have this pleasure?"

I do not look up at my mother, but I know the expression she wears on her face when she is with Francesco: a look of studied blankness. It is one I have seen on the faces of rich men's wives when they accompany their husbands to Mass, knowing all of society is aware of whatever it is they are shamed by: their husband's mistress or his gambling debts. It is the same look I have seen the men display in church as they dip their heads for prayer in carved booths. It is an expression that reveals nothing, says nothing. It is the sign of things that are hidden.

Francesco glares at Mamma as if he would decide his next move. Every sense in my body is alert now, like a mouse hiding in long grass, the shadow of a kestrel circling overhead. I risk glancing toward him and see his full mouth surprisingly curl into a smile. Could it be good news? Perhaps he has made a fortune and is content.

He licks his black lips. "In fact, I was recalled to the city. Palermo has a new inquisitor from Spain: Fernando Afán de Ribera. He's tasked with uncovering the heretics and sinners that pollute our city, and so, the men of Palermo must return and give whatever aid we can."

His smile grows wider. This news appears to please him but there is an edge, like a newly sharpened knife. I can feel the cool steel of its blade. Suddenly, violently, I long for the silence to return but the box is opened now, its contents spilling out. I recall Mamma's words: *He may be one of the* Inquisitori. *Indeed, I suspect this is so.*

"Ribera is charged with the power of God, with His strength, and so his work has already begun here. They call him the 'Avenger of Sin.' He's clearing out those who will not hear the word of our Lord. He's doing God's holy work, Madonna."

Francesco's voice is smooth as the silk shift he wears. He reaches for the glass vessel and pours more wine for himself. In one gulp he drinks it down. He is most alive when he talks of sin. Strange for a man as religious as he. I cannot tell if he notices how we shrink back. Valentina stands at the back of the room still. Her eyes dart between us all, watchful, alert. Mamma murmurs something in response, which I do not catch. I am too busy fighting to stay in the room. Every cell in my body jangles as the waves of panic course through me.

It is then I catch the scent of something. It is a musty smell, of rotting leaves and stale water. An aroma of decay and putrefaction. Accompanying it is a familiar ringing in my ears, a noise that starts low then increases in volume until it is a clambering sound like a bell pulled too long and too loudly. No one else appears to hear it, and I know it is a warning. I look down at my hands. They are there, lying now in my lap. They look like my hands, but they are roughened, stained with something, oils and tinctures maybe, the nails ragged and dirty. Then, they dissolve back into the smooth whiteness of my skin. Just as suddenly, the smell is gone, the noise abates, and the room forms back around me. The meat lies pungent on the table. The candle wax burns its hot, melting aroma.

"Surely we're a God-fearing city?" My mother's voice is light, controlled, but her face betrays her; blanched pale in the darkness. This makes Francesco laugh, though I hear no mirth. I jump at the sudden sound, and he notices. His eyes rush to me. Again, I am too slow, and I catch his gaze before dragging my eyes downward. It is an effort. My grip tightens around the meat knife I hold in my right hand. It would be the work of a moment to plunge it into his heart, except I have no strength. I am feeble as a newborn.

He continues to watch me, as he always does, as he always has.

"Our city is filled to its rafters with sin. Surely you of all people must understand that?" He turns back to my mother at last, a sly grin on his face. He likes to taunt her about her past, her profession, though he too was one of her guests. I do not need to see Mamma's expression to know this slight does not go unnoticed. There is but half a heartbeat before her reply, only the slightest hesitation.

"Of course, husband. My knowledge in holy matters is, as ever, under your guidance."

Francesco grunts again. Satisfied by her answer, he leans forward. He breathes in as if all the air in the room is his.

"I was also recalled to witness a great event, and you'll both accompany me. You should know what all the city is talking of, and so I'll tell you."

Again, a heartbeat's pause.

As I wait, I feel the skin prickle from my neck down to my spine. It is as if I already know but have forgotten the details. A log drops in the grate, casting a shower of red sparks. I jump again, a sight that makes my stepfather laugh out loud this time.

"Yes, there's much to fear, my dear Giulia, if you don't walk the path ordained by our Lord."

I force myself not to shudder as he speaks my name. I try to think of his words as drops of rain that run off me, washing away like autumn showers. Still, I do not look up.

With a sigh, perhaps tired already of his taunts, Francesco continues, though his tone becomes more businesslike.

"The Holy Office has caught a local woman by the name of Faustina Rapisardi. A witch."

Faustina.

Our friend.

This information, these words, swarm like flies in the marketplace. I hear them jerk and twitch. I look up and am surprised to see nothing, just the flickering candlelight.

"They call her a witch?" Mamma repeats the word. It is a curse all its own. There can be no mercy, no way back, once a wife or daughter, mother or sister is given this name. She is branded as effectively as a cow seared with a hot iron. I can feel my hands starting to shake.

"Of course," Francesco says, continuing without pause for thought, without any notion of the cruelty and injustice that is our inheritance as the weaker sex. A flash of rage rears up inside me. It startles me, so used am I to pretending obedience. I have to breathe slowly, carefully in the gaps between his words.

"This woman, this *witch*, is a maker of diabolical potions that have been sold and used to poison the working men of our city. She was caught giving it away in the marketplace and arrested. Her sin is beyond imagining. I will spare you the details gained from her questioning." Francesco dabs his face with his linen napkin.

"There have been rumors for months, of course. Men of all classes wonder if they're safe. They watch their wives, they even watch their daughters . . ."

Francesco looks to Mamma, then to me. We both drop our eyes with the required deference, and something else: a recognition we must hide. He continues, glancing away as he speaks.

"She'll be tortured, then she'll meet her fate at the gallows," he says, rolling the words around his mouth like a comfit. Almost as an afterthought, Francesco pulls a piece of flesh from the pig's bone, the white cartilage surrendering the dark meat. Ripping it into two smaller parts, he puts it to his mouth and sucks its juices.

Our friend, Faustina.

I glance at Mamma, knowing my face reflects the shock she is feeling too, knowing that with my expression, I risk exposing us.

The silence grows thicker. The room seems to darken but it is a trick of the light. The candles still glow. The fire still burns.

Mamma recovers first.

"Then the Holy Office is doing God's work, Amen," she says at last. This time her voice is stilted, but her husband appears not to notice. He yawns and drains the last droplets of good Rhenish wine from his cup. I feel my body begin to shake. It is outside of my control. I look at my mother, panicked.

Without looking back at me, she holds out her hand, signals for Francesco to follow her.

"You must be tired, husband. Come to bed. Your work requires a rested mind and body."

With another great yawn, Francesco takes my mother's out stretched hand.

"With pleasure," he murmurs, kicking back his chair.

As they leave, I know he will glance back. I stare down at my plate, my eyes unmoving. I feel the air itself shift and know that this is when his head turns. I do not look up. I never look up.

Then, the sound of the door closing. I exhale.

I lay my hands flat on the smooth, knotted wood of the table. It feels cool to my touch, solid, unyielding. I stay there for longer than I should, just breathing, waiting for the panic to pass. The candle on the table gutters out.

Our friend is a woman now branded a witch.

Our friend is a dead woman walking.

Worse, and I am ashamed to admit it, I am afraid for myself. With one word she could bring us all down. She could speak my mother's name. She could speak mine. I look up. Valentina is watching me.

# 8

That night, long after the night watchman has hollered, there is
a sound at my chamber door.

Mamma shuts my door slowly, silently, until the bolt clicks
into position. Then, we wait. I hear her breathing, faster than
usual. The flickering light moves toward me. Her eyes are wide,
her pupils enlarged.

"Mamma, what can we do? How did they arrest Faustina?"
The questions fall out of me.

"Shhhh, you must be quiet. We can't risk anyone hearing us."

I snort with derision at this, knowing Valentina will be snor-
ing in her pallet bed, while Whipping Boy will have crept out
to stalk the brothels and taverns. On the nights I cannot sleep,
I creep out of my room and wait for his footsteps. His are the
lightest of all. He appears out of the palazzo's shadows like a thin
specter, his cloak around him. It amuses me to see him thinking
he is the essence of subterfuge while I am watching him from my
hiding place. He returns as the first streaks of dawn lighten the
skies. No wonder he falls asleep during morning prayers, an act
that affords him a beating from Francesco. It never stops him.
Any caged animal longs for its freedom, no matter the price.

"We can't risk my lord hearing us," Mamma says sharply,
drawing the heavy brocade fabric curtains of my bed around us,
as if that would protect us.

"What will they do to her?" I bite my lip and taste blood.

My mother opens her mouth as if to speak and then stops.
She pauses. I realize in this breathless silence that she does not
want to frighten me. I stare at her. The expression on my mother's beloved face is hard to read. There is only a single candle

flame to illuminate the space. She pushes back a loose ten-dril of hair from my thick plait, just as if I were a young child again, and tucks it behind my ear. I am reminded that no mat-ter where we have lived—and we have laid down our heads in many places, from the hovels of Madrid's slums to the splendor of the Spanish court—we have been together, in our own private world. Mamma and me. Our own sanctuary. Until now. Now, the ever-present dangers of a confusing world dance around us. I can almost hear their rasping breath.

"I don't know what'll happen. There are few who can with-stand the . . ." It is here she stops again. "The rigors . . . of questioning by the agents of the Holy Office. We must pray, daughter. We must pray Faustina can hold her tongue. We must pray she finds the sweet release of death quickly."

"But what if she gives names? What if she names us?" I persist. Fear blooms within me like ink spilled on parchment.

"What if they come for us?" I ask, gripping my mother's hand. "We can't stay here and await our fate. We must leave. We must go far from here."

Mamma says nothing. I realize she does not know what to do, and I have to fight my frustration. She looks away again, but there is nothing to see except the heavy drapes, nothing to breathe except the stifling air. Perhaps she can sense this terror's dark shape, its heavy mass unmoving.

"Giulia, we can't flee. Francesco wouldn't stop searching for us. He'd send an army after us—and his wrath upon finding us would be too high a price to pay for our small freedom."

"But, Mamma, we can hide. We have women who are loyal to us in the city. They would protect us."

Mamma shakes her head. "They wouldn't, and they'd be right not to. They'd be hunted too, and if they were caught helping us flee, their lives would be endangered. We can't run.

We have my husband's protection—for now, at least. That must give us comfort. Pray, Giulia. Pray. It's all we can do—and stay silent. Tell no one. Admit nothing. Perhaps this will pass."

"But she was—*is*—our friend," I say, correcting myself when I realize I have all but condemned her. "There must be some way of helping her?"

"No one has friends once they step inside the dungeons. We'll pray for her. Giulia, my love, it's all we can do."

This is not enough. I open my mouth to object but before I can reply, Mamma blows out the flame, pitching us back into darkness. She moves, pulling the curtains aside, her footsteps barely discernible as she retreats back to the bed she shares with Francesco. The door clicks shut behind her. Our sanctuary broken.

# 9

## February 16, 1633

Today we watch our friend die.

It is barely past dawn. Whipping Boy brings in the water for washing. Behind my velvet drapes, I hear his clumsy footsteps, the water slopping over the rim of the jug as he goes. I have not slept. All night, I have waited. I am waiting, not just for Faustina's execution, but to see if our fates are entwined. I am waiting to see if our secrets will come spilling out like a sack of flour slashed open by the baker's knife. The *tarocchi* lie there too, but I do not touch them. I am scared of what they may reveal. I have chosen ignorance. It is a poor protection, of that I am sure.

I know this morning will be long, tense, as we wait for our signal to leave. I wonder if we are always waiting: a woman's lot to be forever existing in the gaps, the pauses between the acts of men. Gattino senses my disquiet. He cannot settle, first rubbing against my hand to stroke him, then, just as quickly, reaching back with his mouth to bite me in a flash of claws and teeth. Eventually, I give up and drop him to the floor as I lie back on my bed. He stalks off, ears back, tail high and twitching.

"Pray for me," Faustina says through bloodied lips. "Pray for me, for I have sinned."

Her voice can barely be heard amid the roar of the crowds, come to watch our friend's death. It is as good as a play. Among the spectators are nut sellers and men hawking *avvisi*. I do not glance at them. Their excitement sickens me. I turn my face away as they pass, though plenty hold out a coin and snatch at the thin parchment. It is midday and the winter sun is lukewarm on our heads. There is a carnival air, like one of the many saints' days our stinking city devotes to Santa Rosalia, the plague destroyer. When offered up to the heavens, the bones of the noblewoman stopped the pestilence that ravaged the city ten years ago, though for months the narrow streets were filled with the bloated, putrid corpses of the dead. Or so Valentina has told me, her eyes alive with morbid delight. According to her, the alleys rang with the sound of ravens cawing, perched upon blackened limbs, plucking out milk-blank eyes. Rats gnawed at faces, plague boils suppurating in the heat. Undeterred by her death five hundred years earlier, Rosalia herself appeared before a man and beseeched him to raise her bones—her jaw and three fingers—and lead them through Palermo in procession. In doing so, the evil fever was halted, and her patronage of the city assured.

Today, the stench of unwashed bodies is overpowering as commoners and nobility alike squash into Piano della Marina. Nearby sits the Palazzo Steri and its dungeons, watching silently as whores rub shoulders with gentlemen, washerwomen, farmers' wives, and nuns. Like us, they are gathered to witness the spectacle that is holy justice, though it is plain more than one form of business will be done today. Harlots ply their trade in the throng, their bright silk dresses and carmine-stained lips proclaiming their wares as they flirt and simper their way to a good meal this night.

"Look away," Mamma says. She sees my gaze follow the painted women standing tall in their *chopines*. I look back and notice she is white-faced behind her veil. We neither of us want to be here, but my stepfather demands our presence. We cannot refuse him. Yet we cannot bear to look at the platform erected especially for the execution, the scaffold pointing upward to the heavens. I know we have failed Faustina; my heart tells me so. She was our friend, *is* our friend. She holds our closest secrets—or I pray she still does. She has been broken by agents who now hold crucifixes that gleam with gold and rubies.

Thankfully, my stepfather is nowhere to be seen. If he was here, he might sense our shock; how we fidget with our sleeves, how we try to look anywhere but at *her*. He has slipped away to shake the hands of dignitaries, the men who have done the work we see here today; Faustina's hair hacked from her head, her body twisted, tormented by these men of God.

We are standing in the section of the viewing gallery reserved for the wealthy. From here, we see as much as the pigeons that swoop down to pick at discarded fruit, the bits of offal swarming with flies, the detritus of the market usually held here. We see people jostling and talking, spitting shells, and arguing. We see all manner of life squeezed into this place.

It was the low beat of the drums that alerted us to the arrival of our friend, who will now be butchered like the pig for supper. Then came the shrieks and howls of the onlookers who had run with the wooden carts that jolted Faustina on her journey to her execution, paraded to the city. Pelted with stones and rotting onions, she would have been jostled and taunted by the shrieking swarms of people surrounding the wagon as it rolled into the square.

When the wagon rolled to a stop, we watched her descend, her gait awkward, unsteady, the strappado having done its work. The crowd, which seemed to grow denser by the minute, pushed and heckled as she made her slow, faltering way to the wooden steps. Faustina wore her own noose around her neck. It dragged behind her as she climbed. Finally, she took her place upon the scaffold.

Now, a momentary hush descends.

We wait; unable to look, unable to turn away. I touch my neck and imagine, for the briefest moment, the feel of the rope, rough against my skin. It is more than an imagining; it is as if the weight of it hangs heavy on me too. My body sways a little as I watch her, the woman who taught me to use a pestle and mortar, who stroked my face so gently. I do not know if her mother is here, her siblings too. I hope they are not. This is no sight for a child and yet the square teems with small ruddy faces and snot-smeared cheeks.

Reaching into a pocket sewn into my skirts, I touch the blackbird's feather, then the edge of the deck of *tarocchi*, some of my treasures, my talismans. I hold them as if they can bring me comfort.

Just then my stepfather returns. His deep black velvets contrast with the bright colors of the noblewomen's silks, the wealthy merchants in their finery, their wives fluttering their fans. Both Mamma and I are at odds with the scene in our muted blue skirts, each earning a look of disapproval from him. Francesco likes us to dress richly, to show off his wealth with finery. Today, we could not oblige him. To dress up as if for carnival in truth would have sickened us. We know we will suffer for it later.

"Pray for me. Pray for me, for I'm a sinner."

Her voice, thin, reedy, carries across the mob.

Then, just as suddenly, the crowd roars as one. Faustina stumbles and there is a cheer, a crescendo of excitement. Her fragility seems to rile the onlookers. People shift and move, the crowd sinuous and swaying. Voices are raised but I cannot tell what is said. I feel the drums in my ears as if they beat beside me. I look down at my feet and expect to see them bare and bloodied, just like before, but all I see are my boots poking out from my robe. I dig my nails fiercely into my palm to stop myself from fainting. I try to swallow but the dust renders my throat dry. Our friend has only seconds left to live.

Then, unexpectedly, her voice rings out.

"Laugh! So many of you will come with me!"

The shock is immediate.

It reverberates through the crowds like the currents that swirl beneath the city's rivers. The Holy Office allows only a few short sentences of contrition from the heretic facing their death. This outburst is unheard of. A scandal.

The hangman looks around for instruction. A moaning goes up from the square. People climb up onto the viewing platforms, surging toward the gallows. Faustina looks triumphant but her victory is short-lived. With a roughness not normally given to a condemned woman at this, her final moment, the executioner grabs the rope and hoists it into position, pulling it tight around her neck. She climbs the ladder with difficulty. The priest's voice can now be heard reciting the Apostles' Creed. The final seconds of our friend's life have arrived. They are ebbing away. Nausea rises.

". . . *soffri e fu sepolto* . . . he suffered and was buried . . ." As these words leave the priest's lips, the ladder beneath her feet is kicked away by the executioner. She drops sharply, clumsily. She chokes. The crowd barely draws breath. It groans again, this time louder. People seem to move as one toward our hanging Faustina, her feet dancing, her hands clawing ineffectually at the thick rope. The hangman's assistant jumps up from the ground below and grabs her ankles, pulling our friend downward, hastening her death. A single act of kindness amid this cruelty. More prayers are heard, increasing in sound and intensity.

There is a loud crack. Confused, I look over and see one of the platforms is collapsing. It takes a moment for those upon it to realize. More of the structure breaks off, and now there is screaming. Spectators fall back into each other. Both wooden boxes, built hurriedly and badly, disintegrate under the weight of the people who climbed on top of them to get a better view. Some might say this is Faustina's work, the work of a witch. People are crushed, lying mangled on the ground, many unmoving. There is panic as people try to escape but cannot move away. Children are trodden under the feet of the crowd.

"Cursed!"

"Cursed by the witch!"

The cry goes up. It is the sound of hunting dogs baying to the horn, scenting the deer in the undergrowth, pulling to be unleashed.

Behind them, Faustina's body jerks, then hangs limp like a game bird waiting for the butcher's hook.

"We must go. Quickly," Mamma says.

I feel my eyes widen with terror.

"We go. Now." My mother's voice is harsh.

I allow her to pull me away from the carnage below. We cannot help, we can only save ourselves. We join the gentlemen, their wives, their sons and daughters, the nobles and churchmen who flee, back to our carriages.

As our carriage moves away, the insides of the door bolted, Francesco shouting orders to the coachman, the same thought keeps beating alongside the thud of my heart: *Did she name us? Are we dead women walking too?*

# 10

Three months have passed since they killed her.

Three tense, hard months as spring followed winter, and still, we waited. There was no work done in the still room. Francesco stopped our day visits to the convent, saying the plants and herbs were not godly work. Mamma stopped us from going at night, saying it would bring trouble to our door. Instead, we went back to our roles as a merchant's wife and daughter. I dropped stitches, while Mamma ordered new sheets, better plates for the table, arranged flowers cut from early blooms in the garden. We walked around Francesco's villa like two stranded ghosts, trailing through the sunlit chambers, dust motes dancing in the strips of glowing yellow light.

Every moment has seemed to contain a threat, or the promise of one. Every moment has also contained the memory of *her.*

Didn't she laugh when I mixed up the jar of face tonic with the salve for San Fiacre's figs, mimicking an old woman applying goats' milk, lemon, and eggs to her buttocks?

Didn't she weep when she told of the woman in her fifth moon cycle, miscarrying her child, the small mess of blood and gristle sliding from her, never to breathe the same air in this world?

Wasn't her touch gentle, her smile contagious?

Grief is the memory of the touch of her stained hand, roughened from washing and sweeping, the dirt on her soles when she refused to wear boots, the crease between her brows as she concentrated on the exact dose of a tincture or essence. It is in everything she ever was to me. When Mamma told me about the poison, it was *her* I felt betrayed by, the sore rub of a secret kept from me.

And now she is gone.

Her absence fills the air we breathe even as her remains lie rotting in a mass grave. Her head will have been removed after her death, disembodying her soul and barring her entry into the kingdom of God. Or so the priests say. But they say many things. Perhaps we will see her the next time we drive over the Ponte delle Teste in our fine carriage, a bridge so called because of the severed heads on view, the recently departed *decollati* serving as a warning to us. Perhaps we will look away, as we did at her execution.

Francesco's gaze has become sharper. He watches us intently as we go about our tiresome chores. He moves through the villa silently as if he would catch us unawares. There is a subdued air in the house of discord. Valentina rarely appears, staying by her hearth in the kitchens, while Whipping Boy turns his face away as if his vague interest in me, his furtive glances, his blushes, have ceased.

My sampler remains tangled. My dance maestro despairs of me ever learning the correct steps. My heart remains in the still room, hazy with the scents of our preparations, with Faustina at my side, humming, with Mamma close by, decanting oils or bundling together drying plants.

Then, one day, the restless, grief-laden air breathes out of my lungs, and I notice it is hot, angered, fuming. Where is my mother? Valentina does not know. Her eyes slide away from me back to the rabbit she will skin. It lies, flopped, limp, on the table surface. In her right hand, smeared with brown blood, is a large butcher's knife. With a swift movement, she slams it down, cutting the right hind leg at the joint. With another chop, the left hind follows. From there she will slice the leg open, using a smaller, thinner knife, peeling back the skin from the pink-gray meat, moving down the carcass, guts sliding out, leaving a lump of muscle and bone for the pot.

Whipping Boy does not know. He is sweating as he piles wood outside the kitchen door. He does not stop to wipe his dark hair nor drink from the well.

She is not in the storerooms, the herb garden, nor the brewery.

I finally find her in the darkened mew where Francesco's hawk perches on its wooden pole. The hawk twitches and flinches as it hears my approach, its face covered by its hood. Eyes adjusting to the darkness, I see Mamma. She is looking at the bird, tethered to the post.

"Mamma?"

She starts as if she had not heard me approach.

"Giulia . . ."

I walk slowly, trying not to disturb the creature but it shifts, skittish, shuffling, its head moving with each new sound. Words have been building inside me for weeks, and now they must come out.

"I can't bear this, Mamma. We're trapped here! Why must we stay inside being watched all the time? Faustina would've hated this. She would've carried on, Mamma."

My mother clucks at the bird. It moves its head with a sideways tilt.

"Mamma, listen to me! They killed her. They humiliated her! And for what? For nothing! Because she helped get rid of bad men? They took our friend, and they destroyed her in front of everyone." I am crying now, a river of tears that I have been unable to shed. I have missed her, but it is more than that. I am enraged, horrified at what they did to her, what they could do to us. It has all got tangled up and instead of fear, I am filled with fire, with a rage so fierce it burns hot in my chest. There is another feeling, one I have not yet allowed myself to understand. It is another grief, but this time, it is for the poison. I miss making it. I miss the ritual and the risk, the sweet sound of alchemy broiling, of the *acqua* forming. This is a strange yearning, and so I barely acknowledge it, but it is there, underneath the sadness and rage. It is the loss of freedom, too, freedom I had not known since arriving here. I miss our night excursions. I miss our shared secret, the shared danger. I feel as if I am living half a life.

"Giulia, enough. I've already placed you in danger, I won't do so again. It's too risky to carry on making the *acqua*. You must see this, *amore mio?*"

She reaches out a hand to smooth down a tendril of my hair that has come loose, but I push it away.

"No, I don't see this! It's always been dangerous! We're protected by Francesco, and Faustina wasn't. It's different for us. We have to carry on for her sake!"

"Giulia, you're a fool to think we're safe!" Mamma says sharply.

The hawk bristles, rustling its plumage, the mottled russet-brown feathers that fold back into themselves again.

I step back, not wanting to alarm the bird, but I am furious.

"You're wrong," I hiss. "We're playing into their hands by doing nothing. Our obedience only serves those churchmen who tortured her." The sobs rise in my throat. "There were many *Inquisitori* there at her death, and none even glanced in our direction! We must carry on."

"Oh, Giulia, you've much to learn. The *Inquisitori* act with stealth. They don't arrest a woman in daylight, in front of her husband, surrounded by her family, her allies. No, they work in the shadows. They take people at night. They take them into their courts and their prisons, and the accused may never know the charges against them until they climb the ladder to the noose. My love, there's plenty to fear."

I stare back at her. I will not accept this verdict. I am sick of waiting, always waiting. Shaking my head, I turn and stalk out. Once the cage door is open, the birds inside must flap their wings and fly, if only for a short time before they are captured again. I long to soar.

That night, the familiar creeping hand slides up my thigh, pushing my night shift higher and higher.

At first, I do not know what is happening. I had fallen into a troubled slumber after my fight with Mamma, and now I am entangled, twisted, trapped. Disorientated, I am unsure what time it is or where I am, until I feel him, and then I know. His fingers are clammy, his breathing heavy. He is in my darkened chamber, moving on my sheets as if invited. It takes a second for the swirling dreams to recede, but when they do, I react as if I am being murdered in my bed.

"Get off me, whoreson!" I shout, repeating the curse I heard in the brothel.

The sharp sting of his slap follows.

Face throbbing, curses flying, we wrestle now, though he has my wrists tight in his grip. I aim, then fire a globule of spit at his face. This only serves to excite him.

"You want to fight me, little savage?" he pants. "*I denti di dio*, God's teeth," he hisses, "you've become stronger, little one . . ."

I spit again but he is already fumbling with his breeches. Trying to kick out, I realize he now has me pinned down. I am panting, not just with panic but with anger that runs molten through my body, crackling like lightning through the branch of a tree.

It is no use. He is still stronger than me. I try again to lash out at him, but I cannot move my legs. Then, I remember.

I fall still, suddenly.

It seems to please Francesco.

"Good, good. You'll learn your place, little mistress," he breathes, his hot breath on my face. I turn away, momentarily study the pattern woven through the thick damask hangings adorning my bed. They smell musty, of dust and sleep. I could trace the thread's journey across the plateaus and valleys of the flowers and leaves that entwine so charmingly, but I do not. Instead, my left arm, now freed as my stepfather forces himself onto me, creeps, silent and slow across the sheet and under the feather bolster. Face still turned, each heartbeat bringing me closer, I concentrate on breathing, just breathing, as my hand searches for that which I have hidden. It is the slender handle I discover first, the wooden crucifix disguising its true purpose. I draw it carefully as Francesco thrusts.

A nun's dagger. Found at the convent, left on the low stone wall of the cloister, between one of the arches. I should not have picked it up, slipped it into my skirts, but I did. I swore to myself I would return it, but I never did. I have not dared use it, until now.

Francesco is panting now. I know he is almost done. I wait until his face screws up and then I pull the blade from its hiding place. Except I fumble. I am too slow. Francesco is too heavy upon me as he drops down. He spots the weapon before I can use it, grabs my hand, his large digits curling around mine, and wrenches the blade from my grip.

For good measure, he slaps my face again.

"Bitch. She-devil. How dare you! It is I who rescued you! Why do you think I married your whore mother? To get you. You were the prize, little savage. You."

Francesco laughs then, ruffles his hand through his hair as he pulls his breeches up and pats round the bed looking for his doublet.

With a final look, he walks out. He does not even think to take my weapon. I do not care. His words, like arrows, have struck their target.

It was me.

It was my fault.

# 11

I do not need to read the *tarocchi* to know what comes next, but they tell me anyway. The cards have whispered to me from their hidden place, and I have ignored them, unwilling to see the future. But now? Now, I have no choice.

I turn over the first: *La Fortuna* again. This time it has reverted to its proper position, the hands of destiny placing the fortunate back at the top, the rest cascading to the bottom. My hands tremble as I pull the next, and I am right to fear it. The tower stands, but only just. It is ablaze and crumbling as a streak of lightning strikes from the heavens. All will come tumbling down. It speaks of change, upheaval, disaster.

It has been two full moons since I last bled. Once again, I have no sheets to scrub when the yard is empty, no shift to soak overnight in lye. Knowing Valentina's beady eyes will learn my secret, I have sneaked down to the cold store to take the earthenware bowl of pig's blood. It is this I wash out of my bedding, pretending my courses have come.

After my fight with Francesco, he has stayed away but I know it is only a temporary reprieve. I expected punishment after that evening, but he said nothing. I would have accepted a beating as penance for my sin of attracting him to us. Perhaps he guessed that, and this silence, this pause, is my punishment instead. If so, he knows me better than I have given him credit.

I have not told my mother about my knife. Francesco appears not to have told her either. I now share this secret with him. A thought that sickens me.

I know the time is coming when I must tell Mamma about the child I am sure is growing inside me, but I have not yet found the words.

As it turns out, I don't need to.

Sitting in the shade of the grapevines that trail the walled garden, I have a small Bible in my hand, but the curling pages lie unread, abandoned to the early summer heat. I am hot, fidgeting and nauseous when Mamma sits beside me on the stone seat. She fans herself.

"Mamma . . ." I begin, then stop. I have barely acknowledged the crisis that will come when my pregnancy is discovered. I have barely acknowledged the fear that comes to any woman faced with carrying a child and surviving its birth. My life, if not already over, is slipping into uncharted territory. I do not know what to fear the most—the trials of labor, the extinguishing of my youth and virtue, or the condemnation I know I will receive. Of course, Francesco will deny ever having touched me. As a woman, I will be discounted, dishonored. Destroyed.

Then, there is the unavoidable fact that I am carrying *his* child. The thought of Francesco's seed growing inside me makes me recoil from myself. And yet, despite this, there is hope: a softness, a space where something inside me grows with this creature.

"You're with child," Mamma says matter-of-factly.

"You know?" I say.

Her fan stops fluttering. She looks at me, then moves her gaze to the villa walls across this ornate section of our garden; the palm leaves, the spilling flowers, the cypress trees. All of which belie the tragedy that is unfolding in our small part of this city.

"I feared this would happen. It was inevitable," she says. There is no shock, no wailing, no gnashing of teeth nor panic. Not what I was expecting.

I fan myself with my discarded book. Should not a young woman like me be preparing for marriage, for a long engagement to a suitor chosen by her father? Should not she be giggling with her sisters as she sews linens that will form part of her dowry, dreaming of faraway places where she will start a new life?

Instead, I have this. This dishonor. This separation. It is an ending, not a beginning. And yet, and yet. There is a feeling, as soft and fine as a spider's web. It hovers close, gossamer threads linking me to the new life growing within. I can sense my child. I can sense *her*. Though my head tells me I am ruined and lost and broken, my heart opens and fills me with joy. I cannot explain it.

"Daughter, I'll help you, I promise," Mamma says. She smiles at me and strokes my hair. "Tonight, put your linen rags up inside you, as you would normally. You must do everything just as you would as if your courses had come. Once Francesco is asleep, we'll leave. Tell no one your secret, my love."

My heart lifts. We will leave. Tonight. I am instantly giddy. Perhaps the cards were wrong. Perhaps the tower was not a warning but an opportunity, an ending to this existence and the beginning of a new one.

As for telling anyone, who is there to tell? I may as well whisper into Gattino's furred ear.

My mother stands up, smooths down her skirts. She is splendid in a deep russet red gown, pearls and rubies around her neck, fine lace covering her bodice, though I know that before the day is done she will be found weeding the herb garden or feeding the pigs.

"And, Giulia, we must be careful. There's uprising in the city, the streets aren't safe. We must keep to the shadows tonight."

Valentina has brought news of tithes set by our Spanish masters from the marketplace. Every day, she frowns as she tells us, so-and-so from this quarter said they saw empty bread stalls toppled, mud and rocks thrown in protest. We are shielded inside these walls. Francesco continues drinking his good Rhenish wine. He still sups from silver goblets. His horses are tacked in the finest Spanish leather. We still eat well each night. We are the lucky ones. Yet, luck is relative, I have discovered.

"Mamma, we're never safe. We always keep to the dark alleys and corners." I sigh, leaning back on the seat, feeling the thrill of a new adventure, a new home—or perhaps we will go back to Spain, to the family of courtesans we left behind. We were happy there, Mamma and me. Just how it was, before Francesco.

Placing my hand on my belly, I consider this. Inside me is the beginnings of a child. Perhaps it already has tiny lungs to breathe. Perhaps it has fingernails and toes, hairs sprouting from its head, eyelashes forming around the green eyes we may share. Later, when the owls hoot, when the light leeches from the day, we will leave this place, jump ship, and all will be as it was.

Francesco balks at the sight of the pouch worn around my neck. He looks at me when I enter the dining chamber, his eyes immediately drawn to the small leather bag of crushed cloves, lavender, and rose petals, which hide the scent of menstrual blood. He drops his gaze as if even to look upon me is a sin.

"I bid you good night, stepdaughter," he says, clearing his throat, his chair leg scraping against the stone floor in his haste to leave. Inwardly, I laugh at his discomfort. For a sinful man, he is the very vision of awkward delicacy. I feel a twinge of triumph, casting my eyes down as any dutiful, shameful daughter of Eve should so that he does not see how I rejoice at his embarrassment—and my small victory. I am the very image of deceit.

We neither of us eat much. Mamma and I sit in silence, each absorbed in our thoughts. Valentina mutters and huffs in disgust at our lack of appetites when she clears away the silver platters upon which the food lies almost untouched, even though what she doesn't finish she will sell at the servants' door later.

Once Valentina's muttering has ceased, and we have watched Whipping Boy's nightly departure—cloak swinging, candle flickering, coins clinking—it is time to leave. I have with me my shell, my coin, a new sprig of rosemary, my blackbird's feather and, of course, my *tarocchi*. I take them for courage, and because they are the only real treasures I possess.

"Come," Mamma says. No candle to flicker. Dark cloaks clutched around us. Coins, perhaps, though we cannot permit chinking. We must make no sound. We are two women alone at night walking through a city that can erupt in violence or rioting at a moment's notice. We have heard the shouts and the glass breaking from inside the safety of our gilded prison. We know there is unrest, and yet we have set out into the dark streets with only our wits.

This night I am emboldened. It is only when Mamma veers away from the harbor that I stop. Question her.

"Why this way? The port, the ships, are that way!"

My mother frowns.

"Come, Giulia. We've little time," she says. She continues walking.

"Stop!" I say. This time my voice carries. "Where are you going? If we're leaving, then better we go by boat. If we travel overland, we'll be too slow. Francesco's guards will outrun us within days, hours even."

My mother looks aghast.

"We aren't leaving, daughter! We're going to the convent. Clara is waiting for us."

"Oh," I reply, thinking perhaps we will pick up the essential herbs, those for childbirth, those for the *acqua*, before we board a ship. I follow her and we move quickly now. There are shouts in the streets nearby, and so we change our route, swerving in and out of alleys, small passageways that a visitor to the city may mistake for dead ends. It takes longer, but we reach Sant'Agostino without incident. Mamma taps out the agreed signal, which brings the nun. Somehow, my mother has got word to her to expect us tonight. Sister Clara gestures for us both to be silent. Her face seems pale in the darkness. From the chapel comes the low voices of the choir as the sisters sing the prayers of Nocturns. We hurry to the still room, which Sister Clara unlocks, giving Mamma the key this time. My mother takes it without a backward glance but the nun hovers.

"Teofania, I must go back to Vigil. I can't linger, my absence will be noted." Clara speaks with urgency, though she has stayed to tell us this. Her words are rushed, harried. "You mustn't come again like this, so close to our prayers. We may be discovered, and if we are, I can't help you."

My mother, in a gesture I recognize as purely hers, takes hold of the nun's hands, stroking them gently, looking into her face as she speaks. In the months and years to come, I will remember Mamma's instinctive care, the gentle attention she gives to her friend. It seems to me, even now, that I have witnessed something unbreakable that exists only between women.

I am young but I know already that we women exist in the black beyond of the stage, behind the thick curtains. As men strut and preen, we make do with what we can, mere supporting players in the theater of life. But what they don't know is what grows in the darkness backstage; the fraternity of women, the collusion of femalehood, the kindred understanding that blooms away from the harsh gaze of men. Mamma places one of her hands against Clara's cheek. The nun winces at first, and then smiles as if it is something she has forgotten how to do. She is already used to the dearth of physical touch that is the holy woman's lot.

"We thank you, Clara. We know this is a great risk for you. We'll be gone long before Lauds, but we needed as much time as possible to complete our task before dawn," Mamma says.

A look is exchanged between them, but it is too dark to see what it might mean. For a moment, I am disarmed. Before dawn? Surely, we should go long before then? Mamma busies herself. I watch as she gathers herbs—rue, black hellebore, parsley, juniper. They are not the ones I expect her to take, and I know what they are used for. I have helped my mother administer them. I know they will make a fetus fall out from a woman's womb in a mess of blood and gristle, tiny bones, and unformed soulless remains. It is mostly whores who need such services, but not always. I have seen women barely ten years older than me who have borne a child every year since they started to bleed. Worn out from childbirth and raising large broods, they come, pleading. We dispense these herbs with instructions to brew a tisane to sip each evening, to help the unwanted child slip out from its unwilling mother, back to whence it came: to the graveyard, or simply burnt in a good fire along with rosemary to cleanse the air.

Every second that passes, I feel a growing unease. I was not sure but now I am. Seeing Mamma take up her pestle and begin pounding, I cannot hold my silence.

"Mamma, stop."

"There's no time, Giulia. Here, take the apron. Help me."

"No," I say.

My mother turns, but resumes her grinding motion.

"Stop." I step forward and take hold of her wrist.

I understand now why we are here. There is no ship. No return to Spain and the life we left.

I also know that I will not take this physick.

There is no sense in my decision, no logic at all. If we do not plan to leave, as I wanted, as I have always dreamt, then this child cannot be born. It must be sent back whence it came—and yet, I cannot do it. Yes, I am scared. Yes, I know my fate is uncertain, my life ruined, but I still cannot do it. Inside me is a daughter. I can sense her tiny heartbeat. I cannot fathom how I know this, but I do. We may be responsible for the deaths of many men around the city walls, but I will not condemn my own child.

My mother is now staring at me as if I have run mad. Perhaps I have.

"Listen to me. I won't do this. It's wrong. It's wrong for *her* . . ."

"What are you talking about?" my mother says impatiently. If she notices I have named the sex of the baby, she does not say.

"I won't do this."

"Giulia, this is impossible! You know you can't go through with your pregnancy! They'll never accept you—or this child. You'll never have a chance of marriage or security."

I turn away.

"I've no chance of that anyway! No boy will ever want my hand; not here, anyway. No merchant family will take me in as their daughter. I'm a bastard, or have you forgotten? But, Mamma, you're right. I can't have this child here, in Palermo, but perhaps I could have it somewhere else, somewhere familiar. I've thought it all through. We can buy our passage on a boat to Madrid. We can sell our jewels and buy horses and ride to the court. They'll know us still, I'm sure of it. I'll have my child away from here, away from Francesco—"

"Giulia!" Mamma interrupts me. She drops the pestle and grabs my arms. "Are you feverish? Are you unwell? You must see this can't be. They'd never let a woman and daughter board a boat without their husband or father!"

At this, I lose my patience.

"Mamma! You've spent your life being used by men, relying on them for your safety and comfort! I won't live that way, not ever. I refuse to! I don't care what it costs me, but I'll walk my own path!"

My mother steps back as if I have slapped her.

We stand, glaring at each other.

I am panting with . . . what? Fear? Fury? The desire to make my mother understand, when even I do not?

"You're a child, Giulia. Did you really think we could run away? Did you really think that was possible?" Mamma makes a guttural sound. "No, Giulia. We'll deal with your situation here and now. This is why we're here."

I take a sudden breath as if I am choking and place a hand on my chest to steady myself. The chamber is warm as heat lingers from the day, but I am chilled to my bones.

"My situation?" I say.

"We'll use the remedies tonight. We'll rid you of this . . . this devil that has been planted inside you against your will."

It is perhaps the first time I have seen the anger my mother feels at Francesco, now directed at me. She reaches for my hands just as she did with Sister Clara, but I snatch them away. I am trembling, cold. Drifting in from nowhere I can place comes a rotting smell, the stench of black bile on a surgeon's slab. It is putrid and dank, like an open grave, followed by a high note that seems to increase in intensity as the seconds pass. I place my hands over my ears, not wanting to hear it, but the screech of it magnifies.

"You're wrong, Mamma. This is no devil inside me—this is a child, this is my *daughter*. I feel like I know her already; she's strong and willful. She wants to live."

I feel oddly calm now, as if I am a tree gripping the mountainside being buffeted by great winds. The sound reaches its zenith, but I care little. I am fighting for my child's life. It is my mother's turn to stare back at me, horrified.

"You're saying you want this?" she says. "Giulia, until the child quickens, you run no risk to your immortal soul if you—"

"If I what, Mamma?" I interject. "If I kill her? If I abort her with our clever herbs? I'll never do that!" I am shouting now, careless of the danger I am placing us in, risking our discovery here, risking Clara's position as well. "We have a chance of freedom! We have a chance of our own family. We could take your jewels and buy passage, husband or no husband. With enough gold, we can escape from Palermo—"

"And be unprotected against sailors, against all who might do us harm both on the journey and beyond?" my mother interjects. "They'll kill us for our jewels. We'll be drowned in the seas, a watery grave for us and your child." Her words strike me, fast as a viper. "You can't have this child. Imagine the scandal. They already despise us. Now they'll destroy us—"

"They despise *you!*" I am moving before I finish. I am trying to open the door, stamping my feet until the key turns in the lock. I look round before I go. I see the herbs. I see a path laid out before me, a path I will not tread. A path where I kill my daughter before she has drawn breath, for the privilege of remaining Francesco's chattel. All hope of freedom, of living a life away from here, buried. I will not let this be my fate—nor my daughter's. Though it is madness to walk away, I do it, my boots echoing on the hard, cold floor. I leave Mamma standing by her deadly plants. I throw open the side door, not caring who might be lurking in the alley. I inhale the night air, my chest heaving. It smells of manure and fish bones, piss and dirt and sunbaked roads, as well as salt from the sea. It smells of a place that has become my downfall. Here, I will be ostracized. Here, I will know disgrace, instead of sailing free across the ocean.

Anger strengthens my courage. I walk the dark streets without fear as my blood is up, like a hound scenting the deer. Gritting my teeth, I run now, suddenly wanting my chamber, wanting to shut the curtains around my bed and wait for the storm that is about to break over my head. There are footsteps behind me, but I do not look back. I run as if I am the doe who knows she is chased by dogs. Perhaps they will catch me, sink their sharp teeth into my neck and rip out my throat.

Perhaps I will bite back, bloodlust rising, eyes flaring, teeth gnashing.

# 12

Francesco is waiting when I return.

Wrenching open the door to the servants' entrance, I almost run into him. He stands, blocking my way.

"Where have you been?"

Falling back, shocked, I look around for another exit. The high-pitched clanging in my head is unrelenting. It sounds like a bell ringing, frantic and urgent, warning me of imminent danger.

There is no other way, so I try to push past him. He grabs my arm.

"Get off me! You're hurting me!"

"Where have you been? And where's my wife?" I know he will hit me so I duck, and his swing lands in midair, making him stagger. He stinks of stale wine.

"Filthy worm head!" I shout, repeating one of the cook's favorite curses.

He seizes a lock of my hair and tugs me toward him. He drags me, stumbling, across the flagstones, then the marble floors of the villa.

"God give you ill fortune," I curse, and he answers: "But He already has, Giulia! He has already given me you and your *buttana* mother!"

I turn my head and try to bite his hand, but he holds me so tight I fear my hair may be pulled from my head.

"You disgust me," I say as he throws me into a chamber I have never set foot in before. I know immediately it is Francesco's study. There is a large mahogany table, set at which is a carved chair of the same wood. A fire is lit, and a goblet sits empty on an ornate side table. There are piles of vellum, yellow and curling. There is a quill, its nib black with ink. Next to it lies a leather-bound Bible studded with gemstones. I rub my skin where he gripped me, the bruise already forming under my now-torn sleeve. He strides to the door, turning a key, placing it into a pocket in his doublet and locking us both in.

"Why have you locked the door?" I say, backing toward the edge of the room, panic building.

Something snaps. Francesco looks at me with those hard eyes, and before I know what I am doing, I change course. I run forward. I lunge at him, kicking, trying to tear at his hair, his skin, anywhere I might hurt him.

"Let me out! Let me go!" I shout. He raises his arms and almost lifts me, throwing me onto a large Turkish rug by the fireplace. Floored, I remember the child in my womb. I pray she is unharmed as I grip my stomach, heart racing, breath short and panting.

"*Santu diavuluni.* Know your place, she-devil. I'm your master, or did you forget?" he says. On his face is a small smile. The heat of my anger dissipates, turns into the slow chill of fear.

Francesco scrabbles about, looking for something. He unlocks a cabinet with the small key he has now located. There is a malevolent pause. The smell is back, this time stronger, overpowering. I lift my head up like an animal to glean its source, but I know it well enough to understand it is another warning. Rancid, like rotten meat this time. The odor permeates my skin. At the same time, the high note, the discordant sound, rings in my ears. It takes everything for me not to fall to my knees, clasping the sides of my head to stop its clamor. I may vomit. My stepfather comes back toward me, oblivious to the noise and the stench, and in his hand is the object he has been looking for: a scourge, its long rope lengths knotted and frayed.

Holding the whip in his right hand, his face is expressionless. At first. Then he smiles as if he will embrace a beloved niece. As he does so, he pulls his arm back. Francesco unleashes the ropes bound together to purge sin from the mortal flesh of monks. The pain is immediate. The violence of the knots as they rip into my flesh is horrifying—accurate, efficient. Blood, hot and sticky, soaks into my shift. I have no time to react.

He comes at me again, and again.

I crouch now under the blows, hearing a tearing sound as the instrument shreds my skin. There is so much blood. There is burning, searing pain. On the verge of blacking out, as the room swims and my cries become stuck in my throat, there is suddenly a noise. The door bursts open. Neither of us has heard Mamma's key turn in the lock.

For a moment, nothing happens. Francesco, whose face is twisted with rage, stops. He stares at me, mirroring my bewilderment.

Then, my mother runs to me, pulls me into her embrace and I cry out with the agony of being held. Francesco steps back and drops the scourge, slick with livid red, which smears the marble-veined floor, the Turkish rug now spoiled.

"My love, my love," Mamma croons as I shake in her arms. She turns to Francesco. "You're a monster! Mortification of the flesh is a sin. The Church itself has banned it so why do you have that . . . that terrible thing?"

As if awakening from a night terror, my persecutor starts. He turns around, then leaves, the sound of his boots ringing on the cold granite surface. Mamma is on the floor beside me, folding her arms gingerly around my frame.

We stay there for a long time, weeping. She strokes my hair and whispers a song she used to sing to me as a child when I could not sleep. It is a sad song about a bird kept inside a trapper's cage. This bird, imagine if you will, is a small sparrow, unremarkable and ordinary with dull brown feathers, beady black eyes and a white chest, whose only beauty is its flight. It has been tricked, caught in a cage woven from sticks, and is bound for market. It knows its fate. It cannot escape and so it sings because that is all it can do. It sings a song so sweet, the trapper's heart is melted and he opens the door of its cage. The bird flies free, back to the skies where it calls and shrieks out of pure joy.

The song used to comfort me, but tonight it feels like a lie. My cage door is shut and bolted, and I wonder if I will die, trapped inside this gilded jail. I tell Mamma to stop, letting the silence grow instead. The fire crackles, spits, and sighs. The moon shines bright through an open window.

I limp to my chamber. My mother bathes the wounds with water of lavender. Carefully, she covers the cuts with salves I have made, before wrapping my arms, my back and shoulders, my neck and torso in clean linens. There are cuts on my scalp, which she dabs, making me cry out again. As she works, I know there are some wounds that can never be healed. I understand what must happen next. Before the thought crystallizes, shapes itself, my mother raises her face to mine.

She strokes my cheek. I wince but I do not want her to stop.

We stare, words unspoken.

We cling together in silence. Somewhere, Gattino leaps upon his prey, hauling a mouse between his claws, tumbling it until the twitching creature moves no more.

# 13

## July 1633

Francesco died as he lived: ostentatiously. He puked. He purged. He moaned and wailed. He cried out to God as he clutched his stomach, complaining of burning pains, and more besides. Mamma forbade me entry to his sickroom, so it was Valentina who brought news of the master as she carried broth and water up the stone stairs, and rank-smelling chamber pots back down. For once, the warring in the kitchens ceased.

Anxious days turned into restless nights. Physicians came and went, shaking their heads, handing over their bills when they had finished with their leeches and concoctions. I would listen to the doctors' whispered conversations in the halls and stairways, each saying how well Francesco looked, how vital, despite the fact he was dying. If suspicion fell on my mother then, as the noblemen of the city visited and were turned away, I was unaware of it. I spent my days reading as I waited for my torn skin to mend, for the pain to settle, though I cannot recall a single word I read. I spent my nights sitting by Valentina's blackened hearth as the strange hush of the house settled over us once more. June had bled into July, and the heat of the city continued to build. The fog of the sickroom seemed to creep through the house, along with a gnawing sense of disquiet. There must have been whispers against Mamma, though I never heard them. There must have been glances and muttered speculation and, finally, suspicion.

Francesco died on the morning of the sixth day of his agonies. He was considered hearty and strong, this man who rode the Spice Route, buying and selling his goods at a profit. Why then would he be cut down in his prime? What mischief was afoot?

When Mamma left the sickroom, her face ashen, her usual composure displaced, we knew what she would say. It was done. Our master was dead, our futures uncertain, though we would not mourn him.

The doctors came to take his still-warm body away. Mamma said nothing, though she must have known our fates were in their hands. The sudden, inexplicable death of a wealthy man could do nothing but raise suspicion, though I was too blinded by my own sense of relief to realize. To me, it felt like a great storm had passed, leaving the lull of its ending in its wake.

How wrong I was.

When Francesco was laid out on the autopsy table, the surgeon sharpening his knife, had they already decided the cause? Teofania's dead husband, waxy and stiff now, was peeled open, probed. Later, the cook told me they found nothing; no blackening of the tongue membrane, no corruption nor putrefaction of the organs, no trace of poison, for that was what they were looking for. How Valentina knew this was a mystery to me, but by then it mattered not anyway.

This did not quiet the voices that grew louder, speaking against my mother. A prominent man's unexpected demise must raise questions, must solicit a response. A man such as Francesco must be accounted for. It was natural for suspicion to land upon my mother. She was his concubine bride. Her beauty, her rise from squalor: none of it could be tolerated any longer.

They came for her in the early hours, only days after my stepfather's death, just as Mamma said they would—at night, in silence, cloaked in darkness.

I heard nothing as the *Inquisitori* came into our house and were ushered up the stairs to Mamma's chamber. I heard nothing when they took her away into their dungeons for questioning.

The cook, her customary scowl wiped from her face and replaced by a kind of aggrieved shock, fumbles for something as she speaks. I stand, swaying in the kitchen, unable to understand that my mother is gone, taken from me, though the words are clear enough.

"They made barely a sound, barely a sound," Valentina sniffs. "They came and took her after the bells of Vigil. I opened the door to three men, their faces hidden by their cloaks. They wore large crosses, so I knew who they were . . ." Her voice trails off as she finds what she has been looking for: a length of linen used for cleaning. She dabs her face almost delicately. It is done with an elegance she rarely possesses.

"They were inquisitors from the Holy Office?" I ask, though we already know the answer.

Valentina's eyes flash at me and I see that underneath the tears is a gleaming, watchful interest. I look back at her and say nothing. *Was it you?* I think. *Were you the informant? Did we have spies above and below stairs? Or was Francesco an inquisitor in truth?*

Before Valentina can say any more, I turn away.

I will not show her my terror. I will not break down in front of her. Mamma and I have never before been parted. I imagine her now in a small, rat-infested cell that drips with dirty water, lying on dirty straw as she awaits their questions, and I want to scream. Grief and fury clash inside me. I must *do* something. But what? I am alone except for two servants, one of whom may have betrayed us.

The cook is crying for the loss of her job, her livelihood, her home, now the master is dead and her mistress locked up. *If it was you, why didn't you think this through? Your prospects are poorer, your future uncertain*, I would like to say. *However did your life come to this, with a concubine mistress lying in a fetid jail and a dead master who made a bad death?*

Whipping Boy sits on the earthen floor in the corner of the room, sniveling. He is crying for his position, the loss of his nights of pleasure and the inconvenience of starting again with another family in another villa.

When I cry, my tears will be for the loss of everything.

Valentina looks up from her tears. She comes over to me and places a hand on my sleeve before I reach the kitchen door. It is the first time she has ever touched me. Instead of the vitriol and triumph at her whore mistress's downfall, which I expected, she looks at me with pity. This gesture is the only kindness she has ever really shown me.

"Giulia, little mistress, there's nothing you can do. There's no hope once someone is taken. You must prepare yourself," she says.

Her voice is surprisingly gentle. I swallow and move away, her words echoing behind me. There is no hope.

Despite this, I find myself seeking out the dense faceless exterior of the prison. I hover nearby. Perhaps I could trick one of the guards. Perhaps I could bribe them or lure them away so I can enter. Every day, I go to the jail. I place my hand on the stone wall, warmed by the sun, and pray Mamma can sense me. Every day, I look for a chance, a way in, knowing with a heavy heart there is none.

A week later, Valentina, her face ashen like her empty hearth, bangs the door behind her, her eyes searching for mine. I stand up from my place at the table where I have been shelling nuts, knowing these next words will form the fire inside which my life will be forged anew.

"Speak," I say.

The cook swallows.

"Speak now," I say again.

Valentina shakes her head, holds her large stomach as if winded but she does not take her gaze off mine. Her chin trembles. I march over to her and grab her free arm. I twist it, my rage appearing as if from nowhere.

"Tell me what you've heard!" My voice is harsh. I would strike her if I thought it might quicken her answer.

"They're saying . . . they're saying that your mother, God have mercy on her soul, will be . . ."

"Will be what?" I demand. My face is inches from hers. I see how all she wants is to climb onto a cart and be carried away to the mountains, to the sister she loves and the simple life she craves. Yet, she is here, in this kitchen, her basket lying now on the floor, its contents—some onions, garlic and other herbs—lying in the dirt.

"Mistress, they're saying she's a witch and a poisoner, and she killed her husband, my master . . . They're saying that in two days' time, on the twelfth of this month in Piano della Marina, she'll be executed."

I let go of Valentina's arm as if I have received a blow to my stomach. Bending double, I hear a long moan like an animal caught in a trap. It is my voice, and I cannot make it stop. I cannot breathe. I cannot think. The room colors yellow.

They will kill my mother.

They will hang her for a murderess, and there is nothing I can do to save her.

Everything goes black.

Valentina revives me with mint tea, heavily sugared, holding it to my lips.

There is movement around me as I pull myself up from the floor. The cook has left my side and is pulling jars from the shelves, wrapping them in linen, clanging and bustling, huffing and muttering. I realize she is packing to leave. I do not blame her. If they hang the mistress of the house, who's to say they won't turn their hawk eyes toward her servants, her daughter, even if our cook is in the pocket of the *Inquisitori*? Who's to say they won't snatch us up and hang us all as accomplices? My barely touched tisane cools in my grip as I watch Valentina.

In goes the silverware. "In lieu of wages," she says.

I shrug. I do not care for spoons or knives or candlesticks. She can do with them what she will. I imagine she will sell them in the marketplace to pay for her passage out of the city.

"Take them. Take whatever you want," I say, sinking my head onto my arms.

The shock of grief comes first. I walk around my chamber for hours, then sink onto my bed, unseeing. If I had ever set foot in the churning seas I traveled upon, I would imagine it feels like this. The harsh disturbance of the cold. The undulating oscillation of the waves. The currents that shift and pull. Then, submersion. Grief submerges me. It is Sunday, the most sacred day of the week. I must wait for Tuesday. I must wait in an empty house, wondering what comes after this, after she is dead. I must wait until the contents of the crucible come bubbling up like molten lava, spilling out and burning us all.

# 14

Tuesday comes.

I have not slept. I cannot remember when I last ate. It is as if my whole life has led to this point. There is an inevitability, a familiarity.

I have been expecting the *Inquisitori* to come knocking, knowing I cannot do anything except obey them. They did not come, or they have not come yet, and so I rise from my bed with some difficulty, my bones as stiff as an old woman's. My belly is still flat, but I hold it, hold *her*, as a mute gesture of comfort, for which of us I cannot tell. I cannot believe my mother will never meet her granddaughter. I feel the loss of this already, the break in the chain of womanhood. My daughter will never set eyes on her beauty, will never know her kindness, her courage, her spirit.

I choose a black gossamer veil that covers my hair. I dare not be recognized as the poisoner's daughter, the wicked Teofania's child. Who knows, perhaps they will try to arrest me too if I show myself. My heart thuds. The heat is unbearable, and it is still early. I dress slowly, carefully, as if each part of my garments is somehow sacred: my shift, my robe, my bodice, my girdle. Then, the veil. Perhaps this is how a novice nun feels as she steps into the strangeness of her sanctified life and the garments that will mark her out forever.

Today, I will bear witness to my mother's life ending. I will watch as the crowds jeer and jostle, as they curse and sway, and I will not take my eyes off her. To do so would be a betrayal. I will be with her until the end, until our story is complete and I am forced to begin again. No one is here to help me. Whipping

Boy left not long after Francesco's death. I have no notion where he went, or where he is now. This time he did not glance behind him as he pulled his homespun cloak around him and walked away. Fear makes strangers of us all, even Gattino, who has slunk off to seek his fortune elsewhere.

Valentina has also gone. She will be halfway to Piana by now.

Time passes and I hear the street hawkers shouting as the crowds begin to gather, so I leave, not bothering to shut the side door behind me. All I have is a purse filled with Francesco's gold, and my cards, my trinkets and my mother's ledger, which is heavy inside the leather bag I have taken from my dead stepfather's chamber. Strangely, the *Inquisitori* did not think to look for such a thing. Retrieving it was my first act once the shock of Mamma's arrest had subsided. It was not well hidden. Any half-wit cleric could have found it under my mother's mattress. There is no new entry, though. Our secrets stay hidden in the book I will keep. It is all I will have left of her.

I do not leave by the main entrance. It was always Francesco's palace, his domain, whereas the lowly door to the alley is enough of an exit for me—a backward glance of a way out.

I step onto the cobbles and almost immediately am swept along by the throng making its way to the square where the Holy Office holds its theater of cruelty in the name of justice. Already the air is thick with the stench of sweat and dung as donkeys bray, goats bleat, and their owners laugh and throw crude jokes at each other. The atmosphere is festive. There is nothing the populace of Palermo loves more than a good execution. Today, they have been promised a spectacle. I keep my head down, my gaze on the ground as I walk. Beggars hold out their hands, or the stumps where their hands used to be. Soldiers hiss at passersby, showing their missing limbs. African men in brightly colored garments spit sunflower kernels. Children born with deformities beg for alms. Prostitutes totter. Old women limp. Children skip.

Overhead, a raven calls. Its harsh, throaty voice is mocking. I make the sign of the *corna* against the bird as a messenger of ill omen, knowing that no gesture, however heartfelt, could change the outcome today.

Next to me, a washerwoman carries her bundle on her head. She winks as I catch her eye, but I look away. She cackles, spits, and continues onward, whistling now. Behind me I hear women gossiping, men laughing, a cacophony of languages and dialects, children whining as we move toward the place where Mamma will meet her fate. Every step sickens me. I want to turn back and run far away from this place of death. But with every step I draw closer to the place where I would stand in place of her, if only they would let me.

All of the city, it seems, has come here to see the infamous murderess die. The pamphleteers are doing good business. I see the glint of coins changing hands, but I do not look at their wares. I cannot bear to see what they have written about her. I keep my eyes fixed to the ground, willing myself to keep going. Still, I have not cried. I know the time is coming when I will. I fear when it does, I may not stop.

Again, the low beat of the drums echo from the entrails of the city.

Again, the shrieks and howls of the crowd follow the cart as it jolts over the cobbled streets.

At first, I see nothing of Mamma. Instead, I smell the backs of heads: their rank, yeasty odor as the temperature rises. I hear

chatter, gossip, raucous laughter, an argument brewing, someone sucking on their teeth. I feel a child tug at my skirts for
coin, the sharp elbow of an aging crone as she pushes past me,
the stink from her person bringing to mind rancid curds left in
the churn too long. Instinctively, I check for my purse tucked
within the folds of my dress and am relieved to find it still heavy.
You cannot be too careful on execution day. I glance up at the
stands where we once stood. I see the high-ranking women and
their daughters who turned their faces from us, their husbands
talking together. I feel like I have died and come back from the
grave to see what happens next.

Then, silence. Or, as much of it as can be in such dense
company. I see the white peaked hoods of the Bianchi moving slowly above the mass of people. The fellowship of Sicilian
nobles walks the condemned to her death. Beforehand, they
will have gone to her in her cell, washed her feet, heard her
confession, and made ready her soul for judgment. Everyone
knows this.

The Bianchi enter the stage first. They walk in procession
before the cart as it lumbers out of the dark, looming alleys into
the harsh sunlight. Their presence ushers in a stillness. The
wriggling, serpentine movement of the masses stops. It is I who
sways now.

I see her: her head is shorn; the scars weeping blood where
once there was beauty and luster. On her back is sacking, daubed
with a large black cross where once was the finest silk and lace.
She is hunched, broken, unfamiliar. I think of her delicate fingers stained yellow with tinctures, the nails now wrenched
off, leaving bleeding stubs. I think of her elegance, dancing in
Madrid not so many years ago, spinning and leaping in front
of a king who could not take his eyes off her, though his queen,

Elisabetta, was sitting beside him. Her legs now buckle beneath
her. I would weep but I do not have time, I must bear witness. I
must keep looking, I must honor her life and remember even as
she still breathes.

Then, the sound.

Intoning the *Miserere Mei, Deus*, the brotherhood, their
obsidian eyes showing through the slits in their white hoods,
appear to halt, though their chanting continues. I do not know
why I have not noticed it before, but I see the destination now:
the platform, the ladder and the noose. I stare as if transfixed.

Movement follows. I see it from the corner of my eye. Teofania di Adamo, my mother, my family in its entirety, begins to
descend from the wagon that carried her as a warning through
the streets of the city. *See! See the murderess! Throw your left-
overs from the week's stew, your discarded onion skins, your rotten
apples. See how she shrinks back from you in her shame! For this is
a woman who dared to kill her husband Francesco by poison!*

She moves with great difficulty. Her elegance is destroyed.
Her beauty is vanquished. They have cut chunks from her
arms with the pliers that run with blood in the jailer's hand.
He stands beside her, grimacing at the crowd, scowling. Blood
runs down the length of Mamma's arms, drips off the ends of
her fingertips where her nails once were. They have brutalized
her, yet she is still a creature of shimmering wonder to me.
Even now, I cannot help but see her again in my mind's eye,
a young woman holding my hand as she teaches me courtly
dances. I can almost hear the first high note from the lute of
the musician she employed to teach me, or the laughter coming from her chambers, which were always filled with lords
and ladies, music, and candlelight, even the Planet King, Philip
of Spain, himself.

All too quickly the spell is broken. Suddenly, the crowd surges forward like flies to a rotting carcass. The air is filled with screams of fury and curses, which drown out the chanting.

*Strega! Diavulu! Buttana!*

*Witch.*

*Devil.*

*Whore.*

I do not know if Faustina gave Mamma's name to her torturers. Perhaps the *Inquisitori* lurked in the shadows, waiting for Mamma to make a reckless move, to expose herself. I do not know if Francesco guessed, if Valentina watched us after all, or if Clara felt called to confess. Perhaps Francesco chose to protect my mother, and when he died, there was nothing to stop the holy men capturing her. I do not know if one of Mamma's clients, the women she cared for, was responsible. Perhaps someone whispered in the churchmen's ears.

There is so much I do not know, but there is one thing I am sure of with a certainty I feel in my gut: I am not safe here. They will come for me.

I stay silent. I do not jeer or jostle, heckle, spit, or roll my eyes as those around me are doing. Already, I feel nauseous as I wait as each second passes. I concentrate on her and pray I will not faint. I stare without blinking now as Mamma stumbles, causing the crowd to shriek louder in delight. The brotherhood leads her up the steps onto the wooden platform. I can see the effort it costs her just to stand. Her legs drag as she moves, each step appearing to cause her great pain. The sun, the odors and noise make my head ache. I dig my nails into the palm of each hand. I must not faint. I must be with her. She will know I am here. She will know I am watching. We are bound together by love, and she will know.

Now, the Bianchi pray for her soul. Here and there, heads lower as the sacred words are said, but not everywhere. For every person who shows reverence, there are scores who continue to talk and shove, chew and yawn. Soon the curses begin again, the prayers forgotten. My throat is dry. My heart seems to be working but I cannot feel it. I cannot register my own stubbornly continuing life when my mother is being robbed of hers.

A woman beside me speaks. ". . . they say the crime was so evil they devised a new method just for her . . ."

". . . they say the authorities have ordered she be killed by strangulation, not by the rope but by hand . . ."

Before I can react to this, Mamma drops down to her knees. I register the man who has been there all along: clad in black, stout, arms on his hips, a hood covering his face.

The executioner.

Bile rises in my throat. The world has perhaps a minute more of Mamma within it. She kisses the feet of this man who will kill her, clumsily, apologetically. I stare and stare at her, trying to see some part of her, but they have destroyed everything that was her essence. She is unrecognizable, even to me. I see only the evidence of their hatred, their butchery.

"*Passus et sepultus est*" (he suffered and was buried) is the signal, but though a rope dangles there, it is not meant for my mother. Instead, the hangman steps in front of her. As the prayer ends, he holds up his hands, coarse and red. He closes those fat digits around her small neck. The crowd gasps. For the length of a heartbeat he holds his position, a player on the stage, his audience enthralled. I cannot hear Mamma choke when, at last, the executioner's grip tightens. People fidget and screech, their voices rising now to a crescendo in the heat. There is scuffling and pushing as people try to see what comes next; the climax of the entertainment.

I am condemned to watch every last gasping second of it. My head feels light. My throat tightens as if I too can feel the pressure of my last breath being squeezed out of me. It is so real I wonder if I will fall to a faint. Mamma grasps the man's hands as if trying to stop him. Someone in the crowd nearby laughs. After all, it is a futile gesture. My hands stray to my neck but I must recall them to my sides. I must not reveal my identity to this crowd. They would rip me to pieces.

Then, unexpectedly, he releases his grip. My mother slumps down onto the platform. A collective sigh issues across the square. The sun is high in the sky now. Many shade their eyes, blinking. Some are even praying. Mamma is alive but barely so, ready for the final act.

*Burn in hell, witch! You're the Devil's whore!* somebody close by shouts.

With a large metal hook, the executioner, with admirable skill, slices her open from chest to pelvis. The crowd gasps again. I dig my nails into my skin harder, drawing blood as her guts emerge. I do not look away. This man, who covers his face with a leather hood except for the slits for his eyes, reaches down and with a flourish, holds up her innards to the now-baying crowd. I keep breathing, though it is an effort. Vomit rises so I spit on the ground. It is almost over. His bloodied hands, startlingly red, now grasp the still-beating heart of the woman who has scandalized all of Sicily. He holds up the organ tenderly for everyone to see.

His work continues, grinding through muscle and bone, flesh and sinew, but I have seen enough. As I stumble away, pushing through the onlookers with surprising strength, I make a vow, one that will become my legacy. I will carry on my mother's work, whatever it costs me, however dangerous, however reckless. I will make Mamma's concoction and no man will ever be safe again.

I slip away from the crowded piazza, down through the pox-ridden streets, toward the port and into the rest of my life. Behind me, in the high sun, in four glistening and bloody quarters, lies my mother's corpse. Within me beats my unborn daughter's heart.

# PART TWO

*"Ubi periculum maius intenditur"*
(Where great danger lies)

—PAPAL BULL *UBI PERICULUM*,
POPE GREGORY X, JULY 1274

# 15

## Rome, June 1656 (23 years later)

*Giulia*

"*La peste!*"

"*La peste!* God save our souls!"

The voices rise into the sky like a flock of starlings.

"*Misericordia!* Mercy upon us, Almighty God. Hear our prayer!"

A woman shrieks. A baby cries. Men grunt. Then, the sound of the whips as they rise, crackling in the air, then fall, their thuds heavy as knotted rope meets torn flesh. There is a pause, an almost audible wince, before they crackle again. My daughter stands beside me as we look out into the narrow Via di Corte Savella. She is tall, elegant, with a proud bearing, so like my mother. Every time she turns to me, I fancy I see the echo of Mamma's smile or frown, and my heart re-forms itself around the grief that has never left, though so many years have now passed.

The flagellants, a group of twelve men, mutter prayers as they walk, their heads bowed, their feet bare, dragging along the cobbles. People line the narrow street, flanked by tall buildings on either side, crossing themselves and praying aloud. One woman is pulling at her hair, while her neighbor shakes her praying hands to the heavens. All are scared. All fear the wrath of a vengeful God who would throw down this pestilence upon His people to atone for our many sins.

The men—for they are all men—stripped half naked, moan as they castigate themselves. They do not have Santa Rosalia, as we did, to fend off the plague. The whips flay. The blood seeps. The sweat sprays, while the baby cries and cries. The sight of them transports me back into that candlelit private chamber where I received the blows these implements of torture bestow with fierce precision.

"Come inside, we've seen enough," I say to Girolama, placing a hand on her arm.

My daughter wears a gown of finest satin. She wears diamonds around her neck. She is altogether the height of luxury and fashion. Beside her, I am sure I look drab in my plain linen, with an apron stained with plant oils wrapped untidily around my still-slender waist.

Girolama brushes off my touch as she would a fly, and I have to bite my tongue.

The arrival of the plague is not a surprise, though it brings fear and famine in its wake. Fields of crops lie unharvested throughout Italy, and the price of bread rises daily. For weeks now, we have heard tell of plague coming up from Naples. It is all anyone has talked about in the markets and washing streams, but we have known all along it was coming—we, the women who practice the secret arts of plants, herb lore, and other forbidden things besides. We can feel the pestilence as it comes upon us, like a miasma in the form of a beast, breathing hot, putrid air over the churches, palaces, back streets and markets of this, the Eternal City.

With a shrug, my willful, determined, stubborn daughter acquiesces. Inside the apothecary our grumbling, irritable Graziosa is warming her ass by my fire. Another, my beloved friend Giovanna, is out in the city helping a woman birth her baby in a slum not fit for cattle.

"What say you?" I nod to Graziosa as I pick up my pestle and reach for a large bronze mortar. "What news of plague?"

Graziosa has startling flame-colored hair with streaks of gray, a neck strewn with icons on chains and tokens of saints' faces that clack as she fidgets. She also has a foul temper. Graziosa helps dispense our remedies, traveling every day across the city, whispering to women at Mass, knocking on the doors of those who seek our skills as wise women. She collects payments, delivers herbs and ointments, and finds us new customers as discreetly as she is able. She has worked for me for many years, and still I wonder why on earth I keep her. With her wiry, twitching frame, she reminds me of a sparrow, a bead of light in her small, brown eyes, one of which squints. Her head moves here and there—never still, seeing everything.

When she first sought me out, my business in Rome was new, though my reputation as a woman who could cure a bad marriage had already spread from the south, creeping like wildfire across the city.

"Are you the one they say can magic away a husband?" Graziosa had asked as we stood, women huddled together in the far reaches of the nave at the church of Santa Maria sopra Minerva as the interminable service rolled on over our heads.

"I know who you are," she continued when I did not answer, a sly expression on her weathered face.

"And who am I?" I replied, careful to keep my voice low. I knew of this woman. They called her the pious beggar, and I already knew she dabbled in the occult arts, selling spells to help make a baby, and charms against *il malocchio*. Women spoke of these things freely at Mass, away from their husbands and lords. Simple magic was widely accepted here once, and many made a scant living selling prayers written as enchantments, or concoctions as salves for heartbreak, or to stop a husband's roving eye. It was—*it is*—a natural part of our world. So different from Palermo, where it was all heresy, and everything that fell outside of the remits of the Catholic Church was banned because it was an outpost of Spain. Rome has been a more lenient mistress, until now, as fear stalks the hovels and palazzos, and Death comes calling. Times are changing—and what was once simple is now deemed sinful.

"You're the one they're calling *la Signora della Morte*, the Mistress of Death . . ." The flame-haired woman grinned, revealing a mouth of rotten teeth.

"I know no one of that name," I said, suddenly cold. I turned away, but Graziosa grabbed my arm and whispered in my ear.

"I know many women who need your remedy. I can help you."

I stared back into the woman's face, trying to read her motives, feeling an instinctive pull toward her, despite her manner. Her eyes were sharp as a hawk's. They still are.

"How do I know I can trust you?" I said, shrugging off her bony grip as we bowed our heads for prayer.

"You don't." She grinned with pure wickedness. "So I'll prove it to you."

And so, she did.

Within weeks, I had more customers than I could manage, and from then onward, Graziosa was as much a part of my small circle as my daughter and my friend.

Our pious beggar is always cold. Even in the early Roman summer, Graziosa covers herself in layers of filthy rags, though I pay her a good enough wage for a decent bed, a new gown, and her supper each night. When she lifts her rancid skirts to heat her spindly legs, the odor of unwashed linens fills the small still room at the back of my shop.

"Open the curtain," I say to my daughter. "Let some air in."

"Though it be noxious and filled with plague seeds, it's better than an old lady's skirts," my daughter says.

I raise an eyebrow at her, and she smiles back at me, unrepentant. Girolama stalks to the door, her skirts swishing, her jewels glinting. Her smile grows as she pulls open the thick velvet curtain that separates the shopfront from our hidden work in the back room.

"I've seen corpses piled up outside the city walls," Graziosa says.

"And how, pray?" I say.

All but two of the city gates are closed for fear of new contagion. No one may enter or leave without a pass. How then could our odoriferous beggar sidle out when even the grandest may not?

Without waiting for an answer, I return to the work I had begun when the flagellants passed by: grinding fragrant and bitter plants—rosemary, feverfew, and thyme. All effective against bad miasmas and foul air.

Graziosa cracks a nut between her remaining blackened teeth and grins impishly.

"Oh, I can go anywhere, my beauty. I can disappear like smoke coiling from a candle. I can come and go as I please. No one notices a little old woman."

"Even one as charming as yourself?" My daughter yawns as if taunting our friend tires her. She was out late last night, returning just before the cock crowed. I waited for her, as I always do, always will.

It does not matter how many times I warn her against shining too brightly, against flaunting her skills as an astrologer. She will not heed my warnings, dismissing them as a mother's fears. Ever since I fled Palermo with Girolama in my belly, I have not stopped running from the *Inquisitori*. Even though we are now hidden inside a small shop in a narrow street that sits in the heart of a great city, I will never stop running.

"Girolama, help me finish these remedies. There'll be many customers needing physick over the coming weeks."

My daughter eyes me lazily, like a cat stretched out in a shaft of sunlight. I remember how Gattino would do that when he'd eaten a good supper.

"Mamma, I'm exhausted. There were so many who wanted my predictions last night."

It is my turn to raise an eyebrow. "Beware your countesses and your dukes. They may dangle coin and favor, but you are merely their plaything," I say.

My daughter smiles, and I see my words have not penetrated her haughty exterior. She appears like a grand lady, but she is not. They will never truly accept her, and this thought makes me shiver. Girolama tosses her raven-black hair and ignores me, as daughters do. I pray she is right, and that her connections, lofty as they are, are enough to dazzle the clergymen who also circle Rome's nobility.

I always leave our argument knowing it is one we will return to. Our work is already reckless, our path already strewn with jeopardy, but I cannot see the sense in flaunting it. I look away from my beautiful daughter, turning back to Graziosa, who is emitting wafts of her own pestilential stench.

"So, what news from Mass?" I ask. "What will our inquisitor pope do to help his people?"

Graziosa spits out a kernel. I watch it land on my earthen floor and roll a little before halting by Girolama's silk shoe.

Rome—indeed, the whole Catholic world—has a new pope: Alessandro the Seventh, famed inquisitor of Malta. He is a man they say watched expressionless as the heretics he burned screamed in agony, their skin melting before his eyes.

"His elevated majesty, *Il Papa,* does not deign to inform me personally." Graziosa sniffs. "But I hear tell of a Chigi brother who will come to the city to rescue us. The word is he will open lazarettos and send us all to die in strange beds, away from our families and loved ones—"

Girolama snorts with derision. "You always sleep in strange beds, old woman," she says. The two eye each other before the elder laughs again. "My mother pays you well yet each night you huddle in rags on the cold stone floor of a different church. How can a lazaretto be worse?"

Graziosa shrugs. "I'll take a hard, holy bed over any other," she says stoutly.

"Your piety is astonishing for a woman who sells poison," I say, throwing my daughter an amused glance.

The crone reaches into her skirts and retrieves another nut. It cracks between her teeth.

"God sees my sacrifice in eschewing a warm bed, depriving my bones and body of comfort. When it comes to Judgment Day, all will be reckoned."

All will be reckoned.

There is now a silence, the sort that carries all the words that are unspoken, a quiet that is flavored and colored by them.

"I saw the death of our Inquisitor Alessandro in the cards last night. The planets also speak of turbulence and death," Girolama says, looking over at me.

"It is unwise to foretell a pope's demise," I counter, looking back at her. "Temper your predictions at your parties. You never know who may be listening. And, anyway, plague is here. There'll be plenty of new graves dug, you don't need the planets nor the *tarocchi* to tell you that."

I return to my mortar, where the resinous stalks lie half-ground, their fragrance filling the small room as the fire burns low.

# 16

A fine wooden carriage draped in velvet and brocade curtains clatters past the guards posted at the city gates. The wheels rumble and judder over the cobbled streets.

Walking with my friend Giovanna, we stop as the carriage draws to a sudden, shuddering halt. Two farm laborers, their carts blocking the street, argue loudly, gesticulating at each other.

"Whoa, there." The carriage driver pulls up the reins. As the wheels creak and the hooves skid a little on the uneven ground, a man draws the curtain and pokes his head out to see what calamity has befallen them.

It takes a mere moment, like the flash of a bird's wing as it takes flight, but when the man moves, I see another sitting beside him. It should be the nobleman with his head out of the window who catches my eye. Instead, light glances off something inside the carriage—a brooch or a jewel of some description—and my eyes are drawn to the man seated in the shade of the interior. For a brief, unexpected moment, our eyes meet, and as they do, I feel the earth shift beneath my feet, a swell like a wave rolling under a ship. I stumble. Giovanna catches my arm, almost knocking the basket out of my hand.

"Giulia," she says. "Are you well? What's the matter?"

Her eyes, the green-brown color of olives, blur. Her face looks suddenly strange, covered as it is by a swathe of linen to filter invisible *seminaria*. Around her neck is a pouch of fragrant herbs to sweeten her inhalations. It seems to move like a pendulum, back and forth, and as it does so, the sound returns.

Not since I was a young woman have I encountered this strange high note, the piercing quality of it that fills my head until it might burst. I place a hand on my temple, willing myself not to faint. Then comes the stench. This time it is a burning smell, as if all around us is alight—the people, their clothes, their skin. Thick oily smoke seems to fill my lungs. I gasp and cough, "What's wrong? My God, not *la peste?*" Giovanna's eyes search my face, but I cannot answer. Just as suddenly, the moment vanishes, leaving its sulfur trail, as the carriage lurches forward, the dispute between laborers concluded, the street clear again. I watch as it jolts away, my body shaking. A legion of soldiers, carrying halberds and flags that flap as they ride, surges past. Upon the fabric is the sign of six mountains and an eight-pointed star.

Who is he? And why do I feel this way?

It has been many years since the Sight visited me. Not since Palermo. I had almost forgotten the nausea of its pull, the deep waters of its echo. Why has this sighting, this most transient of glances, left me shaking?

"Come, we must go, we've work to do," I say, though I am fighting the sudden urge to cry out, to run. From the core of my soul, I want to escape, to get away from that glint, that dark, unblinking gaze.

The bells ring for None as we reach the house we have been sent to in the Trastevere district. We both look up toward Basilica di San Pietro, which stands looking down upon us from its height above the din and heat of Old Rome.

I hold my basket, which contains the herbs and plants we may need today, and raise my hand to knock. I look behind me.

Giovanna glances over each shoulder too. Only an aged woman
carrying washing and a costumed man in *medico della peste*
garments scurry past. The doctor wears a leather hood over
his face, the pouch attached to his hood trailing the scent of
aromatic herbs. I tap on the wood though my hand still trembles. The door opens, and a woman stands there, beckoning us
inside. She wears a dark dress and a grim expression.

"Is there plague here?" I ask. Looking around I can see no
crosses daubed on the doorways, no sign the nearby dwellings
are tainted.

"There isn't, mistress. Quick, come inside before my neighbors see us."

It is a modest dwelling, by no means a hovel, with a good-
sized entrance, and a comfortable chamber to receive visitors,
though we are not directed that way.

"She's in her room; she's waiting for you."

We follow up a set of stairs that leads to the first floor. The
woman who answered the door, the same one who came to
my shop the previous day, leads us into a back room, which is
stifling and airless as the warmth of the day simmers. In the
chamber, there is a comfortable enough bed, and upon it lies
a young woman. She looks to be the same age as my daughter.
Near the bed stand two younger women, whom I assume are
the girl's sisters. Three sets of wide eyes turn to us, reminding me of the tawny owls that nest in Rome's treetops. Owls
are harbingers of death, so I hush the thought, putting down
my basket. Mayhap only one small life, one tiny heartbeat, will
end today.

"You're carrying a child you don't want?" I ask.

Giovanna is already rolling up her sleeves.

The girl nods.

"Lucrezia, you must tell them what you told me," the girl's mother says. There is a look that passes between the two women, mother and daughter, and I guess this is not the first time she has had need of services such as ours.

"My courses dried up, so I knew I was with child again," the girl says, confirming my suspicions. "We tried to get rid of it," she adds. "My mother took me to places with stagnant airs, but it didn't work. Nor did the hot baths and my fall down the stairs, which only left me with ugly bruises. So my lover hit my back and punched my belly, but still it wouldn't come loose."

"Didn't you try to get rid of it with purging herbs?" I say, moving around to the woman's side as Giovanna readies herself with linen strips and moss for bleeding. "We have hellebore, juniper sage, and rue that would've done this much earlier, and much safer. I could've mixed you a tea made of parsley, which also would've done this job without risk or injury."

Lucrezia looks back at me. She has eyes the shape of almonds and skin that glows with both youth and pregnancy.

"I wasn't sure," she says. "My belly ached but it could've been the flux. Then when the blood didn't come, and I had the sickness each morning, I knew. The friar said the incantation he sold me would give me the *aborto*, but nothing happened."

"What friar? What incantation?" I frown.

Lucrezia's mother speaks. "My cousin's wife gave us the name of a friar who promises to charm away unwanted babies with holy words scratched onto parchment and tied around the stomach."

I look over to her and sigh, knowing women will believe anything for the promise of relief from what ails them.

"I'm unmarried," Lucrezia says, matter-of-factly, "and my lover is wed to another. Can you help me?"

Giovanna and I exchange a glance. We are here to relieve this woman of the child in her womb and hope not to kill her in the process.

"We'll try," I say.

"Has it quickened?" Giovanna asks, referring to the animation of the soul of the embryo, the moment where it turns from animal to child in church law. Forty days for a boy, eighty for a girl, who must remain suspended in the slick juices of the womb until she congeals and becomes human.

"For if it has, and it's a boy inside your belly, then what we're doing today is a mortal sin," Giovanna says as she works. What she does not say is if we kill the woman as a result of the methods we use, then we are all headed for the scaffold.

"Open the shutters, it's warm already. We must keep Lucrezia as still and comfortable as possible," I say. Quietly, and only in her mother's earshot, I add: "If she's to survive another abortion, then we must do everything we can to stop fever and pain. You'd do well to send your other daughters to a different room. They wouldn't wish to witness what comes next."

The woman nods, her face pale. She instructs the girls to leave; their eyes are still wide and owl-like. There is the slightest pause, a moment where this can be stopped, reversed. When no one says anything, we begin.

Giovanna works quickly. Together with Lucrezia's mother, I hold down the young woman until she is pregnant no longer. Her cries are muffled by her mother's hand held over her mouth, the clotting, bloody mess of the unborn lying in a bucket. Tears run down Lucrezia's face.

"Hush, child, all will be well. We'll find you a good husband, and you'll give him many sons, and me many grandchildren."

I pray the mother's words are true. I pray she survives the night.

By the time we leave, the summer sun has dipped. The house is stilled as Lucrezia sleeps off the opium poppy I gave her to dull the pain. Its use is banned by the Holy Office as a tool of the Devil, but the Horned One and I circle each other, recognize each other, and so I disobey in this, as in so much else.

"Will she live?" one of Lucrezia's sisters whispers as we make our way down to the entrance. I turn to her, see the worry and shock on her face, and put a hand on her shoulder.

"Pray for her. Pray for us all. Take this to help ward off infection—it's a mixture of dried figs, rue, and honey. Lucrezia must swallow a dose each morning," I say, handing her a small jar.

Just before we open the door, Lucrezia's mother shoos away her daughters and turns to us.

"You're known as *la Signora della Morte*. Don't deny it."

Her hand is on my shoulder. I glance at Giovanna. Her face, like mine, is in shadow.

"I need your medicine, the one that kills rather than cures. I can't let Lucrezia's lover take her again. He won't stay away though he has a wife already. Please, mistress, I must be rid of him. He has no children. Only his wife will suffer, and the gossips say she already has another lover, a tanner from Florence . . ." The woman's voice has dropped so it is barely audible.

"What we've done here today is already a mortal sin. How many more sins do you want on your conscience?" I breathe. The air between us thickens. Outside, the street is busy now as people return home or go about their business. I think of the flash of the clasp, the juddering carriage.

"Giulia, abortion is one thing, but we know nothing of this man. Come, we have done enough here today," Giovanna says. She is staring at me steadily.

I look one way to the mother, who now sheds tears. I look the other and see my friend, her forehead creased into a frown.

"Does he beat her? Does he say bad things to her?" I ask, sliding my gaze away from Giovanna back to the woman. She grabs my free hand; the other holds the basket. Inside it are two small vials of a colorless liquid. Upon them is the face of San Nicola di Bari. If you looked into my wares, unfolded the remaining linen strips, you would find them. Saint's waters, or so they appear. A healing oil they say is secreted from his corpse, which cures anything from dropsy to melancholy. I always carry two. I cannot say why, except it was a habit of my mother's.

Her grip is tight.

"He doesn't, but what he does is worse. Upstairs my daughter lies between life and death. If she survives, she may never bear a healthy child for a man who can make her respectable. How's that better than a beating?"

Giovanna hisses. It is a small gesture, a mere passing of air from her lips.

"Giulia . . ." Her word is a warning.

I take back my hand and place it on Giovanna's arm, squeezing it a little. "All is well."

The glass vial is cool to my touch. I hand over one of the containers.

"Yours is an unusual request," I reply, "given that it's not from a wife wanting widowhood, nor a whore wishing to free herself. If Lucrezia lives, then I see you may need this."

Giovanna shakes her head. She is angry with me, yet I continue. I say the instructions I give to all the women we help: "One drop at a time. One small drop, then a week later, another.

Within a month your troubles will be over." If I listen hard, I can hear the memory of my mother's voice as she said those same words.

Heart beating faster now, I take the pouch the woman holds out to me to pay for the abortion. She reaches into her skirts for more coin, but I stop her.

"I'll charge you for my physick, and for our services as wise women, but there's no charge for this extra service today. I pray to God you'll need it because then your daughter will be alive and well."

"Thank you, mistress. You're an angel sent to us from God," the woman says as she reaches to open the door.

*An angel of death*, I think as we leave, cloaks drawn around us, first checking the street.

Outside, Giovanna unleashes herself.

"How could you do that? We don't know her, except for her coming to the shop to ask for our services! We know nothing about this man either."

"I pitied her. I felt sorry for her. Giovanna, her daughter may die tonight. I couldn't bear if Girolama was left the same way, with the same choices . . . Forgive me for ignoring your wise counsel. I won't do it again."

Giovanna's face un-creases itself. At this, she manages a smile. She knows as well as I that this is most likely an empty promise. I look back at my friend's face. In the shadows, there is a trick of the light. For the briefest moment, I see Francesco's expression, his unwavering, unwanted attention, the attention I brought to me and my mother. I have to swallow down the taste of bile, remembering I too had no choice. I feel the hatred against him swell inside me, and I know I feel the same toward the man responsible for Lucrezia's state.

Strangely, Giovanna nods as if she understands. With that gesture, we are back in rhythm together. Just then, another flash. This time it is a flare of black, darkest blue and white; two magpies arch their wings, screeching as they move skyward. We stop and watch them go, swooping toward the lush gardens of Il Vaticano.

*July 1656 (by Giulia's hand)*

*Lucrezia Fabbri, aborto (Giovanna)*      *7 scudi*

*One vial of acqua (Giulia)*      *No payment*

## 17

*Fabio Chigi, Pope Alessandro VII*

There is a burst of movement as the birds swoop past the window of my chamber in the Palazzo Apostolico: magpies, their wings outstretched. Momentarily, I am stopped in my labors, the papers I am poring over temporarily forgotten in the delight, the joy of their flight. Up here, I am close to the heavens, or at least, I like to think so, as I sit at my desk in my papal suite, considering the dispatches of the day and my replies as Holy Father, God's representative on earth.

A sudden rap on the door of my private rooms startles me. One of my officials, of which I have many, makes his reverences, announces the arrival of my brother Mario.

"Send them in," I murmur. I turn the key in the lock of a small cabinet that has been built into my desk where I keep my most private things. I place it under the marble skull that sits by the pile of parchment and documents in well-ordered piles upon my desk. My great friend, Gian Bernini, carved a small contour, a dip underneath his masterwork—a space for this key alone, my most valued possession.

Smoothing down my white papal robes, adjusting my papal ring, touching my papal cap gently to know all is in place, I rise.

My brother appears in the doorway. He takes off his plumed hat, prostrates himself, as does the man who follows a mere step after him. I flick my gaze over this person, then back to Mario's bowed head.

"Brother," I say, raising my right hand in a gesture of benediction. I hold out my hand, and he kneels before me, his thin
lips touching the golden ring. The stranger steps forward.
"May I present to you Inquisitor Stefano Bracchi."
My brother steps back and the stranger kneels and kisses
the ring, made to my own design with our Chigi emblem:
six mountains and an eight-pronged star etched in gold. His
mouth is full, his eyes quick and intelligent. He walks like a
man of high birth. He has thick black hair and the tall, strong
frame of a man used to hard riding. He wears a plain cloak,
though I notice the clasp is inlaid with precious stones.

"You are welcome here," I say.

Only weeks earlier, I had written to Mario, ordering him
to Rome to vanquish the pestilence as he did in Siena. There,
he created quarantines for the sick and dying, closed all public
business except worship, and rid our home city of the suppurating corpses, the crosses daubed on doorways, the terrible
sight of plague boils. Inside my letter was another message,
a secret message. *Bring your spies*, I wrote. *Bring your execu-
tioners and your investigators.* Plague is not the only sickness
in Rome. Heresy and witchcraft grow untethered like a can-
ker. This pestilence is God's punishment on Rome, and I have
vowed to uproot it without mercy. *Bring the physick that will
cure this great city, and all will be forced to swallow it.*

"Your Holiness, thank you for inviting me into your presence." His voice is low, subtle, his dark head bent in supplication.

"And how was your journey? Arduous, I imagine? I'll have
refreshments brought to your chambers," I say, gesturing for
them to rise.

"It was as nothing compared to the work we must do in
Rome," says Mario. "There must be immediate measures taken.

My men have entered the city days before my arrival. I've placed guards at every gate, and they're all now closed to prevent the spread of contagion. I've identified two possible sites for lazarettos. These measures will be implemented immediately, upon your command, brother."

If I experience a slight thrill at hearing my older brother, one who was praised by our father for his skills in the saddle and with a sword, asking for my permission, deferring to me as his authority, I do not show it.

"Under my direct supervision, you'll have everything you need to enact measures against *la peste* from this moment forward. You're Rome's new health commissioner, and you'll save our city. But—" And here I pause. "It's perhaps Bracchi's work that will be the most vital. For God is punishing this city for its sin and corruption, which has been left to grow and take root for too long.

"Stefano Bracchi, it's your job to hunt down heresy in all its forms. This is God's work, but it's also the work of the State, as well as the Holy Office. We must have obedience alongside devotion . . . What say you?"

I see he is not flustered. He is not overwhelmed by my majesty, nor that of the palace and its finery. He looks like a man born to power, and yet I have made inquiries, and he is merely the son of a trader in leather, though one who was prosperous, if not wealthy.

"All those who stand against the codes of the Church, all those who work with the Devil, who cast spells and tell fortunes, all those who flout the rules of the Catholic faith will be brought to heel, Your Holiness. My spies will infiltrate everywhere, into every large household in Rome, casting my net, which will catch witches, sorcerers, and practitioners of black magic as well as criminals and lawbreakers."

I nod.

"This is holy work, indeed."

After I have watched my new inquisitor leave with that inde-finable self-assurance I have never been able to claim, though I was born into one of the highest families in the land, I walk to the window of my apartment. People cross the space in front of the basilica, but one stands out: a woman. She stops and stares up, almost as if she is looking for me. Her hair is the color of the wheat fields on the lands of my birthplace. It hangs low down her back, though she wears a plain *trinzale* that does not quite manage to contain its waves. It is untamed, escaping the sheath. As if she senses my gaze, she pulls up her hood and vanishes inside it, but not before I have glimpsed her beauty. If I were a lesser man, I might feel lust at the sight of such a woman, but I conquer myself. I compare her dignity to my mother's—and her charms: her strange green eyes, or so they appear, though she stands too far away to be sure, the sheen of her skin, the hair that cascades to her waist, begin to fade away.

I shut my eyes. I breathe. My time is here. My work begins.

# 18

## Giulia

I wonder if I am being watched. I feel strangely sure I am. I draw my hood over my hair, feeling exposed, though I am but one of perhaps twenty people or more crossing the square in front of Basilica di San Pietro and the papal apartments. Glancing upward, the windows of the palace stare back, blank, unseeing. There is no movement within, but I cannot shake this notion.

Giovanna has gone to Mass after leaving Lucrezia. I have decided to walk through Rome. The air feels different, as if the wind has changed direction and is blowing in upheaval. It feels as if a tempest approaches, the atmosphere charged, intensified, expectant.

There are fewer people on the streets than before the pestilence arrived, but there are still plenty of us who must carry on, buying bread, praying at Mass, seeking work. Little has changed, except that the daubing on the doors appears daily, and the plague doctors stride around, their black robes swaying, their long canes pointing in their direction of travel.

Each night, the plague carts judder. Those pulling them call, "Bring out your dead." What would the dead say to being dumped down onto another rotting corpse, groins against faces, legs entangled with arms? Would the dead object? Or would they laugh at the incongruous sight? Blackened limbs. Buboes that weep pus. Pale, graying faces staring endlessly. Would they see this as their final performance in a life spent on the fringes of the stage, as small parts in a greater play? These unmoving corpses are people we once knew: the baker from across the piazza, the brewer and butcher, their mouths now quieted, their bodies swollen with disease. Would they think this a good death? Would they look down and pity us?

To us, the dead are silent. And perhaps it is best that way.

I walk the meanest, narrowest streets once I am over the Ponte Sant'Angelo, the bridge where Archangel Michael, carved in stone, mingles with the bodies of the executed. I am not sure what I am seeking, but I know I must move, and keep moving. Now and then, I fancy I hear footsteps close behind me, but when I stop, turn, inspect the *vicolo*, there is no one, or at least, no one who looks out of place. There are always mothers with gaggles of dirty children, swiping at one or more with large, reddened hands. There are always washerwomen, drunks, the occasional soldier or young boy carrying messages. As I walk, I feel the potion humming to me, and though I brewed a fresh batch only a few nights ago, I decide to make another. This yearning for my mother's *acqua* is both a confusion and a comfort, and it is with me always.

I change direction, knowing now where I will head. Tonight, I will invoke my mother's spirit and dance with her as the potion seethes, as the owl hoots. Under cover of the plague, I have become bold, seeking out new clients and offering my solution to women's woes more openly than I ever have before. For who can say if a death is one thing or another in these troubled times? Who can tell if disease is sent from God or the Devil? This pestilence has given my poisoners the chance to peddle my wares without fear of discovery. Women, impatient for *la peste* to do its work and kill their husbands, are terrified they may die too, before their freedom is obtained. While God may be in no hurry to rid the city of its cheating, grumbling, cruel masters, they are. And so, they come to me, and I am pleased to help them. As men die every day and my services

remain undetected, as laborers fall down in the fields and the
sepulchers fill, I will make more *acqua*, and I will shed my own
tears for what is lost to me.

A boy stops in front of me, wiping his snot-streaked nose on
his sleeve. It is as if he reads my mind and appears before me like
a fairy child. I give him a coin and whisper to him the message
I wish delivered. He scampers off, giddy with his new riches,
leaving me to follow behind.

Later, I pass under the curved arches and columns of the front
portico of San Pietro in Vincoli, my veil covering my face and hair.
I make my way to the statue of Moses, carved by the great artist
Michelangelo, which sits as if waiting for my arrival. I flick my
gaze to the marble horns at the front of his forehead. Each time
I come here, I wonder if these horns were the Devil's rather than
the light of God, as if this is a joke at the worshippers' expense.

Just like last time and the time before, I hear the soft tread of
Padre Don Antonio's approach, I feel the whisper of his breath
and the movement of his hand as he crosses himself and mutters
a prayer. Just like I always do, I turn to him, slipping the coin
purse to his other hand hidden by his cassock. When my hands
meet his, I am always surprised by their coolness. We stay there,
for a moment, joined by the merest touch. He drops the purse
into his garments, brings out a small package. I take it, our skin
brushing against each other.

"Bless you, my child," he murmurs.

His gaze is soft as he watches me. I return it, frank and
open. I feel we understand each other, though little is ever said
between us.

"Thank you, Father," I say piously.

Padre Don Antonio has the face of a well-fed man, with a small, sculpted beard and hair worn low by his ears. He stands with a straight back and has the look of a man who carries much knowledge. His expression is set in a weary smile as if he sees everything yet is surprised by nothing. He nods his head, but does not turn away.

"Mistress . . ." he begins.

"Yes, Padre?" I say a little breathlessly. It is a long walk up to this church that looks over the remains of our ancient forefathers.

He smiles again. "Have a care," he says.

It is I who drops my gaze, feeling my cheeks redden. He walks on as if there is nothing between us, and our meeting is that of any parishioner and her priest. The package contains crystalline white arsenic.

I bob a curtsy to the altar, to the chains of Saint Peter that sag in their reliquary, a symbol of entrapment, a symbol of eventual freedom. I think of the padre's brother who supplies the poison, working in an apothecary shop somewhere in Rome. If I wonder why both would risk their necks for this illicit enterprise, I stopper my thoughts like dough sealing my earthenware vessel. It is not my business to know their secrets.

I walk out. I do not look back.

Even though I made the vow to my mother as I fled from Palermo that I would continue her legacy, I was reluctant to continue her work at first.

I launched into the uncharted seas of my life, washing up on the shores of Naples, carrying a baby and penniless except for the satin gown on my back. For months, I did little but grieve and survive.

To make the potion meant I would truly acknowledge her death, to know she would never stand beside me again, watching, teaching, praising me. I was but a child, begging for sustenance, sleeping outside convent doors as my belly began to swell—and I knew I could not face that. At least, not yet. A kindly nun took pity on me, learnt of my skills with herbs and took me in. They were a poor fraternity, a small convent of elderly nuns, and could not afford to feed an extra mouth. I had no dowry to become a novice, and so I taught them everything I knew about making remedies for fevers, for skin rashes, for ills of the digestion and much else besides. Before long, I had the key to the apothecary, and I would make up creams and ointments to sell. Yet still I did not touch the crystalline white arsenic, used to whiten skin and kill vermin. I did not touch the nightshade, which some call the devil's berry, flowering as it does under the cover of night. I did not look for those selling game birds, their flesh puckered with lead shot.

The ingredients sang to me, though, but I closed my ears. I was not ready.

Then, one day, a woman came to the convent, asking for the young mistress who made such efficacious salves. Her face was draped with a veil, but we were alone in the apothecary, and she removed it.

A livid purple bruise flowered around each eye, one more yellow than the other. Her lip was badly cut and there were smears of fresh blood on her cheek. She pulled up her sleeve and revealed her wrists, small and pale under the bruising that was shaped like the large fingers on a large hand.

"This is my husband's work, mistress. I don't come here to frighten you." She paused. "Though you're younger than I imagined. I've need of your physick. Only your ointment has restored my skin each time . . ." She swallowed. Collected herself. Then continued. "Your skills as an herbalist are admirable, but I don't know your name?"

"I don't have a name," I said. The words almost choked me. I had no name now that Mamma was gone. "I'm orphaned and without friends or family."

Her eyes were dark, her manner elegant despite the pain she must have suffered. She nodded, and I saw that she understood. I noticed she did not look resigned, as many do when faced with a brutish husband, and this struck me, even as I was quashed by my troubles and my grief. I saw a woman who had no choice but to submit, but had found herself here, with me, the ingredients of the deadly *acqua* pulsing on the shelves.

We looked at each other as if we shared some great secret, some confidence the rest of the world must not guess, though she could have had no notion that poison had been my apprenticeship. I felt Mamma beside me in that moment. I felt her phantom breathe into my ear, her spirit eyes watching me, her presence nearby—and I knew what I had to do.

I drew in my own breath. I felt suddenly calm. I knew which path to take, a path that would be impossible to turn back from.

"Madonna, there's a way I can help you, if you have the courage." We stared into each other's eyes as the air formed jagged around us, though there was a stillness that settled over us too, like a veil floating to the ground. Just then, the prayers began. The cloistered nuns raised their voices and floated their song to heaven. It was as if God Himself willed it, as if He blessed this path.

"How can one so young help me?" the woman murmured.

I did not answer that question, saying instead, "I've a potion that'll cure your husband's ill treatment of you. Four drops spaced each a week apart. Each drop placed carefully and secretly in his wine or his soup. He'll suffer but he'll have time to make his peace and set his affairs in order, Madonna. And you, you'll be free."

The woman, whose name I did not discover—such things were not important—drew in a long breath. The air in the convent smelled sweet that day: incense and freshly harvested herbs mixed with perfumed soaps for washing, tinctures, balms, and tonics; a heady mix of scent and bitter oils. She pulled her sleeve back over her injured arm, her veil back over her damaged face, and she nodded.

That night, when the nuns had finished their evensong and the swallows had returned to their nests, I turned the key in the apothecary lock, making sure no one could disturb me. As Mamma had taught me, I tied a rag over my mouth, and I prepared the *acqua* for the first time alone. I was overcome as I worked, not by the acrid smoke of the distillery, but by memories of Mamma. I wept for her as I slowly, tenderly, mixed the poison until, at last, there was just enough belladonna to seal its potency. I felt like I was home again, though with a loss so deep and wide it almost swallowed me whole. From that moment, the die was cast. There was no turning back.

"Thank you, young mistress," the woman said when she returned. This time her face was covered with a thick lace veil. I passed the small jar into her hands and shook my head.

"No thanks are necessary, Madonna, only caution is required. Do as I say. Give the remedy slowly. Care for him as any loving wife would." I echoed my mother's words, each one a ripple of grief.

She pressed a single scudo into my hand. I shook my head—after all, Mamma had rarely charged for this service—but the woman looked at me, and even through the material I could see the pity on her face.

"Take it. You'll need it," she said, looking down at my belly.

Perhaps that day was ill-fated. Or perhaps it was the day the stars shone brightest on me. Who can tell? It was the day I began my own trade in poison—in justice, freedom, and death. Over the years since that moment, I have learned to hide the light of my vengeance, my thirst for justice, performed in the only way a woman can: in secret, away from the fathers, husbands, confessors, and lovers who own us from the second we are born until the moment we die. I have never been sure whether my need to avenge Mamma's death and the guilt I carry is stronger than my desire to save the women who come to me. Perhaps it does not matter. The ending is written the same.

*January 1634 (by Giulia's hand)*

*Bruised woman,*

*one vial of acqua (Giulia)*          *1 scudo*

# 19

"Did she survive?" I ask Giovanna when she walks in many hours later, pushing the thick velvet drapes aside. Dressed in her faded widow's weeds, she looks weary. Dropping her basket down on the wooden table, my friend looks back at me and manages a smile. Giovanna was called away from Mass, and sent word to me here, at the shop, saying she would be late and not to wait up for her. I always wait, for all of them, as if somehow my vigil will keep them safe from harm.

"It was a difficult birth. The baby lay the wrong way around in her belly. She survived her labor, just. The moss staunched the bleeding, though I can't say whether childbed fever will take her. She's too young, and too weak."

"And the child?" I say, throwing another log onto my small fire, which is lit to take away the chill of this autumn night.

Giovanna sighs, pulls up a stool and sits beside me.

"By the time I left, the babe was suckling at her breast. She looked half-starved, though. I'm worried her milk won't be enough."

This is nothing new. Many of the young girls whose labors we attend barely have a scrap of meat on them. Newborn babies die because there is nothing to feed upon, and none can afford a wet nurse. The price of wheat doubles as people drag out their dead, as plague cadavers pile up in the streets and the lazaretto on the island of St. Bartholomew is filled up.

"I will send her some goat's milk and a posset to enrich the blood," I say.

Girolama makes an irritated sound. I arch an eyebrow and look over at her. She is grinding cloves, ginger, and rosemary.

Together, their scent is acrid, intensely so. Perhaps I will send her this remedy too. It is a bad time to birth a child, with the plague showing no sign of waning. In the streets, they are burning clothes and bedding, books and parchments from the houses of the dying. The air is choking and thick.

"What say you, daughter?" I ask. "Do you object to us helping these girls? They have little except for the babe in their arms." I am tired, irritable, and my daughter's manner grates.

"I say nothing, Mamma, except I wouldn't let a poor man put his seed inside me for a smile and a hot supper. These girls, they're all the same. They make their own fate." Girolama looks away, a small smile playing about her lips. I see she is pleased with her retort. She thinks she is a *saggia*, a cunning woman, indeed. If she sees the irony in her statement, being born from a mother who had no choice at all, whose fate was determined by her father, then she ignores it. My daughter knows what happened. I have not spared her the facts of her birth. I have not given her a fantasy of a kind father who died when she was too young to remember. I have given her only truth. Yet, she does little enough with it.

I snap at her. "Then you're as foolish as they. Poverty is not their fault. Men's desires are not the fault of those they desire. These girls, as you call them, know of no other life. It's what they've been born to. They're the ones left with babies to feed while *la peste*—or the alehouse—takes their husbands or lovers. They're guilty of nothing but trying to love and be loved." At which point, Girolama, who calls herself *La Strologa*—the Astrologer—snorts with derision. I am forced to hold my tongue even though my daughter exasperates me. Sniping will get us nowhere.

Girolama throws me a look, her dark eyes flashing, as they do when she does not agree with me, and I catch my breath. At these moments, I see my stepfather Francesco before me as if he had stepped out of the past, up from his deathbed, trailing the rank air of the tomb behind him. Then, as now, I cannot breathe, and I must step away, compose myself, come back to her anew to resume our many small battles. My daughter is willful, determined, impatient. Perhaps she is more like me than I care to admit.

I have mixed a draught for Giovanna, and when it is ready, I gesture for her to stay seated and take the hot liquid. It is a tisane, infused with honey and chamomile to sweeten her rest. She sweeps back her chestnut-brown hair and smiles again, though I can see the worry for the new mother and baby etched on her face. My friend never birthed a child of her own. Though she has seen three husbands go to their graves, all from natural causes, none ever planted a child in her belly. She has told me little about the men except to say that her third, and last, was a feckless lover who could not keep out of other women's skirts.

"I'll go back tomorrow morning and check on them both. I'll take them the milk and medicine, and any bread if we have spare." Giovanna yawns. "But there's something else, Giulia, and this is for your ears too, Girolama."

"What is it, *amore mio?*" The flame leaps up, small sparks shoot upward into the soot-blackened chimney.

Giovanna seems to rouse herself. Her gaze, when she turns to us, is alert.

"Inquisitors have set up a stand in Campo de' Fiori, inviting people to come and confess their sins. I saw them as I passed, at even this late hour."

"Inviting them . . ." I echo.

Giovanna nods, sips the hot drink.

She puts the cup down carefully, but I see a slight tremor. Is she scared?

"There were two priests, and people were lining up to speak to them. One of the men wrote down what they said, and the other walked the square, telling people to repent and confess, to tell the Holy Office everything they know about their sins—"

"And those of others," I finish. In my mind's eye I see the carriage from this morning, the gemstone brooch, the look from dark eyes that bore into mine. I feel the tingling of the noise that only I could hear, marking the Sight and its warning.

"Giulia, I spoke to the herb seller, and she said there are priests in each square across the city. What does it mean?" Giovanna says.

She is looking at me with curiosity, guessing I am distracted. Girolama looks over to me too. The moment vanishes as quickly as it came, like the light from a snuffed-out flame. My daughter wipes her hands on the apron that covers her satin robe. Her insolence has vanished. She gets up and walks over to Giovanna, taking her hand and stroking her hair. My friend is a second mother to my daughter, yet sometimes they fight like she-cats. Not now, though. Now, I see the love Girolama bears for her as Giovanna leans her head against my daughter, and they both wait for me to speak. Behind them the rows of stoppered pots and ceramic jars are barely visible in the darkness. Inside them are healing plants: rue, cinnamon, thyme, lavender. Inside the jars are unguents, salves, and rose water, their scents mingling together—sharp and sweet, bitter and floral.

I shuffle in my seat.

"Perhaps nothing," I say, and yet I know this cannot be true. Inquisitors are always at work in the city, but this is different. This is the beginning of something.

The sound of a carriage, its wheels jolting to a halt, interrupts our reverie.

Girolama strokes down her fine gown of deepest blue and pulls on a shimmering velvet cloak of the same color, a gift from one of her aristocratic patrons. She pretends to bow to me. Her hair is braided back off her face, now covered with a black veil. Black kohl is smudged around her eyes. She looks impressively magical. In one hand, she holds a deck of *tarocchi*, wrapped in a purple silk cloth. In the other hand, a purse embroidered with golden stars.

"Mamma, don't stay up. I won't be back before dawn."

I have urged my daughter to shine less brightly, but she is as incapable of this as the sun. She radiates in the glow of the aristocracy's interest, and I find I do not blame her for wanting to blaze in those high-ceilinged rooms lit by good beeswax candles, dazzling with light and color, perfumed with heavy-scented musk and bergamot. Just like the palaces of Spain in my childhood. But in these darkened times, we must have a care. We must watch for *il malocchio*, in case its malevolent gaze turns toward us.

Yet, caution is a word my daughter is still to learn.

Not for the first time, I think that three strong-willed women in the same household is ever a recipe for discord.

"I'll wait for you, my daughter, as I always do." When I look at her, the Sight eludes me. I wonder if it is because I do not want to see what lies ahead. Born under a Black Moon. Living a cursed life. There may be much I want hidden from my gaze. "Be careful," I say, suddenly awkward, unsure.

"You worry too much, Mamma," she replies.

The fire spits. Girolama is bright, canny, bold. She is ambitious for fine things, for fine people, for a world that is just out of her reach. When I think of her tonight, her face flushed with candlelight, a goblet of wine in her hand, the cards laid out on a carved table inlaid with glass, I shiver. But what else could I expect? I taught her to read the *tarocchi* as a child. Then, when she was a young woman, I taught her to make the liquid that we are known by, though she seems indifferent to its seduction, its pull. Perhaps I am grateful it is so. My daughter wishes to shine, whereas my potion—and our clients—must stay hidden. Perhaps this indifference will keep her safe, and she will find other ways to forge her future, away from my *acqua*, away from my killings, away from the whims of men and their desires. She seems to care little about the women we help. She wants only to raise herself high and higher. But will she fall? Will she tumble down? Will we all?

# 20

I have another set of cards.

I brought them with me from Palermo as a girl of fourteen summers with my stepfather's child in my belly, and they have stayed with me ever since. I wait until Giovanna leaves, then lay out my *tarocchi*, their gilded edges torn, their colors now faded.

They seem to call to me tonight. I take this as a sign I should read them and so I turn the first. The room starts to swim in front of my eyes, and I am seized by a terror so fierce I could faint.

The Tower.

Forked lightning hits the crumbling edifice as all falls to the ground and is destroyed. It is a warning of turmoil, disaster, ruin. The same card I saw the night I ran from Mamma and the convent still room, and into Francesco's clutches. Heart beating, I try again and turn the next. This time I see again the same card that I pulled all those years ago, which I have pulled many times since: *Il Papa*, the Pope. The symbol of authority, dominance, obedience. The final card: *Il Diavolo*, the Devil. Contradictory, tricky cards that return more questions than I ask.

My hands shake. The cards weren't calling, they were goading me. Nausea and shock collide, and I feel disorientated. With fumbling hands, I gather the cards together and pack them away, wishing I had not revisited them. Now I feel the tug of the future, crumbling like the tower, unsure of my fate at the hands of destiny.

## 21

*Alessandro*

Bracchi's footsteps ring on the polished marble.

I sit, watching his approach from the splendor of the papal throne. To each side of me cardinals and envoys gather. Some hold documents, some contracts that need my signature. Some hold essays and arguments that whisper of Earth's passage around the sun and other heresies.

"Your Holiness, Stefano Bracchi is here for his audience with you," Cardinal Camillo Maretti says, bowing. Maretti's serene manner, the dignity of his years, his doctorate in both canon and civil law, separate him out as a man of honor among the factions and rivals that compete around me. Of all the men at my side since my pontificate began—and there are many—he is the most steadfast, trustworthy, calm. I would trust him with my life.

I extend my hand.

Bracchi kneels before me and takes my hand, kissing the ring in obedience.

"Your Holiness," he says.

"Thank you for coming, Inquisitor Bracchi. How fares your work catching Rome's rats in their sewers?"

The man looks up at me, and I swear I see something: a quick intelligence in his gaze. I wonder if I need to look into him, though the necessary checks were completed months ago. He has an unblemished record.

Bracchi gets up, bows and steps back.

"Your Holiness, I take great pleasure in reporting to you that more than a hundred spies are now working in the city.

They've fanned out into every neighborhood, every quarter and district. The Holy Office of the Inquisition also has a network of informants working out of Santa Maria sopra Minerva, and we've had many come forward to confess their crimes."

"Good, Bracchi, very good."

"The prisons are full, Your Holiness."

I look past him now at the French ambassadors, the Spanish too. They preen and scowl, mutter and fidget, and I am just about to call Louis XIV's stooge, Cardinal Mazarini, forward when Bracchi addresses me again.

"Your Holiness. Forgive me, but I must speak with you on a matter that may be . . . concerning . . . though I cannot yet tell."

He does not pause or wait for my permission to proceed, like all the others. He has a curious self-regard for someone born to a merchant.

"Our inquiries are at an early stage," Bracchi interjects. Before I can answer, he continues. "There are rumors."

"There are always rumors," I say.

"Men are dying in great numbers," he says.

"There's plague in Rome. What else do you expect?" I say, about to dismiss him.

I think of the skull that sits on my desk amid the piles of letters, the quills and missives, its white marble sheen looking for all the world like bone. I think of my carved coffin, the sarcophagus that lics underneath my bed, awaiting my final ascent to spirit.

"Your Holiness, yes that's true, but *men* are dying. Many more than women, and many don't show any of the usual signs of *la peste*. Officials and barber surgeons across Rome are reporting of otherwise healthy men suddenly succumbing to an illness for which there appears to be no cause. They're saying men have died this way for years . . ."

There is a pause. The envoys have stopped their preening and scowling, their muttering and fidgeting, and are staring at Bracchi as if seeing him for the first time.

"Men die all the time. Much disease is mysterious to us, known only to God," I say, yet I gesture to him to move to the side of the room. I get up from my throne and step over, shooing away the officials and clergymen who follow me wherever I go. Lowering my voice and placing an arm on Bracchi's shoulder, I urge him to continue.

"Your predecessor, Pope Innocent, knew about these deaths, the manner of them being unusual, but nothing was done. I've written to every surgeon, everyone who performs autopsies, and every priest in Rome, ordering them to report anything suspicious to me. This way, we have eyes and ears at the mortuary slabs as well as in the confessional box . . ."

Here, Bracchi stops and directs his clear gaze to me. He has acted without my express permission. He has taken it upon himself to order my priests to break penance. I know he challenges me to object. The confessional is a sacrament, instituted by Christ. To pass on information is to break the sacred bond between sinner, priest, and God.

Yet break it we must.

I do not say this. I hold Bracchi's gaze. Eventually, he coughs, lowers his eyes, and waits for my response.

"Do you mean to suggest these deaths may be caused by diabolical forces at work? Could this be sorcery?"

For a moment, Bracchi looks around the throne room. He takes it in, as if he has only just noticed the red velvet hanging behind my gilded throne, the priceless antique vases, the thick-veined marble and Baroque splendor of the ornamental tables and footstools. He sees, as if for the first time, the plush scarlet padding on my golden throne, the papal throne—its power, its majesty.

"Your Holiness, I don't know but I suspect there's foul play at work. I've opened an investigation, if it pleases you to continue?" As he finishes, bells start to clang, one chiming as another rings, a cacophony of sound announcing the canonical hour of Terce. I find I have to raise my voice to answer.

"Of course, you must persist. Keep me informed as you progress."

I am about to turn back to more pressing concerns, the pile of papers and documents that require my signature and approval, though they must now wait until after prayers. But he speaks again.

"The reports I've been given so far all say the same thing. The corpses look perfectly preserved. There's no bloating, no blackened membranes, no rotting of the organs. In every way, they look full of vitality and health, except they're dead. It may mean nothing . . ."

For the briefest moment, we are both silent.

"Perfectly preserved," I echo.

Of course, this is unusual, but many causes of disease lie outside our understanding, are inherently heretical as they may question God's creation, God's divine destiny for us all.

Eventually, my reply comes, in the form of a dismissal.

"I have confidence you'll unearth any wrongdoing, Bracchi. You may leave me."

I turn away but not to my work. Instead, I am seized by the desire to sit with the skull Gian created for me, to look upon the precision of it—the caress of its marble surface, the forensic description of its humanness. I wish to stroke it, to kiss its contours, to revel in its cool beauty.

Then, and this comes from nowhere, I see the hair of the woman outside the Palazzo Apostolico. I see her eyes that avert themselves, the hood she swiftly covers herself with. She comes to me as a ghost would, silently, then slips out of reach.

"Your Holiness, are you quite well?" one of my officials asks. Maretti has taken my arm as if I am faint. I look around and see the men of importance I am surrounded by, and my senses return.

"I am well," I say, allowing a small smile, a gesture to reassure.

I allow myself to be led to San Pietro, to the worshippers who await me, my heart thudding inside my heavy silken robe.

# 22

*Giulia*

Crossing Campo de' Fiori, I carry my basket close to me, my hand inside it gripping the remedy I am on my way to dispense.

I walk quickly through the narrow streets of Rome, swerving around stray chickens and lines of washing that sag overhead. Bells from a nearby convent sound for Terce, the clamor rippling across the rooftops. Though it is early, already the smell of unwashed bodies, incense, and excrement—both human and animal—is overpowering.

Red crosses are crudely painted on doors as nearby a priest reads out the names of the dead. I weave past small alleyways, where women beckon from the darkness. The sight of them, with their curled hair and rouged lips, softens me, reminding me of long-ago days.

Head lowered now, my cloak pulled around me, I walk onward, knowing each stone and icon, each dwelling and tavern all the way to my destination: a narrow street on the banks of the Tiber where the tanners reside. Where once I may have glanced behind me, checking no one was following, now I hurry onward, fear of catching plague seeds overcoming any caution as to the nature of my business. I am careful to keep the linen scarf over my nose and mouth.

I pause at Piazza di Ponte, where the ornate arches of Ponte Sant'Angelo span the river that is our watery heart. Each winter it floods the surrounding roads and buildings. Each summer it falls back, turgid and glistening. It is the place where pilgrims cross, passing the papal dungeons buried deep inside the bowels of the Castel Sant'Angelo, as they go.

Something catches my eye.

A movement beside me.

I stop. Pause. Wait for the motion to reveal itself.

A small boy bounces out of the gloom, grins up at me, his teeth white against the grime of his face. I throw him a coin. He ducks down, fast as one of the black snakes sold in the square. I see the metal glint of the coin flash sunlight before it disappears into the recesses of his filthy clothing. He wipes his nose, smearing snot, leaving a trail like a snail's up his sleeve. I cannot help noticing the sleeve is ragged and patched. His arm, where he has scratched a rash, is red and sore.

"I can give you something to soothe your skin," I say, remembering I have some of the balm containing the comfrey plant in my basket. "Or you can crush basil leaves with a little clean water to make a paste . . ." Before I finish, the boy casts me a look I cannot decipher and runs off.

I look around. It is late in the morning now and the fishmongers are packing up, the remains of their catch starting to stink. Likewise, the butchers lazily swipe flies away from the brown-stained packages that now only attract the attention of cattle; the pigs and goats tied to the gratings by the bridge. Two carriages attempt to pass each other, both drivers shouting directions as another urchin hollers an insult. In the confusion, I choose my moment to cross the open ground, past the people, the animals, the wooden stands, the towers of bottled produce and discarded vegetables that rot on the ground.

From the other side of the piazza, at the point where the road I seek begins, I can see the tower of Tor di Nona prison. And as I walk toward the square tower, I catch sight of three drooping shapes. Three condemned men are strung up from the battlements like pheasants on market day. Underneath each rotting cadaver is a scrawled sign, stating their name and crime: *Cesare the tanner: heretic. Horatio the wine-seller: occult practices. Niccolò the sailor: heretic.*

Again, I stop, though I feel exposed away from the shadows. Bile rises in my throat, and I want to turn back. From here, I can see the shaded doorway of the place I am expected at—the butcher's shop—and yet my feet will not move. I cannot walk past the dangling corpses or the walls of this notorious prison. They say, at night, you can hear the cries of prisoners. If you listen hard enough, while the city sleeps, you can hear the ghosts of men rattling their chains as they shiver and groan.

A sudden noise. I jump, almost drop my basket.

I turn to the source of the sound.

A shutter has been flung open. A window in the house I must visit. Inside, I see a woman's face and I know she has seen me too. I hear the scratching of knives from the workrooms nearby, the sound of industry, of men working. My feet move, and though I feel I may faint, I find I can walk.

The front of the shop is empty except for the remains of the day's business; a bloodied wooden table, the unsold carcasses already thick with black flies though it is winter and the raging heat of summer has abated. The stench of meat is strong—bestial, sweet, and sickly—but I wait. I know I must move again but my body defies me, and I feel a whisper at my neck and the high note that serves as a warning. It is accompanied by the sudden smell of dirty, dank water, as if the Tiber is eddying at my feet. The reek is so strong now, and the sound so high, I wonder if I truly will faint.

Fear rises within me. I sense danger. I have no notion how or why except that it is akin to a hare scenting the air, catching the presence of a fox as it crouches in the undergrowth. I am about to turn away, sickened by the stench, but there is another noise: a child's footsteps behind me.

The same woman, her face pale, her expression fearful, comes down the stairs from the upper floor and stands before me, gesticulating and calling me forward. Still, I cannot move. Every muscle, tendon, bone, and organ all rebel now. They all come to a halt.

"Come, come inside," she says.

I glance behind me, but the owner of the footsteps has vanished.

# 23

In the dim light of the narrow shop, the woman points to the stairs.

Without a word, I follow her. As I do so, I feel strange, woozy. It is as if the waters of the Tiber creep against my feet, dragging on my skirts as they begin to drown me. I keep climbing upward, though it is an effort. When we reach the top, I look down at my gown and am surprised to see it dry, patterned with the usual dust from the road at the hem.

This woman, whose name I do not know but who appears to be the mistress of this house, shows me into a small, clean room. There is a single bed, and a chair with a Bible placed on the seat. A simple rosary hangs on the bed frame. The shutters are closed, making the light slant inward in slivers.

For a moment, neither of us speaks. I feel the sudden urge to leave. Perhaps she senses it because she grabs my arm just as I feel my body begin to turn. Her grip is surprisingly strong for such a slight frame. She holds me, but I wrench my arm away.

"Forgive me," she says. "I didn't mean to hurt you."

My throat feels dry. When my voice comes, it is a choking thing.

"The men hanging outside. When did they start doing that, parading the dead like meat on the butcher's stall?" I have said the words before I remember where I am.

The woman looks to the side as if they are strung up against her own wall. She shrugs.

"For a while now, mistress. The *Inquisitori* . . ."

"The *Inquisitori*," I repeat.

The air seems to suck out of the room.

"What ails you, mistress? Why did you ask me to come here?" I say, stepping backward, away from the side where the ghosts of the drooping men sigh. This woman took me aside at the market, asked for my help. Giovanna knew her as she lives within the same streets, and so I agreed to come.

The woman looks at me. She has an angular face, not unattractive, with black eyes and hair that curls down her back. I realize she is younger than I expected. I still do not know her name.

In response, she lifts her skirts. Her thin legs, her sallow thighs, are smudged all over with purple and yellow bruising.

"My husband's a devil. It's he who should be hanging on that wall, mistress. See how he treats me?"

"I'm sorry for your troubles," I say, moved by her plight, yet still I feel the urge to leave this place. I glance around. There is nothing outwardly to trouble me, but the Sight says otherwise. Why has it returned after all these years? Why now?

There is no answer. The sight of her wounds, the purpling flesh, brings to mind the discarded lumpen joints that lie below: the speckled white of the fat, the darkening red of a limb as fat flies swarm and feast. I know I am being warned, yet I find, almost to my surprise, that I am my mother's daughter still. I know I will help her, despite these tremulous visions.

"He'll kill me, mistress. One day, he'll do it, I'm sure. I've asked around for someone who has knowledge of herbs and plants, someone who can help me. The women at Mass whispered of you. If you can't help, then I should dig my grave."

From somewhere in one of the workshops there comes the sound of something dropped. A male voice shouts. A dog barks. Sweat prickles my skin. Nodding, I open my mouth. What words can I say?

My words will not right the wrongs, only my potion has the power to do that.

"The Church and your family won't give you a divorce," I say, "and so you're left with no choice but to accept these punishments as your lot or choose a way that'll imperil your soul. It could lead you to the gallows." I do not intend to sound harsh; at least, I think I do not. "Think carefully, Madonna. Both of us have been warned. The men hang there plain as day. They can't speak. But if they could, they'd tell us to think again."

The woman drops her eyes and appears to consider this. She brings her hands up, shielding her face, and it is then I realize that she is praying.

"Madonna," I say softly now, "every moment I stay is a moment we could be caught. I can leave now and we never speak of this again, but know this, I can't answer to God for you."

She looks up at me. Her face is streaked with tears, but her mouth is set firm. I think of her bruised legs, her impossible choice, and I pity her.

"I'll do it. I've no other choice. If I don't, then it'll be my grave my family will mourn over. Better it's his."

I am already reaching into my basket. "The medicine will do its work, but don't rush, I implore you, however desperate you are to be rid of him. One drop tonight, another in a week. Four drops will end your troubles. Say nothing to anyone, not your mother, not your sisters. This is between us—"

"And God," she finishes, meeting my gaze. Her eyes are fierce, bold, utterly unrepentant.

"And God," I say, the word catching in my throat. "May He forgive us both."

I hand her the vial, sealed with wax, still cool from its storage place in the back room of my shop. The face of San Nicola stares back at me, his arm raised in prayer and supplication, his gaze direct.

"If your husband asks, this is a bottle of holy water to sanctify your union."

I turn to leave. I have been here too long, but she takes my arm again. Before I can shake her off, I realize what she is doing. In her other hand is a small purse weighty with coin, which I push away. My instincts tell me I must go.

"Don't look for me again," I breathe.

Stepping out into the street, I am almost surprised to see December sunshine forming cool puddles of shadow by the walls of the shops and houses that lead back to Piazza di Ponte.

Here, I stop for a moment. The water slaps against the banks of the Tiber as boatmen and passengers haggle, boats sway, and gulls caw. The market has almost vanished now, packed away until the next day, leaving only the stinking vegetable and animal remains to be pecked at by birds and foraged by urchin children.

I take a different route back, skirting the streets and alleys, stalking the narrow lanes, but as I walk, I hear a man's voice.

"Mistress, stop."

I walk faster.

"Mistress, stop. I'm an officer of Rome and I order you to stop!"

His footsteps echo behind me. Closer. Closer. I can hear him pant. I stop. I wait.

The man is wearing a doublet made of thick Florentine wool. Francesco himself would have taken the measure of this man, costing his doublet, his hose, the velvet cap, the flamboyant white feather curving over it, almost touching his swarthy cheek. It moves as he speaks.

"Mistress, my name is Captain Tommassoni. I have orders to inquire as to your business today."

"My business," I say, still as a mouse as the shadow of the falcon moves overhead.

"Well, all citizens and their movements. Pray, where are you going in such a hurry?" He steps closer to me, and I feel his hot breath on my neck as I turn my face away. He stands too close. He appears to be enjoying the proximity. He smiles, strokes his mustache, his eyes traveling up and down my body.

"I'm on my way to Mass at San Lorenzo in Lucina. I didn't want to be late," I say, looking away.

"On your way to Mass. A godly woman, indeed . . . Now, what, pray, is inside your basket?"

There is a pause that lasts the length of my heartbeat. I swallow.

"Look inside—just a few simple remedies to help a friend with fever," I say.

I hold out the basket; my heart beating, my chest moving in and out. He takes it, looks through. Picks out the package of powder of wormwood.

"Open it. Taste it," he says, his eyes challenging.

I unwrap the small parcel and lick the end of my finger, careful not to look up, to see this man watching me. I dip my finger into the powder and bring it to my lips.

"Good . . . good . . ." is all he says.

Just then, someone shouts, "*Ladro! Aiutami qualcuno!*" (Thief! Help me, someone!)

Reluctantly, the captain looks behind us. I hear more footsteps, moving faster, and more shouting.

"Thank you, mistress. I must attend to this," he says, moving away as the thief escapes into the narrow alleyways.

For a moment, I cannot move. I look up and at the corner of the street is an icon hewn into the crumbling stone wall. The Madonna and her child look down upon me, their gaze pitying. *Thank you*, I breathe to her, uncertain, strangely reverent. I am not usually taken to worshipping this virgin woman who birthed a baby. Yet, perhaps as a woman, she, more than most, would understand what it is to be the object of male scrutiny, to be told who she is and why she is. For a brief moment, we are complicit, and I thank her for that. I thank the gods also for my decision earlier this morning not to include two vials of *acqua*, as is my usual way, as was Mamma's way. I am left with the sensation of a storm having blown through, leaving all scattered in its wake. This time, I do not trust it. This time, I am on my guard.

# 24

Back at my shop, we have a visitor.

Maria Spinola is the newest member of my circle, one who flits in and out of my shop, the brothels she works in, the taverns and churches she seems to dance through. She is known for going out with the fairy folk, supernatural beings whom she tells us she is intimately acquainted with. To look at her, you would know straightaway. She wears her long brunette hair scandalously loose. Entwined within her thick tresses are shells, birds' feathers, and colorful ribbons. On her face is a faraway expression, as if she sees nothing except magical beings. I know this to be false. She is a prolific thief. Maria can spot a pocket watch or a purse on its string in the further reaches of the playhouses, where she flirts charmingly with lords, bishops, and gentlemen, relieving them of their valuables before they can blink.

She is standing now at my hearth, stirring the great cauldron from which emanates a most pernicious scent. Girolama storms past me as I enter, pushing the curtains aside, forcing me to breathe in the thick odor.

"I can't stay while she's making her filthy witch's brew!" My daughter stomps past me, skirts swishing, arms gesticulating. She is making the sign of the *corna*, and I am unsure if she jests or if she is making the sign against *la sfortuna* in all seriousness. I watch her go without expression. I have taught her to fight like an alley cat, to claw her way through life, surviving and making her own luck, as I have had to do. It is no wonder she feels at liberty to express her feelings at every opportunity, though I cannot help a sigh escaping from my lips.

"Maria, the stench is unbearable," I say, pulling the material back to cover the doorway. "What in the name of the gods are you doing?" I choke on the fumes. This is no metallic smell. It is the earthy, sharp odor of something natural, but something diabolical too. "Aren't you meant to be out helping Giovanna? She has two births she must attend, and she's in need of another pair of hands, even those as quicksilver as your own."

Maria looks at me, her eyes like a bird's, twitching and shining. "Giulia! Why are you so cross?"

I do not say that I have had the narrowest of escapes from the police, whom we all know defer to the *Inquisitori*.

"I'm making a new poison for you. Can't you see?" She tuts as if I am the fool. I arch my brows and set down my basket. "So many are coming to us. Three women this week already came to the shop asking for your special remedy. The same number at least came last week, and the week before that. We must think of new concoctions to brew."

As I walk over, covering my nose with my sleeve, I peer into the mixture and see a toad bobbing in the steaming liquid.

"You're boiling a toad? My God, Maria, have you gone mad? Does Giovanna know you're doing this?" I gasp, backing away, fighting the urge to laugh. If the Holy Office could see us now, we would surely be dragged to the noose without mercy. The sight of such a complete picture of witchcraft as this half-deranged whore and her familiar simmering in the blackened pot makes me want to double up with mirth. Maria looks back at me and catches my mood. She bursts into girlish laughter and does a jig for good measure. Seeing my surprise, she dances over, takes my hands, and we swirl around, cackling like *streghe* in truth.

When Giovanna walks in, dropping her shawl onto a chair with a weary gesture, she stops. She stares. Her mouth drops open.

Maria—hair flying, shells clacking, eyes cast to heaven as she swirls—throws out her hand and gestures for my friend to join us. Despite the black circles under her eyes, my beloved Giovanna lets herself be drawn into our circle. She takes my hand, and together, we move and sing the words women say at the washing stream. *Who will we marry? Will our lovers be strong and rich? When will good fortune come?*

We laugh and dance and chant as the toad boils and the steam coils, the fire blazes.

Graziosa is the next to appear, but she seems entirely unaffected by our gaiety. She sniffs. She seats herself down in my chair. She spits the shell of a nut into the hearth. The mood evaporates.

"There's news of *Il Papa*'s inquisitor," she says, "this man whom his exalted self, Alessandro the Seventh, has set loose in the city. They say he's a clever man, a pious man . . . They say he's commanded surgeons and even priests to report to him, their wives and daughters too. We can consider nobody safe anymore."

I let go of Maria's and Giovanna's hands. "And today I was stopped in the street and questioned," I say.

We all glance at each other, panting from our exertion.

"What else do you know about this inquisitor?" I say, holding my hands against my waist and waiting for my heart to steady.

Graziosa spits again. Without answering my question, she continues, "I heard something else at Mass. Lucrezia's lover is dead, and his wife is shouting through Rome that he was poisoned."

My gaze meets Giovanna's. She warned me. She told me not to give Lucrezia's mother the *acqua*. Have I endangered us all because I would not listen? At least now I know that Lucrezia survived.

"We must watch our backs," I say, my eyes sliding back to the fire, which burns low. I think of the butcher's wife and her bruises. I think of Lucrezia and her blood-smeared thighs. I shudder and know I would give my remedy to them even now.

A crow lands effortlessly on the window ledge, his black presence filling the small frame. Then, just as suddenly, wings flapping, eyes blinking, he departs, emitting a raucous cry.

"We're being warned," I finish.

*December 1656 (by Giulia's hand)*

*The tanner from Lazio's wife,*
*one vial of acqua (Giulia)*      *No payment*

*The salt seller's mistress,*
*china root for the lungs (Graziosa)*      *2 scudi*

*One vial of acqua (Giovanna)*      *No payment*

*The butcher's wife,*
*one vial of acqua (Giulia)*      *No payment*

# 25

A week later: footsteps.

I step quickly to the curtain, breathing a little faster, and pull the drapes aside. Though these are the blackest hours between Vigil and Lauds, I recognize the shapes of two of my sisterhood.

"Were you followed?"

It is my first question these days. Where once I would have asked how the woman was, how it went, whether she understood our instructions, now there is this question: Are we followed?

Maria shakes her head absently. Graziosa spits.

"If we were, they couldn't catch us," says the older woman.

They have been out, delivering remedies, skirting the city walls to avoid the inquisitors' stalls, which teem with repentant souls begging for a place in one of their stinking jails. Giovanna, Girolama, and I have been sitting up, waiting for the women to return.

"Don't worry, Giulia, *they'll* protect us," Maria says, humming to herself as she moves into the room.

Even though the satin of her gown is faded, the lace on her bodice mended, her stockings darned, she has the air of a lady, someone born far above her station. Maria was born in the slums of Palermo, though we did not meet there, nor in Naples where she lived before arriving here, in Rome. I knew of Maria for years before I realized she could be useful. It takes wit and resilience to dance between the worlds she inhabits, flitting from lover to lover, from church to playhouse to tavern, from gentlemen in finery to innkeepers in darned linen, from nuns to gentlewomen, to whores—all with a smile on her face and her cleverness hidden.

"Who is protecting us, Maria?" I ask, watching her closely.

She giggles, then darts me a look that reads like a challenge.

"The beings, of course! They're near us even now. Can't you hear them? They whisper their blessings. They watch over us all. They watch over my daughter for me."

"You have a daughter?" I ask, sure I have never seen her with a young girl.

Maria's eyes lose their brightness suddenly.

"Isabella. She died, not far from here. She was in the orphanage because I couldn't afford her keep. One day, I would've got her back. I promised I'd return for her."

Graziosa turns to the fire.

I feel the thud of loss as if it were mine.

"I'm so sorry, Maria, I didn't know. Forgive me, I spoke without thinking." I move to embrace her. She folds into my arms like a small child.

"She was eleven years old, a beauty! The nuns said she had weak lungs, but I'll never know what took her. She's safe now, past any pain. Sometimes, I see Isabella in the corner of my eye, and she's smiling, twirling her skirts, a flower crown in her hair." Maria's voice is muffled. She draws away from my arms, her eyes shining with tears.

Graziosa looks back at me.

"Oh, Maria," I murmur, "you must be so tired. Come, let me make you a paste of honey and fig to sweeten your dreams tonight."

Giovanna puts her hand on my arm.

"Sit, Giulia, it's late. I'll make the mixture."

I look over at her gratefully.

Maria sits down beside me. Graziosa appears to be praying as a rosary clicks between her bony fingers. Girolama is watching us all and I see something in her gaze.

A glint of silver. With a long movement, Maria pulls a chain from a pocket concealed within the fabric of her gown. At the end of it is a watch pendant.

"So beautiful, just like my little girl. I'll keep this for you, my darling," she croons.

We none of us speak. I wonder if her spectral imaginings, her communing with fairy folk, began when her daughter died. In many ways, Maria is like a child herself, or perhaps a magpie: part scavenger, part iridescent creature with this shining new piece that she has somehow lifted from a rich man's clothing.

Maria has a talent for stealing, yet I never see any improvement in her situation. Her husband appears when he needs money and leaves her again when it has run out. She has many lovers, many of whom do the same: they take her coin, then disappear. They are cruel whoresons who deserve no less than a drop or two of my *acqua* but Maria always forgives them, and so they crawl or swagger back eventually. Maria's heart is kind, though her methods are dubious, her moods mercurial, erratic, maddening.

My daughter speaks. "You should get rid of this madwoman! She's half gone with the fairies she loves so much. Who knows who she talks to? Who knows if she's loyal?"

So it was scorn I saw in my daughter's eyes. If she makes a good point, then I do not acknowledge it. I dislike Girolama's cruelty as much as the men who prey on our Maria. She is right, though. Since the inquisitor arrived, none of us has slept well in our beds. We check every alley we cross. We look over our shoulders on the way to Mass. It is as if we are expecting the Holy Office and its devils to breathe down our necks each day, dangling the noose. We are all wary and unsettled, and this sniping between us is becoming wearyingly regular.

Maria Spinola at first appears not to hear, continuing to inspect the treasure she has pilfered.

"Fuck you," she says then, without looking up.

"Girolama, why must you bait her so? What has Maria done to you?" I snap. "Leave her alone."

If violence could be caused by staring alone, then my daughter would have murdered me many times over. She stares at me now. Her temper flares, hot and instant, just like her father's. Girolama spits on the floor.

"Fine manners for *La Strologa!*" I say acidly. "Do you spit in front of your noblewomen in their gold carriages?"

"Don't blame me if she brings trouble to our door." Girolama's hands are on her hips like a fishwife down at the riverside.

"Quiet your serpent's tongue! We don't know who may be listening. If anyone, it's *you* who endangers us! Telling everyone of your powers, your predictions. You're nothing more than a rich woman's pet," I say, regretting it instantly.

Girolama throws me a look of pure malice and stalks from the room. Seconds later, the door to the shop slams as she leaves. I stare after her, half-wondering whether to follow my daughter. As if Giovanna reads my thoughts, she shakes her head, gestures for me to sit, to be calm, though I feel anything but.

"Let her go. She'll be back soon enough," my friend says, "and you speak the truth!"

"Truth that's hard to hear," I say. I can feel my heart slow from its thudding, but the bitterness of regret lingers.

Graziosa chooses this moment to crack whatever she has been chewing between what is left of her teeth. The sound brings me back to myself, and I realize I have forgotten to ask her about the visit to the brothel in Piazza del Popolo. I turn to our pious beggar, still shaken by the exchange with my daughter.

"How was Celeste de Luna?" I say. The renowned courtesan, who works out of one of the largest pleasure houses in the city, often sends for our help. It was Maria, who sometimes sells herself there, who brought in Celeste's custom, and she is one of our best-paying clients.

Graziosa swallows her mouthful before she answers. "What do you think? She wasn't scratching her cunny this time so we needed no tinctures against the French disease . . ."

I wait for her to get to the point. Giovanna, who is getting ready to leave for her pallet bed and wool mattress, puts a hand on my shoulder. I take hold of her palm. It is cool, the skin roughened. I feel her wrist. The pulse is steady though faint.

"You're tired, my love. Get some rest," I say and we share a small smile.

"Mistress Celeste is a famous beauty but even she can't keep a man if she wants to," Graziosa is saying.

I hear her as if she is in another room a little way away from us. Giovanna and I smile again—this time there is something impish in our gaze—and I turn back, because now the old woman's words are making more sense. Now they sound important. They contain something I need to hear, though I am not yet sure what it is.

"She has lost the favor of a wealthy client—you might say a *holy* client—and relies on us to restore his favor."

Graziosa looks up from her rosary beads. She looks between Giovanna and me, and I see sharpness, a sureness in her words as if I am reading them on a vellum page. Something is announcing itself.

"A holy client . . ." I echo. Then: "What did you give her?"

Every client is written into Mamma's ledger still. Into her book of secrets, I record every name and every remedy given, and by whom, just as I did when I was learning my letters. I know I must write this down, the low hum in my ears tells me so, though I do not know what it means for us. Graziosa drops a velvet pouch upon the table. The sound of it is weighty, swollen with coin. "Two love philters: one to administer in the cardinal's wine, and another to give on the tongue as love play. We've taught her a charm to bring him back to her, which she must repeat throughout each day," she says.

"A cardinal? Celeste has reached high this time," I murmur, scooping up the purse to share out the coins. The humming is still there, a shadow of a vibration.

"There'll be more business done," says the old woman, dropping her skirts and making ready to leave. "Many of the girls were asking about our services. We told them if they need help, they must come to us by day under the pretense of buying perfumes or skin-bleaching lotions. They'll come. Their livelihood may depend on such simple magic. They must procure clients or starve. They must cure themselves of love-longing or tempt their suitors back."

The remedies sold to Celeste are a simple mix made of rose water and basil to encourage love, and cardamom brought by sea from India to invoke desire. Together they have been simmered over the fire and wished into being by Maria's pagan prayers.

I often ask myself whether these incantations work, or whether they are merely providers of comfort or hope. Perhaps it does not matter. Perhaps the spell is present in the desire of each woman, in the strength of their longing for the outcome.

Graziosa, her bad eye squinting, her hair bleached by application of acid of rhubarb, tangled and dirty, walks in a series of jerky movements to the curtains. Maria gets up, and together they make their leave, out into the night streets.

"Walk a different route," I call after them, reaching for the ledger and a quill. They both have vials of poison hidden in holy bottles, to administer to women who have approached us: the weaver Cecilia, the dyer's wife Teresa. All of whom I trust. All of whom I doubt.

When they have gone, I turn to Giovanna and find she is watching me.

"What is it?" she says.

"How did you know there's something on my mind?" I reply, smiling.

Giovanna shrugs. "I've known you a long time. Tell me, what are you thinking?"

I fidget. Pick at a thread. "Laura, the baker's wife off Campo de' Fiori, came to me. She wants to buy my *acqua*." My voice is low. Nearby, a goat bleats, a night watchman calls. "She has a new lover and wishes to be rid of her husband."

Giovanna frowns. "Is he bad to her? Does he beat her? She can't just get rid of him because she wants another."

"She says he is good to her," I say.

There is a pause now. The sharpened point of my goose feather quill accepts the ink, draws across the page. I have the day's work to record, and so each night I write, and as I do so, I imagine my mother is sitting beside me, watching my letters, the way I loop my *a*'s, my *e*'s, how I slant my *l*'s too far to the right as if they are rushing across the parchment.

"I want you to give her a vial but charge her. This is her choice and her conscience," I say, eventually.

Giovanna's smile disappears. "No, Giulia, I won't do that," she says. "It's one thing to kill a man who deserves it, who uses his fists, who flaunts mistresses or lovers in front of his wife. It's quite another to kill in cold blood, just because she wants to . . ."

I press too hard and there is a slight rush of ink. The letters I have written merge with the blot. It soaks into the paper, and I watch the words disappear.

"Is there a difference? The outcome is the same." I stare now at Giovanna, and it is she who drops her gaze first.

"But you'll be killing an innocent man . . ."

There is a longer pause. It stretches out in front of us. Inside this pause is everything we would want to say to each other, though no words are yet formed.

"Is there such a thing?" I say as the candle gutters out.

*January 1657 (by Giulia's hand)*

*Celeste de Luna, 2 love philters and*
*a spell for a lover returning (Maria)*      *10 scudi*

*Cecilia, the weaver,*
*one vial of acqua (Graziosa)*      *No payment*

*Teresa, the dyer's wife,*
*one vial of acqua (Maria)*      *No payment*

# 26

Standing on deck, shading my eyes, my hair streaming behind me, I feel the elemental pull of the sea that sparkles and washes beneath my feet, bringing me to my new home across the sea from Spain. Salt stings my eyes, though I see him watching me, always watching me. Does he watch everyone this way? His gaze is ever-present, omniscient, but I am drawn so far into the swell and motion of the sea, the thrill of the endless horizon, that I quickly forget his scrutiny. I am busy being entranced at finding the ship's cat watching me with gray-flecked eyes from behind a coil of rope—a scrawny, pitiful creature that, faltering and shy, walks over to me at last and now sits, purring in my lap. He gobbles up the titbits I bring him from our meager meals, and for hours on end, I forget about Francesco and his unwelcome attention. Then I catch sight of him, standing on deck, his small black eyes following me. He cuts a somber figure dressed entirely in black velvet, his face unsmiling, but he holds little interest for me in my still-playful world. Just as I reach my hand out to stroke the cat, the scene changes.

Now, I am running. My chest is tight, heaving. I am sure there is great peril, and I must escape. As I move, my breathing quickens, my heart pounds and my palms sweat. I begin to slow as each leg has to work harder to move. Each lung has to expand and collapse with greater effort. Behind me, someone is breathing heavily. Labored, rasping breaths. Confusingly, there is the scent of incense and musk. I struggle to turn my head, to look back at whoever is on my tail, but I cannot slow down. I must keep running.

Panicked, I force myself to look up. I appear to be in a church, yet I have no notion how I got here, and I do not recognize it. There is a vaulted ceiling above me. I see candles, their flames moving slowly as if enchanted, their wax dripping, languid, smoking.

A loud clang. I realize I have knocked something in my haste to flee. Out of the corner of my eye, I see a large golden cross lying on its side on the flagstones. Where are my bed hangings, decorated with patterns woven through the damask? Where is my bed? Where is my chamber? Where is *Mamma*?

Just as the questions form themselves, I realize I am no small girl, I am a grown woman, and I have run up against an obstacle: a large altar draped in shimmering silk cloth. I sense my pursuer getting closer, though I still cannot see who it is who chases me.

There is a blur of white robes, a flash of a golden ring. An eight-pointed star hovers over six mountains. It vanishes. Smoke coils from an incense holder. It is like being inside a drawing, the charcoal smudged, but there is one thing I can see. The cap is perched on his head, unmoving. It is the papal cap.

# 27

It is always at this moment that I wake with a start. For a moment, I am disorientated.

"Wake up. Mamma! There's someone knocking at the door."

I stir at the sound of my daughter's voice. The echo of the dream recedes. I am confused. I realize I am seated in a chair by my hearth. I must have been waiting for my daughter to return from yet another night with her noblewomen.

"Mamma!"

I blink, look up at my daughter, who is still dressed in her finery, this time a black gown that seems to soak up the light with the sheen of a raven's feathers.

"Daughter?" I mutter. The nightmare still hovers. If I shut my eyes, I would find it there, behind my eyelids. I run my fingers through my hair, which hangs long and wavy down my back. From Via di Corte Savella, I hear the sounds of the day: street hawkers shrieking their wares, a woman yelling from a window above the nearest brothel before slamming the wooden shutters, a man's response, his crude curses prompting a shout of laughter; a city awakening.

"Mamma!" Girolama is impatient. She stands, her hands on her hips, her dark hair tumbling to her waist now, the braids loosened, her black eyes fierce. She looks every inch the image of her father. Then, at last, I register the commotion. BANG. BANG. BANG.

"Mistress, I know you're in there! Let me in! I need more of your medicine! Mine cured my marriage and now my sisters want your remedy!" The woman, whose voice I now recognize as the butcher's wife, laughs raucously at her own wit. Girolama and

I exchange a look of horror. I race to the shop front. My hands are clumsy as I fumble for the lock, snapping it back forcefully and wrenching open the door. The woman almost falls inside. I seize her arm. Before she can say another word, I half-drag her into the back room.

"What's this racket? I told you never to look for me again!" I almost choke on the fear that rises now, its taste bitter.

"But mistress, your *acqua* worked! Time has passed, and still no one suspects! I'm free of that brute! He'll never again raise a finger to me, and it was so easy, so quick."

"Shhhh, have a care. Half the alley will hear you!" I say, but she carries on.

"You saved me, mistress. You freed me, and now I want to do the same for my sisters. They're all ill-married and want their freedom, freedom the Church doesn't allow us!"

"Lower your voice, hag!" Girolama says. She strides up to the woman, whose name I still do not know, whose name I do not want to know. "Lower your voice, and leave. We won't help you again. You were told not to come. If you don't leave, I'll kick your ass so hard down the length of this street . . ."

"You wouldn't dare!" the woman replies, jutting out her chin. "If you did, I'd shout as loudly as I could that your mother is the famous Widow-Maker, the one who peddles death. I'll tell everyone she's responsible for all the new widows who wear their weeds to Mass each Sunday! Oh, you wouldn't dare kick my ass, for I'd see you hanged for your deadly brew."

My throat is dry. I clutch at my neck as if the noose is already there, rough and heavy against my skin. I try to swallow and fear I will choke instead. My heart is hammering in my chest. She threatens to expose us, though it would put her in danger too. In fact, she may already have done so with the racket she created. I pace the room. We need to get rid of her.

She knows too much. She knows my secret business, and where we are based. She must have followed me back here the day I went to dispense the *acqua.* How could I have been so foolish not to check? In my haste to return, I was careless. I led her straight here—and now she calls for more of my potion.

For all that I am a murderess, though by proxy, any thoughts I have of slipping something into a glass of warmed wine to calm her shrieking vanish as soon as they arise. She has made enough noise to call down the *Inquisitori* themselves, and I would not be caught with my hands holding a vial of liquid, siphoning each drop.

Looking over at my daughter, her face furious, I know she would not have the same scruples, and I am glad that I am the only one with the key to the cupboard. I glance up at the shelf containing the glass jars. Behind one of them sits this key, though it is not visible from here. The butcher's wife watches me. I snap back my gaze. Her eager eyes dart everywhere now. Girolama would throttle the woman with her bare hands if she thought it would silence her, but we need to keep calm. We have risked exposure enough today without this harridan shouting the place down. My daughter bars the curtained exit, waiting for my response, but my mind is blank with fear. It is the woman who speaks first.

"I have coin. My sisters will pay. They lack for nothing, except the means to rid themselves of their husbands. They suffer as I did. You'd be doing them a good service. You'd be helping them to be free of this pain, this terrible life. Their husbands drink away their money. They spend their earnings on cheap whores and cheap ale, then they beat them when the money runs out. Is this a life for any woman?"

I have dreaded this moment, this discovery of sorts. I have mulled over what I would do if someone spoke up or spoke out.

I have played with it in my mind during long nights waiting for my daughter to come home, or my circle to return, and yet I find, now it is here, I cannot act.

Her voice has, finally, dropped to a whisper. She steps toward me, her face an expression of pleading. I look at her as if she is caught inside a soap bubble, out of reach, her mouth moving yet I do not register the sound.

Something gets through.

*They beat them when the money runs out.*

*Is this a life for any woman?*

Though I am repelled by this butcher's wife, I hear these words, and anger rises in me again. Despite this, I feel a strong desire to leave her presence, and I am reminded how I felt in her home. Was the Sight warning me of this outburst? Or was it warning me of something else, something that is yet to come? I begin to pace again. The movement is reassuring. Each foot still moves, one in front of the other. Each hip joint rocks and sways. Each breath comes quickly now.

Then, the butcher's widow grabs my wrist. I notice her black gown, the lace hanging down over her hair.

"Give me the *acqua*, Mistress of Death, and your secrets stay with me."

I am aware of an intake of breath. It must be mine. Then again, it could be Girolama, who has stepped toward us as if she will wrench this woman off me.

"If I leave empty-handed . . ."

At this point, Girolama cuts in. My fierce daughter would be a match for Satan himself, but she has met a formidable opponent in this blackmailer.

"If you leave empty-handed, then what? Don't you think we'd name you if we're taken? Don't you think your head sits uneasy on your head, if we're questioned? Don't think we'd

save you. I wouldn't suffer the strappado for the likes of you,"
Girolama says.

The two women stare at each other now like two mastiffs
in the fighting ring: teeth bared, hackles rising. I would not
wager on either to win against the other, though I fancy the
widow has the upper hand, the trump card. I place a hand on
my daughter's sleeve.

"We don't want your coin. Take the vials and leave. You
wouldn't be so stupid as to implicate yourself in murder. We'd
deny it. You'd deny it, though they'd kill us all anyway. This is
the last time I'll help you. You may bring the dogs of hell down
upon us and I'll not give you any more of my *acqua*. Leave now.
Use it sparingly. Never come back."

I open the cupboard and pull out two small bottles stoppered with wax and paper with the saint's image painted on
each. I see the woman's expression now: exultant, jubilant, sly.

Without a word she takes them and secretes the poison
inside her bodice. My daughter steps aside, gestures for the
woman to leave.

"Go, hag," she says.

The woman casts her a look of pure triumph as she passes,
holding her skirts like a lady. I can feel Girolama's anger about
to boil over, and I know it will erupt as soon as this woman
is gone.

I am right.

Seconds after my daughter has locked the door of the shop,
first checking outside for anyone who might be too interested in
our business, she marches back.

"Daughter, I know what you're going to say—"

Girolama speaks over me.

"She must've followed you back here, and you didn't think to
look behind you! You, who tells us every day, 'We must be on our

guard. We must use our instincts to protect our circle, we must keep trouble at bay!'"

I stare back at her. Girolama has a way of playing with the rings on her fingers when she is agitated. She takes one and turns it around, the gemstone disappearing then reappearing. I feel the sudden urge to stroke her brow as I did when she was sick and feverish as a child. She paces just like I did. Her skirts seem to absorb the light.

I am about to interrupt, to say that this might be the last we hear of the woman, that she has what she wanted and that is the end of it, but Girolama continues. She spits out the words.

"And that was the last of the *acqua*. Why did you give it away so freely? She wouldn't have reported us. She has too much to lose!"

Girolama is rightly angry. I hesitate before I reply. My daughter is passionate and willful. She lives her life inside her emotions, from one extreme of feeling to another. The storms pass through quickly, though. I know in an hour she will be calm, but until then, I can do nothing except nod my head, and hope she softens.

"Yes, daughter. I made a mistake. I hope she's now silenced, but you're wrong, I don't trust her. She's a fool but I can't believe she'd risk her own life, and that of her family, though she's shown she has a loose tongue. There's nothing we can do now, except perhaps pray. Pray to our gods in secret. Hope the whirlwind blows away. Hope this is finished."

I glance over at my small altar, in truth a shelf above the hearth upon which sit my offerings; a thick-spiked spruce of rosemary that has almost lost its scent, a blackbird's feather dusty with age, my *tarocchi*, the shell from Madrid, and several coins.

Girolama looks at me doubtfully, and I find I share her disquiet. Perhaps it has occurred to my daughter too. Perhaps she and I are of one mind, one question. That question is: Is that woman a spy? Was she sent to entrap us by the *Inquisitori*? Surely if she was, she would have gone to them before now. She implicates herself by asking for more. No, she knows where we are, what we offer. If she was a spy, we would already be behind the bars of Tor di Nona, wouldn't we?

Then, I look around for what I realize is missing. There is a gap, a space where my friend should be.

"Giovanna should've been back this morning. She said the woman had borne several children before this one and it should be an easy birth. If this is so, where is she?" As I speak, a cloud falls over my vision, the floor seems to sink beneath my feet, and in that moment, I know something is wrong.

# 28

It is clear Giovanna is not home.

The shutters of my friend's lodgings near San Lorenzo in Panisperna are shut, and when I knock, no one comes. A rangy black cat mews as it wanders past. There is washing hanging from the windows, some strewn across the alleyway, which dims the light further though it is morning still. I am about to walk away when a woman wearing a dress that is not much more than rags opens the door. She appraises me before she points to Giovanna's apartment and shakes her head.

"They came early this morning. They wore fine cloaks and good leather boots. I watched through a hole in my wall. I saw her walk out with them."

"Who were they?" I say, feeling the icy grip of panic.

The woman looks at me again. "I think you know who they were. I'll pray for your friend. She's been kind to me. She's the only one who could soothe my baby boy when the colic was bad." She nods as if we understand each other, then she shuts the wooden door, disappearing back into the dark corridor.

Standing there, unsure what to do or where to go, it strikes me how little I know about my greatest friend, the woman I love as a sister. She has told me a little about her past: the three husbands; the death of two of them; the betrayal of the third. The usual disappointments and tragedies of a woman's life. But I realize now there is one thing I have never asked her. Why did she join with me in making poison? If she knew the dangers, then why?

We met in Naples. Giovanna was a customer at the convent, buying my herbals for her work as a midwife. She saw my condition, and she offered me her lodgings, knowing the nuns would abandon me when they discovered my secret. When my birthing pains came, it was she who stroked my back, who reached between my thighs to guide out the child. Lying back on Giovanna's simple pallet bed, she placed my squirming infant upon me, the cord still pulsing between my blood-streaked legs. I was fourteen years old. I was a mother, without family except for my baby girl and this new friend.

That night, I wept for the ache of my mother's love. I wept for the agony of Mamma's absence, for the guilt I felt at her death. For the rage I felt that burned within me; deep, festering. Girolama, plucked from the air like the supernatural creature she was, would never know her, but she would know her loss because it was part of me. From the moment she was born, my daughter and my friend became part of my vow to wreak revenge: learning the ancient ways of cunning women. Perhaps the Devil rode within me that night. Perhaps he too suckled at my breast as my fierce love for the mother who would never hold my child scorched my soul.

It was Giovanna who soothed Girolama when I needed to sleep. She comforted her at night when wild dogs roamed outside, barking and fighting. She did not abandon us when I told her my biggest secret: who my mother was (for the name of Teofania di Adamo had carried on the winds across the ocean to Italy and beyond)—and who I am too. I told her about my poison. Then I showed her how to make it. Our friendship was sealed in alchemy as we brewed my deadly potion. Perhaps she had seen much suffering: women left to bring up children, birthing mothers who cannot hide their bruises, trapped wives, neglected daughters, abandoned mistresses. All of them bound to the laws that keep us imprisoned in our roles. Perhaps she saw my work as sacred, as a natural antidote to the lives we women

must lead. I have never asked her. I hope to God I get the chance
to do so.

There is only one person I can entrust with my concerns.

"What brings you here again so soon?" Padre Don Antonio says.

His eyes search my face. He smiles that same knowing, tender smile, and I find myself leaning toward him as if I would
enfold myself in his arms. In this second, I would drop all that
I am to step toward him and find shelter in his embrace. The
moment passes as soon as it arrives. Instead, I speak.

"Padre, thank you for seeing me."

I cross myself and bow my head as another priest walks past.
My hand traces the cross: left to right to forehead to stomach, as
my eyes slide to the floor, a gesture so familiar and yet strange.

"My friend Giovanna de Grandis has disappeared," I whisper. "Her neighbor says she's been taken . . . Please, whatever
you can discover about her . . ."

The padre looks away for a moment, then he steps toward
me, takes my arm, draws me to the side of the chapel. His touch
feels shockingly intimate. I almost stumble as we move. There is
a sick feeling in my belly. He knows something.

"There's been gossip," he says, confirming my instincts.

The nave is quiet now, except for a few worshippers muttering prayers.

"What gossip?" I pull my veil a little farther over my hair.

"The talk in noble circles concerns a cardinal. Someone very
close to our illustrious pope. Cardinal Camillo Maretti saw a
courtesan he's been . . . enjoying . . . add a powder to his wine.
He forced her to confess, sure it was something sinister. She told
him it was a harmless love philter, insisting she'd made the elixir
to bring them both satisfaction in the bedchamber."

The humming begins again. There is a smell of burning, though perhaps it is from the lit candles clustering together near one icon or another. My heart begins to hammer. It pulses. I can hear it in my head as my whole body reacts to this. A cardinal. My beloved friend. Could this be the holy client? I am unable to swallow yet I do not know what the connection between them might be. The padre looks at me as if he sees inside me: my beating heart, the fear pulsing now with the desire to run . . . but where to?

"What's this to me?" I manage to say. The sulfurous smoke of the thin church candles spirals black in the gloom.

"Mistress, rumors of a circle of poisoners are reaching beyond these streets and alleys, and into the finest chambers in the city."

"And who's this courtesan? What's her name?" I urge, feeling my body sway. The keening sound fills up my ears, my head, my lungs. I am nauseous, clammy. An elderly woman hobbles toward the church doors. I see her turn and bob a curtsy to the altar. As she does so, I see she will spill the contents of her basket. The moving candle flames seem to intensify then shrink back.

The priest moves away, but behind him trail the words I was expecting to hear.

"Celeste de Luna."

Back in my shop, Girolama is waiting for me. I do not have to explain anything to her when she sees my face. Indeed, I do not understand why this Cardinal Maretti, Giovanna, and the famous whore Celeste have been mentioned in the same breath.

"The *Inquisitori*?" she says.

I nod, sit down heavily on my chair, before standing up again and grabbing for my cloak.

"I'm going to see Celeste."

"Celeste de Luna? Why her? Anyway, you know how it works. She calls for us, it's never the other way around. She's practically a princess."

"She's a hustler and a whore, and she may've cost Giovanna her liberty, or worse, her life."

My daughter does not hesitate. "Then I'll come too," she says, already pulling her cloak over her gown.

I shake my head. "It may be dangerous. We may already be watched." What I do not say is *And your temper may boil over like milk left on the stove and wreck our chance of information.*

Girolama shrugs as if the Holy Office and their agents are mere nuisances and my warnings pointless.

"I'll come," she says. "I know Celeste from the parties we both attend, and she's more likely to talk to me. "

I cannot argue with my daughter's logic, and I find I am grateful for her company as we head to the north of the city, our cloaks pulled around us.

Piazza del Popolo is teeming with young men in various states of inebriation. Under the lofty heights of the obelisk, gentlemen seem to be gathering in packs, careless of the fact it is not quite noon rather than nightfall. On their arms are women wearing colorful gowns, their hair in peaks like horns, their shoes like wooden stilts, towering over their male companions.

"The brothel's this way," I say, crossing over the square. A young man heckles us as we pass, and I make the *fica* with my thumb poking through the fingers of my clenched fist. He staggers back as if heartbroken, clutching his hands to his chest and laughing.

"Another time, beautiful mistress. I'll await your desire."

We ignore this fool and walk to one of the stately buildings leading off the piazza. Its grand entrance looks more like that of a palace than a pleasure house. Out of nowhere, a woman who is perhaps ten years older than I, with elaborately styled hair, sparkling with jewels, and a gown of carmine silk, approaches. She looks at us as if two ghosts have walked into her parlor. There cannot be many women who walk in through the front doors. She gestures for us to follow her to a side chamber. I had forgotten what luxury looks like, what it feels like. The sight of the tapestries from Turkey, the Murano glass flutes, the pianoforte carved from nut-brown wood with a delicate gold filigree pattern, all serve to render me mute. They remind me of Francesco's villa, our gilded cage, and for a moment, I am silenced. It is Girolama who breaks this enchantment.

"We've come to see Celeste de Luna. It's important," she says, her neck straight, head held high, as haughty as this madam who holds her face to the side as if she would assess us. Her faint eyebrows arch almost to her hairline.

"I'm afraid that's not possible. Celeste is our most glittering star and is indisposed at this time of day. I'm sure you understand." Her voice is melodious, her smile perfection, though it does not reach her eyes.

"We have to see her," Girolama says again, but I see this madam is not convinced by us, and so I speak.

"Tell Celeste de Luna it's *la Signora della Morte*. Tell her we must see her. There can be no delay."

My daughter looks at me as if I have succumbed to lunacy. I have announced to this woman, this powerful, important, well-connected woman, that I am the one they call the Mistress of Death. Something in the air shifts. I sense that the tide has turned and is flowing in our favor. The madam nods. There is a small smile playing on her lips. She walks out, leaving us staring after her.

"She's gone!" Girolama says.

"She'll be back," I say, popping a sugared almond into my mouth from a gilded dish of sweets.

"But, Mamma, what have you done? You've exposed us!" My daughter swings round to stare at me.

"I have, daughter, but I'm gambling that this is a house of secrets, and this one, at least, may stay within these walls."

"And if it doesn't?" Girolama's eyes are fierce.

I look away. I do not want to say that it may not matter, that our secrets may be ours no longer. Giovanna may have been put to torture. She may have said anything to the *Inquisitori* by now. I think of Faustina. I see her broken body jerking, suspended from the noose.

"Come this way, please." A boy, who does not look older than I was when I arrived in Naples, beckons from the doorway. His skin is as black as the night. He wears a green fitted doublet and hose and carries a small golden tray.

"Thank you," I say, and let myself be led through rooms that ring with laughter and gaiety, where candles burn though it is the day, and music drifts through the tall-ceilinged chambers. If I shut my eyes I could be back in Madrid, laughing at the antics of a player on the king's stage, but I am not in Spain, in Philip's easy, fun-loving court. This is Rome. A place of power and intrigue, of vice and perdition, and I do not know what awaits us.

# 29

Celeste de Luna, concubine to the wealthiest men of the city, languishes on a daybed as her music master plays the harp.

As we enter, she looks up, casting her deep brown eyes over us. She is a magnificent creature, even one as bored as she appears. Her honey-colored hair is braided back off her face, emphasizing her high hairline and smooth ivory skin. She wears a rose-pink silk gown that slips off her milk-white shoulder.

"Why have you come, *Signora della Morte*? And why did you announce yourself thus? Is life a game to you? Don't you care who knows you?" Her voice is a sleepy drawl. Now that my eyes have adjusted to the shaded light of the room, its curtains pulled to block out the day's sunlight, I see shadows under her eyes that hint of a busy night's business.

The maestro stops playing. The notes fade into nothing. His eyes flick to my face, then to the ground.

"Don't worry, Lorenzo here is mute. He can play like an angel from God's heaven, but he can't speak. Isn't that a curious thing?"

"The curious thing is that our friend Giovanna de Grandis has been taken," I say.

Celeste looks up. At first, she looks confused, then I see the name register, and her expression changes.

"You may leave, Lorenzo," she says. Her voice has changed. It is harsh now; commanding.

We wait until the music master has bowed his way out of the room. As soon as the doors are shut, Celeste leaps from her bed and grasps my hands.

"You mean the Holy Office has arrested her? *Mannaggia a te, Camillo!*" she cries.

"Who is Camillo? What does he have to do with Giovanna, who even now may be stretched on the rack or breaking her own arms, strung up by the rope?"

The woman is pacing now. The lustrous braided hair hanging long down her back moves as she walks back and forth across the rugs in dainty silk slippers.

"Camillo, why did you betray me?" she says, before stopping and turning to us. "He's a cardinal created by Pope Alessandro, and closest to the Holy Father. For a short time, he was my lover, and I hoped he'd remain so. He's a charming man, or so I thought. It was for him that I bought the love potions from Maria and the old beggar, but of course I know Giovanna well too. She saved me from motherhood—many girls who work here have needed those particular services. When Camillo caught me putting the philter into his goblet, I panicked and said Giovanna's name. He assured me he'd say nothing."

Fury rises in me. I feel it surge upward, becoming anguish by the time it finds my heart.

"Then he lied to you."

My daughter has, until now, stayed silent. "What will they do to her?" she says.

I hear the voice of a child rather than that of a grown woman. I forget that my impetuous daughter loves Giovanna as much and as deeply as I do.

From a nearby room comes the sound of merry laughter. A woman sings a ribald tune, the men braying in response.

"If she holds her tongue and keeps her nerve, perhaps nothing," I try to reassure Girolama.

"For a simple love spell, they may try to frighten her, but without evidence . . ." Celeste shrugs, as if this is, indeed, a game.

I see Girolama is comforted by this. She looks at me and her eyes are filled with tears but she smiles.

"See, Mamma? They have no evidence. All will be well."

I try to smile back. What she does not know is what I gave to my friend last night. Upon Giovanna's person was the vial of poison destined for the baker's wife, Laura. Though we had disagreed, Giovanna acquiesced, and told me his death was on my conscience, to which I shrugged. His death and a thousand others, perhaps. All deserving. All guilty of those crimes only husbands, fathers, and lovers are capable of: cruelty, mistreatment, neglect. In doing so, have I condemned my own beloved Giovanna? If I could open up the jail and swap places, I would do this without hesitation. I pray that our friend had completed her task before the vultures of the Holy Office descended, knowing in my heart she had not.

Time moves slowly.

The hours pass. Sometimes, I find I am circling the small room at the back of my shop, passing the shelves of ointments and remedies, passing underneath the bunches of fragrant, drying blooms, then the hearth, then the curtain, then back past the shelves. In the corner is my cupboard where I keep the dangerous things, the forbidden remedies. I try not to see it, though it remains stubbornly there. Then, just as I feel I cannot pace anymore, I find I have slumped into my chair, my skirts sinking like an egg custard. A great darkness overwhelms me, and I feel like I am sinking, just like my skirts, and I cannot imagine how I was ever able to move. Through all this, Girolama is uncharacteristically calm. She is preparing a stew—we have not eaten for many hours.

"When will Graziosa return from her pilgrimage?" she asks as she sprinkles wild thyme and salt into the pot. "Come, help me, Mamma. Stir this while I cut garlic."

Without any notion how I get there, I find my right arm is moving in a circular motion. At the end of it, a wooden spoon is gripped in my hand. As my arm moves, I find I am saying a prayer—or perhaps it is a spell—to bring Giovanna home to us. It is a plea for protection, for safety, for redemption.

"Who knows where she is, or when she'll return?" I hear myself say as Girolama chops. When she is done, she walks over, dips her finger into the supper of beans and vegetables, and sucks it.

"Definitely more salt," she says, pushing the garlic cloves into the stew, and reaching for the dish of white crystals on the table. On it are my good knives, my pestle and mortar and simple kitchen ingredients—the salt, lemons, a bowl containing eggs, a carafe of goat milk. "Our pious beggar often disappears for weeks at a time, returning with a neck heavy with new icons, and a temper more foul than before," Girolama snorts.

I throw her an exasperated look, and realize I am coming back to myself. I feel like I have been away on a long journey. My back is sore, my neck is tight, and I feel the kind of exhaustion that a new mother feels: wide and endless as the sea.

"Bring me the bowls," I say now, but my daughter does not take the hint to stop her spite.

"Who knows anything about the old witch!"

"Hush! To call her a witch is to condemn her—and we don't know who might be listening!" I say, burning my hand on the pot as I ladle thick soup into Girolama's waiting bowl. I cannot imagine how I will eat this; bring the spoon to my mouth, move the stew onto my tongue, chew and then swallow. It seems like a task that is far beyond me.

"They say she's had more husbands than all of us put together, though I can't see how. She's as scrawny as she's bad tempered, but who can guess a man's predilection?" my daughter finishes, arching her black brows.

It is then I see the cards, sitting there. How did I not spot them before? I must have taken them down from my altar earlier, but I cannot remember. The day has become a blur of waiting spiked with fearful imagining. The backs of the *tarocchi* are richly decorated with gilded edges against a midnight-blue backdrop. The sun, surrounded by her jagged beams, shines on the back of each. They are my only real treasure—and they seem also to be *waiting*, if cards could do such a thing.

Girolama, as if she senses it too, places a hand on one of them.

"What are you doing? Let's leave the cards quiet tonight, they won't bring Giovanna home," I say, feeling oddly nervous at the sight of them.

Instead, Girolama turns the card over.

The air seems to still, the room to vanish. It is the same card, always the same card.

*Il Papa.*

I drop my bowl. The stew spills. A rat leaps out of his hiding place in fright. It flees, its long tail disappearing into a small, dark hole in the wall.

# 30

*Alessandro*

Most Noble and Illustrious Mother,

As ever, I write to you with my love, and with the knowledge that I have lost the greatest of women. As ever, I write to you of the emptiness I feel, knowing you are no longer beside me. It has been twenty years since you left me and ascended to Heaven. Twenty years of grief in which my only comfort has been the act of taking up my quill each night so I can finally be alone with my thoughts of you.

These are wicked times, Mother. Our enemies lie within as well as without. They are like snakes in long grass, lying in wait; fangs bared, spitting poison. The *Inquisitori* tell me men are dying though *la peste* shows signs of waning. My brother, Mario, whom I have elevated to the title of commander of the Papal Army, tells me there are fewer brought to the lazarettos each week.

High-born men as well as the low born die in ever-growing numbers. Gentlemen, priests, clerics, merchants, traders, innkeepers—their corpses pile up and the sepulchers of the city are full to overflowing. We know not the cause, and my clerics tell me the streets and churches of Rome are filled with young widows, flirting and simpering, their grief hidden as if it never existed at all.

Bracchi asked for another audience, which I was pleased to bestow upon him. His spies are combing the city within the walls, into each dark alley, into places you could not conceive could exist—places of degradation, of misery and poverty. Places where prostitution is rife, where children wallow in filth and dirt, where thieves and pickpockets circle their victims like vultures in the desert. Here, I am told, there are rumors. These rumors have spread from the hovels to the ballrooms of this city's noblemen, and beyond. There is talk of a deadly enterprise in butchery and slaughter. Streets away from where I am sitting now, in my private quarters situated in the grandest chamber of the palace in rooms befitting my status, there is devilry afoot.

He tells me a circle of poisoners works somewhere in this most holy city—a fact revealed by a repentant sinner to her confessor. This woman, this Delilah, spoke to her priest, who reported directly to Bracchi. She said she secured a potion that could kill a man in four drops but did not use it. This woman, who did not give her name, said it was given to her by those who declare themselves the saviors of their sex. Without any more information than this, we are blind, and I told my inquisitor so. I urged Bracchi to seek her out and bring her into his rooms for questioning. He refused me this. He does not want those responsible to know we are on their tail. I have indulged him, but time is running out. Men are dying. Those set above these churls by gender, by class, by dignity.

My great friend Camillo Maretti tells me it is commonplace for those of the weaker sex to dabble with philters and elixirs, for love and for jealousy, to cure abandonment and hatred. He knows of a woman named Giovanna de Grandis, who deals in these sordid methods. I informed Bracchi, who brought her into my dungeons, though to no avail. She carried nothing but a vial of holy water, confessed nothing and knew of no poisoners. A thorough search of her apartment revealed nothing, and so she has been freed, but Bracchi has caught the scent, of that I am sure.

It is my avowed mission, perhaps the most important of my reign, to unearth these heretical witches, to bring them to the light of righteousness, to strip them of their unnatural powers and show them the power of Rome, the glory of God and the justice they must face, as we must all do, at the feet of the Lord Almighty.

I will find them, Mother. I promise you, I will find them.

Your loving son,
His Holiness Alessandro VII

I look down at my letter, knowing there is much I have not said. The ink is drying on the thick vellum, the quill still in my hand, but I know the words will remain unwritten. I have a yearning, a sinful yearning. I have lustful thoughts. I want to share these disturbances, for that is what they are, with someone, and yet I have no one else except Mamma and she is long dead. I want to write and unburden my soul of the yearnings of my body, the terrible lusts of the flesh that started in earnest when I saw that woman in the square. She hid herself quickly, but not before I caught sight of her hair, the color of the wheat fields that sit outside the walls of the city I was born in. It hung in waves. It rippled down her back. Her eyes, when I caught sight of them, appeared green, though she was too far away to know for sure. This glimpse, this uncertainty, only serves to tantalize, to seduce. She looked up at me and it was as if she looked straight into my soul and saw something precious, something primal. If only I could tell Mother of this strange, impossible, unlikely fixation, perhaps it would disappear. Perhaps the dreams I have of her, night after night, would vanish. How can I dream so vividly of a woman I do not know? What fire has she set alight in me? What sorcery has she cast upon me? When I place my letters to Mamma away in my hidden drawer, I am locking away my secrets. It is then she appears again in my mind's eye. That glance. That direct gaze. Then, I am overcome with longing I cannot sate.

I imagine stroking her hair and I quiver. How can I say these words to you, Mamma? How can I long for your maternal caress while my skin burns for a flesh-and-blood woman with eyes the color of the sea?

I place the feathered quill back down on my desk. Perhaps I have a fever.

# 31

*Giulia*

"Giovanna, you're home safe! They've let you go," I say, throwing my arms around my friend, breathing in her familiar warmth, the scent of the apothecary, though there is another odor. Something bestial. Something of squalor and dirt. What did they do to my friend in their stinking jail?

It is almost a week since she was taken. A week within which I have mourned and raged, wept and hoped for this moment, thinking it would never come. Curiously, at the very moment I wanted to command the Sight to show me if she was alive or dead, it gave me nothing: no sign, no hint, no warning. I did not dare to pull the cards. Instead, I prayed with the fervent worship of a child. I prayed to our gods, our deities: the mountains, the ocean, the arching sky above our heads, the river as it sparkles in the sunlight. We have no names for our gods, no rituals nor prayer books. We have no Bible. We worship the power that grows the seed in the soil, that uncurls the flower's petals, that makes a child grow in its mother's womb, which breathes death as well as life. We worship with a reverence that is simple and joyful and—naturally—heretical. I have been taught by my mother, and she by hers, and again and again back into history. The properties of plants, the times to pick, the times to grow, have been whispered to me through a long line of women, and with it has come this simple religion of ours, this delight in the raven's flight, the moon and her silver glow.

I draw back to look at Giovanna. "You look pale! You must not have eaten for days. But have they really let you walk free?"

My daughter, Maria, and Graziosa, who has returned from her pilgrimage as truculent as ever, all swarm over. We are like honeybees around a flower, each buzzing with relief and happiness.

"Sit, my love. Girolama, prepare Giovanna a draft. Graziosa, bring over the chair. Maria, bring bread and some of that goat cheese from the market," I say.

Giovanna places her head on my shoulder. I could weep with joy, and find, in truth, the tears are already flowing.

"What did they do to you?" Girolama says as she mixes the soft floral herbs that will bring our friend comfort.

"Very little," Giovanna says, smiling. "Yes, I'm hungry, but they didn't torture me. They let me go. They found no evidence of witchcraft."

With this, Giovanna looks up at me from her seated position. She guesses the others do not know about the vial that was secreted in the faded widow's weeds she wears.

"Eat now. Gather your strength and praise our gods that the *Inquisitori* failed to see what was in front of their faces," I say, knowing we will speak later, when the others go about their business dispensing remedies.

When the others have all gone on their way—to Mass, to the washing stream, to the market—I sit next to my friend. She is tired and so I will make up the truckle bed at the back of the shop. I do not want her going back to her lodgings this night, in case they return for her.

"Why did they free you?" I murmur.

Giovanna looks over at me. She sighs and shrugs. "Who can say? They had no evidence and so they let me go. It's the law."

I nod.

Except, the law is not for the likes of us.

"They found the vial of *acqua*?"

Giovanna turns to me. "They did. I was intending to deliver it to the baker's wife early that morning, though you know my feelings about giving it to her. I was going to slip it to her before he was awake to prepare the dough for rising, but they came before cock crow. They ordered me to accompany them to the jail by the Tiber. I was shaking in my boots. They searched my clothing and found the vial. I told them it was a bottle of holy water, just as we've always planned. They didn't think to test it nor taste it."

"Where's the vial?" I say.

Giovanna shrugs. "They had it. No doubt, they threw it away. They must've done, for otherwise I'd be strung up with all the other unfortunates across the city.".

I shudder. Can my friend really have escaped their scrutiny so easily?

"Giulia, don't worry. I'm free. They believed me, and they found nothing they recognize as poison or witchcraft."

The words all make sense but underneath them I feel the pulse of something. Can the *Inquisitori* really be so easily fooled? Decanting the poison into bottles with the saint's image on the side appears to have worked, as we always intended it should. And yet.

"Did they ask about Celeste de Luna?"

My question makes Giovanna start. "How did you know?" she says.

"Padre Don Antonio told me her cardinal lover saw her put something in his wine. We went to see Celeste. I asked her what happened, and she said she panicked when ordered to give a name—"

"And she gave mine," Giovanna finishes.

"Yes," I say, frowning.

"What's done is done, Giulia," Giovanna says, and it is as if she is comforting me. "I am alive. I am here. That's all that matters."

I should welcome this miraculous escape. I should give thanks for my friend's freedom, and yet I cannot. I do not trust this peace. Perhaps I do not trust anything anymore.

The deep shadows under Giovanna's eyes tell me I must stop my questions.

"You must sleep now. I'll prepare your bed and watch over you. You've done well to say nothing." What I do not say is *Let us pray it was enough.*

The next morning, our circle gathers. A coven, indeed.

"We can't assume we're safe," I say. "Even though they let our friend leave"—and at this, I smile over at Giovanna, who still looks pale—"we must cease all trade except the medicinal herbs and cosmetics. It's too dangerous to dispense my *acqua*."

"Mamma, you worry too much!" Girolama says. "The *Inquisitori* know nothing. Why else would they free her?"

"I don't know, daughter. That's what scares me," I counter. I know what I'm about to say will anger her. "And you can't go to your noblewomen, nor your parties, not now. It's too risky—"

Girolama explodes before I have finished. "No! I won't stay here night and day, chained to your hearth and the apothecary! I have clients who depend upon me. I have . . ." And here she stops.

"You have . . . ?" I say. Is my fierce daughter blushing?

"Nothing, Mamma. I have nothing," she says, but I see she is rattled.

"You've met someone," I say, softly this time.

An emotion I cannot name passes through me. It is like tenderness, and it is as if every part of being a mother has distilled into this moment. Girolama, my only child and a woman grown, is in love. She has stepped into her own life, and though I have expected this, I find I did not prepare myself. My heart aches. There is a space where all that is unsaid sits, and it is here my words stay; they do not come.

"Does he have a name?" I say eventually. "My love, you know you can't see him, at least not until time has passed and we know more—"

"More? There's nothing more, Mamma! Giovanna left without charge or intrusion. We're free to carry on. And yes, Mamma, I've met someone. We're in love and he wants to marry me."

There is a shocked silence as the words settle in the air between us all. Maria is humming to herself, but her eyes are bright. Graziosa is sitting in front of the wall of shelving. A serpent coils in its vessel. An aborted fetus floats nearby and tendrils of plants spread their languid arms in the oil they are suspended within. Giovanna stands up and moves to my side.

"Giulia's right. We can't risk attracting any more attention. My name is known to them. It wouldn't take a clever man long to link it to yours, and to all of our names. I'll carry on with midwifery. Graziosa will dispense remedies for toothache and gout. Maria will do the same. Giulia will see customers in the front of the shop. Everything else must stop. No scrying, no fortune-telling, no *acqua*—nothing the Holy Office could object to."

"They'll always object," Girolama mutters, but I see she is won over.

"So, who's this man who wishes to marry my daughter?" I say to Girolama after the others have left.

Again, my daughter blushes.

"His name is Paolo . . ."

"Go on," I say, adding powdered wormwood to a poultice along with cinnamon, nutmeg, and cloves.

"He's handsome. He's witty and well connected, and he loves me . . ."

I sense there is something else, something sharp like the cold blade of my knife.

"Go on," I say again, waiting.

Another pause.

"He's a nobleman . . ."

"A nobleman," I repeat. My words are suspended between us as we both consider this impossible news.

"Mamma, he loves me, truly. We have a marriage of minds. He's promised he'll wed me when his family agree." I have never seen this expression before on Girolama's face. She looks besotted. She allows herself a smile, while her black eyes sparkle. She plays with an emerald on her finger. It is a new gem, one I had not thought to ask about. Now, of course, I realize who gave it to her.

I am torn between the desire to shake Girolama and the desire to comfort her. Do I need to tell her this will never be? She is a clever young woman, but she seems blinded by affection—and by his promises.

"And when will that be?" I say instead.

We look at each other. My daughter shakes her head as if to dispel my meaning.

"He promised me," she says.

I find I do not have the heart to tell her otherwise. A lordling will never marry a fortune teller, even if she is *La Strologa*. His family will never allow it. In her heart, I think she knows it too.

As if reading my mind, Girolama says, "You're wrong, Mamma. Paolo tells me every night that we'll soon be together.

He says I'm a goddess come to earth to save him from a terrible marriage to a plain countess in Genoa."

"Have a care, Girolama," I reply. "While we may have slipped from the Inquisition's clutches this time, we must still be on our guard. You don't know who this man really is and who his family works for, whether it be the State or Church. We don't know if we can trust him. I'm sorry, daughter."

If Girolama curses me under her breath, I pay no heed. I pretend I do not hear. I would have done the same.

# 32

The injustices do not stop.

Every day for months, women come to my shop, or they speak to one of my circle as they go about their business. Every day, another bruised wife, or bored lover, or angry mistress, or neglected whore, comes to me, begs me to give them the cure for their troubles. Every night, I sit by my cabinet when the others have left, the key playing in my hand, mulling things over.

The *Inquisitori* have not come. It looks as if we slid out of their sight like eels from an upturned pot. And yet, there is a baseline, a vibration. It speaks to me of knowledge acquired, though it is a tremulous sensation. Still, I wait, my shop selling only physick for ailments of the body. I do not trust the silence, the waiting, though for what? Surely, if they tested the "holy oil" in Giovanna's vial, they would already have come? Perhaps it is only because they haven't yet found us.

In this gap between then and what may be, I think about my mother. I think about her caution and how she stopped dispensing the *acqua* when Faustina was taken. I think about how much she cared about the women she helped, and I also think about the poison. In some way I cannot explain, I know the poison *chose* me. It claimed me as its own creature that first night my mother taught me to make it. Mamma never talked about it that way in the months following. She used it to help women, to sympathize with their bad marriages and cruel menfolk. She was not avenging anyone or anything.

How different it is for me. For me, it goes deeper. It always has. I *miss* my poison. I *miss* thinking of its journey, slipping into a carafe of blood-red wine. Sliding drop by drop into the broth simmering on a stove in a gentleman's kitchen. I miss hearing it sigh as it travels down a throat, past the *pomo d'Adamo*, the bite of Eve's forbidden fruit that is forever lodged in a man's throat, down toward the stomach where it becomes an acid—invisible, silent, deadly. I admit I am in its thrall, but there is guilt here too. I have stopped dispensing and those women I could have helped are now without protection. I wonder what my mother would think. After all, Giovanna was set free. Faustina was not. The danger was different, or it appears to be. Even of this, I cannot be sure.

I wonder how many women have died since we stopped dispensing my *acqua*, how many could have been saved, though at the cost of their menfolk. Perhaps it does not matter. Not to God, anyway. What is one sinner's death, as opposed to another's? It matters to *me*, though. Every whispered plea, every sight of a bruised wrist or a black eye, every used, bored, abandoned woman, stays with me. The poison also stays with me. Why did it choose me? What darkness lies within me that answers its call?

I know we should continue to be cautious. This poison, this *acqua*, was my mother's curse—as it is now mine.

Opening the cabinet is easier on my conscience than I imagined.

It takes a mere moment to slip the key inside the small hole, to turn it, to open the door again. Inside, there is a good quantity of lead shot and vials, a row of images of the saint in permanent benediction, but no arsenic. The main ingredient. The king of poisons.

It takes a mere moment to realize what I am about to do. Breaking my own command, I pull on my cloak, step out into the piazza and call over a child with a cap worn so low over his face, I cannot see his eyes. He takes my coin, listens to my whispered instructions and, with a nod, runs ahead of me. Delivering a message. Telling the priest, I am on my way. If the rumors are true, then he will not be at San Pietro in Vincoli tonight. No. This priest of mine, this renegade churchman, will be engaged in other services, in another place outside the city walls, away from the watchful gaze of his fellow priests. I have a long walk ahead.

When the sky darkens, the city changes from a place of merchants and traders to one of pimps and pickpockets.

Giovanna and Graziosa are attending a breech birth and may be many hours, while Maria is selling small charms in the form of pieces of parchment written in tiny, birdlike markings, a language entirely her own and sold for *baiocchi* in the taverns. Girolama is most likely sulking in her more prosperous apartments in Trastevere.

My destination is northeast of the city. It is perilous, my way uncertain, for I am heading to a church that sits outside the walls, Sant'Agnese fuori le mura. There I will cross through Porta Nomentana to meet Padre Don Antonio. I will walk through the night, there and back. As I go, I will send up invocations to the gods who watch over us cunning women, and I will ask for Mamma's protection. By her grace, I will not fall victim to the cutthroats and swindlers who loiter and mingle with the good citizens of Rome. I carry a purse heavy with gold, and so must be vigilant. I also carry a small knife, one I have carried on me since I was a young woman—sharp, sheathed, tucked inside my bodice, its handle shaped like a crucifix.

The streets are busy, and I pass through the center of the city with ease. I reach the place where three streets converge at the fountain fed by the Acqua Vergine. Weaving through narrow streets, I reach the Pantheon, its columns misted as if by a gray veil of centuries past. Harlots catcall. Drunks stagger. Inn-keepers holler. Soldiers swagger. A woman carrying washing glances over and falls into step behind me before disappearing into the night streets.

I keep going until I reach streets that are less familiar. I clutch the purse hanging from my waist and keep going, each tread hesitant, wary of every sound. The buildings fall back to reveal open ground. My leather boots stumble on the uneven road. I pass convent gates, bolted shut for the night. The way ahead is dark, lit only by the flames from an occasional torch in its sconce. I sense I am close, and within seconds I see the city walls looming out of the darkness. Two guards sit by a small fire, laughing, swigging from bottles. I stop, hesitant. Then, out of the black shadows I see a monk dressed in a brown homespun habit, his hair made bald on top, his eyes searching for me.

I step forward, and he sees me. He nods, and I know I am safe. Together, we approach the guards, who look up, unconcerned and uninterested in us. I hold out two *giuli*. Gold glints in the firelight. They nod and I throw the coins to the ground as the monk and I walk through the gate one of the men is holding ajar. On the other side, I realize I have not yet exhaled.

It does not take long to reach the basilica.

It is unassuming from the outside, with a plain frontage, though it is hard to tell in the black of night. Somewhere a bell tolls. Somewhere a baby cries, though the sound is faint. A dog yelps.

"This way, but you must be silent. The priest is conducting a special ceremony."

But the monk steps away from the church and through a small archway. He leads me outside, toward a small domed

building that looks like a mausoleum. He pushes open the door
and beckons me to follow. Heart thumping, I step inside. The
circular domed space is almost entirely black except for two
small flames that seem to be hovering above a single altar that
stands underneath the height of the dome. As my eyes adjust
to the darkness, I see they are not floating, they are held by
someone, a woman. She is naked in the light of the two black
candles she holds in her outstretched hands. Her body is startlingly white. My first thought is she must be cold as the chill
of winter still lingers, though it is spring. Her eyes are shut, her
legs apart revealing the thick black hair between them. Shadows rear up and fall back as the priest, dressed in a black cassock, is revealed by his movement. He walks to the prostrate
woman and places a chalice upon her stomach.

*This is the chalice of my blood.*

Padre Don Antonio is performing the Black Mass, an act
that would see us all hanged. The priest's voice rises now up into
the damp air, and I feel the sudden urge to run. The monk, sensing my alarm, puts a hand on my arm. His touch is surprisingly
gentle.

"Wait, mistress, he'll be finished soon. All is well."

Biting my lip and tasting the metallic trace of my own blood,
I step back and feel the cold stone walls that circle this place,
yet I do as he commands. Oh, I am not naive. I know these
masses take place in the churches that sit away from the center
of Rome, away from prying eyes and the spies of the *Inquisitori*. I know Padre Don Antonio is also an exorcist who, for
the right price, will perform any number of illicit ceremonies,
supply any number of illegal services, including the reason I
am here tonight. This is the first time I have seen it performed,
though. There is a jolt of something in my belly as I watch,
something akin to jealousy, though it is an odd time to feel

this way. I have known him many years now. A chance meeting in a tavern, not long after Giovanna, Girolama, and I arrived in this seething, stinking city, and a deal was struck, a pact made—some might say, with the Devil. Without Don Antonio we may never have begun our trade. Without this priest, we might have been washerwomen, scrubbing dirty hose for a few coins by the washing stream. Some might also say that would have been a better life. A decent, law-abiding life, though one of long hours and meager pay, pottage for supper, and a rough, lice-filled bed of straw to lay our heads upon each night.

Why should a man born into wealth and power sink to doing the Devil's work for coin? Why would a man born into privilege ever consider trading in poison, with a woman like me? He may be high born, but he spends his nights mixing with those of us who live in the filth and gutter of Old Rome. In another life, I might want to know him, I might want answers, but in this life-time, I think nothing, seek nothing, or at least I try to. It is safer that way. I do not ask questions. Ignorance is protection, though a poor one.

This sacrilege—this desecration—is a grave sin. It is the profane cousin of the most sacred act of God; turning bread into flesh, wine into blood. I watch now as if caught in a spell. The woman is still, too still. For a moment—the length of time between heartbeats—I am convinced she is dead, and I am witnessing a sacrifice. But then she moves her arm, the candle flickers and I see my stupidity. How could she hold them aloft if indeed she had been slaughtered? My mind is running away from me. I inhale deeply, trying to steady myself, though I feel shaky and troubled. Yet I do not leave.

# 33

Mass ends.

I hear a carriage arrive out front and realize it must be for the woman. Of course, to afford this service she must be wealthy, ennobled even. Perhaps she longs for a child and can conceive no other way. Perhaps she prays to the Devil for the love of a man who spurns her. Perhaps she prays to exit this life, to escape her gilded cage. I can only guess at her reasons.

I jump when a black shape appears in front of me. He pulls back his hood and reveals himself as the priest.

"Padre," I murmur, unsure who may be listening.

"Mistress," he replies, smiling, as if we had merely met by chance.

"You have what I've come for?" I say.

"Of course, mistress. As ever, I have what you need, though I've told you to have a care. These are troubled times."

For a moment, neither of us speaks. I hold his gaze. It is forthright, direct, a challenge without hostility. Tonight, he seems more a man than a priest. He wipes sweat off his brow and his cassock sleeves fall back. His arm is strong, though stained with blood now. I step toward him. I almost offer my face up to his. No one except for the monk would know. It would be another of our secrets. But, as I move, there is the sound of horses whinnying and the racket of a carriage's wheels turning. The driver's voice shouts a command. A shape moves, hurries into the carriage and then they are off. The noblewoman safely inside, back to whatever it is she is missing in her life. I turn back to Don Antonio. He is watching me strangely. As a man does to a woman he desires.

It is my turn to smile. "My packages?"

"Your packages, of course." He continues to study me as if he is an artist sketching my likeness. I continue to smile. Then he reaches for something the monk holds out to him. I had barely noticed the presence of the other man.

He hands me two parcels, double my usual quantity. I do not have to tell him that more women come to me than I could ever hope to help, especially since we ceased that part of our services. Somehow, I sense he understands me, though how he does is, again, unfathomable.

In exchange, I hand him the purse, retrieving it from within my skirts. Just as I am leaving, his hand touches my arm. I stop. Turn back to him. What now? Is there another part to this bargain?

"Mistress, there's someone who wishes to meet you."

This is not what I am expecting. "There are many who seek my services, Padre."

"But, of course, mistress," he says, looking away for a moment. "I'm the confessor for a young noblewoman."

"What is this to me?" I say, stepping away. He does not remove his hand from my sleeve.

"Perhaps she's nothing to you. Perhaps, on the other hand, you can help her as you've helped so many others. She'll pay whatever you desire."

I look back at the priest and wonder what this means. He urges me to caution, and then this.

"A noblewoman? How could I possibly be of service to her?"

He smiles again, moves closer so I can smell him underneath the incense. His scent is faintly bitter; sweat mingled with an indefinable maleness.

This time, I hesitate, suddenly uncertain. He releases his hand, and I feel the imprint of it on my skin still.

"Meet with her," he says, his voice a mere breath of air. "Listen to her. Perhaps then you might see her as a woman, just like you, just like your family and neighbors, though hers is one of the greatest in the land."

"She won't be like my family and neighbors. She could never know us or guess at our lives," I say. My lips are cold. The air seeps damp and mildew from the tombs under our feet. It is as if Rome has vanished, leaving us here, our negotiation under way, surrounded by the dead.

"Don't ask this of me. My circle—"

"Tell them this is the price of my services to you, if you must tell them something. I cannot forsake her. She is not a woman who can choose her fate."

"Can any of us?"

"Please, help her for my sake."

I take a moment. Breathe. The night air fills my lungs then hisses out.

"This is a terrible risk," I say.

"But I ask it of you," he replies.

So, this is a negotiation, of sorts. I nod. The terms are clear, though one thing is for sure, I will breathe no word of this to my sisterhood.

"Send her to my shop. Tell her to let it be known that she seeks a cure for a woman's malady. I'll speak with her."

The priest nods now. There is a slight sigh from the shadows; a shuffle of air. I look but see nothing. A rat, perhaps. The monk, possibly. I do not linger. Every second we are here is one filled with danger of discovery, though the night is at its blackest. As I turn to leave, I know he stares after me.

As I begin the long walk home, I try to untangle the night's events. For the padre to ask me this, the first time he has in all the years of our strange acquaintance, I understand there must be much at stake, much I do not know.

Walking back, the sky pales orange, the night already disappearing into day as I cross through the city walls. This time, the guards look up. Their eyes follow me as I make haste. I hurry as if the hounds have been unleashed already and are snapping at my heels. There is a feeling growing inside me: that I must run, keep ahead of that which lopes behind me; teeth gnashing; jaws drooling. Helping a woman of noble family and birth is a risk beyond anything I have ever taken. Whomever she wishes to administer my cure to will be of equal birth, will have status, family, wealth. I have kept my circle safe enough dealing with ordinary women, women without these things, women who are invisible to all but us. This woman will not be invisible. These are muddy waters. The path ahead is perilous. I wonder why I did not say no to the padre. Did the night air make me dizzy? Did it make me foolish enough to agree? The packages, hidden in secret pockets within the fabric of my skirts, knock against my legs as I go, reminding me that there is no safety for women like us. To think so is foolish indeed. The risk might be greater, but it is always there.

My mother comes to me as I reach familiar streets. She hovers beside me as, yawning, I fumble for my key. She sighs against my skin as I sit down in my chair, knowing I will not sleep, knowing I will say nothing of this to my circle. Let them sleep and dream sweeter dreams. Let them go about their business without fear, at least with less fear. Let them be ignorant for then they will have nothing of this to say if they are taken. The thoughts hover like dust from the mausoleum as the new day dawns, sanctified now by the clamor of bells ringing across the city.

# 34

The air moves, rearranging itself around the figure who stands now in the doorway of my shop. Noise from the street seems to quiet. Even the horses standing in the piazza, bridled to a gilt-edged carriage, are silent. For a moment, the light appears to shimmer, but perhaps it is the richness of the woman's silk skirts colored vibrant red. Her sleeves are long, her *camicia* made of silk, her veil flowing over her rich brown hair. Or perhaps it is the diamonds at her throat, the rubies and strings of pearls that seem to wink as she steps inside, next to the large ornate cross that hangs around her fine neck. Her scent fills the room. It is a heady mixture of musk and bergamot; strong, spirited, lingering.

"*Nobildonna*, may I assist you?" I say, breathless.

Her robe alone costs more money than I will see in my lifetime. This creature takes another step, clutching a velvet purse now to her breast. She is the only customer in the shop, and I thank the gods for bringing her when business is slow, just before I close between midday prayers and afternoon Mass, when the heat of early summer starts to dissipate.

"Thank you, I'm here to buy creams for my complexion. I am told to ask for the Sicilian with skills in herb lore," she says, looking around. She takes in the rows of earthenware pots on their shelves, the pouches of herbal mixtures, the bottles of tonics and syrups.

"You're welcome, *Nobildonna*—"

"*Duchessa*," she corrects, smiling.

"*Duchessa*," I say, dipping my head. "I have skin lotions and creams that'll treat any ailment."

She is plump, comely, and girlish. Her voice is sweet and soft, her face framed by ringlets. A delicate blush lies on her cheeks, and as she moves, the rich material of her dress whispers. Hush. Hush. I see why Girolama feels such fascination for her aristocratic clients, though I cannot truly explain what lies at the heart of my curiosity, except for her startling wealth.

She moves slowly as if unsure but comes to stand in front of me at my wooden table where I measure out mixtures and wrap my goods. I cannot help but compare her finery to my working robe made of rust-colored linen, a brown kirtle laced with blue ribbon, and an apron to cover my skirts. My neck is bare of jewels, and I remember from my days as a rich man's ward how heavy they feel around the neck, how weighty and cold. Her scent is intoxicating, her manner halting, regal.

She is not alone. A woman stands by the door, watchful.

"Wait there, Lucia."

This woman is used to giving commands. I am about to object, saying Lucia may prevent others from entering if she loiters in the doorway, but, of course, this must be a private transaction.

"My confessor tells me you are the only one in this city who can give me the medicine I desire."

I cannot help it—I look around as if an inquisitor and his devils might be hiding in the shadows. But there is nothing there.

I nod. "You'd better come this way, *Duchessa*."

I pull back the curtains and gesture for her to follow me. She comes alone. Her maidservant stays, barring the door.

The woman's skirts brush my furniture: a three-legged stool; a carved chair, its velvet padding worn at the edges; a long wooden table, stained with tinctures, upon which sit my pestle and mortar. Chopped stalks and dried flower petals lie scattered. A knife stained and ready for cleaning, a damp cloth and a candle stub.

Despite this, I find I am not ashamed to admit this high-born woman into my world. This space is mine and mine alone. I have made a successful business in cosmetics and herbals, an almost impossible task for a woman, and I have done it without the help of a father or husband. I find I am comfortable with this creature sitting on my roughened furniture, spending time by my small hearth.

She does not appear to notice the quality of the furnishings. She sits elegantly on my chair and pulls the gossamer veil off her face. She is beautiful with dark eyes, a high forehead, her eyebrows plucked and arched as is the fashion. Beautiful except for faint smallpox markings which, though faded, still mar her skin. Her eyes are pleading and, for a moment, I am dazzled. This woman, this rich, powerful woman, needs me—and the feeling is bewitching.

I gather myself. I am not some young chit made insensible by this imbalance of power between us, by this aristocrat bestowing her favor upon me. I guess that she lives her life in palaces and villas. It is a far cry from the world I inhabit here, away from prying eyes, feeling safe only in the darkness of small, crooked streets, though I still remember days when it was not so, when I too wore skirts that swished and jewels that sparkled. Those days are long gone now. Now, I am unrecognizable to the society I left behind—and I am grateful for it. What counts, I discover, is that I recognize myself more than I ever did as a stifled, entrapped stepdaughter of a wealthy man.

I wipe my hands on my apron, pulling it from me—I can, at least, remove that symbol of my lowly status—and glance in the mirror above the hearth. A woman approaching the end of her thirties stares back at me. She is still striking. My hair is still wavy and long, my skin still fair, my lips still pink and full, but it is my expression that has changed. There is grief there still; I see it lurking in the recesses of my gaze. But there is strength there too, and courage. I see it in the tilt of my jaw, the length of my neck, and the eyes that stare back, the challenge in their gaze.

I realize I am distracted. The woman is looking at me.

"How can I assist you?" I ask. Her eyes are those of an innocent, a young woman of perhaps twenty years old. Yet, she is here—and I know already that she will ask for my *acqua*. Perhaps her innocence is as much an adornment as her jewels.

When she speaks, I find I am wrong in my assessment of her. She is direct, concise, and candid—it is clear we are speaking as equals, though not of a sort anyone outside this room might recognize.

"My name is Anna Maria Aldobrandini," she says, "and I need your help. May I speak plain?"

"Speak, *Duchessa*," I say.

Anna Maria Aldobrandini, a woman from one of the highest families in Rome, perhaps all of Italy, looks around my apothecary, nodding as if she likes what she sees. Even the snake skins drying, hanging from the wall, do not appear to disturb her.

She moves a little; her silks rustle.

I wait, wondering if this is a dream and I will wake to the sound of my neighbor's goats and the bells for prayer.

Her lip trembles just a little when she finally speaks.

Haltingly, she says, "My story is nothing new. I was married at the age of thirteen to a man thirty years older than me. My prospects and my destiny lay in the hands of my parents, of my family and their interests. In this, I am no different from any woman of my rank."

Here, she stops.

Pauses.

There is a faint sound, like a ribbon sliding across exposed skin. No one else is here, but I glance toward the door.

"I don't pity myself, mistress. At least, I haven't, until now."

"So, what's changed, *Duchessa*?"

When she looks up at me, her face is flushed, and her eyes well with tears.

"You must understand, I've done everything they asked of me, *he* asked of me. I've lain with him, though he is old and ugly and his breath stinks. I've nursed him through winter agues. I've obeyed him in everything . . . but I can't obey him any longer."

"Forgive me, *Duchessa*, but what's this to me?" I say.

My heart is thumping now. One word in her husband's illustrious ear and I am dragged into the papal dungeons. Can I trust her? *Mamma, can I trust her?*

"This is everything to you. This is your work, as much as being married to an old man has been mine. I need my freedom. I need my life, mistress. Only you can give me this. Would you deny me the only happiness I've ever known? I've found the man I want to give myself to, body and soul. Without him, my life has no meaning."

As she finishes, her hand moves to uncover something from her robe: a purse, which she places down beside me. The sound of it is weighty, solid. It is the sound of a fortune.

I look back at her, caught in her filigree net, the words she spins, the coins she offers, and I wonder again why she trusts me. Perhaps of the two of us, she has more to lose. Suddenly, she stands up, starts to pace the small room.

"I can't, *won't*, stay married to the duke."

The air grows heavy. I look down at my hands, so like Mamma's, stained from plant oils, small cuts and nicks from the knives I use to chop and slice them. I know her family will never allow her a divorce. The idea is inconceivable.

"I must be free of this marriage, this pain, mistress," she breathes. "I must be free to love the man I'd die for."

There is a brief silence; a point of calculation, where we both weigh up the possibility that presents itself. She, *la duchessa*, thinks: *I have nowhere else to turn.* I, Giulia, think: *Is this a trap?*

Perhaps now is the moment that everything that has come before has led to. Perhaps this strange scene—two women, alike in mind and bearing, and so different in status and wealth—is the culmination. How did it all come to this? How did every decision, every small act, every step forward, bring us both to this place, to this time? It is astonishing to me. Destiny is at work, but what does this mean for us both? However improbable this meeting, nevertheless it is taking place. In that second, her riches and splendor drop away and I see a woman with a heart that yearns for freedom. I see a woman like me.

"I will help you," I murmur. "But there is one question I would ask of you."

"Ask me anything, mistress," the duchess replies.

"Why did you come? I mean, why not send a servant or your waiting lady? Why risk being recognized?"

She smiles and her face is transformed back to the beautiful young woman she is. "I wanted to be sure of you, mistress. I wanted to meet you and see for myself. There are many I don't trust, even in my own house. I can't be sure who reports to my husband," Anna Maria continues.

"You've suffered much," I say. My hand trembles.

She comes over to me and takes my trembling hands. I notice the six rings she wears, signs of her betrothal and wedding: pearls, rubies, gold. Tears course down her soft cheeks. Her full red lips part and she falls to her knees, silk mingling with the strewing herbs on my floor.

"You must help me. You must free me from this tyranny. Allow me to love another, mistress. Help me marry the man of my heart, for I'll surely die of sadness if I can't be with him."

With this, she shudders, places her forehead upon my out-stretched hands. It burns as if with fever. "Padre Don Antonio says I can trust you, and only you. My family will kill me if they discover my purpose here. I'll kill myself if I have to stay with the duke. My life, my fate, is in your hands, mistress," she whispers.

I send up a quiet prayer to Mamma: *Show me what to do . . . The danger is great, the greatest yet, but she needs me . . . Mamma, speak to me, what should I do?*

There is no answer, or none I can determine. I look down at this spoiled, adored child who now faces the stark truths of womanhood. I see a neglected wife, a girl forced to become a woman. Well, I know how that feels. Taking hold of her head, I lift her face gently. Her eyes are pools of deepest brown. Her lashes long and thick. Our hearts beat. Our blood moves and swirls, traveling through our bodies that pulse with life, with vitality. Our breath quickens, and we are, for a brief moment, complicit.

"How do I know you won't report me? What guarantee can you give for my safety? You ask much of me, *Duchessa.*"

"Please put aside our differences. I speak to you as a woman, one who's trapped and desperate. If there was any other way, I'd take it, but there isn't. Please, you have to believe me. Why would I tell anyone when I'd implicate myself in doing so? I've come here to beg this of you."

As she speaks, the sound begins again as if it never stopped, as if it was always there.

My head fills with the high note.

"I'll send word to the padre. You must do everything in the way I instruct."

For a moment, I wonder if she has heard me, but then she places her cheek against my palms, leaving my skin wet with her tears. Anna Maria (noblewoman, duchess, murderess?) takes her leave of me (poisoner, sorceress, witch), and as she does so, she whispers a prayer.

"God save you," she says, and I shiver.

It may be the detritus of human and animal waste thrown into the streets and alleys, but suddenly there is the familiar sweet rotting smell of decay. I look over, aghast, at this woman of high birth who knelt before me in my back room. She stares back, uncomprehending. Just as I think I cannot take another inhalation soured by the foul air, the scent vanishes, shrinks back into the usual odors of Rome's back streets. Just as my head cannot endure another second of the noise, it too recedes like the waters of the Tiber each spring. At each new turn, the scent and the sound come to me. I understand they are warnings. I also know I have to help this rich-born woman, because she is me. All of them are me. Perhaps destiny sends me these odd imaginings, these portents and signs knowing I can only ignore them because not to do so would go against who I am. I am reckless. I am forsaken by righteousness. I am dark and avenging and powerful. I am also alive and, if not free, then as free as any woman can be. Perhaps it is the latter that is the most dangerous.

*May 1657 (by Giulia's hand)*

*Anna Maria Aldobrandini, Duchess of Ceri,*
*one vial of acqua (Giulia)* 25 scudi

*Eight vials to women at Mass*
*(Giulia)* No payment

*June 1657 (by Giulia's hand)*

*Eleven vials dispensed in the shop*
*(Giulia)* No payment

# 35

*Alessandro*

"The Duke of Ceri is dead, Your Holiness. A sudden illness, an unexpected tragedy."

Bracchi, now governor of Rome, is walking two paces behind me as we move through the corridors toward the basilica, where I will lead Mass.

"There are already rumors—"

I stop, as do all those who follow in my wake.

"Please, leave us," I say, and churchmen scatter, murmuring.

"His widow, the Duchess Anna Maria Aldobrandini, insisted an autopsy was performed to quell the gossip that's been circulating throughout the city," Bracchi says, a little breathless. "It's rumored he was poisoned at her hand. The barber surgeons who performed the autopsy confirmed there was no natural cause of death that could be found, though no sign of poison either."

He pauses. The silence between us grows, then shrinks.

"His organs were intact, his skin flushed with vitality. It's the same as the others. Always men. Always with an appearance of vigor—except—"

"Except they're dead," I finish.

Bracchi, for once, appears lost for words.

"Yet no trace of poison or foul play is found?"

"None," he admits.

"And the widow?"

"Grief-stricken. All accounts say she's inconsolable, but that's not all they say." I wait for Bracchi to speak. He steps toward me. "Your Holiness. My spies tell me she has a lover, a rogue far below her named Santinelli. They say she plans to wed this minor noble-man. She has a motive, but without questioning her . . ."

We are straight to the point.

The woman in question is one of the highest in the land. To arrest her, to accuse her of dealing with witches and poisoners, is to slander her noble family.

"We must tread carefully," I say.

In truth, I am alarmed. Horrified. A duchess and a witch. If there is even a grain of truth in the whisperings, it means rebel-lion. I pause. Bracchi stares back, each of us unable to speak.

"When it comes to it, she shall, of course, have papal immu-nity," I say, thinking out loud.

I cannot bring myself to order this interrogation. It is beyond anything reasonable. It would remove the support of a powerful family, and there is no proof at all I can bring to them.

Bracchi nods. We understand each other. She cannot be impli-cated, but at the same time, we must learn whom she deals with.

"Let me think," I say, dismissing him.

There is a slight hesitation as my inquisitor, the governor of Rome, looks like he will say something. He changes his mind and, instead, bows. He turns and walks away, the tread of his boots echoing as he goes.

The duchess working with poisoners? The *audacity*. It is intoler-able. It is impossible. It is an affront to society and the Church. It is an abomination, if it is true.

I barely notice the arms and hands around me, dressing me in ceremonial robes. Voices speak. "This way, Your Holiness." "To the side, Your Holiness." The *falda* lies under the alb and is held off the floor by trainbearers. I am draped, girdled, trans-formed into God's creature. But my mind is far from here. It is writing the letter that will alert the Aldobrandini family. It is forming the words that will invite their daughter into my chambers for questioning. I wonder if I will ever be able to set them to paper.

Later, after the Mass, I retire to my private chambers to meet Cardinal Camillo Maretti, my great friend. I wish to show him plans Gian has drawn up for me of the new piazza he will create in front of this basilica.

When Camillo arrives, his manner is subdued and he appears to be in pain. His skin is graying and his face looks gaunt.

"Camillo, what ails you?" I say, rolling back the parchment, thoughts of the colonnade and my family's emblem etched in stone vanishing.

"It is nothing, Holy Father. Please forgive me, just some stomach pains, some gripes," he winces.

"You are suffering, my friend. Let me help you. I'll call for assistance. Bring wine. Bring lemon water," I say, and one of my many servants slips out of the room.

"You are too kind," Camillo says and he winces as I take his arm.

"Help will come. All will be well," I reply, and feel my stomach twist as I realize I do not believe my own words.

There is a knock at the door and two nuns appear, one with a flagon of water, another who walks over to Camillo, who is breathing heavily now.

"Take him to his chambers," I command. "Send for my physician at once."

I watch as he shuffles out, a hand gripping his stomach. I find I am shaking.

The next day, my physician appears just as I am making ready to take Mass. My friend has rallied and will walk out to take the air. "This is pleasing news," I say as clergymen arrive, as my entourage forms. Moving to the basilica is a blur. I see the tops of people's heads as they bow. The movement of the incense holders. The sunlight that dazzles, then the darkness of the nave. As I hold my arms aloft, I pray for Camillo. A gnawing sensation grows inside me.

# 36

*Giulia*

The Duke of Ceri lies still.

The face of his corpse is flushed a rosy pink. Covering his skin, a dewy sheen. A countenance made ruddy by riding and hunting. Though nearing fifty winters, he looks vital, as if merely sleeping, looking for all the world like he will get up, mount a horse and rejoin the hunt. He lies in an open coffin underneath the gilded heavens of Santa Maria sopra Minerva, while all of Rome files past to pay their respects.

"My God . . ."

I cross myself.

"What is it, Giulia?" Giovanna says.

"We must leave," I say.

"But I want to see this duke." My friend pushes forward. There is a crowd. Faces turn. Someone shoves an elbow out.

"Giovanna, please, we must go," I hiss.

She turns to me and stops. She looks back at the casket, the bejeweled corpse lying within, the flickering altar candles on their ornate stands. Her expression changes. She grabs my elbow, tries to drag me aside but there is no room.

"What have you done?" she whispers.

I stare back but cannot say the words.

"Giulia! What's wrong? What have you done?"

"Only what was right . . ." I stumble over the sounds. None of the words make sense.

"My God," is all she says, before glancing back to this man of power and importance. A man who lies dead at my hand.

"Many have said your water blesses the dying with the appearance of beauty, of youth and vitality. I haven't believed them, until now." Giovanna is shaking her head. "How could you? And behind our backs?"

There is nothing I can say.

My brow feels hot. My heart pounds. I would pace but there is no room.

What have I done?

"I'm sorry." I want to say more but there is new movement. A woman draped in black lace walks through the crowds, parting them like Moses commanding the sea. Beside her is a man she is leaning on.

*The widow!* a voice says.

*Look how she weeps. She's like a player on the stage!*

*Pantalone in skirts,* says another.

Anna Maria Aldobrandini lifts her veil and holds a handkerchief to her eyes.

I shrink back. Giovanna is staring at me as if she does not know me, her face a picture of horror.

Oh, the performance is convincing indeed. Even from here, I can see *la duchessa* is a consummate actress. The long note of her wail echoes up into the vaulted ceiling. She staggers, almost falling into the arms of the man who walks with her. He is wearing a doublet of deepest black, with seed pearls sewn into thick velvet sleeves. His fingers are covered in rings as he steadies Anna Maria, takes her arm, leads her forward, his head held high.

"Who's that? Giulia, who is she to you?"

I stare back at my friend mutely, unable to speak.

We are murderers and this is our proof. More than this, we have—*I have*—meddled in affairs of state. Giovanna looks at me and her face is pale. It mirrors mine; the shock, the recognition,

the truth of our trade. A dynasty is changed. A future reimag-
ined. The balance of power and state—altered. All because of a
small vial of colorless, odorless liquid. I brewed it alone. I have
dispensed many more in secret since passing hers to the padre.
How many more widows have I created?

The duchess is a model of grief: the dainty tears, the sor-
rowful gestures. I cannot stomach the sight any longer. The
pageantry, the boldness of his death, the absolute theater of her
suffering. It is all so obvious, so exposed.

"We go. Now," I say, urging Giovanna.

As I turn to leave, there is a woman barring my way. She is
older than me by ten years or so, with a face I dimly recall, but
cannot say why. She smiles as I try to pass but does not move.

"Can I help you, mistress?" I say.

"Perhaps you can."

She looks me up and down. I have seen many women eye me
this way, as if I would seize their skinny, cunt-whipped husbands
from under their noses. I eye her back, though I can feel the
room beginning to swim in front of me.

"There are some here who'd say you're *la Signora della Morte*,
the one who sells a certain liquid . . ." Her dialect is unfamiliar.
She looks over at the body, then back to me.

"Then they're wrong," I manage to say.

I try to move forward, before the buzzing sound starts,
though I can feel the vibration of it humming inside me. The
woman places a hand on my arm as I pass.

"Are they, pretty one? Are they wrong? I don't think so, do
you?" There is an odor about her person I do not like. It is the
acid reek of the chamber pot. I push away her hand more forcefully than I intend.

"I know no one of that name."

My voice is sharp now. If she will not move away, I will expand into the space between us. I will roar and knock her down like the giants of old that roamed the hills of Palermo.

"Take your gossip back to the privy where it came from," Giovanna spits at her, grabbing my hand.

Hers feels warm in my icy grip. She pulls me out of the basilica. We neither of us look back, but I know the woman stares after us. I feel the heat of her gaze, the sly curiosity. Once outside, we do not stop walking. We head away from our quarter, away from the alleys and narrow ways that lead to my shop or our lodgings, and we circle the city. We do not stop until we reach the stone arches of the Colosseum that reach endlessly into the sky.

"She hasn't followed us," Giovanna gasps.

"No," I say. "Not this time."

# 37

Darkness has fallen.

Giovanna and I make our way back, dodging people and horses and carts and carriages. Everywhere, there are people. A mother soothing her crying infant. Two men arguing in the street. Women talking across an alleyway as they hang washing from their windows. You might think the pestilence would have carried them all off to their graves.

Every five paces, Giovanna stops to check, but something has happened to me. The horror I felt seeing the dead man, and the weeping widow, has evaporated. The duke lies dead. A dynasty changed, a woman freed. I see the power of Mamma's poison, the scope of it. Fear has melted away, changed to wonder and something akin to pride. It was me who altered the path of this noble house. Me. A nobody.

In my mind's eye, I see Francesco's face. It is startling white, glassy eyes staring at nothing. Forever open and unseeing. Though I never saw my stepfather's corpse, I imagine him dressed in his black velvets, laid out in that coffin, and I feel a burst of joy. I feel no remorse. Instead, I feel giddy, powerful, free.

It is clear to me that Giovanna does not.

Her face is pale, though not as white as my image of Francesco. She keeps looking around. She is nervous and unsure, while I am exhilarated. She skulks in the shadows while I feel like skipping. See what I have done! See the power of my poison! I could sing up to the rafters, except I do not. I move through the city with Giovanna, scuttling like mice until we reach the piazza outside my shop. There are children kicking dust and fighting on the cobbles. There are always children here. One—a young boy—looks up. The light is dim, the candle flames behind shuttered windows emitting a mean glow. I cannot see his face.

"You did what?" Girolama stamps her foot in rage.

Graziosa whistles. She grins, showing her blackened teeth. She shakes her head and she hoots with something akin to delight as I deliver the news.

"My God, what were you thinking? She's a duchess. He's a duke!" Girolama pants, walking up and down, a swirl of fury.

"He *was* a duke," my friend Giovanna says softly.

My daughter paces the room. Back and forward. Back and forward. Her skirts swish. Her jewels glint as she moves. Her expression is one of absolute horror. Finally, she turns to me.

"You forbade us from giving away the *acqua*. You ordered us all to stop! You sent me back home, away from my friends, away from my betrothed!"

"You killed the Duke of Ceri," Graziosa whistles again.

"I sold my poison to Anna Maria," I begin to say.

"Oh, Anna Maria is she now? Will she come for supper as well?" Girolama flares.

"Please, be calm," Giovanna says, holding her hands out, a supplicant to my daughter's temper.

Girolama ignores our friend. "Why did you do it? Was it the money? Did she pay handsomely for your betrayal? Were you enthralled, just as you accuse me of being? Come on, Mamma, tell us."

"There's nothing to tell. The duchess came to me. The padre wanted me to help her. I wanted to tell you all, but I thought it safer this way."

"Safer?" Girolama is beside herself. She spits the word at me. I step back.

"I'm sorry. I had to help her, it's . . . it's . . ."

"What, Mamma?" Her voice is incredulous.

"It's who I am. I help women to kill men—and, my love, so do you." The words fill the space between us. They are jagged, pointing words.

"That isn't what I do!" Girolama retorts. "My work goes far beyond your inheritance potion! You're the Widow-Maker, but I'm *La Strologa*. I can read the heavens and cast a fortune. You can do little but take away life." .

"Then, tell us, *La Strologa*, what comes next? Are we safe? Will they guess it was I who gave the widow my *acqua*?"

Girolama stops. She glares at me.

I have often wondered if Girolama will teach her daughters the recipe, handing it down from mother to daughter through the ages. I see in this instant she will not. She is blinded, dazzled, by those people in high places she calls her friends. My poison is a shadowy, subtle thing. It infuses, silent and hidden. It steals life. It holds no thrall for Girolama, who flouts her charms and her skills. Perhaps it is best this way, though the knowledge makes me strangely sad. As for her talent understanding the planets? I have long guessed it is entertainment rather than knowledge.

They all watch me now: Giovanna, Girolama, and Graziosa. My coven, my sisterhood, my beloveds. I feel the invisible thread that binds us together thicken and tighten. I would trust them all with my life—as they do me. Yet, I have lied to them. I have betrayed them by dispensing my *acqua* in secret.

I walk toward my fearsome daughter and pull her into my arms. She folds into me, reluctantly at first. I feel the rigidity of her soften, and like a small child, she lays her head against my shoulder. The warmth of her black hair, the slowing of her breathing, reminds me of long-ago days when she fell asleep against me: the slow, steady beat of my heart calling her into her dreams. Giovanna comes up behind me and I feel her arms encircle us both. Graziosa shuffles uncertainly, somewhere in the room. Closing my eyes, I imagine a rope that draws us together, its fibers braided and twisted into strands. The anger between us unspools and, for a brief moment, there is harmony.

I send the women back to their quarters, feeling we are safer apart until the fuss dies down. That evening, I make a new batch of *acqua* alone.

I speak to my mother as I wrap the linen around my face, feeling as if I am wearing a shroud. *Mamma, why did you teach me this? Why did you pass on this dangerous inheritance? Was it not enough for us to take terrible risks for the wives and daughters of Palermo? Why give me the power to choose between life and death?*

I ask the same questions as the night hours deepen but they fade away as I work. This is where I belong, in the alchemist's chamber with metals, herbs, plants, and remedies, waiting to be dispensed, for maladies to be diagnosed and treated. For injustice to be seen and avenged.

I build up the fire. I pour water into the earthenware vessel and wait for it to steam. I add the first ingredient, the lead shot, and the alchemy begins. When the arsenic dissolves and the belladonna drops are administered, the long high note of the liquid sounds. It speaks to my heart, the one that grieves still. The room is warm. I wipe my brow. There is light from two candles placed at either end of the table. The pot, now stoppered with dough, is cooling, its contents settling. I could end this right now. I could throw away this solution, give the arsenic back to the padre's apothecary brother, discard the antimony, but I know I will not. This point of clarity is sudden, like a shaft of sunlight reaching through a break in cloud cover. It is not really the women that I do this for, perhaps it never has been. Oh, I have convinced myself—and all the others—but as I stand here, alone with my remedy, the justifications fall away. I do this because the poison is part of me. It is as close as I will ever get to my mother, but it is more than a sum of missing parts. It is like a limb or a thought or a sensation. It is as much an extension of my ability to breathe as it is anything else. It is my anger made physical, my hatred made liquid. Its flame never dwindles. If I ever forget, all I have to do is close my eyes and the images come to me: my mother kneeling, large red hands around her slender neck, my stepfather staring at me while my mother stands beside him, Francesco loosening his doublet. I understand that I will not rest until every deserving man tastes my elixir, no matter the cost, no matter the danger.

Over the coming months I supply more and more of my *acqua*. It is as if time is running out, and I must act—and keep acting—and keep the flame of my anger burning.

# 38

*Alessandro*

It is apparent something is stirring. There is a flurry of movement. People talk all at once, their manner urgent. "What is it?" I say to the flock of cardinals that hovers close by. "And where's Camillo?"

I am poring over a text that veers dangerously close to heresy, making small, neat marks in the margins as I read.

It takes me a moment to register that no one answers.

"What, pray, is disturbing the peace?" I look up and see the faces of clergymen staring back at me. His eminence, Cardinal Bandinelli, a man created by me, steps forward, bows his head, speaks softly.

"Your Holiness, it gives me no pleasure to say this. Camillo Maretti . . . the cardinal . . ."

"The cardinal?" I look up, reluctant to turn away from the scratches made by my quill.

"Cardinal Maretti is dead. He passed away in the early hours. The physician was called, but nothing could save him."

I stare back at Bandinelli uncomprehendingly.

"He's dead?" I say. "Nothing could save him?" I echo.

"Yes, Your Holiness, and it grieves me greatly to tell you . . ."

There is muttering behind him. My mother's spectral hand lies now on my shoulder, her touch cold from the catacombs. *Camillo is dead*, I think, and the words make no sense at all.

But there is more. I can feel it building in the air around my desk. The plague is vanquished. I held a ceremony to thank God for delivering us, yet still men die in droves.

"Say it," I command, blinking. "Speak."

Bandinelli, his mustache and small beard trimmed expertly, the frown lines cutting deep into his forehead, looks back at the cardinals before attempting to speak again. He clears his throat. I look from him to them as if the words he is reluctant to say will reveal themselves.

"Your Holiness, there's talk of poison."

I stand up now. Papers scatter. Vellum falls to the floor. The room appears new, as if I have never set eyes on the ornamental vases, the gilded cross, the red velvet drapes, the chairs of shining walnut. It is as if I have never seen this space before. There are voices now. Cardinals and emissaries murmur around me but the words are indistinct. In my mind, I imagine Camillo's body as if I am standing in his bedchamber: the waxy sheen of his skin stretched over bone and muscle, his mouth slightly parted, the terrible stillness.

"Your Holiness?"

"Send for Bracchi" is all I am able to say.

The governor walks toward me, his face grim. He kneels and I extend my hand, though it trembles. His mouth grazes the ring. He did not come straightaway. Hours have passed, but they seem to have disappeared in no time at all.

"Please accept my condolences. I know Cardinal Maretti was a great friend of yours," Bracchi says, eyes lowered.

Still, the words do not seem to penetrate. Camillo. *Where are you? Where have you gone?* Perhaps of all men on earth, I should know this.

It occurs to me that the governor spoke before me, the pope, but I find I can disregard it. I do not care. This feeling is familiar and unwanted. It wells up and constricts my throat, my mind, my heart.

Bracchi nods as if he understands all.

"It's my duty to inform you that an investigation has begun into the manner of Cardinal Maretti's death. I was with the surgeon while the . . . the autopsy was performed this very day."

Bracchi shifts as if uneasy. I stare out of the window as sunlight leaches from the sky.

My governor of Rome coughs. He continues. "The body looked perfectly preserved. There were no tumors, nothing to suggest a natural cause."

In the silence that follows, something grows, some understanding of something as yet unsaid.

"And an unnatural cause?" Now I find I can say the words, the white heat of anger rushes through me. It catches me by surprise, and I am glad I am seated—the velvet padding against my back, the golden throne supporting my arms, the seat stopping me from fainting.

Bracchi looks up as if he guesses, though I know I appear perfectly composed, my hands folded in my lap, sitting in my papal finery, the murmur of clergymen behind us.

"There was no corruption to the organs, no blackening of membranes, but there was something . . ."

"Something?" I say, leaning forward.

"The cardinal looked as if he was in the finest of health, a most extraordinary and strange sight."

"How can this be?" I say.

It is as if I have awoken from an enchantment. My heart beats wildly. Buffeted by tides of grief, I can barely speak. I have lost my greatest friend. My only friend.

"Witchcraft," Bracchi says.

# 39

*Giulia*

Something has changed.

I can feel it on the air, in the snap of a bird's wing, in the growling of a neighbor's dog. I can hear it in the clang of bells for prayer. I can smell it in the breezes that come off the harbor from faraway lands. Somehow, I have been safe, kept hidden, but now that protection has drained away. How do I know this?

I saw it in the sign of the *corna* made by the oil seller in Campo de' Fiori when I approached her stall. I saw it in the whispers and sharp glances of mothers and their daughters at Mass. I saw it in my daughter's face when a thick vellum note arrived to say her presence was not required at her patron's villa. Something has changed.

Despite this, women come every day. Word of my poison took flight during the pestilence and now is unstoppable. As the danger grows, I find I am zealous rather than afraid. I grow more determined to right the wrongs mankind deals out to women each day, rather than less. There is comfort in killing. There is truth among the lies. Whatever happens, despite everything, I will continue.

*August 1658 (by Giulia's hand)*

13 vials dispensed at the washing stream
*(Giulia, Giovanna)*                    *No payment*

*September 1658*

*Isabetta, the boatman's wife,*
*one vial of acqua (Graziosa)*          *No payment*

16 vials dispensed at Mass
*(Giulia)*                              *No payment*

*November 1658*

*Isabetta (the boatman's widow, on behalf of*
*her sister), one vial of acqua (Graziosa)*
                                        *No payment*

*Six vials dispensed in the brothels of*
*Old Rome (Maria, Girolama)*            *No payment*

# 40

There is a great banging on the shop door.

We freeze.

"They've come for us," my daughter says.

I hush her, gesture for her to carry on eating, to appear normal, as I stand up from the table, legs shaking.

"Wait there. Stay in the back," I say, smoothing my hair back from my face. My legs walk. My arms reach out for the curtain, parting it, then drawing it together again. My body moves toward the door, then I hear my voice, though it seems to come from another source.

"What's this commotion?" I ask, as if I am a normal shop trader.

"Open up! It's Graziosa!"

Relief overwhelms me.

"Quiet down! Be patient," I snap as I open the door.

Before I can speak again, the old woman who runs our errands falls into the shop. She is wailing.

"All of Rome is talking of the butcher's wife and her sisters!" Graziosa is gabbling. She wrings her hands, sobbing and looking about the room blindly.

"All of Rome is saying what?" Girolama, who has appeared from the back room, guides her through to my chair by the hearth.

"You must calm down. You must tell us everything," I say, trying to hide my alarm. "What has the butcher's wife done now?"

At this moment, Giovanna walks in. She stops and stares at us.

"What's happening here?" she asks. Even the sight of her reassures me. She has been in my life longer than even my mother was.

Graziosa gulps down air, then speaks.

"There are new rumors in every square, every marketplace, every tavern because of what that harridan did! I don't know why it's happening now, so long after you dealt with her, Giulia. Perhaps she has a loose tongue? Perhaps she has boasted to her friends and neighbors? I don't know, but people are saying openly that there's a circle of poisoners at work in this city, and that the butcher's wife used our potion. Many who hear the rumors know this to be true. Perhaps now they don't deny it! There were rumors when the Duke of Ceri died, of course—there have always been rumors—but to speak openly, plainly, to look at me as if I am a threat to *them*. This is new, Giulia. This is all new. If our circle is common knowledge, then it can only mean one thing—"

"We are exposed," I finish.

"Deny it to whom?" Girolama cuts in before I can say more. Since receiving the missive from her patron, she has been subdued, but every day, I see small signs her spirit is returning: when she curses the baker for burning our bread, when she snorts with laughter at a shared memory. "None of our customers would dare speak. If they do so, they implicate themselves. It has always been our salvation."

Giovanna and I exchange a long look. Perhaps it was so. But now?

That must be why Girolama's party invitations have vanished, melted away like butter left too long on the sill. That must be why the oil seller made the *corna* to my face.

"They'll hold their tongues, they have to," I add, pretending to a calm I do not feel. There is a quiet agitation to my fear. I am a mouse caught in a falcon's glare. If the women we serve fear *us*, then we are truly in danger.

"You worry too much!" Girolama has one eyebrow raised. "There's nothing to fear. The old woman talks of rumors, nothing more. So what if the butcher's wife and her sisters have boasted!

Who can prove it was poison? Who can prove it was anything but a summer fever? My friends will protect us if there's any more to this than marketplace gossip. Paolo will come for me. As soon as he hears there may be danger, he'll take us all away, and all will be well."

I can feel my temper rising, along with my astonishment, but it is Giovanna who speaks.

"You're wrong, Girolama. If there are rumors, then there are *Inquisitori* listening to them. Any one of those rumors could lead them here, to us," she says. "Don't think for a minute any of your fine friends will rescue us from anything. We mean less to them than pigs grazing on slops, for at least the pigs can be butchered for bacon!"

"Peace, Giovanna," I plead. Though why else would they send the gilded, scented note dismissing my daughter's services?

For a moment we are all silent. Dread is like mist moving across the sea. It fills each corner of the chamber.

"There are other rumors."

We all turn to look at our wizened crone.

For once, she does not seem pleased at the attention.

"The cardinal was poisoned. Everyone is saying so." Graziosa looks around at us, from face to face, her icons shifting as her scrawny neck moves.

"Cardinal Maretti was Celeste de Luna's estranged lover," she adds.

"We know this," I say.

"But do you know that the love philters didn't work? They were discovered by the cardinal, who brought all hell down upon Celeste, saying she was trying to poison him. Or so the whores in the brothel opposite say. I talk to them. They know everything that happens in this city. Celeste was in fear of her life—and so she waited until the fuss had died down and then she poisoned him, with your *acqua*, Giulia. The marks of it are unmistakable. The corpse never shows any sign of decay. If anything, it looks healthier, with rosy cheeks and a sheen on the skin. The whores say the cardinal's servants have told them he looked better in death than in life . . ." Graziosa says.

"But who gave her my poison?" I ask the old woman, exasperated. "For I did not." I can feel panic growing like mold on week-old rye bread.

"I don't know, but my guess is our Maria gave it to her. She works in the same brothel when the mood takes her. She must've heard of Celeste's troubles. The cardinal had stomach cramps for weeks, and a terrible burning pain. Celeste must've doctored his wine little by little, with Maria's help."

I begin to pace the shop, up and down.

"We must be careful. We must act with ever more stealth. We must make sure we're always taking different paths through the city. We must be ever more alert, must stay in the shadows and move across the city under cover of night. We can't risk being recognized."

"Whatever Maria did, we're already hunted," Giovanna says.

"Mamma! Giovanna! You're both wrong! There's no proof it was us—or the *acqua*," Girolama says.

I place my hand on my bodice, trying to breathe while my mind races. How could Maria have stolen the *acqua* from under my nose? It is always locked away, but I keep the key nearby. I cast my eyes over to the jar inside which floats the aborted fetus, behind which sits the key. It would not have been difficult to find it and open the cabinet.

Suddenly, there is another noise at the shop entrance. Footsteps sound, then the curtain moves to reveal Maria, as if the Devil Himself had sent for her. Her smile falters as she sees us staring back at her.

Girolama is the first to speak. "Did you give *acqua* to Celeste de Luna?" Her voice is harsh.

Maria looks confused, then I see it.

"Stop, daughter," I say and walk over to her.

There is a bruise, livid and yellowing, on Maria's right cheek. There is a cut on her arm and dried blood in her hair.

"Your husband, he's back, isn't he?" I say softly, to which she nods, tears streaming down her face.

My daughter opens her mouth to speak.

"Enough questions. What's done is done. Get me the salves, daughter. Giovanna, make Maria a soothing draft. You'll stay here tonight, *amore mio*," I croon to our friend.

She takes my hand as if a child being led to the warmth of my hearth. Not for the first time, I wonder why Maria does not use our remedy to end her troubles, though I know she has a loving heart toward this man—a man who deserves much less and gives her nothing except pain.

"It's my fault," I say. "I should've kept a closer eye on my remedy. Don't blame Maria, she adores Celeste and would do anything asked of her."

"But what do we do?" Giovanna says as she strokes Maria's hair and hands her a small goblet of wine warmed over the fire, sweetened with spices and honey. "Surely, it's time to stop giving out your poison? There are too many things going wrong, too many rumors. If the women of this city turn on us, we're in grave danger. Surely, now is the time to stop for good?"

Girolama dabs ointment on Maria's cuts. Graziosa looks away. I say nothing.

"Giulia, you're reckless. With every vial you supply, there's one more chance of being captured." Giovanna looks over at me.

"My mother didn't stop! She never abandoned those who needed her. In her memory, I must do the same." Even as I say this, I forgive myself the lie.

"But she died for them, Giulia," Giovanna says, "and each time you dispense the poison, you bring us all closer to a death sentence."

The air is tense. Giovanna stands facing me.

"She did," I say. "I don't deny it."

"Then, why, Giulia? Why go on taking these risks?"

For a brief moment, I ask myself the same question. Why can't I stop? As much as my anger drives me, my guilt does too. My mother died and I was unable to save her. I let them take her from me, and I watched mute as she was killed by the man I brought to our life with his unnatural desires. It is my fault. It is all my fault, and so I must atone—and I do not know how else to do this except by bringing justice to abused women and death to their men.

"Because I can't stop. Because I owe my mother this," I say, eventually. I feel the wet itch of tears as they course down my face. "I'm scared, Giovanna, I admit it. I'm frightened but I won't stop. Don't ask this of me."

I move closer to my friend, take her work-roughened hands, her fingers as stained with tinctures as my own. From her skin comes the astringent scent of rosemary and thyme. She lets go of my grip. Dabs away my tears with a gesture of infinite tenderness. I feel my strength returning, my soul hardening.

"If my life ever meant something, then it can only be this work I do. There's no freedom nor justice for women except by my hand. We've seen how powerful the *acqua* is. We saw the duke. It killed a cardinal—"

"You can't be pleased to deal in death, Giulia! This is necessity, or justice, or whatever you want to call it. It shouldn't be about power!" Giovanna drops my hands. Steps back from me. There is a gap between us I have never felt before.

For a moment, there is silence.

My voice, when I speak, is harsher than I intend.

"I'll continue to do my mother's work and supply freedom and vengeance to the women of our city. I'll give them the poison they require to end their marriages, marry their lovers, or bring pain and misery to those who've ill-treated them. I won't falter now. I won't tremble. It's my birthright—and yours too. It is our duty to women beyond this small circle. Who among us would turn any woman away? Who among us wouldn't do the same in their position?"

I look around fiercely.

"We carry on."

*Date unknown (by Giulia's hand)*

*Celeste de Luna, acqua, quantity unknown*

*(Maria?)*                                        *Payment unknown*

# 41

*Alessandro*

It is late.

For a moment, I am disorientated. Looking upward, I can feel the wide space, the extent of the air above me. Moonlight streams pale shafts of light through the windows of the dome. A hazy light, making soft the darkness. I am reminded of the volcanic stone used to build this marvel of the Catholic faith: the earth subjugated to Christ. Elsewhere there is the black of night, pierced by candlelight. I know above me there are four medallions—Matthew with the ox, Mark with the lion, Luke with the angel, and John with the eagle—though I cannot see them. Above them still, the night sky is depicted in azure blue with gold stars, but they hover and shimmer far out of reach. My mind is reeling and spinning. Tonight, I am a stranger to myself.

Footsteps on the great marble floor. They are mine. I move again, and the sound echoes, fanning out and disappearing. Perhaps there is no one here but me, but then again, I recall a worried look, another: frowning, someone half-running behind me, calling to me to take some rest. But I cannot rest. My beloved friend is dead. I cannot stop because when I do, it is the earth under my feet that seems to spin, and I am scared I will fall and keep falling into the darkness below.

"Your Holiness, are you ill?" a voice says.

I look over. Out of the blackness steps a servant. Another beside him.

When I do not answer, they exchange a glance, a signal. One turns and runs, his boots tapping on the stone.

"Your Holiness?"

It is not apparent to me why they are here. I gesticulate, hoping he will also go away but he does not move. My knees are suddenly cold. I am kneeling but I do not remember dropping to the ground in the holiest place in all Christendom. My face is wet. When I bring my hands to my eyes, I discover I am weeping.

*Mother.*

I was expecting to call upon Camillo, wherever he is in God's Kingdom.

*Mamma.*

But the image that comes to mind is not my dearest friend, the cardinal, nor is it my mother. Instead, I see she who torments me, that sets this wretched fire alight inside me. Her. That woman in the square. She turns but her features are covered by her hood. I search and search for her. In every Mass I take, in every service I give, I look for her. She is never there.

Time must be passing, because I am now lying on the floor of the basilica. This time, I do not hear the sound of a person approaching.

"Your Holiness? It's Governor Bracchi. You're unwell, Holy Father. Let me take you to your rooms."

A hand reaches down. At first, I do not take it. I am praying now. I am beseeching the Lord God to hear me, to take away this confusion of pain and desire.

"Your Holiness. You must be moved. You can't stay here."

"I can't stay here," I echo, and I look up into Bracchi's intelligent face, his keen eyes that seem to see under my skin.

Then, everything falls back into place. I am suddenly horrified. What am I doing here?

"Help me," I say, reaching up to him.

In my chamber, I am now pacing as Bracchi watches me. He hands me a Venetian glass goblet, but I look at the red liquid within and I balk at putting it to my lips.

"We will never speak of this."

Bracchi bows in response. He says nothing.

I put the glass down, careful not to let its contents touch my skin. I shudder and wonder: *Would Camillo be alive today had he shown the same caution?*

"This is a grave matter, a terrible crime. The cardinal's death is inconceivable. If you are right—if this is witchcraft at work—then the situation is worse than I thought, coming as it has to the heart of our church, and our state. Who will be next, Bracchi? Will it be you? Will it be me?"

Bracchi still says nothing. I feel anger rising now. My governor has failed me. He has failed Camillo.

"We must take action—swift, decisive action. The death toll rises every day. We cannot let this go unpunished." My head throbs and my cheeks itch with the salt from the tears I have wiped away.

"Holy Father, what would you have me do?"

I pace again but this time my ragged breathing has calmed, my head has cleared. Whatever temporary madness of grief overcame me, it has turned to cold fury. Like a Medusa, I stare back at him, willing this upstart inquisitor to turn to stone. But he is not the disease. The remedy I seek must be swift and it must be harsh.

"Cover the city with public notices. It is now my command to the people of Rome. I order them to step forward. Anyone caught harboring heretics or witches will be punished. Our time working in the shadows has gone. Bring this hunt into the light,

Bracchi. Show the populace they cannot hide. This way, we will unearth them—and any who defy me will suffer the consequences . . . and Bracchi?"

"Yes, Your Holiness?"

"When you know who these witches are, make a trap. Catch them with this Satanic potion. Catch them and let Camillo rest in peace."

I am panting as I finish. I stand now, in my majesty, my troubled state forgotten, my grief subdued. I am *Il Papa*. I am the closest to God on this earth. I will have order in my territories, the chief of which is Rome. This time, we use my methods of extraction.

# 42

*Giulia*

The winter sunshine is warm on my neck as I walk toward Trastevere. A carriage jolts into the piazza carried by four black horses, nostrils snorting, heads nodding. I pay it no heed and continue on my way. Each day, I take a different route, attend the service in a different church. I know they are seeking me, like a deer knows it is hunted in the forest. Prowling behind me, I sense the watchers, their hooded gaze, their hurried steps, yet I never see anyone follow me. They are skilled, covert, hidden, but I know they are there. My heart reaches out into the spaces around me, and I know they are there.

I am walking through the winding cobbled streets as shutters are flung open, as birds flutter onto the roofs, as people hang washing and gossip, gesticulate or fight. I am on my way to the basilica of Santa Maria. The bells call the devout for prayer. A flock of gulls rises into the blue of the sky.

It is then I see the women, dressed like crows.

Widows appear from doorways, from carriages, around street corners. A sea of black veils and mourning dress. Perhaps the city's widows blended into the everyday tragedies of *la peste*, but now . . . Now it is different. Now, our work is plain for all to see. It is as if I am seeing them for the first time, and I feel my heart begin to pound.

That is not all.

It is once I have crossed the river, which sparkles as it washes under the bridge, that I see them.

It is my first sight of the notices.

They have been slapped on the stone walls, one after another. In front of me, one corner peeling already, is the proclamation.

I stop. Blink. I wonder how I have not noticed them before. Perhaps they were put up this morning before dawn. Perhaps they have been there for days or even weeks. I have not ventured far from my shop.

I look down each alley and they line the walls there too so that nobody—not even I—can pass them by. Now comes the sound, at last. I have been expecting it. It pierces my head, building from a low vibration to a high-pitched noise. I grasp at my ears, cover them, cry out. People look at me strangely. A toothless gray-haired woman laughs nearby, staring directly at me as if she knows my thoughts. A man glares, swearing as he pushes past when I stall like an ox at the plough.

## NOTIFICAZIONE

# À PUBLICA UTILITÀ

For the health and liberation from poison of the people of Rome.

A most grotesque butchery has been afflicted upon the men of this great city. A circle of female poisoners, hags and witches led by la Siciliana, has subjected their victims to a poison of such evil that hundreds may have been slain.

Without taste or odor, the diabolical potion is brewed and dispensed, and renders the afflicted with such agonies that death is a welcome relief. The discovery of the ingestion of this witch's brew comes only with violent stomach cramps and vomiting. The slow-acting venom may be administered by Delilah to Samson, in broth, wine, or ale.

Beware good citizens, and know you are hereby commanded to report any or all witches and heretics, and all those you know to be guilty of the injury of men and the State, to the authorities!

The city of Rome renders to the world an example of extreme piety and devotion to our Lord God. These witches will be brought to holy justice!

My feet begin to sink again, each step as I turn away feels more sodden, more treacherous than the last. I am sinking into the silt of the Tiber, as the green-gray water froths, as the riverbed closes over my face, suffocating me. I breathe and find I can almost feel the grit of sand and detritus washed in from the mountains.

I stagger back, and I run this time. I run and run until I have crossed back over Ponte Sisto. The drowning feeling washes back, away from me. The sound withdraws like pebbles on the Tiber's banks, into the twisting water, going back into its depths as they move away out to the sea.

*La Siciliana.*

The Sicilian woman.

They know of me. How long before they know my name?

# PART THREE

*"Ubi multae feminae, multae veneficae."*
(Where there are many women, there are many witches.)
—*MALLEUS MALEFICARUM*, KRAMER, 1484

# 43

*Giulia*

My first breath was a gasp, a sucking-in of life itself, or so Mamma told me when she was sure no one was listening.

This thought comes to me as I run from the notices, away from the shock at seeing the proclamation. I slid out from between her thighs slick with blood and sweat—crumpled, determined. I did not cry. I did not shudder or wail. There was no need for the midwife's deft handiwork. I pushed myself out, sticky and smeared with the birthing, ready to take my place in the world.

That inhalation claimed my space, my inheritance, though I was but the bastard of a notorious courtesan—a girl who could never take her place in society. My mother squatted on the birthing stool, held by the women she worked alongside; the whores who fought like alley cats for the attentions of the men upon whose livelihoods they depended. Outcasts who now mopped her brow with water of lavender, its oily tang settling over the animal reek of the chamber, its fires blazing, its heat stifling. They held her hands. They prayed. Rivals they might have been, but this was their private arena. Away from the false smiles, the sideward glances, the lascivious theater of their trade, a bond was formed between them. As Mamma moaned through the surging pains, as her legs trembled and her hips thrust downward, those women cooed and soothed, brought lemon water and shed tears as my head appeared. Mamma said she wept tears of joy when I was born, strong and lusty. If she had known what was to come, who I would become, would those tears have been for sorrow?

Unsure where to go, I veer through the streets, choosing the narrowest and meanest, as if they could still protect me. I stop, finally, panting. I have reached Piazza Farnese, and so I take a moment's rest, hoping to hide within the endless motion of people going here and there. The sands of time are running out for me. I know this, and perhaps this is why I dwell upon my birth. I want to clutch at time, to pull it back toward me like fibers of wool on my spindle.

The players arrive unannounced, their cart jolting across the cobbles. They spill out in a confusion of painted, wigged, costumed creatures. They are young and they look hungry, their faces hollowed out by the years of poor living during the contagion. Already their painted faces are smeared, their once-colorful costumes now faded and dusty from the road that brought them here.

Their play begins, as it always does, with salutations to the crowd. Scaramuccia speaks, his voice echoing around the square.

"For your delight and delectation, we present to you the players of the most famous and commendable troupe, *I Corvi*, the Ravens . . ."

At this, a small figure, a child dressed all in black with rags sewn down his sleeves to make wings, appears and proceeds to flap and caw and peck. The audience gasps, though it is a poor costume and, we discover, an indifferent play. I should leave. I am too exposed here among people, in the sunlight, but my body will not move. Will not obey my command to flee. I breathe in, then out. There are people around me, but I cannot comprehend them, their aliveness, their loudness. I barely notice as the play continues.

Then I notice him. He looks directly at me. There is a holler from the crowd. A child shrieks. A man spits. Another curses his friend, gesticulating. This man still does not look away. There is no attempt to hide his . . . what? Scrutiny? Interest? He has a face I cannot dislike—a strong face, a frank expression. His eyes gleam, though not unpleasantly. He is broad-shouldered and dark, wearing a plain cloak, but I see the shine of the stones on its clasp. He looks at me and I do not feel I can turn away again, yet I know that I should. His gaze unmasks me— both to him and to myself. Does he know me?

Arlecchino jumps and twirls, and I realize I must go. I must find the others and warn them, if they haven't already seen the notices. How can I have delayed so long? It was foolish to think I could outrun my panic. I stand up as Rugantino declares for the couple to half-hearted applause. Colombina somehow conjures the energy to clap and laugh. The players throw flowers they have picked on the roadside. The scene starts to melt. My head feels strange, woozy. I pray I do not faint in the square and have my purse cut from my skirts.

A crow passes overhead as if its motion has slowed, as if the world has paused, as if time has frozen for a heartbeat. Oily black wings flap. A large protruding beak opens. *Caw. Caw.* The bird of ill omen has come to me, and as it does so, I look up and catch the black gleam of its eye. Though the day is warm, I shiver.

Suddenly, as if the moment never happened, as if the crow and its warning had evaporated into the blue skies, color and life roar back into my ears, into my vision. The audience cheers and throws coins. The players wipe their faces. The press of bodies against me is overpowering. I look over at the man, but he has gone. I look up to the heavens, and the crow has gone. I must leave before it is too late—or perhaps we are long past that now.

Breathing is difficult but I start to push my way through. An old woman turns to admonish me, her open mouth revealing a single decaying tooth. A young woman with red plump cheeks carrying a child that bawls tuts as I shove past, apologizing as I go.

Then, recognition dawns. The crow's message is delivered already. Word comes to me in the form of Padre Don Antonio, who stands barring my way. His cassock is bleached white in the sunshine. His face is partly covered by his cloak.

You cannot go back. They have them all.

At first the words make no sense. *Caw. Caw.*

You cannot go back.

They have them all.

I am transported back to a time long ago when inquisitors took my mother. This time, it is my daughter, my circle of outcasts and wise women that have been taken. Not so wise. Not so cunning. The priest is telling me that they have all been captured and taken to Tor di Nona. My head spins, just as it did before when Valentina told me Mamma had gone. My throat tightens and I fear I may pass out, just as before. Those I love are taken from me, just as before.

My daughter; they have my daughter.

The priest has looked everywhere for me. He takes my arm and pulls me through the crowd. At the side of the square is a woman selling bread. Stupidly, I stop. I tell the priest I need some for our supper. He looks at me as if I am a half-wit. I insist we must have bread, but almost as if he planned it, the stall holder shouts something at me. This time, I have no trouble discerning the meaning.

"*Strega!* Be gone, *strega*! I won't serve you, witch!"

People look round to see the source of the commotion. I stare blindly at the woman who is refusing my coin. A sudden thud and I am tipped off balance, knocked sideways. It is only the speed of Padre Don Antonio's response, grabbing my arm again, that prevents me from falling. I look up, dazed. A young boy, his skin inflamed, his rags grimy, looks back at me. I recognize him. This is the urchin that I saw in the street when I approached the shop of the butcher's wife, my vial of *acqua* rattling in my basket. This is the urchin who has carried messages for me, who plays in the piazza outside my shop. His face is sharp, his gaze unapologetic. He shoved me, and I do not know why. He stares, and I cannot look away. He is my adversary and yet I do not know him.

I do not have time to ponder the meaning of this, of all of this. Behind me I hear the actors shaking their hats, making the few coins dropped into them clink.

"Giulia, we must leave this place. We're in danger—terrible danger. You must find sanctuary. The *Inquisitori* are hunting you."

I stare at the padre. These words feel foreign to me. I do not respond. I cannot.

"Listen, mistress. I'm told men are asking after you in the alehouses and markets. My brother tells me four sorceresses were captured this morning, two at their dwellings and two at the villa of a noblewoman who was used as bait to lure you into a trap. They set you up. They know what you do with your potion, and they convinced a rich woman to pose as a client. They were seized when they tried to give her your remedy." I think of the carriage drawing into the piazza, the four black horses, and wonder if the bait was carried inside. Where was the Sight? Where was my warning?

If I ever forgot that this man standing in front of me, this priest, was from aristocratic stock, then I remember now. There is much he knows, and I can only guess at those who have whispered in his ear. Perhaps his family knew to warn him. Perhaps he reads the signs and knows they may be on his tail too.

"I'll go into hiding," he says, as though guessing my thoughts. "My family name and connections make it necessary."

"But why did you come to warn me? You've put yourself at risk of discovery, Padre?" I ask, confused, my head reeling.

"There's no time to explain, except to say I've watched you, knowing what you do and why. There are many cruelties in this world, and we share an urgency to put them right, even to avenge them. But you must listen to me. They have all of your circle, all of them. Giulia, you must go now, there's no time to waste."

I look at the clergyman as if struck dumb. My mind is filled with questions. Who betrayed us? How did they know where to come, who to find? How did they discover my name? There is no time to think; instead I must act. Finally, his words make impact. It is the first time the priest has called me by my name, and, oddly, it is this that chills me most. I pull my arm away.

"Giulia, they know about you. They know about your work. Assume they know everything. They're saying you're a witch and a sorceress, and you cast bad spells. Your reputation has spread like fire through dry grass."

My reputation.

Witch.

Sorceress.

Perhaps I always knew that one day, the women of Rome would betray me. Of course, they would speak if commanded to by their father, husband, or inquisitor, or if threatened with arrest. They have looked away from me and my sisterhood in the street and marketplace. There are many who do not want to be reminded of their deeds, of the knowledge we possess.

Perhaps it was not always so, but then the pope unleashed his
*Inquisitori*. Even so, my heart is sore at this betrayal. The risks
we have taken to help so many, and for what?

"My reputation," I repeat.

"There's always someone who'll speak with a forked tongue,"
the padre says. "There's always someone who'd sell your name
for coin or to avoid the torture chamber. Surely you know this,
of all things? Please listen to me now." He grabs my hands, startling me. His hands are large. This time, I do not pull away. "I
don't know the details and there's little time to guess. Perhaps
one of your clients betrayed you. Or the death of our wealthy
benefactor's husband prompted further investigations. Perhaps
the rumors have spilled out from these streets and into the ears
of the cardinals, perhaps even the pope himself. It may be all
these—or none of them. There's no time to find answers. You
must go!" His voice is soft now. The bread seller eyes me still.

I look back at the priest and wonder again why he has come
looking for me. I do not know this man beyond our secret business, yet he may have saved my life today.

"But where should I go?"

"Go to the convent at Trinità dei Monti. Tell Mother Superior Innocenza I've sent you. She'll take you in. Our families are
connected through bonds of marriage. She will not forsake you.
But go, Giulia. Go now."

"Yes, go, *strega*!" the stall holder says. She spits for empha-
sis. I do not wait to hear more. Already, people are casting sideward glances at me. I cannot stay here and risk being lynched
by a mob made excitable by the dirt pageant. I turn and leave,
picking up my skirts to walk faster. As soon as I clear my way
out of the piazza I break into a run, and I do not stop. I pass
the fountain in Piazza della Trinità dei Monti, staggering up
the steep hill under a canopy of trees, my thighs burning. It is

one of the grandest churches in the city: rich, influential, built by Louis of France more than a century ago. I can barely speak by the time I stand in front of the two bell towers that loom in ornate splendor over me.

Breathless, my ears still ringing with the bread seller's curse, the same one thrown at my mother, I hammer on the wooden door.

# 44

## Alessandro

*Is it wrong to want you?*
The knotted rope flays my skin.
*Is it wrong to desire you?*
Blood runs down my back. I try to muffle my cries as I pull the *flagellum*, the scourge, out; gouging, lacerating, slicing.
*Mamma help me. It has been years since I saw her in the piazza, looking up at me, but my desire has only grown . . .*
Another lash, another stroke of the discipline, its seven cords unleashing more agony—the mortification of the flesh made real. My private penance for my sinful longing, the longing that never recedes, the longing for sun-drenched hair and eyes the color of water.

It is the dead of night.
The Papal Army soldiers stand outside, unmoving. They guard the palace, lit by torches that flicker and dance, though there is no breeze. The swallows are silent, nesting in the eaves. The bells are still in the hours between Compline and Vigil, the time when everything in God's world pauses, when even the trees and stars and oceans hush to praise Him.
I am alone in my private apartments, unable to sleep, wrestling with my unnatural desires. I beg God to free me of my spiritual pain by releasing it in the realm of the physical—with a bloodied whip and a scarred body. I am sinful, subjugated. I can find no peace as soon as the fires are lit and the day closes. It is

then that my yearnings consume me, and I have lately sought a way to tear them out of me.

The knotted rope ends thud as they land. I force my arm, which is shaking now, to swing another blow down onto my blood-streaked back. This time, the pain forces me to my knees. And again, and again. The cords whip through the air, each representing one of the seven cardinal sins: *lussuria*, lust; *gola*, gluttony; *avarizia*, greed; *accidia*, sloth; *ira*, wrath; *invidia*, envy; and *superbia*, pride. All of these have I felt. One among them dominates my waking nights. One of them, perhaps the most powerful of all the deadly sins, runs through my veins and fills my head, my heart, my loins. The sin I carry in my heart is like a burning flame. It ignites me. It chars me.

Oh God, on nights like these, I know you have turned away from me, your vicar on earth, your chosen one. How can it be that you have risen me so high but plague me with lust so deeply? Is this my punishment for reaching these heights? Is this the great test you have set me for this life? If this is a test, I am failing it, Lord. I am failing.

I collapse forward, the blessing of the cool marble floor meeting my face. I do not know how long I stay there. Each evening before retiring I ask for a bowl of water and a clean linen cloth to be brought to my rooms. I do not say why I need it. No servant has ever questioned, would ever presume to question me. Similarly, when it is removed the next day, a mess of blood and sweat contained within, no questions are asked, though I see their quick glances toward me, confusion then dawning understanding. Each morning, I awake in sheets that are stained pink, with a bloodied shift, and yet none asks why. Perhaps they choose not to see.

I rise up off the floor, exulted now, without sin, relieved of the burden of my hunger. I feel the scarring, exposed and weeping. I feel the monstrosity of my actions, and yet I know I will be here again, will experience this wretched penance again, if not tomorrow night, then soon.

Next, the discipline must be put away. Dabbing at the blood now congealed, now drying, I handle the cords with reverence, as a caress. They free me of my sin. They remind me of Christ's suffering. They bring me back to God, to righteousness, though the price of their power is almost more than I can bear. They remind me of the seven virtues; accompanying each sin as its opposite. For lust there is *castità*, chastity; for gluttony, *temperanza*, temperance; for greed there is *generosità*, generosity; for sloth there is *diligenza*, diligence; for envy there is *gratitudine*, gratitude; for pride there is *umiltà*, humility. Make me humble, Lord. Make me a man in your image. Make me forget, blessed Virgin.

There is enough space to lie the scourge inside my private drawer, the one containing my letters to Mamma, and her handkerchief, which I stole from her bedchamber the night she died. I open it slowly, wincing. Here it is hidden from any but my own eyes. It must remain my secret. We are not Spanish. We do not revel in displays of bloodthirsty penance. In Rome, we conduct ourselves with quiet reverence, with dignity. So, it must be my secret. As I push the drawer back, concealing my shame, I catch sight of myself in a carved mirror. My eyes are bruised-looking, my face pale and gaunt. I tease my mustache, the only real vanity of mine, and see my hand is covered in flecks of blood. I see a man vanquished. A subject of God subdued, though my gaze stares back at me steadily. I see a man who knows his strengths and his weaknesses, and who carries the weight of the Catholic world on his shoulders. I see a high-born man who has taken his place in society and, yet, I also see the shadow of his past, lingering.

# 45

*Giulia*

I am taken in by the convent on the hill.

It seems the priest's name can buy me a freedom of sorts—for now. Mother Superior Innocenza escorts me through the cloister to her chamber, closes the door and turns to me. Her face is lined but she wears the black veil with dignity and authority.

"I know who you are," she says.

My head is buzzing like a hive before its queen leaves and the swarming begins. I am rendered speechless, without words or thoughts as fear hits me in great waves like those of the sea crossing so many years ago. The pitch and crest of the past undulates and swells beneath my feet. It has washed in and is drowning me. Maybe I always knew it would end this way. From the moment I was born, a shadow was cast over me. Outcast. Whore. Witch. Poisoner. I am also Daughter, Mother, Survivor, Healer, though those parts of my history will never be written, of that, I am sure. But now, all I can think of—all I can conceive—is that they have Girolama. They have my circle.

"Who am I, Reverend Mother?" I say in a small voice.

What I want to say is *Where is Girolama? Where is she?*

I have to find my daughter. I have to find my friends. I have to avoid the holy devils who wish me ill. I do not know how or where to start.

*Where is she?*

"Sit, child, and I'll tell you who you are," she answers, not unkindly. I find I am shaking all over as I sink into a chair, the face of the bread seller leering from my mind's eye.

*Strega.*

Witch.

The same curse chosen for me as for Mamma, as for Faustina. This night, I wish for that power and find all I have is a basket empty of bread and the clothes I stand up in. There is nothing here to form a witch's brew, nothing to tempt the Devil into carrying out my wishes. I find I have nothing. I have no home. I have no friends except this nun sitting in front of me.

"You're the woman they call *la Siciliana*. All of Rome talks of you. See, even I, a servant of Christ, know the gossip from the market stalls and fishwives. But then, we nuns are invisible. We have ears to listen and tongues that stay silent. They say you're still beautiful and have hair that ripples like heads of wheat in the fields. They speak truth. They say you've come from Palermo to wreak deadly revenge upon mankind, but for what reason they don't know. They say you're the daughter of Teofania di Adamo. They call you *la Signora della Morte*, the Mistress of Death, the Widow-Maker."

I nod. I cannot deny it. I have heard all these names, and more, though few have ever dared say them to my face—until now.

"When they covered the city walls in public notices telling of your poison that acts so silently, it made every citizen in this place think. Do you know what they began to realize, my child?"

I shake my head. I am mute.

"They became scared," the Mother Superior continues, though I am barely listening now. Close to fainting I concentrate on breathing as panic seizes me.

*Where is she?*

"They understood at last that they might suffer the same fate as the Duke of Ceri. They began to say, 'Why not me?' They realized that anyone with coin, or perhaps even none at all, could obtain your wares and do the work only God in His infinite wisdom may do."

She speaks and I try to untangle her words, but none of this is what I want to hear. She tells me nothing that is of any interest or use to me. *They have my daughter*, I want to shout. *Listen. Hear this. They have her, and I do not know if she is alive or dead.*

"Only the Lord can decide our fates, Mistress of Death," the nun continues. "Only He can decide whether we live or die, and the timing of our entry into the blessed state of heaven or the fiery depths of hell. They saw they couldn't control you, child. They started to imagine their own deaths at your hand, and that's when the tide turned. You may have been protected by the silence of those you served, but no longer."

The nun speaks with a soft voice, though her message is clear and sharp as water from an icy well. There is nowhere for me to hide. I am alone and almost entirely friendless. I look up at her. Our eyes meet almost as equals. I am the first to look away.

"What will happen to me?" I ask. It seems like a question she will want to hear.

The nun smiles. "They can't touch you here. This is consecrated ground. This is sanctuary. They will not enter. I won't allow it. Be thankful, my child. God sees all our sins. None can cast the first stone."

I look down at the flagstone floor and realize I have no future. I am trapped, here in the convent, in a sacred place of holy women, but I am trapped as surely as if I was in one of *Il Papa*'s jails.

I am shown to my own small chamber by a novice nun who will not catch my eye and does not speak. I find I do not care for her disdain. Or is it fear? The cell is bare of anything except a wooden cross on the wall, the body of Jesus nailed to it in eternal suffering, and a thin hard bed.

Though I am tired to my soul, I find I cannot sleep. Instead, I walk the room, thinking only of my helplessness, my agony at the thought of what they are doing to Girolama, to Giovanna, to Maria and Graziosa.

But it is my daughter I pray for most fervently. This time I pray to their God, not our gods. I pray to the Mother Superior's God, to the inquisitors' God, the pope's God. This time, I beg forgiveness, as well I should as it is all my fault. It was I who carried on my mother's legacy, and I who instructed my circle how to make it. I have as good as killed them and, tonight, I cannot reconcile this thought with the knowledge that there are fewer bad men in this world. My recklessness has put everyone I love in danger. Everyone. My heart feels split into two parts: the slice that regrets all of it, and the part that regrets nothing, which rejoices at their deaths. *How can they be two parts of the same whole?* I ask their God, *Am I forsaken?* There is no reply, or none I can decipher. I ask Him, *Is my daughter—are my sisterhood—forsaken?* Again, I feel nothing, hear nothing. I keep praying until the first light of dawn, when I fall, at last, into troubled slumber.

# 46

*Alessandro*

My mother says my first breath almost never came.

I was pulled out from her noble body by the family physician, who pronounced me dead on sight. My skin was blue, my body cold. A silence rippled out from the black-robed surgeons in attendance for this, my most illustrious birth. Standing in my mother's great chamber, their faces lit by the flames of the beeswax candles, the shock was palpable though not unexpected. Perhaps they crossed themselves, their expressions carefully neutral, their hearts hammering underneath their velvet-clad bodices. Perhaps they knew they would incur the wrath of my father, Flavio, a formidable man and head of our dynasty. Perhaps they held their breath, as I held mine.

Then, the cry. Woken as if by God Himself. I do not know what prevented me from immediately claiming my life, my inheritance. Heir to the illustrious name of one of Italy's foremost banking empires, if not the wealth, which by then was in decline, though it was never once spoken of in front of me. My mother, weeping, at first with grief and then with happiness, held me to her, proclaimed me her favorite, her miracle, and kissed my small forehead, or so she told me many years later when we were alone, sitting by the loggia as the sun set over the Tuscan countryside and the sky was streaked orange. She smiled over at me, her hair gray, the bloom of her skin faded yet still beautiful, still proud, haughty, regal.

I smiled back, knowing myself the favored one. Knowing her love was mine, truly mine, above all others as I raised my goblet to her: a queen among women.

Nothing was ever too good for me.

How many can say, as I can, that they were held at the baptismal font by a celebrated artist? Wailing in Francesco Vanni's arms as the shock of cold holy water trickled down my forehead, bringing me to God almost as if I were a cherub from one of Vanni's drawings.

Now, I smooth down my thick robe. It is early and I am walking through the Vatican gardens, enjoying the cool morning air. My mind has calmed. The wounds on my back are healing, and I have not felt the urge to use the scourge for days.

"Forgive my intrusion, Your Holiness, but the governor of Rome seeks an audience with you on a matter of a most urgent nature. He says he must speak with you today."

Cardinal Andrello genuflects as he approaches. I subdue my wish that this was Camillo approaching, bringing me news.

My thoughts have been resting upon the latest missive, which arrived early this morning by weary riders from Spain. The letter, its seal miraculously still intact, was not political in nature. Indeed, it surprised me with its forthright religious inquiry. A delegation of bishops had written to ask permission to come into my presence and present their arguments for a more thorough, more severe process of persecution for heresy. They write from the land that created the auto-da-fé, the act of burning heretics at the stake.

I have ruminated on the contents of the letter as I walk through my Eden. Exotic plants vie for attention. Somewhere

close by, the sound of water cascading. Scents emanate from
the *viridarium novum*, the medicinal garden. Here, the healing
powers of God's plants are studied. Botany becomes akin to a
new science as medical men learn about our Creator's world,
and all within it.

I offer my ring to Andrello. He bows his head to kiss it.

"Please, Cardinal, take a seat with me. You look flushed. You
must be calm, tranquil in this place," I murmur, waving to him
to take a nearby seat.

We sit like two old men taking the air. We turn our faces
toward the dome of Basilica di San Pietro, and, for a moment, we
are entranced, like two newly ordained deacons witnessing the
true beauty of God for the first time.

"It's magnificent," I say.

"It is, Holy Father," Andrello replies.

We both fall into silence as if sitting here together was our
intention. The cuts and sores I have inflicted upon my skin sting
as they mend. I breathe in deeply and smell the freshness of the
air away from the stews of the city. Radiant light fills my vision.
Lush greenery. Exquisite architecture. Yet, in my heart, truly I
find little real peace.

After some moments have passed, I speak.

"Tell Governor Bracchi I'll give him his audience today. You
may go now."

Andrello stands up and smooths down his cassock. He bows
before removing his person from my presence. I watch him go,
walking back toward the Vatican, knowing Bracchi will be waiting
for me. He must wait. We are all subject to God's time, to His plan.
My governor must learn patience, as we all must. I am as a teacher
to my pupil. I sit. I stay and I think of the letter. Perhaps we have
been too lenient, and Rome is at risk of appearing weak to the
outside world. If this is true, as the bishops tell me emphatically it

is, then this cannot continue. Perhaps these clergymen are right, and we must enforce a new severity in our dealings with heretical crimes, with witchcraft and sinners. There is much evil and darkness to ponder amid this heaven on earth.

Time passes. I stand, awkwardly. A servant offers his arm but I refuse it, shoo him away. Walking slowly toward the basilica, I send the man ahead to warn Bracchi of my approach, to tell him to meet me under the dome we have just admired, exalting our meeting and placing us at the very heart of the Holy See. If I recall lying there, prostrate, begging for God's help, I choose to forget it.

My footsteps echo on the patterned marble floor as I approach. The sheer scale of the basilica—its nave, dome, chapels, altars, and tombs—reduces every man in comparison. Even I.

More footsteps. Bracchi approaches. If he too remembers that night, he gives no indication.

"Holy Father, I thank you for granting me an audience." The governor is an impatient man. He speaks quickly, his mind racing before him. He bends on one knee, as he must do when approaching the pontiff. I hold out my hand and he clasps it, kisses the papal ring, starts to speak again. I stop him.

"Governor Bracchi, what news do you have that's so important it interferes with the business of the day?"

I see him smart, but he bows his head. His voice is slower, calmer. Inwardly, I rejoice at his taming, though I give no hint of my satisfaction. No man can demand the attention of a pope. He must wait until it pleases God for me to see him. My pupil is learning, though I see something as yet unformed within him. Should I worry about him? Checks have been made, reports have been written. He is a pious man, a forthright and judicious man and one without blemish. Yet, there is something.

He asks for permission to speak. I grant it.

"Your Holiness, we have them," he says, his voice barely able to hide his triumph. "We have them all except one."

"Who do you have?" I reply. Nearby a bee hovers, a leaf curls. Bracchi stays on one knee.

"We have four of the witch-women who've imperiled the men of our city for so long. We've caught them, and they've given us their leader's name. They're in our dungeons awaiting the next stage of our questioning. They'll answer for their crimes, Holy Father."

For a moment, I am seized by the strange desire to exclaim my delight, to grab this man and embrace him. I turn away, briefly, to regain my composure. I flinch as I move and hope he does not see.

"You've captured those who are the source of this filthy butchery? If this is true, then we must praise God. And yet, you say there's one still at large. Why do you come to me? Surely, you'll hunt down and capture this jezebel?" I almost spit the word.

"The jezebel is a Sicilian named Giulia. Her mother was a poisoner, and we have her in our sights," Bracchi says.

The judge shifts. I see he is uncomfortable. Perhaps his knee hurts. Perhaps his back, too. I keep him where he is, giving no sign that he may rise to relieve his discomfort. God asks all of us to learn what it is to suffer. He asks us to endure, to forgo the pleasures of the flesh, of the body and the mind, and so our spirit grows and our hearts find courage. This, I know. It is scored into my flesh by the whip. Again, I am this man's teacher. I see he struggles with his learning.

"My spies followed her. She's taken refuge at the convent of the Santissima Trinità dei Monti. My men and agents for the Holy Office tell me she's there now and is under the protection of the Mother Superior. She's been offered sanctuary. I've sent officers to ask Mother Superior Innocenzia to give her up, but she refuses. I come to you because I have no other way of luring the rat from its hole."

Our eyes meet. I gesture for him to rise.

For a moment, I am unsure.

*Lord, how do we flush out this villain? God Almighty, hear my prayers and guide me.* I send up my prayer and gaze at the towering vastness above us, which appears to be as high as Heaven itself. It hovers as if weightless. I am reminded of the Tiber on a day such as this, when the sun sparkles as it crests on its way through Rome from the heights of the Apennine Mountains down to the Tyrrhenian Sea. A thirst comes upon me, and it is then that the idea forms, as if channeled directly from our Lord and Savior. I turn to Bracchi and smile. I gesture for him to approach, to come closer so my words do not carry across the breadth of the building.

"Your officers will spread rumors in the taverns, the markets, the boatyards, the shops, and piazzas. They'll travel into Old Rome and give word that this poisoner Giulia Siciliana threatens to poison the city waters and will wreak her revenge on all mankind. They'll say she's run mad with her lust for killing and cares little now whom she destroys. They'll say we must all fight to free this devil from inside the sanctuary walls and crush her before she can do the work Satan himself commanded of her. Go, and tell your men to leave no corner of the city untouched by these stories. She'll poison the water. We'll all face our deaths if we cannot enter the convent. They will gather. The people will take fright and they'll storm the wooden gates. With them will be my army on horseback, but they'll remain outside the church. I can't be seen to break sanctuary."

Bracchi looks at me as if seeing me for the first time.

"But hear this," I say. "None is to harm her. She must come to your care untouched. She must be interrogated properly. She must confess all freely. That way we avoid creating a people's saint of her. We'll stop any who say she was lynched and is made a martyr to the women of Rome. We must destroy her carefully, with precision."

I can see my governor is shocked by what I have said to him. I do not trouble myself to explain further. I have given my orders, and I expect them to be carried out. Together, we will bring down this foul wretch. Her time has come, her reign of violence finished. No more shall the good men of this city tremble before they take a sip of wine or a spoonful of broth. No more shall men fear those set by God below him: his wives, daughters, servants. Together, we will persecute this jezebel and kill her for her wickedness.

Even so, I command a legion of new tasters for my supper. I post papal guards outside every chamber. I watch each servant ever more closely.

# 47

*Giulia*

I pace, then weep.

I lie staring at the whitewashed walls for hours, then fall into a restless slumber. I speak Girolama's name to invoke her spirit, but nothing comes—no sign, no portend, nothing at all. Then, I feel as if I can live no longer and would prefer a heretic's death to this waiting.

I follow the hours of the liturgy, listening to the nuns as they chant their prayers, joining their services, hovering close by. None speaks with me, except to tell me when it is time to eat, pray, or sleep. None looks at me directly. Their gaze is always positioned somewhere close by—the foot of the cross, the hem of my gown, the arch of a doorway. I prefer it this way. I am already outcast. I am already condemned. Their refusal to make me visible feels like truth. Perhaps I am already dead, and this is the purgatory they speak of.

Only Mother Superior Innocenza calls me to her study to sip a goblet of wine after the prayers for None. Perhaps we would have little to say to one another in another lifetime, but in this, we find we have common ground.

"How do you bear it?" I ask, not many evenings after I arrive.

I am beyond all sense now, helpless: veering between fits of weeping and blank terror for my daughter and my circle, and despair at the thought of never seeing daylight outside of the convent grounds again. The walls remind me of our villa in Palermo, the gilded trap that encircled Mamma and me. The convent is the same. After three days, I wanted to scream and batter down the doors, to run as fast and as far as I could, to gulp in freedom, to run to the prison holding my beloveds and beat it down.

I cannot imagine how it is possible to become content, as all the nuns appear to be, in such a place, within such strictures. I miss my plants, my remedies, my potions and tinctures. Here, the apothecary door is kept firmly locked, and though the smells I am so familiar with—the pungent floral scents of lavender, clove, chamomile—drift through the passages and walkways, mixing with the tang of alcohol for preserving, for liniments and tonics, it only serves to widen the gap between this life and my own. A life that is now lost to me.

I have had time to chew over that life, to peer at it from every angle, to dissect it and pull the meat from the bones of it. I regret everything, and I regret nothing. I always knew there would be a high price for freedom, and that is what I gave my poisoners. They had few options without husband, father, family, status, name, or wealth to protect them. There was no respectable living available to any of us and they came with me, learned my trade, willingly. I am still guilty. I have endangered them, and our clients, in this endeavor. I have also given them a life, however risky and shadowy, away from the strictures of the marriage bed or the veil. Were we brave or foolish? Are we culpable, as the holy men will say we are? Even after stripping my life bare, like a joint for the pot, I cannot tell. There is no living to be made except as whores or wise women—and both are perilous, scandalous and without protection. Yet, everything comes back to this: I am guilty. We are all guilty—and my friends will die because of me.

"Mother Superior, how do you bear this?" I say again, sweeping my hand around her office, which is richly furnished with a polished desk and two ornate chairs, a fireplace and shelves that are filled with manuscripts.

It is the books that astonish me. These are her only real possessions, apart from a large gold cross upon which Jesus weeps ruby tears, opulently. They line the shelves in clutters and piles. The convent life is one of the few places a learned woman can be free to seek the wisdom she desires.

"I never wanted to become a cloistered nun, Giulia," Innocenza says, for I have given her my name. It is all I have left. She looks back at me with her direct gaze, and I find myself flattered. This woman of high birth appears interested in me, appears to treat me as an equal, though society places us far apart. "My family, though wealthy, had my older sister to marry off, to enrich with dowries and land. For the rest of us, our future lay behind the wall. It costs many times less to send a girl into the Church than it does to buy a high-born husband. I begged for marriage. I pleaded with Father to allow me a respectable husband, without fortune or standing, just so I could travel out of the confines of my life. I so desperately wanted a taste of other places, other sights and sounds. I wanted to become a mother one day, to have children of my own. My pleading was ignored. It was decided by the time I was eleven that I would enter a convent.

"I was given my wish in one way. Only a year or so later, I was summoned by the abbess of a convent many miles away, and in holy obedience I went. For many years, the cloister was my jail, and I resented it. But time went by, and my anger faded. Slowly, surely, the jewels of the Catholic faith revealed themselves to me. They were laid bare by the women who had come before me. Their quiet strength, their wisdom and courage, their shining faith showed me how childlike I remained. Only through my own surrender was I able to become who I am today. I conquered my rage. I crucified my image of myself as a daughter of a noble house, and in that crucifixion, my soul was reborn. I had to die and be reborn, just as Jesus Christ died for us, to bear our sins. I was redeemed, though it took many years."

The nun is suddenly quiet. She studies me now by candle-light. A cat hisses somewhere. Her face looks strange but perhaps it is the fading light.

"Perhaps the same fate may lie ahead for you?"

I stare back at her. She sips her wine and sits back to let me absorb this simple sentence.

The same fate.

I think what she means is that perhaps I might, one day, take the veil. Perhaps I might crucify myself on the cross of obedience and submission. Even as the thought arises, something inside me quashes it. I know myself. I know I can never do what she has done. I will never bend my will to her God who looks down on us from above, who sees everything, or so the Bible says.

There is a brief silence before I find the words to reply in a way that she might understand.

"My fate was determined the day I was born, that's what I believe, Holy Mother," I say, pulling my fingers through my long hair. It lies heavy against my back, though the convent is cool enough.

"I know they'll kill me, just as I know they'll kill my daughter and my friends. Our fates are different from those of women like you." This time I shrug, making Innocenza frown.

"I don't believe that, Giulia. Our Lord says we can all be for-given. We can all enter the Kingdom of Heaven if we submit ourselves to His will, if we have faith."

I almost laugh. "Mother Superior, I'm past redemption! You know what I've done. If He knows of the deaths I've caused by proxy—hundreds, perhaps thousands of them—then your God won't let me pass into this heaven you speak of."

A blackbird sings its throaty evensong, though it is the last days of winter and the first of spring. *La merla*, her white feathers forever blackened with soot, or so the legend of *i Giorni della merla*—the Days of the Blackbird—tells. We both look up at the window and see a flash of dark wings as the bird leaps into the sky. For a brief moment, the window is filled with motion and feathers, claws and yellow beak. Then the bird is gone.

Neither of us speaks. The air feels odd, unsettled. Then the abbess looks over at me, as if she sees the shadow of my thoughts.

"I don't believe your prophecy of your life, Giulia," she says, standing up and walking to the window. "It's within God's power to forgive you, even if you can't forgive yourself."

"But, Holy Mother, I don't seek forgiveness. I seek truth! Every woman I helped had no other way, and if they did?" I shrug again. "If they did, then it was for their conscience, not mine! None of the men ever asked for forgiveness. None of those who caused injustice did, either, so why should I? The only thing I have cause to regret is that I was not clever enough to stop them catching us. The only thing I regret is that they have my daughter and my friends."

Suddenly, all is clear. My life is presented to me as if on a silver platter. My heart is sure, and my actions knowable, fathomable. I realize, sitting inside this sacred place with an abbess, that I would do it all again, despite the risks.

"I can't bear to stay here a moment longer, unable to save my own child. They'll torture her. They'll probably kill her—and there's nothing I can do to change her destiny. That's what I regret now, and only that, Reverend Mother."

Tears run down my face. Grief washes over me. Keening, I bend over and find myself on all fours on the cold floor. The Mother Superior does nothing. She does not attempt to comfort me. She does not try to tell me easy lies, to say that God loves me, and this is all part of His design. She does not move. She watches me as if curious, though I sense she is acting as witness to my suffering; and in doing so, elevating it. I am a disciple of pain in this moment. Strangely, I am deeply moved by her stillness as the tears come and I clutch my waist trying to breathe.

When I am finished, I wipe my face on my sleeve and crawl back up onto the chair. Still, the nun says nothing. I sense no judgment as perhaps I did the first day we met. She does not move. She is like a holy woman in a fresco: still, calm and patient. I am the opposite, as it appears I am destined to be. My face feels sore, my eyes still weep fat tears, my nose runs and my heart breaks anew with each breath I take.

"They have my daughter. I might as well be dead."

Innocenza nods as if she understands completely, and yet how can she? How can she know anything of my life, of what I am capable of, of what it feels to have birthed a child, been a true mother?

"I'll pray for you, Giulia," is all she says, as if, again, she reads my thoughts and finds them wanting.

I do not walk down to the chapel for Vespers, nor Compline. I lie on my hard bed and think hard thoughts. I recall every argument I have had with my daughter, and I regret them all. I picture her, and the others, and I am seized by fright.

I know they are in grave danger, that much I can feel, though the Sight is an unreliable ally these days, and has all but abandoned me. I know they are still alive, though I cannot sense any more than this. When I shut my eyes, I see only the endless black of the void. There is one thing I have with me, one thing that I have hidden inside the convent, behind a loose stone in the walled garden. My *tarocchi*. I had taken to carrying them with me, perhaps as a lucky charm, perhaps as comfort. Who can say?

The images of the suns are faded, the midnight-blue edges ripped and torn, but they still vibrate with secret knowledge.

When the bells chime for Compline, I wait until the prayers begin, the sound of female voices rising and falling as they worship. Then I sneak out. I find the stone and, looking behind me to see I am not watched, I pull out the part that covers my cards. They are wrapped in linen. I secrete them under my veil. They are calling me. They are bringing me back to the old ways, the old wisdom.

Though I am breaking every law, every code, in this sacred place, I find the old ways sit as easy with me as ever. My lineage, that of a cunning woman, a midwife and herbalist, stretches back: woman to woman, healer to healer. I draw the deck out of its cover, setting aside the old blackbird's feather, the shell and coin, the trinkets that have followed me through my life to this place, and place the cards on my bed. I check again to see no one has followed me, but the corridor outside my chamber is empty. The prayers lift upward. The evening closes in.

I sit, tracing my fingers over the beloved symbols. Here, *L'Amore*, the Lovers, stand, Cupid above them, raining down his arrows. Here, *Il Mundo*, the World, the final card of the major arcana, a naked woman floating, suspended between heaven and earth, surrounded by a wreath. She is watched from each corner by the four evangelists: angel, eagle, lion, bull. A sign of the ending of things. A sign of wisdom and completion. Here, *La Morte*, Death, the Grim Reaper's skeleton brandishing a sickle, reminding us of impermanence, of endings, of failure. They whisper to

me. I do not know how much time I have before the nuns realize I
am not there and seek me out. I decide to pull one card, just one.

A slight hesitation, then I draw. The card lies face down on
my bed linen. My hand trembles as I turn it over. The image is
unmistakable, though this card is aged and ripped. The figure
wears the triple tiara. His right hand is raised in a gesture of
blessing, his spiritual dominion absolute, unimpeachable, ever-
lasting. On his face, an expression of stern authority. In his left
hand, a gilded triple cross. It is the Hierophant. *Il Papa*, the Pope.

He is coming for me.

# 48

The sound of jeering reaches us first. Then the shouts: men's voices.

The noise reaches us within the church walls as we prepare for Compline. I am standing at the back of the chapel. The night bells ring, low and soft. Then, the prayers. They echo and sway, surrounding each of us, lifting up to the rafters.

... *I have sinned exceedingly, in thought, word and deed, by my fault, by mine own fault, by mine own most grievous fault* ...

Then, a banging, a thumping. Someone, some people, are hitting the doors, battering them. It takes a moment before we understand they are trying to break in. Several of the nuns look around but our Mother Superior does not move. She holds her head high. Her voice rises higher, louder, and the nuns, as sheep before a shepherd, follow her lead.

... *The Almighty and Merciful Lord grant us pardon, absolution, and remission of our sins* ...

*BANG. BANG. BANG.*

Then the clatter of metal objects hitting the church doors. Then the curses follow.

"Give up the witch! Give up the poisoner who fouls our water. Give her up to us!"

... *He that dwelleth in the secret place of the most High shall abide under the shadow of the Almighty. I will say of the Lord, He is my refuge and my fortress: my God; in him will I trust. Surely he shall deliver thee from the snare of the fowler, and from the noisome pestilence* ...

"Send out the sorceress. Send out Satan's bride for she'll pay for her crimes! If she doesn't come, we'll take her!"

*THUMP. THUMP. THUMP.*

Then another voice. A voice of authority.

"Open these doors, I command you in the name of the Holy Father, Pope Alessandro the Seventh!"

For a moment, a mere heartbeat, a breath, I see consternation. The white faces of the nuns shrouded in black veils over their linen habits, crosses around their necks, turn to me. I stare back into the eyes of Innocenza. She does not move. She stands as rigid as a statue of the blessed Virgin. Without hesitation, she begins the psalm again, from where it stopped. Some of the nuns join her, but not all.

*. . . He shall cover thee with his feathers, and under his wings shalt thou trust: his truth shall be thy shield and buckler. Thou shalt not be afraid for the terror by night . . .*

There is a roar. This terror of the night is real and here among us. I can feel the presence of the mob like an animal about to attack, its hackles raised, its hot breath on my skin. The high-pitched noise comes, as I guessed it would, then a burning smell so intense I glance around to see which of the candles has caught, knowing even as I do so, that the Sight has returned to me. With it comes fear.

Mother Superior Innocenza stops chanting now. The nuns' voices die away instantly, and they stand, we all *stand*, looking around, unsure what to do next.

Innocenza is the first to move. She strides away and, without thinking why, I follow her. I should have run in the opposite direction. I should have hidden in the crypts, in the cellar or the privy. Instead, I turn and follow in her wake, knowing as clearly as if the message had been scribbled down that I must face whatever this is, because the Sight tells me so. It nudges me onward, the sound in my head so loud now I may retch, the burning smell choking my lungs.

The Mother Superior marches toward the great door of the church. As realization dawns, nuns scatter like black hens. She stops, then draws breath.

"You will not enter this chapel! Who are you to dare break sanctuary? Step away from the door!"

There is a sudden hush from outside. Murmurs. A lull.

"Step away from this door by Almighty God!"

She throws her voice out of this sacred place and into the crowds that are waiting beyond the safety of our defenses. Her audience is stunned into silence. She would have made a fine queen, holding herself as a regent would, haughty and strong. Then, into the hush, she acts. Taking the iron bolt, she pulls it to one side. It drags into its new position, and when it scrapes to a halt, Mother Superior Innocenza, abbess and nun, shoves open one side of the door and steps outward. She is alone. She is unafraid.

"What's the meaning of this disturbance? It's the Holy Office of Compline. The sisters of the Santissima Trinità dei Monti basilica are praying. Who disturbs their prayers? Who'll explain why you disrupt the peace of God's house this night?" She is magnificent.

I stay in the shadows behind her, but I see the flames of the torches. I see the glint of metal—knives, poles, and pitchforks. I see men's faces—and some women too. Many men, many torches, many weapons. I cannot help myself. As a moth zigzags toward a flame, burning its gossamer wings, I step forward, pulling my veil over my hair.

At first, no one says anything. Then the crowd parts awkwardly, and there before us appears a man wearing armor that reflects the orange fires as they leap in their torches. Twilight has fallen. Perhaps that is why I am slow to notice. Perhaps my mind lags behind my senses, but I see them now. Behind this man, this captain, are many uniformed men. Each wears the colors of the papal guard—red, yellow, and blue—under their polished armor. Each carries a halberd.

"You've been ordered by Pope Alessandro the Seventh to release the woman known as Giulia Siciliana and give her to us. We will not leave until she surrenders herself."

So, they have discovered my name. Did they torture my loved ones to gain this information?

The captain's lip curls as he speaks. He spits on the ground and smiles. Several members of the rabble give low cheers, shake clenched fists, scowl, and grimace, many of them female. Their hatred astonishes me, though what was I expecting? I, who am used to the protection of women. I, who am used to being guarded by their silence. I have lost that protection. I have lost their fragile trust.

"I will not break God's sanctuary."

The Mother Superior stands firm but I see her tremble now. Time seems to pause, and in that moment, I feel the throbbing of my pulse, the beat of life itself within me, and I know what I am about to do.

"My men may be ordered by *Il Papa* not to break sanctuary, but there are many here who would risk damnation to put an end to the killings. You'll give her up, and if you don't, they'll take her."

For a moment, I wonder if I will faint, or laugh, or vomit. My legs begin to shake. Before Innocenza can respond, I submit to the high note that seems to waver now. It runs through me, through every cell in my body, compelling me onward toward my destiny. The Sight is back, telling me what I have to do—and even without it, I would not endanger the lives of the nuns who took me in.

I step forward.

I remove my veil.

My hair is lit by the fires and shimmers gold in the torchlight.

I say these words; perhaps they will be my last.

"I am Giulia Siciliana."

There is a gasp, followed by renewed cursing, hollering, spitting, and the shaking of fists. It would be comical in a play, but this is no theater. That part is to come. I know what follows. I will be imprisoned. I will be tortured. I will be interrogated and put on trial. I will be killed publicly for everything I have done, and, in that knowledge, I find I regret nothing. I wonder, finally, if this is how freedom feels.

I look at the Mother Superior, who returns my gaze steadily. We both nod. We know this is where the play finishes, where the last act begins. It has only ever been a matter of time, of waiting. We know my death is a certainty, and so let it begin.

I step downward onto the earth and the crowd parts again. Two guards greet me, their stakes aloft, their faces grim. All I know is that I will see my daughter, my friends, my circle, though this is surely the end.

# 49

*Alessandro*

Most Noble and Beloved Mother,

We have them all.

Five sorceresses. Five poisoners who have, with coldhearted malice, butchered their betters with their deadly concoction. They may not have administered the poison, but they brewed it and dispensed it. They eased along the demise so wished for by treacherous wives and daughters across the city and beyond. They hoped *la peste* would hide their maleficent deeds but, by the Grace of God, it did not, and they will now pay for their sins, of which there are many.

I know you will be smiling in heaven, Mamma. I know you will look down on me, your son, and see what I have achieved for the glory of God, and Rome, and perhaps all Italy. These serpents in the nest were not just murderers, dear Mother. They were asps in the bosom of the Church and the State, spreading false hope and dangerous ideas to those set below their husbands, fathers, confessors and brothers. They planted the seeds of dissent, of rebellion, of bitter disagreement, and even worse, of independent thought and action. For does not the revered work of the Reverend Kramer, the *Malleus Maleficarum*, the Hammer of Witches, say when a woman thinks alone, she thinks evil? Does not the text reveal the carnal lusts of women like these which drive them to union with the Devil?

How many great minds may have been lost through the spite of women? We will uncover the details. We will discover their networks, their accomplices. We will unearth them all in the name of God Almighty. We will use as many methods as we deem necessary to obtain the purity of truth.

These witch-women have robbed the men of Italy of their deserved rest, their peace of mind, in the very places they should be comforted, revered, obeyed. How dare they, Mamma! Do they know what they have done? They have torn a hole in the very fabric of society—and this is their real crime. The arrogance! The deceit of these blackhearted sirens!

I allowed Governor Bracchi an audience today to give him our thanks, to give him those commendations I know men of his station might wish to receive from such as I, their vicar of Rome, their channel to God Almighty.

No words can express my disgust, nor my joy, at the knowledge that tonight, as I light a candle and think of you, the five hags hunted for so long are meeting their fate. They will languish together in Tor di Nona. Let them have their last moments. Let them squirm and rage. Let them quake and buckle, then tomorrow, oh tomorrow, they will begin to answer for their corruption without pity or mercy. The interrogation starts at dawn. I have commanded Bracchi to bring me daily reports. Why cannot all women be like you, Mother? Why must they claw and scratch at us, hoping to raise themselves, hoping to cut us men down?

You were the greatest of your sex, Mamma. Though beset by the weaknesses and frailty of body and spirit, you rose above the state God was pleased to bestow upon you and became a beacon of piety and strength for all women to emulate, though they could never hope to attain your dignity, your intelligence, your forthright wisdom. I leave you now. Perhaps tonight, I will rest without the aid of the scourge. Perhaps tonight, my unnatural desires for the woman who has snared me in her feminine net will abate, and I will sleep. I will be at peace.

Perhaps.

Your loving and faithful son,
His Holiness, Pope Alessandro VII

# 50

*Giulia*

They handle me roughly.

I am dragged, pushed, spat upon. I am shoved, kicked, leered over. My robe is torn, and they laugh. The jailors find my distress amusing, but all I care about is the first glimpse of my daughter's face.

The stone walls drip rank water. The slabs that make up the uneven floor are strewn with filthy straw. Rats scuttle. Prisoners jeer and wail. The stench of the makeshift latrines, a bucket in each cell, mixes with the stink of the unwashed and lice ridden. Bars rattle as I pass. A woman hisses, half beast now perhaps. Another curses, yet I walk, my shoes slipping on the piss-stained stones, a fat jailer pushing me forward.

There. I see her at last. Her long hair is unmistakable. Black and sleek still, hanging down her back. She turns at the sound of my footsteps.

Tor di Nona prison lives up to its reputation. The walls leech unhappiness and fear. The cells were surely made in imitation of purgatory: a place between, where we are already half-dead. They are dark, dingy, dirty.

Some of the women have their hair hacked from their heads, blood still drying on their skulls. Others have already been tortured. They lie unseeing, deep inside their own arena of pain. Torches line the corridor, and they flicker, throwing dark shadows into the far reaches of this hovel. The smell is the odor of poverty and horror, somewhere between human sweat, dirt, and feces.

For a moment I am reminded of the clients Mamma used to take me to see: the dwellings barely fit for their animals to inhabit, where the stench of stale sweat mingled with days-old pottage and excrement. Somewhere in that cacophony of smells was the sour odor of fear. What other calamities may befall them? What last dignity might be taken away? What new pain or disaster might strike? The difference here is that these women know what will happen next. They know they will be led to the torture chambers where they will repent and be broken. They know they will never leave except to be huddled in the cart that drives them through the streets to the place of their execution. They know their fate—as I know mine.

"Mamma!" Girolama falls into my arms like the little girl she once was. I hold her tightly as I used to. The prison door bangs shut behind me. I stroke her hair, whisper false promises into her ear as I used to. We stand, swaying together.

I open my eyes eventually and see Giovanna. Next to her, Graziosa squats in the corner, a wild look about her eyes, and over there is Maria too. She who spins ethereal thread with her hands, her eyes vacant, her manner resembling a confused, dreamy child.

"We're happy to see you, Giulia. We thought you were dead," Giovanna says as she steps over to us, putting her arms around me and my daughter. Girolama continues to weep, and I find myself shushing her like I would a baby.

"The guard, that whoreson, told us you'd been killed by a mob in the center of Rome. They told us your body was ripped apart, your tits spilling out, your cunny exposed for all to see," my daughter says, spitting at the bars and the fat jailer who leers at us just beyond them.

"Well, at least he has an imagination," I say. "And I'm glad to see your spirit is still intact, daughter. As you can see, I'm whole. I'm alive, though for how much longer . . . ?"

"But where have you been, Mamma? How did you escape them for so long?" Girolama says. I see she is touching her hands, trying to play with the rings on her fingers that are no longer there. "*Amore mio*, I as good as became a nun. They knew where I was. The Holy Office sent a delegation of men to speak with the Mother Superior of the convent that harbored me, but she refused to hand me over to them. Then, they came with a mob, on the direct order of *Il Papa*. That's when I gave myself up. Holy blood would've been spilled that night if I hadn't. She was brave, but she was no match for an army."

"But, Mamma, how did you know to hide? Who told you of our plight?" Girolama puts her head on my shoulder, and I kiss her again.

"Padre Don Antonio looked for me. He risked his position, perhaps even his life, to find me and tell me to go."

"An unlikely savior," Giovanna says.

We share a sad smile, an understanding of sorts.

"Can you see what will happen?" Maria says, finally recognizing me and coming over to us. Her hair is matted with pieces of straw entangled in its mane. She has a strange look on her face, halfway to madness. She hums after she finishes speaking as if trying it for the first time. Giovanna and I exchange another glance, then I shake my head.

"No, Maria, I can see nothing. There's only blackness ahead. I can't see a future at all."

For a moment we are all silent. Our thoughts are interrupted by Graziosa, who suddenly shrieks, then falls quiet again. Maria walks off as if in a daze.

"So, tell me what happened. How did they catch you all?" I ask, still holding Girolama as if I will never let her go.

"They knew everything, Giulia," Giovanna says. "They must've been watching us for weeks, perhaps months. Someone has told them about us, or perhaps many have—who can tell? A new client came to the shop just after you left that morning. She said she was the maidservant of a fine lady who lived in a villa just out of the city. She said her mistress was beaten by her sadist husband, who'd force her to lie with his exalted friends in debauchery and lust. She said they hurt her—and she needed an urgent remedy for her situation. We believed her."

"I thought you didn't want to dispense any more *acqua*?" I say.

"I didn't," Giovanna replies, "but you weren't there. I wasn't sure what to do. We believed every word the girl said, so Girolama and I went with her in her fine carriage. Graziosa and Maria hadn't arrived yet. The maid said there was little time before the husband returned and we had to hurry. It was my fault we were all taken. I'm so sorry, Giulia. I failed us all." Tears run down Giovanna's beloved face. I am torn between wanting to hug her and shake her.

"You mustn't blame yourself. It was I who forced you all to continue, knowing how much danger we were in! I guessed they were following us, but I couldn't stop," I say. "If it wasn't that trap, another would've been set. There's nothing any of us could've done except to leave Rome and go far away, but it's too late for that, and anyway, they would've found us one day."

"They took my things; they dragged me out by my hair." Maria's voice is that of a child.

I release my daughter and go to her, stroke her tangled tresses and whisper soft words in her ear. I turn back to Giovanna.

"In truth, I'm weary of this life, living as a fugitive, living in the darkness of the night streets, of the back alleys. We'll go to our deaths knowing we tried to help. That there are many women of this city who lead better lives because of it. There are many women who would not be alive had it not been for my mother's remedy."

Giovanna nods. Girolama's expression is hard to read.

"We were always marked, my loves, from the very start. Our only power was in the evasion, the very fact we existed at all and did what we did. In the convent, I had time to think. There was nothing else to do except pray! Oh, I have taken more risks than I should've. I've been reckless with our lives, but was there any other way of living?

"When I first made Mamma's *acqua* in Naples, I knew I'd taken a dangerous path, and would endanger any who worked with me. I knew this and yet I chose to make it. I gave it to a woman who may have died without it. But don't think me noble. I've done this for my own reasons too. I can't explain, but the poison is part of me, and I serve it, its potency and power. It also meant I could live independently because, at first, I charged for it. I would've starved without it.

"It gave me a life many woman can't have: without husband or father to dictate every action, every thought and deed. I'd seen what that was like. My mother lived under my stepfather's thumb, and before then, she was a plaything for gentlemen and even a king, but none of it bought her happiness or freedom. The *acqua* was my chance at that, and I took it. And yes, I've been responsible for the deaths of many men, perhaps thousands since then. That is not the only crime, though. Our crime has been to exist on the outside. Our fates have been sealed all along."

There is silence when, at last, I finish speaking. I look around. Tears are streaming down Girolama's face, but her gaze is direct, open, as she looks back at me.

"I love you, my friends. It's the honor of my life to be here with you, having done what we've done. It's a miracle we've survived thus far," I add. "I'm proud of what we've done. I'm proud to say we righted the wrongs of men. There have been so many."

Maria is chatting to herself under her breath as I hold her. It is then I notice her gown is torn in several places. I can feel her skin through the garment. It is clammy and cold, though the jail is as hot as the infernos of hell.

"What happened?" I say.

Maria looks at me blankly, and I realize she is lost to us. She has taken herself inwardly to a place I cannot reach.

"The guard took her and used her for his pleasure," Girolama says. She spits on the floor. "He knew she worked in the brothels—he must be a frequent visitor. They're animals here. They're lower than beasts in the fields."

Graziosa stays where she is, squatting. Her colored hair is now dank, her gray roots limp and lifeless, the fiery color faded. Her eyes dart around the cell, appearing to see everything yet I wonder if she sees anything at all. She does not seem to recognize me, and I wonder if she has lost her mind too. They call this place "the pit" and I see why. Moldy breadcrumbs are scattered on the floor and there is an empty jug of water nearby. The remains of a meal, if that's what it can be called.

"Courage, sisters. They can beat us and force us to confess, but they can't change our hearts and minds. Never forget our freedom lies elsewhere, in the thoughts we have, the actions we've hidden, the love we've felt. The Church may mutilate and debase our bodies, but it can't touch our souls, and that's what frightens them. We have our own gods. We have our own ways. Our safety has only ever been within ourselves. They can't rob us of that."

"They can do much to hurt us, though," Giovanna says quietly.

"If an inquisitor so much as lays a hand on me, I'll bite his testicles off," Girolama says with unexpected relish.

There is a moment of hush before, suddenly, we three begin to laugh. Perhaps it is the image of my daughter pouncing on a churchman. Perhaps it is the sheer helplessness we know is our current state that would make that course of action impossible. Or perhaps it is the joy of hating, the stinging beauty of anger and cold rage and killing. We laugh together, clutching our sides, crying tears of desperate mirth, while the other inmates and jailers look at us as if we have all run mad. And perhaps we have. Perhaps we have.

# 51

My name is called out the following day.

I have been expecting it. They hope to break me first, as leader of my circle, as the woman who began it all.

I barely slept overnight as we lay on the floor, Girolama in my arms, amid rats scuttling, lice crawling, and women weeping. The jailer stands, grinning, iron keys clanking on a chain around his sagging waist. He beckons, pointing a thick finger at me, and I get to my feet, brushing off the straw and dirt as if it still matters. I have not eaten anything, nor has a sip of water passed my lips since I arrived. My head feels woozy.

My hands shackled, I stumble behind the prison guard as he slouches his way up the steps toward a chamber at the back of the building, scratching his ass and whistling as he goes. As we rise, the tower becomes less a prison and more a set of rooms lined with books and rolls of thick, milk-white parchment. It is incredible to me to think that the business of pain and punishment happens below this calm, efficient place. I am directed into the prosecutor's chamber. There is a doorway that opens to a balcony, below which is the Tiber. A fire smolders in the hearth.

A door to my right has been left open, perhaps so I can see the thick rope of the strappado hanging from a hook, a pulley, in the roof. It is also known by another name, *il tormento*. I stand— awkwardly, defiantly, trying not to look.

Then, I realize.

It is him.

It is the man who was looking at me so intently in Piazza Farnese the day I fled to sanctuary. It is the man whose eye I caught in the carriage on the day the Sight returned to me.

He is sitting before me at a huge table which is piled with papers, documents, and a large leather-bound Bible. When he looks up, his gaze is direct, steady.

"*La Siciliana*," is all he says.

I do not know how to answer him, and so I say nothing. I am determined to be clever, to dance around his questions, to defend myself and my sisterhood from this *inquisitio*. Underneath, though, I am scared to my marrow.

In truth, pain frightens me. When I gave birth to my daughter—despite Giovanna's expert midwifery—I experienced what it is to be swallowed whole by agony. Even now I recall the pounding waves, the endless contractions. The moment where her head crowned and I felt like my body was tearing in two. All of that pales before the threat of the rope.

"What am I to you?" is all I say.

I stare back at him, though I am trembling, I cannot help it. I know he sees it, but there is something in his gaze I am drawn to. It is not the look of a cruel man, I think, though time will tell if I am right or not. There is an intelligence to him, a curiosity even. I know that their aim is for me to confess. It is not enough to know a thing in order to prosecute. By law, they must have a signed confession to execute me. In this, at least, I have some say, though I know this is only a delay—they will find a way to kill me whether I speak or not.

"My name is Stefano Bracchi and you're here by invitation of the Holy Office of the Inquisition."

By invitation.

He continues, "You're being detained in the papal prisons because I've long suspected you're the woman they call *la Signora della Morte*, the one who makes a certain poison, which has been sold across Rome, and perhaps elsewhere in Italy, for many years now."

He pauses as the effect of his words sink in. It is as if he can read my mind, see my terror. There is no one in all of Christendom who would not fear being the guest of the Inquisition.

I hear a noise behind me. A man dressed full in black enters, carrying a large leather-bound book. Its pages are held shut by an ornate clasp.

Without looking in my direction, he sits at the back of the room. He opens this book. He coughs, then begins to turn the pages until he stops, finds his place and looks up, waiting for this to start.

He must be the notary, the man who will record this conversation. It will be filed as a record of this *inquisitio*, one that will be read maybe many years from now when this is reduced to a few scratchy words and blots of ink, and our lives will mean nothing more to its reader than any written story does. I almost break down at the thought of this. Somehow, this fading of life and hope and passion into yellowing parchment and blotched ink feels like a tragedy.

I think of my friends, of those women who have come to me. I think of the warm blood in their veins, the sweat on their skin, the laughter and sorrow on their lips. All that life, that hope and hunger for living. Will they stand here too? Will they be followed, captured, tortured, paraded, then murdered? Oh, I know how this story ends. I could almost grab the quill and write it myself in the notary's sheaf. Then, just as I am wondering where I would begin, I remember another book, a ledger, where all my secrets are hidden, where all our names are writ beside our remedies. I was foolish to keep it, incriminating us as it does. I do not know why I did not burn it when I left Palermo. It was the only tangible link to Mamma I had, so maybe it was not so surprising after all. Despite that, I realize that if they have it, I cannot protect my circle with my silence.

Almost as if this Bracchi official can read my mind, he picks something up from behind a pile of books. I feel the room begin to swim in front of my eyes. The sounds are strange. As he approaches, it is as if his footsteps are coming from far away. The room goes black.

I do not know how long I lie on the floor. When I pull myself out from my faint, nothing has changed. All is the same. Stefano Bracchi, this man who represents the most feared institution in all of Europe, is standing in front of me, looking down on me, not unkindly. In his hand is my ledger—my book of secrets. He holds out his free hand to help me up, but I refuse and crawl up from the floor where I have fallen. There is no sound except a roaring in my ears like the ocean surging.

"You'll place your hand on the Bible, and you'll swear to tell the truth. If you lie you imperil your immortal soul. Do you understand?"

I nod.

I place the flat of my shackled palms on the Bible, now held out to me by this man. The metal around my wrists is surprisingly heavy, and it is an effort to lift them. He holds this Bible in one hand, my ledger in the other.

I say the words. I swear to his God that I speak true. The words mean nothing to me, but he seems satisfied. He nods to the notary.

"We have this evidence of your crimes," Bracchi adds, almost as an afterthought.

I nod again.

He puts the Bible down on the table and opens the ledger. A page falls open and I see Girolama's childish writing, her first attempts at forming her letters, spelling out the name of a customer and the price paid. I could weep at the sight of it, but I hold myself steady, waiting for the next blow. It comes quickly.

"We have this book and it's a very helpful book. It contains the names of every customer of yours, what they paid or didn't pay, what they bought from you and those who supplied it. It contains the word *acqua*, which, if I'm informed correctly, is the name of your poison. Am I right?"

We are straight into the heart of the matter, then.

I say nothing. I do not acknowledge this. I do not blink. I remember to keep breathing.

The inquisitor nods.

He comes closer. I catch his scent—leather, incense, musk. His eyes are deep brown, his face is strong. Not in this lifetime, but another, perhaps.

"Giulia." He smiles as he says my name and I think suddenly of the padre. I wonder where he is, whether he managed to hide behind his noble family. I see the curl of black hair at this man's nape.

"Giulia, you can't fight this. You've fought for so long, I know you have. Your life is survival. It's hard but there's also been joy and peace in it. But you must understand, your road has ended, Giulia Siciliana. It has ended here, with me. You'll find peace again in another life if you trust in God Almighty, as I do, as we all do."

His voice is like liquid molasses, rich and sweet. I know I cannot trust this man. I am not some foolish girl whose head is turned by a fine jawline, a masculine physique, but in this moment, I wish I was.

"Make your confession, receive absolution. You can then receive the sacraments and return your soul to God."

I do not move. I do not say a word. My thoughts will not be revealed to him. I swallow with some difficulty, but I say nothing.

"Please, Giulia, you must help me. I don't want to hurt you, but I must order you to tell the truth. We must have your confession, the law demands it." His words sound like a caress now. He speaks softly as he holds my book—Mamma's ledger. It is all I have left of her. It is all I had left of her.

"I have nothing to say to you, Inquisitor," I say, my voice small though my head is held high, my back straight. There will be no more fainting fits. I feel strength flooding back to me. I remember who he is, what he stands for, whom he serves, and I pull myself up. If this man notices my new resolve, he says nothing.

"I'll ask you again. Please, I don't want to hurt you. I've watched your friend Giovanna since we released her. Do you know why I set her free, though I guessed straightaway the liquid she carried with her was your infamous poison?"

I look away. I say nothing.

"I'll tell you. Because I wanted to be sure that you were the woman we hunted. My agents had followed you—and others— for months but we had no real evidence, until Giovanna de Grandis was arrested, that is. I let her go. I reported to *Il Papa* that it was manna from the bones of San Nicola, just as you intended us to think. I wanted to give myself time to understand you, to know what it is that drives a murderess to commit these grave sins. I wanted your friend to lead us to you, even if I risked the lives of other men in doing this. But there was no new evidence, not for many months. You stopped your trade in poison, I think? You've been one step ahead of us for so long, Giulia, until now."

Still, I say nothing.

"Giulia, I know you. I know what moves you, what drives you forward. I know your mother died in Palermo at the hands

of the Spanish Inquisition. I know her legacy—and your vow—
has been to avenge her death. How do I know? I have a brain
to work this out. I've watched you and, I admit, I'm fascinated.
Please, tell me everything you know, tell me the names of every
woman who approached you and where they live, and I may be
able to help you."

His honeyed words drip and ooze but now I feel light as air.
There will be no information from me. There will be no kind
words that will tempt me. I stand here for the women of Rome,
and I will take their secrets, those not written in my ledger,
anyway, to my inevitable grave.

"I'll tell you nothing," I reply.

# 52

He steps toward me, a knife in his hand now.

The blade is clean, sharpened. As I inhale, he steps closer still until he is standing before me. The table of the room is still piled with sheaves of parchment covered in rows and rows of words and letters writ by a neat hand with black gall ink. The fire still smolders. When he moves, I flinch, but he only walks behind me, slowly, carefully. I can feel his breath on the back of my neck. He strokes my hair, his touch barely discernible, in a gesture of unimaginable intimacy. He grips a lock tighter. He pulls my neck back but only a little. Then, he cuts.

Thick waves of hair fall to the floor as he gently, gently slices through my long tresses. They fall in a blonde cloud at my feet. As I exhale, he strokes my neck, my shoulders, moving the hair off me as he continues to work until the blade is cold, stinging, against my scalp. I do not look down at the floor now. I cannot move. I am spellbound by my transformation at the hands of this man who is making me into a condemned woman.

The notary has stopped his scratching. The sounds from the river dissipate. There is only this moment, the slow removal of my flaxen hair, my greatest treasure, or perhaps not. Perhaps that title would go to my daughter, who will be cut down like my hair, leaving nothing of me behind at all. This thought sidles into the room and settles itself down, to be examined as the judge works. I have never before considered what it is I might leave behind, even that I might have something precious enough. The realization that it is too late arrives and settles down too. There will be nothing except the scribe's careful notes. There will be no record of the life I have lived except for these documents that will bring judgment upon me. I do not realize I am crying until the last of my hair has gone and I am shorn.

The governor walks round to face me. His expression is somber.

"I'm sorry for what I must do, Mistress Giulia," he says. He glances at the scribe, and the trembling quill is withdrawn from the parchment, held away from recording this most strange conversation. The inquisitor is apologizing to me, and yet it feels natural, as if we were both born for this tender scene, just like the *innamorati* in the square.

I do not answer. I cannot. I am floating in a place beyond words. My head feels faint, and I feel the salt itch of tears as they slide down my cheeks.

"I'm sorry, mistress," he says again.

This time, he puts the knife aside. He takes hold of the laces of my bodice. He tugs to release the first knots and then begins to unlace them. My breath is now a gasp. My heart thuds low and fast. There is a slow dance to his undressing of me. It takes a few jerks and the bodice is freed. I am invited to step out of my robe and, holding on to the inquisitor's hand, I let the fabric puddle on the floor. I stand in my *camicia*, holding his gaze.

He pushes my shift down to the floor, gently, leaving me naked in this room, in this place. There is a sigh in the air, a lament perhaps, or the wisp of desire. The silence is broken by the sound of Bracchi picking up his knife and walking back to me. He traces the scars that still run down my back.

"Stay still, Giulia, or I'll cut you," he says.

I wonder what he means but then I recall it is not just the hair on my head that will be removed. He kneels before me now, his face close to my body. I know what it is to desire a man. After Francesco, I declared I would love no one, but over the years, lovers have come and gone, though none have left me breathless as I am now. The blade is cold against my secret place. It glides, cutting away the hair only a lover may see. He moves slowly and I hear him breathing, feel it hot against my skin. The knife slips and I wince.

"I'm sorry," he says as he wipes away the blood.

Looking down, I can see he is using his own white linen shift to soak up the livid red cut. He staunches it and continues, this time a little slower. My breathing returns to normal, and I discover I feel no shame at being naked before two men I do not know. There is a power in it, the power of the earth and the trees, the oceans and rivers, where the heart of the natural world beats. I was born in a courtesan's chambers. I grew up in a palace harem. I am no shy, God-fearing maiden. I am blood and bone, nerve and gristle. I am the sky and the fields, the mountaintops and the curving bay. I am alive and, in this moment, I fear nothing.

As if knowing this, the notary looks away, but I see him glance back, now and then, when he thinks I am not looking.

"Look all you like, scribe," I say. My voice rings clear.

He looks up, startled, suddenly uneasy. I realize I have scored a victory when he turns away—and does not look back.

The inquisitor looks at my body with a lover's gaze, and yet he is preparing me, though for what? I have heard before that the *Inquisitori* strip their victims before the torture begins. They shave away the bodily hair and then the *afflitti*, the condemned, are ready to face the thumbscrew, the rope, the beatings and starvation. I wonder which method he will choose. It hardly matters.

Back in the cell, my beloveds crowd around me.

Maria seems better, more like her old self. She fidgets and pulls at her hair, but she is here now, not away somewhere with an imagined fairy king. She is shocked at the sight of me: bald, covered in a length of sacking, shivering, my hands now released from their manacles. Girolama's eyes are wide in shock, I imagine, for the dawning realization of what lies ahead for her, for them all. It is Giovanna who comes straight to me and places an arm around my shoulders.

"What did they do to you?" she says. Her eyes are wide, they search my face, my shaven head.

I shake my head. "Nothing, my old friend. They didn't put me to torture, though they kept the door to the chamber open so my eyes could see their tools. No, they did nothing except shave me and dress me in this . . ."

I could laugh at the absurdity of it all as I take hold of the sacking as if it were a fine gown and curtsy.

Giovanna and my daughter exchange a worried look.

"I'm fine, I promise. I haven't lost my mind, at least, not yet," I say and smile.

My heart feels light, I cannot deny it, as if a new path is emerging and I realize with relief it is one I am happy to walk.

"She's delirious," Girolama mutters darkly. "Sit, Mamma, take your rest."

"But what of Graziosa?" I say, ignoring her.

I see that our friend is floundering. She has become a hunched crone in the days and weeks she has been here. Fear has taken something vital from her, though I cannot be certain what it is. She scratches through the dirt looking for imagined crumbs. She whispers to the rats, to the stones and spiders, that she must be free. I can only feel pity for her now. Perhaps she is going somewhere beyond pain, beyond the physical, and if so, I am grateful for it. She is the elder among us. If anyone is to be spared the rack, I hope in my heart it is her.

There is now a constant, palpable feeling of dread. There are also more earthly concerns. The privy bucket is full to the brim, and I have to breathe through my mouth so I don't retch at the stink of it. There is the *squeak, squeak* of our rodent captives, those who enjoy dwelling in dark, dirty places. Perhaps we are like them after all.

"What happens now?" Giovanna says. Her hair hangs unwashed and greasy down her back. Her clothes are grimy, her skin filthy. She has lost weight—they all have, in the weeks they have been detained here. I can feel Girolama's ribcage as I hold her.

"They'll question us all now they have you," my daughter says. "They were waiting to capture you, or so they said." She turns her face to me.

There is nothing I can say, except the truth.

"Yes, they will."

There is a pause. From somewhere in the jail comes the sound of a woman wailing.

"They said they were going to kill you, and when you were dead they'd kill us too. They said our reign of terror is over and now we'll pay for our crimes. They said they'd drag our bodies through the dust . . ."

I feel a tight sensation in my throat and cannot find words to reply.

It is Girolama who breaks away from holding me. "You should've left Rome," she says. "You should've run far away from this. Now, you'll die a murderer's death with us all. You should've saved yourself."

I hold her proud face in my hands.

"Never would I leave you. This is our darkest hour, but we'll face it together."

"Then your heart is too big, Mamma, and you're a fool," my daughter says, and, together, we share a slow smile.

I may be a fool. I may be many things, but I am also a liar.

I do not tell my broken circle, my daughter and my friends, that the inquisitor has my ledger. I let them rest this night ignorant that the very evidence needed to damn us is sitting on the inquisitor's desk, and it will hang us all.

# 53

*Alessandro*

Most Noble and Beloved Mother,

How I wish I could command you down from Heaven to sit with me this evening. I have witnessed a most remarkable tale of sorcery and murder. I have heard from the very mouth of a duchess, a confession of the most heinous and grotesque manner.

This day, finally, I bestowed papal immunity on the Duchess of Ceri, Anna Maria Aldobrandini, a young widow with a most unsavory character and reputation. The supremacy of her birth as the great-grandniece of Pope Clement VIII has protected her from scandal since the sudden, and unexpected, death of the duke, and her hasty remarriage to Santinelli. Were it not for her family being one of the oldest, wealthiest, and most powerful in this kingdom, she would be languishing now in the papal dungeons with her co-conspirators.

You see, Mamma, questions were being asked about the duke's death even before her scandalous remarriage. The rumors carried across the city, whispering that the duchess had used a witch's brew to kill the husband she despised. The rumors magnified when she married her young lover, so that I was finally forced to act. I have waited months to question her. Bracchi urged me to do it for his Congregation on Crime— the trial that will scandalize the whole of Christendom. I could not! She may be foolish. She may be a murderess, but she is powerful and protected. I have had to tread carefully.

With great care and delicacy, I approached the Aldobrandini family. Naturally, I promised the noble-woman would not be held accountable for her crime, if indeed she had committed one. We arranged for the duchess to visit me privately. She came, penitent and shamefaced, as she should. Oh, Mamma, if you could have seen the young woman's face, hidden by a black veil as if she could hide her guilt that way! Dressed richly, her fingers jeweled, her neck heavy with pearls, she begged forgiveness from me for what she was about to say. She prostrated herself on the mar-ble floor. I held my hand out for her to kiss the papal ring and, while doing so, she lifted her eyes upward to meet mine.

To a mortal man, she has everything calculated to seduce and beguile the senses. Her eyes are large and her lashes thick. Her hair is dark and shining, her neck white and long. Her cheeks are rouged a deli-cate pink and her lips are full and sensuous. Even the marks left by smallpox do nothing to detract from her beauty. Any man would fall for the charms of this siren, this faithless Delilah, yet, to me, she is only ever a shadow of womankind standing in the glare of your sun, your majesty, Mamma. She could not enchant or beguile me, because the greatest of women holds my heart, though I am troubled nightly by imaginings, by memories of the woman with rippling hair and sea-green eyes.

I let her prostrate herself before me. I let her feel the coolness of the floor, the coolness of my attention.

Eventually, though, I allowed her to rise. She was humbled, I saw that, yet she had an abominable spirit that
seemed unquenched by her intolerable actions.

Once I reassured her that no punishment would
befall her, the truth fell from her lips and the nature of
her degraded soul was revealed to me. She insisted she
wanted to unburden herself of the truth. She told me
she confided in her confessor about her marital woes.
She told me the noble duke did not charm nor please
her. She said he was old, ugly, impotent. She told me
she fell in love with Santinelli and, as a woman, she
found her calling in worshipping this man, this upstart.
The duchess, tired of her marriage to the esteemed
duke, sought out the services of the Sicilian poisoner.
But how did she do this, Mamma? How did the highest
in the land meet with the lowest?

A certain Padre Don Antonio was her confessor.
Long have I heard whispers about this priest and his
unnatural practices. Long have I ordered his black
masses be hidden from scrutiny. He may be surprised
to learn that I have known all along that he performs
Satanic rites for those with coin enough to pay him.
Naturally, I could not expose the priest as his clients
who submit to the black masses held in their honor are
nobles. They are misguided, but they too are rich and
powerful. They too must be protected.

The beautiful duchess told me her confessor
assured her he could help her solve her "problem."
This siren pretended hesitancy. She said she was
afraid, but the priest reassured her none could uncover
her crime and her husband would die a good death,
in time to make confession and absolution. From the

tears running down the duchess's face, though partly
hidden by her veil, one might have thought she was
sorry. From the expression, the lament in her voice,
one might have thought she was full of regret. But,
Mamma, I could see no sorrow for the late duke. I
could see no real piety, no modesty, which is so prized
among womankind.

She told me the priest acquired the poison from *la
Signora della Morte*, the Sicilian. She said she did not
know where this woman lived nor where the poison
was made. Perhaps I believed her, perhaps not. It mattered little if she was lying. Perhaps she was protecting
the Sicilian in a conspiracy of the feminine, of women
filled with bile and hatred against their betters. Bracchi knew where the poisoner was. His sources led him
there. His spies had been following her. He picked up
the trail of this witch and saw her dealings. And then,
a woman came forward, the wife of a butcher. She confirmed the place where the potion was brewed, and its
ingredients, and so all the pieces fell into place—and a
trap was set. Our laws dictate we must have evidence to
convict both criminals and heretics. This is not Spain.
We do not assume guilt and tie them to the stake, fanning the flames beneath their feet.

I digress, Mamma, but my emotions run high. I
lost a friend, a cardinal to this witchery, though the
doctors assure me old age was responsible for Camillo's death. In my heart, I know the truth.

Anna Maria Aldobrandini fidgeted. She pulled at
the fabric of her silk gown. She wrung her hands, as
she confessed all to me, the conduit to God Almighty.
She confirmed every thought Governor Bracchi had.

During confession, the clear, tasteless poison contained within a small glass carafe was slipped into the duchess's hand by this priest. She told me it was but a small matter then to administer the *acqua*, away from the servers who taste the duke's food at every meal. Of course, the duchess would be privy to the working of her household, would be well placed to find a way to slip the poison into the duke's wine. She said her maidservant Lucia acted under her instructions, adding two drops to the duke's wine as they sat together one evening, eating an intimate meal. The serving girl will, naturally, be dealt with. She said that was enough to induce the first bouts of vomiting and fever. Then, as the duke's condition worsened, she refused to let the doctors come close. It was while she was pretending to nurse her husband, as any good woman must do, in his sick chamber, that the last two, fatal, doses were given. Within a week, the duke was dead.

The family begged me to keep the duchess's name out of the public investigation. For months, I let the Aldobrandini beg to save the duchess from both scandal and punishment. I let them plead with me, and when they had pleaded just enough, I granted it on the condition that their daughter of rank and fortune takes holy orders. This woman, who has in cold blood murdered her husband, will walk free and will repent her sins for the rest of her life within the arms of the Church once her new marriage is dissolved. It is a fitting, and dignified, end to this, the scandal that will shock all of Rome.

When the duchess had finished, she mopped up her tears. I thanked her and only then did I inform

her of her fate, her future, which had been decided
by myself with the approval of her family. She was
silent for a moment before standing up abruptly. She
curtsied, then turned and walked away. Her head was
high, Mamma, not at all like a woman humbled and
shamed. No thanks did she offer for her salvation.

Tonight, as I finish my long letter to you, as I prepare to blot it dry and then put it away carefully into a
cabinet that holds my letters to you, I take your handkerchief. I bring it to my cheek. I breathe in, knowing
there is little trace of you left, but hoping, always hoping, the scent of you might return. I will sleep with it,
with you, by my pillow.

Your most humble and obedient servant,
His Holiness Alessandro VII

# 54

*Giulia*

They say no one can withstand the *strappado* for long.
Bound by ropes, arms pulled behind the back and suspended by a rope attached to the wrists, the victim's weight
creates the torment, pulling their arms from their sockets. It
is an instrument of exquisite torture, and it has been used on
Giovanna. My dearest friend lies on the straw, her arms hanging lifeless and unmoving. Any movement causes her to wince and
groan. I stroke her forehead, still bloody from being shaved,
anger flowing through me like the lava from Etna, and yet I can
do nothing. Bracchi has revealed himself at last. He is not the
tender, reluctant questioner I met. He is a player on the stage
of this theater, an arch villain who hides behind the curtains.
He waits until the last moment to pounce onto the boards, glittering with malice and malignant ill fortune.

Giovanna whimpers. Every breath brings her an agony I
cannot mend, yet she has managed to speak a little. She tells
me Bracchi knows everything. He knows about the duchess.
He knows about Padre Don Antonio. He knows all our secrets
and yet the law says he must hear them from our own mouths.
My silence is my only power now, my only refuge from this
horror. It can serve only to obstruct their justice. It cannot save
my circle because they have the ledger and will force confession out of them. Yet, I will not speak. They will not have that
victory over me.

I imagine the notary scribbling down each word that was drawn from Giovanna's mouth as she screamed. Did he record the pain? Did he describe her cries in the pages of his transcripts?

"I told him we bought the arsenic to make cosmetics, to make skin-whitening creams . . ." Giovanna coughs and goes silent as if these few words are too much.

"Shhhhh. Save your strength to endure this, my friend," I say through cold lips, knowing the price of her lies. "He's a monster. Bracchi's a devil. I'd kill him with my own hands for hurting you." As I say the words, I am trembling with rage. "I wish I'd taken your punishment. This is all my doing. It's *my acqua*. It should've been me."

It occurs to me that perhaps this *is* my punishment. Perhaps Bracchi does know me as he says he does. Perhaps he has seen into my heart and understands I would rather face torture alone than watch my beloved circle suffer. I see he is a clever man, cleverer than perhaps I realized. I have underestimated the Holy Office of the Inquisition.

"This isn't your doing." Giovanna turns her head to me. She reads my thoughts too. Tears stream down her face.

"It is, it is! It was I who taught you the recipe. It was I who told you we could never be caught as long as our clients held their tongues! It was I who showed you how to brew the liquid. This is all my fault. I've never asked you, Giovanna. Why did you join me in this enterprise? Why did you come with me to Rome? You could've stayed in Naples, working as a midwife and living a good life."

"I chose to stay with you when you left," Giovanna rasps. "By then, you and Girolama were my only family. As for the poison . . . I was weary of the misery I saw, the broken women and their impoverished children. I was weary of trying to help but knowing I could do nothing. It wasn't a big step, moving into your world, learning your craft. I already knew herb lore, and so this side of it was a natural part of that knowledge. Besides, I knew what it was to be betrayed by a man, to have your heart and hopes crushed. I'd had three husbands before I was nineteen, and only one of them I chose. He broke my heart, he cheated and took everything I had. The *acqua* was my salve, too . . ."

Giovanna breathes with difficulty. Her face is twisted with pain, while her arms hang limp from her dislocated shoulders on the filth of the floor. I don't dare touch them or try to fix her, and so, instead, I trace a single teardrop, gently, down my friend's pale face. Her eyes are dull, her hair lank, her skin bruised, but she is beautiful to me, even now.

"Hush, *amore mio*. Hush and save your strength. We don't know what may lie ahead."

"Giulia, don't look so sad. I wasn't free to walk my own path, until I met you. See? I knew what I was doing and, like you, I find I regret little, though we gave false hope to the women we helped. We told them a better world was possible. We helped women kill their husbands or lovers so they might find the freedom that we yearned for. We gave them hope, and that's the cruelest thing of all, because there's no freedom for women. We scrabble for our dignity, we beg for our pride and no one . . . no one is ever listening."

I watch my friend sink her head back down to the floor—spent. Girolama is squatting next to us, but until now she has stayed silent.

"When the marchesa hears of our capture, they'll pay for this," she says.

"The marquess?" I say, at first confused, then her meaning dawns on me. "Oh, you mean your noble friends? They're long gone! They won't save you, or any of us. No one has friends when they're inside the Inquisition's dungeons." I remember words spoken to me many years ago by Valentina. My heart lurches in my chest. It hardens.

"They will! When they realize what's happened, they'll rescue us! I've told the guards to watch their backs."

"And what do the guards say?" I ask.

Here, my daughter drops her fierce gaze. "They laugh. They're idiots and they'll pay for their ill treatment of us. When Paolo comes . . ." Girolama stops. It is as if she has heard her own words at last.

"My love—" I start to say.

She stops me. "Don't, just don't." She gets up, walks to the wall, her face a picture of anguish. "They'll come," Girolama says, eventually, but her voice shakes.

I look over to the corner where Graziosa scratched in the dirt. They took her this morning and she is still not back from questioning.

"We must pray our friend's still alive, or if not, has passed to a better place," I say.

Girolama looks back at me, and we exchange a strange look, realizing I have wished for the death of a friend. This place seeps into the soul like dank river water through the stones in winter. It draws out every bit of unhappiness and fear held within. It has a character all of its own. It is more than the stage we walk across and within, it is the whole world, and like a creature from the deepest seas, it encircles us, pulling us ever further down into its watery depths.

At dusk, Graziosa reappears. She is carried to the cell by two jailers who grunt and curse as they throw her to the ground.

Girolama, Maria, and I run over. What is left of her lies crooked and broken.

"She's been racked," Girolama says, her voice reflecting the horror I feel.

Graziosa's breath is shallow; her eyelids flutter, then close. She is halfway to death already.

"Perhaps she can't feel anything? Perhaps she's gone beyond pain, God rest her soul," my irreligious daughter says.

"They've done this to an old, defenseless woman to warn us. They're sending us a message. They're showing us what they'll do to us if we don't talk—or perhaps even if we do."

Light slants through the small window high in the walls of our jail in the shape of the bars across it. Outside, there is the commotion from the river—bargemen shouting, passengers cursing, the slap, slap of the water against the thick stone walls.

# 55

The next day, it is my turn again.

"It doesn't matter what you do to me," I say, as if we are speaking as friends in the market or the tavern. "I'll never confess. You may break every bone in my body. You may tear off every nail from my fingers. You may strip me, beat me, whip me, but I'll never give you what you require. I'll die before I say anything."

I meet his gaze. He has the decency to blush a little and look away. He is a handsome man. He has a presence about him that I cannot find repulsive, and yet he has inflicted torture upon my friends, and so naturally, I despise him. Strangely—and perhaps this is an echo of my old intuition—I also sense his humanity. He is intrigued by us. I presume he could have killed us all a long time ago, and yet he did not.

"Why didn't you arrest us months or years ago, when your spies first encountered us? I'm assuming the small boy, the urchin, was one of your network? I'm enough of a fool to have tried to help him. And there was the woman who approached me while the duke's body was laid out. I recognized the stench. It was the piss she used to soak dirty linens. She'd followed me too, hadn't she?"

Again, this feels like an intimate conversation, not at all like an interrogation.

He smiles, and I see his teeth are white against his olive skin.

"Giulia Siciliana, I admit I knew of you—or at least, of your poison—for a long time. The plague hid your business well, but not well enough. Women began talking in the confessional about a liquid that could kill a man in four drops. Surgeons reported to me strange deaths where the men, always men, looked radiantly alive, and yet they were lying dead on the mortuary slab. It was then I knew we had a new foe in our midst. Silent and fast-acting, leaving no trace. For many months, we were puzzled, looking for this assassin, this maker of poison. Meanwhile my spies picked up the scent.

"I suspected you had a hand in the Duke of Ceri's death, but still no proof, except for the single vial of your *acqua* from the abortionist de Grandis. I thought the same about Cardinal Maretti. But when my agents came to question the prostitute who names herself Celeste de Luna, they discovered she'd vanished. Run away, taking her secrets with her."

"What's all this to me?" I say.

He glances over. Continues as if this is another pleasant interlude. "More and more priests came to me with stories of women buying poison. More and more surgeons wrote to me with news of unusual deaths. Always men. Always looking healthier than in life. I knew if we found you, we would find the heart of this matter.

"When the pope commanded his people to inform against you, the tide turned in our favor. Your clients were loyal to you, Giulia, until, finally, they weren't. Of course, you led us to many of them, and we'll arrest them all in time, but I admit, I wanted to see what you would dare to do, where you would dare to tread. I was the cunning cat, biding my time, and you were the mouse, scuttling around the dirt floor . . ."

He pauses for a moment, takes a breath.

I feel faint. My head spins.

"Perhaps I should've captured you earlier, but I admit, I enjoyed watching you, Giulia. You're unlike any woman I've ever met before."

I look over at him.

We are back in the same room as before. This time the hearth is empty. The door lies open so I can see the rope, the pulley, the possibility of what is to come. The desk is piled high. The notary scribbles. My ledger sits on the desk in full view, and it is open. I do not recognize this page, but I see my own handwriting. I have to squint as the light, though not bright here in the back of the prison, feels harsh after the darkness below.

"Why did you do it?"

The words finally untangle themselves. I experience a new sensation, as if none of this is really happening. Perhaps it is the contrast of the warmth and sunlight to the dark chill of the dungeons below.

If I could, I would say I chose freedom, but this amounts to a confession, and so I don't. I remain silent.

He raises an eyebrow.

He stands, leaning his back against the table. I am opposite him, alone, also standing. One step forward and I would be close enough to feel his breath on my skin; another step and I could touch him. The notary coughs. The quill scratches, then falls silent, the line complete.

What happens now?

Will he drag me into the torture chamber, or does he rely on others to do it for him? How did he do it with Giovanna and Graziosa? Does he get his hands dirty?

Eventually, Bracchi runs his hands through his thick black hair. He looks like a man, if not tormented, then challenged. I guess the cause. He has to interrogate me. He has to instruct his officers to force confession from me, yet he finds he cannot. Perhaps he sees me as a woman rather than a witch. I cannot be sure. He says nothing, but I take it as a small victory on my part. But how long will it last?

"You're an intelligent woman. You know you couldn't have hoped to get away with your trade forever. Your own mother was executed as a witch and poisoner. Your own mother slayed her husband with the same mixture! Were you so desperate to follow in her footsteps?"

This inquisitor moves suddenly, and for a moment I think he will strike me. Instead, he moves round to his desk and clasps the back of his chair.

Mamma's face flashes in front of my eyes. Then, I see her kneeling before the executioner; large red hands around a small neck.

I feel dizzy. Dust motes swirl in the air between us.

"I won't give you a confession, Inquisitor. There are many reasons why a woman might do the things you accuse me of, but I won't share them with you. My secrets will remain my own. They're not yours to discover."

I stare back at him, defiant.

He blinks. Then he sighs, and I wonder if now is the time.

He glances over to the door behind me and shouts out, "You may bring her in."

# 56

For a moment I do not recognize her, but when she scowls, the face of the butcher's wife is revealed to me. She marches in, appearing unfazed by her invitation to appear before the Holy Office of the Inquisition.

"You know each other." It is not a question.

I turn my gaze to her. She looks drawn, though I sense an eagerness, too. I turn away.

"I don't know this woman," I say.

"She's lying. This is the hag they call the Mistress of Death, the mother of the sorceress Girolama. She supplies the *acqua*."

I look at her again. Her eyes gleam.

"Madonna, you're mistaken," I say and cast my eyes downward. My head throbs. I have an intense thirst, making it difficult to swallow.

"She's lying through her teeth!" the woman, whose name still evades me, says. "I saw her many times at Mass at Santa Maria sopra Minerva. My friends told me not to go near her because she's a *strega* and a poisoner! I saw her deal her wicked potion to many women. I never bought it from her, though she tried to sell it to me. But I was too afraid to say anything."

I look over at the inquisitor. He knows as well as I do that there is a listing in my ledger, though it does not state her name. He knows as well as I do that she is lying, and he is hoping that I will help him prosecute her by telling him about our dealings. But I will not do that. I have not spent my life protecting the women that come to me, however disagreeable, by spilling it all now. I say nothing. I will say nothing until the moment my neck meets the noose.

"I've nothing to say about this woman. I've never met her before."

I wonder what this butcher's wife gains by trying to implicate me. Is she hoping that by doing so they may look leniently upon her now that she has given them this information? I do not know. I do not care. Exhaustion, fear, hunger has left me empty, hollowed out like a dying tree.

The inquisitor speaks. His voice is languid, sanguine, utterly calm.

"And yet, this woman who stands here before us, whom you say is a stranger to you, knew where you kept your poison. She was able to tell us where the key to your secret cabinet was hidden, and what you kept in there. It was this woman who led us to the vials of *acqua*. Yet still, you deny knowing her."

So, the Sight had not failed me. It came to me when I met this woman, and now I know why. She was destined to betray us. When Giovanna was first arrested, Bracchi may have had my potion and suspected it was the poison he was seeking but he had no way of linking it to me, to us. This butcher's wife became that link. She led inquisitors to my shop, to my sanctuary, and in doing so, she broke the bonds of womanhood. She betrayed us all—and this is why I was warned away from her.

I shake my head, though it is all clear. Even knowing this. Even knowing how I disregarded the Sight to help her, I find I hold no anger toward her. I have no desire to implicate her and tell the truth. It is enough that we are caught. Let those who can flee do so, whether culpable or not.

"I say nothing, Inquisitor."

I lift my gaze now to his. The shrew speaks, oblivious to this dance between us.

"I was a respectable wife, and I'm now a grieving widow. He was a virtuous man, a good man. He treated me well. I had no complaint of him, which is why I didn't approach this woman for her services."

Her lies flow from her lips. She killed her husband, and she gave my potion to her sisters so they may do the same. And now, it seems, she cannot stop talking.

"I've had many ask for my hand since he passed, but my feelings of loss prevent me from entering marriage again so soon."

She looks satisfied, perhaps pleased with her performance. I am reminded of Colombina smirking behind her hand as the falsehoods rolled from her tongue. I stare at the judge, as if to say, *Look, we all know why we're here. You want me to finish the scene with a confession, with drama and mayhem. You want this woman dragged to the cells to join me and my sisterhood. Well, know this, Inquisitor, I won't do it. I'll tell you lies and you'll have them recorded in your book, but lies they will remain.*

I can see we are of one accord. He knows my thoughts just as I am starting to know his. He will have to dismiss this lying wench, and his prison will have one fewer resident tonight.

Stefano Bracchi sighs. He wrinkles his brow. He strokes his chin. Finally, he summons a guard, and the woman is led away. She throws me a sharp look as she goes, still grumbling.

But the inquisitor is not finished with me. I sense the climax of the play approaching. The curtains are raised and are about to fall. He claps his hands and a man lumbers in. This time he has a large dead dog in his arms. The dog must have expired days since; I can already smell the decay.

As if this is the finale, Bracchi reaches for a vial. I recognize it as one of my own. The saint is there, the colorless liquid inside, though the vial is empty. It might be the one confiscated from Giovanna when she was released, or it could be the one taken when she was caught in his trap. It might also be one they found in my cabinet. Again, I find I care little for the details of my case.

He had hidden it behind his pile of papers. His interminable pile of confession, of evidence, of lives that will end at the pope's command.

"You know what this is. I won't trouble myself to explain except to say that we found this on the person of the woman known as Giovanna de Grandis when we lured her to a noblewoman's villa to arrest her in the act of selling it."

So, he waited until the trap was sprung to test my poison. A curious lapse of judgment. Again, I do not care, except to realize that this lapse has given us time, has probably kept us alive for longer than I care to recall.

"De Grandis told us it was to remove blemishes. She told us it was to whiten the complexion. I didn't believe her. I administered several drops on to the meat fed to this dog. It was kept in one of our cells for the experiment. The next day the dog was breathing with difficulty and had vomited up his meal. So, I laced another bowl of meat with more of the potion. Each time the cell was opened, the dog's suffering had increased. I opened the cell door myself and found his body lying by the untouched bowl. Proof that your *acqua* is deadly. Proof that your concoction is lethal to animals and humans alike. What say you, mistress?"

With difficulty, I turn my head away from the stricken creature, my heart swollen with grief for the torments it had suffered. But it changes nothing.

"I say nothing, Inquisitor."

# 57

*Alessandro*

Most Noble and Beloved Mother,

The *interrogatio* has begun.

The net has been cast. The haul has been dragged in, struggling against the pull. Those trapped inside are finally facing holy justice. There is a sweetness to this day—a victory emerging. Though they wriggle and twist, the poisoners and their clients are beginning to talk. The evidence is being collated. The time of their reckoning is approaching.

I break off, put down my quill briefly. I breathe Rome's air as if all of it is mine.

Today, I go to the prison to cast my eyes upon the witches that have terrorized Rome, to hear their confession. I will hide my identity. I will see them as a man looks upon the evil of women. I will rejoice in the work of the Lord.

Mamma, I will write more tonight, once I have, like Daniel, stepped inside the lion's den. I await God's angel, closing the mouth of the beasts, bringing divine protection to us all.

The odor of the jail is the first thing to hit me. Human waste, blood, sweat—an unimaginable mixture of evil odors. I hold a fine silk handkerchief to my nostrils as if this would prevent the stench from reaching them. Then, the sight of the condemned as they bark and snarl like the beasts they are, reaching through the bars in the doors to their cells, like imps from the flames of hell. The air is sour. The noise of their groaning and crying echoes through the chambers.

"Stay back, Your Holiness," says Governor Bracchi, striding before me. The flagstones are slippery. I am careful with each step, and so I drop behind. The inquisitor has to stop and wait for me, my borrowed cloak dragging in the filth.

Then, we reach the monsters' lair, the cell holding our witches. There are guards outside the doors. There are bars on the windows, but I wonder if it is enough to hold them and their devilry.

As if reading my thoughts, Bracchi says, "There's no escape, for either a mortal woman or one using sorcery. There's no way out except through this door, and it's guarded night and day. Your Holiness, did you still wish to see them?"

He peers at me, as if he senses the terror that has seized me. It is so profound, so deep, I almost turn and flee. Yet, I cannot. I am God's representative on earth. I must find the courage to continue.

"Your Holiness?"

"I'm quite well, lead me to them," I say though my throat constricts. I pull the cloak I am wearing over me, hiding my robes, and hence, hiding my status and position. I am not worried they will recognize me. I am a distant figure when I take Mass or look down on the crowds that gather each Sunday from the balcony of my apartments. Without those symbols of the papacy—the liturgical vestments, the cap and cross—I am reduced. Without them, I am just a man.

Bracchi opens the cell door. There is an old woman lying on the straw, her mouth open, her eyes glazed, and I wonder for a moment if she is dead. There is another who lies close by, propped up against the stone walls that run with moisture. She is breathing, but her face is set into an expression of pain. I saw it on my mother's face when she was close to death.

As I wonder how Bracchi can tolerate this proximity to those he interrogates, there is a whooping noise from the corner. I see a strange creature, surely a messenger from Satan. She babbles and fidgets, pulling at her hair, which appears to be decorated with shells and other strange adornments. I step back, revulsion overcoming me. A rat runs underfoot.

There are two women standing. One is shorn, the other has long black hair. For a moment, they do not move. I am panting now with the heat of my cloak and the fear that engulfs me. Never before have I been so close to evil. Never before have I been so close to the clutches of the devil. The one with dark hair spits onto the filth-strewn straw. Then, the other turns.

Though her hair is hacked off, her scalp smeared with dried blood, I would recognize her anywhere.

It is her.

It is the woman who looked up at me from the precincts of the basilica. Though it is dark and wretched in here, the color of her eyes startles out from her face. They are the color of the ocean. They are green and clear like water.

I stumble back, my courage failing me.

My nights have been plagued with thoughts of her, with sinful, lustful thoughts of this woman, the hair she used to have, the eyes that stare back at me now. I have been bewitched. I have been seduced and used by a witch. The room starts to spin as I recoil.

I see Governor Bracchi turn to me.

He takes my arm, signals to another officer, and together they remove me from this den of sin. Perhaps I am delirious, but I hear myself cry out.

Bracchi shouts an order.

"The Holy Father is unwell. Call a physician!"

# 58

*Giulia*

The man inside the black cloak was familiar to me.

He walked in with Bracchi, a churchman come to take confession, or so the inquisitor said. His thin, angular face, his mustache, his small, manicured beard, was visible in the gloom of the cell. Our eyes met, and I knew he was someone to me—an enemy, perhaps.

The buzzing came with force. A sting from a thousand bees. A buzzing that swooped down into my head, and yet I was sure we had never met before. He fell back, overcome by the squalor, and something else. I saw it in his eyes, though we were caged together for the briefest moment. I saw a man who had risen high. I saw an eagle slicing through the air, wings flapping as its talons reached down to pluck its supper from the grass. But who was the eagle, and who the prey?

As he fell, he threw out his hand and I saw the ring. A heavy gold ring, far too valuable for most clergy, with an insignia I'd seen before: six mountains, and above them a star.

I turned away as Bracchi and the churchmen left, knowing what would happen next. I had felt it in the air. I had felt the feathers that spanned my wings tip and splay as I rose into the sky. I knew who he was. After all, the *tarocchi* had warned me all along. They had seen him coming.

# 59

*Alessandro*

Mamma,

I cannot eat. I cannot sleep. I am beset by terrors of the cruelest kind. Your face—or is it hers?—comes to me when I try to rest. Your eyes—except now they are hers—stare back at me from the mirror.

This woman defies my authority, and that of the Church and State. She will not speak. Every day she is alive and refusing to confess is another day this witch stalks the earth, bringing mortal terror. Bracchi insists he should continue, this time with the methods he has used on her coven, but I have ordered him to bring forward the execution. The spell must be broken. Her death is the only way I can be free.

God give me strength to act as a pope because I cannot as a man. She has robbed me of my reason and courage. She has used witchcraft and sorcery upon me. For why else would I be in such pain? Why else would I suffer these longings?

The governor came to me after the physicians had pronounced me well in body and mind, declaring the foul airs of the prison as the reason I stumbled. I waved them away and turned to the man entrusted with upholding holy law. This is what he said:

"Giulia Siciliana refuses to speak. Is it Your Holiness's will that I proceed to other, more persuasive methods?" Bracchi faltered. I sensed a hesitation. "We have confessions from three of the women: Maria Spinola, Graziosa Farina, and Giovanna de Grandis. There's enough evidence to hang them, yet the Sicilian will not speak, and so we will question her daughter next." Bracchi said all this as he knelt at my feet, his head bowed so I could not see his expression. "Your Holiness, in Roman law, we can't prosecute without confession, unless an exception is made . . ."

I nodded. I am aware of our laws. I am also aware that I can override them with a papal decree.

I stood up. I walked to the apartment window. I looked out over the hills of Rome, the basilicas, the bells, the tiled roofs and trees, the glistening Tiber moving in and out of view. I knew I could not instruct Bracchi to rip her apart with his torture implements, and it surprised me. I have hunted her. I have thought of that moment, her capture and trial, with restrained eagerness. Now it is here, and I find I do not have the stomach for it. I want her dead, and I want it done swiftly. Yet this weakness surprises me. If you were beside me, Mamma, you would have no hesitation in calling for their tongues to be forced to talk. You were ever a woman of virtue, of belief that could not be shaken by simple human impulses. Yet, you are not here. You will never stand beside me again, and I alone must decide what happens next.

Sometimes, I wonder if I could slip away, find the edges of the river, fill my pockets with stones. Each step into the water bringing me closer to you. Each step, down into the waving riverbed, sinking into thick silt, would send me to you. A mortal sin. An unforgivable crime against God. A child's longing for his mother.

Keeping my face turned to the view so that Bracchi did not see my indecision, I said, "The poison-makers show an abominable spirit, a contempt for righteousness, a despicable disdain of all that is holy."

I saw her face as she turned to me in her cell: the dirt-smudged cheeks made hollow by hunger, the green eyes that pierced my flesh and my soul, the refusal to bend to my command, the tenderness of a sackcloth gown and bare feet amid the cold, the dirt, the filth.

I drew breath. I prayed, and that is when the words came to me.

"This Giulia Siciliana displays an obstinacy and outspokenness that means she would withstand the strappado, and as such make mockery of the method. I fear her daughter will show the same refusal to talk, though question her if you must. Given the enormity of their crimes, I will issue a decree, one that will expose them to the usual punishment of hanging, even without confession. What is sure is that they will all die."

It was as much as I could say. I have been bewitched and so she must die. Why is it so hard, then, to say these words?

Mamma, sometimes I hate you for leaving me.

# 60

*Giulia*

When they take Girolama, I draw the cards I smuggled into the jail in the secret purse of my skirts.

Knowing they would take them off me, I hid them under stinking straw before they stripped me and replaced my robe with sacking. I wait for my daughter's cursing—her shouting for Paolo who will never come, for her illustrious friends who have abandoned her too, her flailing and biting—to die away, then I reach for them. The deck speaks to me as if our conversation has never stopped, only drifted away until this moment. I lay them face down on the damp stone floor. I stroke their aging tattered surfaces, and, like a breeze drifting in from the orange groves of Palermo, they whisper, they call to me.

When I turn over the chosen tarot, I am surprised.

I was expecting the skeleton figure of *La Morte*, Death, the black shapes of ravens circling, cawing overhead.

Instead, I gaze upon a woman with long hair the color of wheat, adorned simply in a blue gown. In her left hand, held aloft, she holds a star.

*La Stella.*

I wonder if the spirits that dance and skip around these messengers are laughing at me. I wonder if the cards themselves have run mad, this place sapping their powers too.

*La Stella.*

An optimistic card. A card of divination, of secrets and wonder. A card of light overcoming darkness, of reaching upward into the heavens, of coming through great troubles and seeing hope and radiance at the end. It is a card of alignment of body and mind, a card of hope, faith and trust. I understand nothing. I can see no future, no cycle of life in this toothless platitude. Yet, this card says something of intuition and magic, and reassures that divinity is behind all that passes, and will ever come to pass.

The Star.

Why does it visit me in these, my final hours?

Puzzled, I scrabble the cards together quickly as a guard approaches with the day's bread and wine rations, though none are meant for me. I have discovered the inquisitor's punishment and it is starvation—that and the cruelties he inflicts upon my beloved friends. I barely register hunger anymore. My head has taken on a lighter, empty feeling, which is not unpleasant, and I am comforted—oddly—by the reading.

Many hours later, Girolama returns. I see they have not harmed her. She holds her shaven head high, though she too wears sacking instead of her silk skirts now, and is barefoot.

"Whoreson! God give you ill fortune!" My daughter has a fine voice. She curses at the guard who scowls but does nothing more. Even he, it seems, is cowed by Girolama's rage. "You're a devil and a dog whore!"

I cannot help raising my eyebrows. I did not raise my daughter to throw around profanities like a sailor, though it amuses me now.

"They didn't put you to torture," I say, holding a cup of water to Graziosa's mouth, leaning her head up gently from where she lies, dribbling and muttering. I break a piece of the stale bread and soak it in the liquid until it is a mush so I can attempt to feed her. "Graziosa, you must eat. Can you hear me, old friend? You must eat—"

"Leave her," says Giovanna, who has at least recovered her senses, if not her movement. "She's beyond our help."

Even Girolama pauses as we look at the woman who lies in the dirt, her olive skin sallow and bruised, her breathing shallow. Outside, a river rat squeaks, a cat pounces.

I am roused to temper suddenly. No one will save us. We have helped so many over the years, and no one will come. I feel desperately sad for my daughter, for us all. The humiliations, the dirt, the sleeplessness and terror have taken their toll. I want to die, and quickly, that much becomes clear to me now. I have lived with too many secrets for too long, and I am tired of it all. There is nothing except the void, as the Sight has told me. This time, I listen to it.

"Did you confess?" It is Giovanna who speaks. Her voice is thin, reedy.

My daughter turns to her and rushes over to stroke our beloved friend's face.

"I didn't, Giovanna. I spat at them as they cut off my hair. I swore and fought them. They needed three men to hold me down," she says, and I cannot help but smile. "It would take more than the strappado to open my mouth, and I told them so."

"Then you're fortunate that they believed you," our friend replies.

Girolama looks shamefaced as she realizes what she has said. Graziosa coughs and moans. Her eyes flutter as if she can hear us.

"Shh, save your breath," I say. I place Graziosa's head gently back down on the straw.

"Then, we neither have confessed," my daughter says, now enlivened. "This means we won't hang. The law requires confession!"

Giovanna and I exchange a glance, just as if we are tutting over my wild daughter's sayings or actions in the still room. But we are not in the still room now. We are far from our spices; our herbs and plants; our remedies, tinctures, and essences. We are far from our home, our sanctuary, our safety. This time I speak softly. "They'll hang us all, daughter. They'll find a way. You must adjust yourself to this. You must adapt, as we all must." Girolama opens her mouth as if she will sting me with a retort, and then closes it again. Perhaps she finds there is nothing to say. We fall into silence. Someone close by groans. Another bangs something metallic against the bars of a cell door. There is a flurry of activity from the river, a wedding party perhaps on their way to their celebrations. Shouts of glee and catcalling ring over the waters. Meanwhile, we are like statues as the enormity of our plight comes home to its nest, as it glides downward to where acceptance is waiting, where Death is waiting.

# 61

That night, I have a dream.

I am fourteen years old and sitting in the lavender-scented gardens of Francesco's villa in Palermo. The sun scorches. My Bible lies unread, wilting in the heat.

I watch as my mother walks slowly toward me, singing softly as she comes. Her beauty surprises me, as it always does, always did. She plucks a rose, picking its petals off as she comes closer, her song growing louder, pale pink petals drifting languidly to the ground as she crunches the gravel underfoot.

Before I can speak, the scene changes. A ship is leaving harbor, and I am running as fast as I can toward it. I am seized by the knowledge that I am meant to be on that boat, heading out toward the horizon. I know I am in great danger if I do not get on board, yet my legs feel heavy, and heavier with each step; my wet skirts drag downward, more weighted with each movement. I know I cannot make it to the edge of the port in time. I feel sure I am shouting and waving but they do not see me. The captain turns away; the rigging, the sails, the ropes all engaged to move forward and onward, leaving me behind on the harbor wall. The spray from the sea is like a fine mist; the wind lashes my hair.

Then, I am inside the still room of the convent, and Mamma is there. Sister Clara scowls, then disappears as if she is a phantom. There is a quarrel. I am shouting again and now I am running, running, panting.

Francesco's face veers up and I am captured. The scourge appears, as does Mamma, and there is blood, so much blood. I know I am moaning but there is more to come.

The dream turns into something else: a visitation perhaps, a memory of what took place many years ago. It forms itself—swirling into being—and I see myself creeping into Francesco's chamber. It is dark, the household silent. A dog barks in the street. I tread lightly, my skirts brushing the marble floor as I walk to my stepfather's rooms, though I wince from the pain of my injuries. The door creaks as I open it. I freeze, but no one comes. Inside my gown, I have a pocket, and in this hidden place is a small glass vial. The vial contains a colorless liquid, and when the dough is eased from the neck of the bottle, there is no odor to speak of. Just a few drops, yet my hand is shaking. I look back toward the doorway, expecting him to burst in, yet still, no one comes.

I pour too much. The wine in its vessel has taken all the liquid, and there is nothing I can do to remedy it. Trembling, I place the vial carefully inside a piece of linen and bury it in my folds of silk, taking care that none of the liquid touches my skin. It is done. Hardly able to breathe, I back away from the wine and his goblet, laid out for his pleasure tomorrow. Each footstep takes me farther away from my crime. I click shut my door, and fumble in my large chest, wrapping the vial in another piece of linen, a cloak I think, hiding it at the bottom. Teeth chattering, heart thumping, I pull back my linen sheet and slip inside, not caring that I am still fully dressed.

Then, back in the dreaming, I see the boy urchin's face, the one with the sores on his skin. He grins. His teeth are white, his face grubby, and I wonder if I always knew he was the inquisitor's spy. This time, he lets me dab salves on him, though still he grins, still he hisses: *strega*.

The rotten smell of the river drifting in awakens me from this nightmare, these visions. Then, the sudden squawk of a night bird. I lie awake, remembering how my mother died for me, for my crime, remembering I am a murderess in truth.

# 62

## Alessandro

Mother, they die today.

Mother, these wicked women will pay for their crimes, and all shall witness the glory of the Church and State. I will breathe the air of the city, the heart of God's empire, knowing it is mine, all mine.

I have ordered a stage be built in Campo de' Fiori upon which the gallows will sit, so that all may watch, just like a theater, just as if it is the final scene of a great play. I have ordered the transcripts of the investigation be locked away in the papal dungeons of Castel Sant'Angelo, never to be opened except with my written approval, so nobody may learn the method of making this poisonous potion. The recipe will remain a secret, buried in the past.

I have ordered the pages of *la duchessa's* testimony remain unnumbered so they may be removed from the notary's transcripts, so there may be no trace left of the history of her dealings in sorcery and poison. Likewise, with the priest Padre Don Antonio. His part in this tragedy will not be written. I am told by his family he died of a fever and is buried in the family vault, and so he will lie undisturbed by the tides and swells of history. No one can know that the Catholic Church harbors occultists and criminals.

Mother, I clutch your handkerchief and hope for the scent of you, the floral musk haze that surrounds my memories of you, that will always remind me of you. There is little trace beyond the odor of age and dust, but I never stop trying to find you. One day, when it pleases God to release me from this mortal body, I shall rise to Heaven's gates and I shall find you. With love and reverence, I leave you now. The candle is lit. The flame leaps. The heat is stifling as I sit alone, as I think of you, as my heart yearns for you. Every night, I pray to be reunited with you. I lie against my coffin that still waits under my bed and I beg our Lord to take me to you.

Mamma, I will pray for their souls. I will pray for mine. I will pray that the torment of your absence is relieved by God Almighty for I cannot do it, I cannot do it. Thoughts of you remain, though it is she who torments me, the devil who stole my peace, who almost toppled my reign.

It is many days since I last purged the longing I feel for her from my body and soul with the whip, but I know, tonight, I will be subject to its cruel mercy. The scourge awaits me in its drawer. The blood upon it, dried and brown, will mix with my living blood—yet it does not cure. It does not heal. It merely quiets the calling, the longing, the sinful love I bear for her still.

Alessandro

# 63

July 5, 1659

*Giulia*

They come for us before dawn. I am awake, though the others are still dreaming fitful dreams.

We are ordered by the jailers to rise, then dress, then walk. Girolama half-carries Graziosa, while I help Giovanna. Maria stumbles behind us, humming. They have spared her the worst of their torture methods, except the *sibille*, a rope tightened around her fingers until she said whatever they needed her to say. Maria's mind wanders and ambles somewhere else, somewhere away from this place. We have tried asking her about Celeste de Luna, whether she stole the *acqua*, whether she gave it to the courtesan, but she says nothing that makes any sense, except the name of her long-dead daughter. She trills and sings like a songbird and so we leave her to her madness. We none of us know what she muttered in the ears of the inquisitors— whom she implicated, what secrets she may have spilled— but again, it is of no matter. They were always going to end it this way.

We are taken to the chapel of the prison. It is dark, though a candle is lit on the altar. Footsteps ring on the flagstones as we arrive, and we turn to see the hooded figures of a line of men walking toward us. Each holds a candle that appears to hover in the darkness. Each throws a ghoulish light, casting the shadows of their features upward. Their heads are lowered, and when they stop, one of them steps forward to speak.

"We are a confraternity of noblemen. We, as a brotherhood, are here to help you repent your sins and prepare for a good death. We are here to help you become resigned to God's will. We are all sinners. May God forgive us all."

I notice the jailer guarding us is grinning as these words seal our fates.

"Prepare for a good death?" my daughter repeats.

Before anyone can answer her, a sudden commotion draws our attention. It is the clattering of horses' hooves. A rider appears brandishing what looks like a rolled-up sheaf of parchment. With peculiar haste, the messenger dismounts and hands it to the cloaked man, the leader of this brotherhood. He takes the missive. The wax seal cracks as he breaks it, opens it, reads it. When he says the words out loud to us, I already know them as if I had conjured the letters myself. It is a decree signed by His Holiness, Pope Alessandro VII.

The words tell us we are condemned.

The words tell us we are to be put to death at the Campo de' Fiori today.

The brief silence that follows is broken by a noise rent from my daughter.

Girolama begins to scream. She curses *Il Papa* at the top of her voice. She flings insults at the Roman courts, the churchmen, the whoresons and bitches who betrayed us. She marches up to this man, a nobleman perhaps. She rages at him.

"You've no legal authority to hang me! I didn't confess anything! You can't put me nor my mother to death, it's against the law!" If anyone notices that she does not defend our friends, then, wisely, they say nothing. She continues to rail at the man who, with sublime patience, stands there, saying nothing.

I am impressed, though I am also reeling. It is hardly a surprise and yet the notion of being alive one minute, then ascending the ladder to the noose and breathing my last is suddenly deeply shocking. Where will our breath, our spirit, our aliveness go once the deed is done? Oh, they may do what they like with our bodies afterward, and they surely will, but what happens to our character, our nature, our very *essence*? This, the moment of my reckoning, is the moment I find myself pondering life's great question, though I have had many long night hours to begin this inquiry. Awaiting news of my fate, I did not wish to confront it, yet now I have no choice. I would laugh at my timing, but it is not amusing. I would cry but I cannot find the strength. I am, therefore, in a state of suspended existence, a pregnant pause, if you will. I am here, and yet I have been told the exact timing of my death. How many are fortunate enough to know this?

Giovanna is leaning against me, weeping now. Perhaps the end will be a relief to her, her pains and agonies will at last be over. Graziosa is slumped on the ground as Girolama continues to screech, issuing a wide range of profanities in the general direction of these hooded men in black robes. How calm they are. How still. I watch my daughter as if she exists many miles away. I feel a sense of curiosity but nothing more. I know this is shock. I know that once the waves of it have rolled in across me, I may curse and flail, but for now, I bear witness.

But what of Maria? She seems to understand. She is pulling her hair out in great clumps. She is quaking and groaning, and so I leave Giovanna and go to her. I try to shush her, but her lamentation grows louder. She cries like a small child, with fat tears that seem to quiver on her cheeks.

"Where are my friends? Where's my beloved, Paolo? Why hasn't he come for me?" Girolama wails now.

The man who appears to lead this confraternity watches her, his expression pitying. He is an older man with a distinguished face, a large Roman nose, and a tall frame.

"Where's the marchesa who promised her protection? Where are the noblewomen who said they'd give me their favor? Where are they? Damn them to hell! Damn them all to hell! Was I just an amusement for bored wives and gentry? Was I their pet to be patted on the head and offered a treat?"

No one speaks.

No one would dare.

Girolama looks at me and I see the little girl who screwed up her face and screamed when she wanted something she could not have. My heart casts out to her. I scoop her into my embrace. I smell her hair, her skin, and grief unfurls inside me. I do not care if I live or not, but I cannot conceive of a world without my daughter. My headstrong, willful, stubborn daughter. My pride and my joy: my life. The horror of the unthinkable events of this day now seem brighter, sharper. They are going to butcher my beloved Girolama and I realize I cannot bear it.

"But it's a waxing moon, a sign of good fortune," she says as a sob, to which I have no reply.

The heavens mock us from above, as they are wont to do, and the Wheel of Fortune turns again, casting us downward into the depths below.

It takes moments to understand that I am crying. Girolama raises her tearstained face to mine, then looks down. What she sees is that, in my hand, I carry the dagger shaped like a crucifix, the one I stole from the convent all those years ago. I hid it alongside the tarot cards, underneath the filth of the straw. It is still beautifully wrought, its handle bound in leather. The blade is thin—it would be a matter of a mere moment to slice across an artery, or a neck, and release the pumping thick blood, finishing what the Inquisition and its agents started.

"But, how do you have this? How have you hidden this from them?" she asks me. We share a smile.

"The same way I hid the cards, daughter." I grin, thinking of them as they lie in the filth of the cell floor. Knowing I shall never cast eyes upon the *tarocchi* again brings me comfort. They have said everything they need to say. And, finally, I have listened.

Then, one of the men, one who hasn't yet spoken, starts.

"She has a knife!" he says.

A brief pause, then chaos ensues.

One of the men steps forward and tries to grab the weapon. Graziosa shrieks, as if she understands. Maria begins to sing again, her voice wavering above the din, its volume increasing, becoming higher and higher. Girolama smiles at me, and I wonder if I will do it. And if so, who will be first? Should I pierce the man's chest, see his look of surprise followed by realization, then terror? Should I lunge at my daughter and save her from the hangman's noose? Or should I turn the implement upon myself, a violent act of revenge, escaping the law we so deride, depriving the Holy See of the pleasure of seeing my pretty ankles dangle above the crowds? I do not think even I know. There is possibility and danger. There is hope and fierce anger. There is retribution, rage, and revenge. All here. All held in this space, as time slides onward.

I hesitate, then step back. Girolama's eyes glint black in the low light of the dancing flames. I hold both my hands up and drop the knife to the floor. The sound seems to reverberate through the jail, fanning out into the narrow streets, across the banks of the Tiber, toward the squares and palaces, the churches, crypts and convents. Across the city it goes, leaving no chamber, no tavern, no boatyard nor tannery, no washing stream nor servant's quarters, no monastery nor butcher's block untouched by its ring.

Then, nothing happens.

No one moves.

Girolama and I stand, looking straight into each other's eyes, and I wonder, *Did I do the right thing?* I do not know the answer. Maria stops her song. Graziosa falls quiet. Giovanna looks between us and, oddly, she starts to laugh, quietly at first, but it builds and so we turn to her. Her reaction goes against everything, and yet I feel it bubbling inside me too. It is a plague of mirth, a contagion that spreads between us. Maria is next to take it up. She starts laughing, cackling wildly. Graziosa mouths something but whatever she is saying is drowned out. Girolama hoots. She is bent double as we laugh and laugh and laugh. From the tail of my eye, I see the men of the confraternity glance sideways at each other, unsure what to do next, unsure how to cure us of this affliction.

We are laughing because it is the beginning of the end. It is time for our story to finish. The curtain is falling, the audience is hushed, awaiting the final stanza. The dagger is kicked, and I watch it spin away. I am seized by the guard. I try to bite his hand, but he is too strong and he grabs me round the neck. Yet, even as this is happening, still we laugh, as if the gates of hell opening up before us are just a moment's distraction, a mere object of amusement at the end of a long journey. The black gates creak and groan as they widen. Inside the sulfurous flames, the yells and shrieks of sinners burning, of their suffering, are drowned out by our laughter.

They take us each aside to write down our confession. None of us are shy anymore. There is no point in holding back the heinous nature of our activities performed in the broiling stews of Rome. In fact, we take great care in detailing our many crimes: our poisonings, abortions, scrying, fortune-telling, our curses and spells. No names are given. They will have to take the trouble to seek those out themselves. This, at least, may be a protection for some.

History may remember us as a troupe of evil-hearted witches, but we are women who live and breathe and love. This is not recorded on the parchment by the noblemen wearing monks' clothing who smell of horse sweat, musk, and fine leather. Our thoughts, dreams, hopes, and visions are not there on that paper either. We exist now only as evidence, as a set of gruesome details, each more nefarious than the next. They do not speak of the women we saved, the beatings we stopped, the babies we breathed life into. They do not speak of the peace our remedies gave, the relief and gratitude from those we served. No, our actions are judged by men in hoods who represent a church that does not recognize us except as sinners and she-devils. But we know. We know our gods whisper in our ears that all is seen, all is well, and death is a small thing, a gentle step into another realm, and we are comforted.

As my confession, such as it is, is finished, I am asked to sign it. I hesitate, the quill in my hand, the ink pooling on the nib, and I realize I do not possess a family name. As my natural father was a mystery to me, and to Mamma too, I was never given one. My mother went by Francesco's name, Di Adamo, but that is something I could never do.

"Mistress, you must sign or be condemned to hell. I urge you to write your name, if indeed you can."

The scribe is not being unkind. Many women of my class and status are unable to write their letters. He does not know I grew up in a court dedicated to art and culture, to learning and literature. I was able to read my letters before I was four, to write before I was six. But what do I write under the lines of his small, neat lettering?

Then, it comes to me.

Born without a father, I have only my mother's name; I have Teofania.

For ease, for simplicity, I put the quill to the parchment and I write: *Giulia Tofana.* The scribe nods and I hand him back his writing tool, a crow's feather, sharpened.

It is late in the morning before we each receive the sacrament. Then, our coverings are taken and replaced with sacking daubed with large black crosses. We stare now at each other as we are transformed into the condemned. Our laughter has dissipated. It was just a moment of hysteria, and it has gone. I cannot take my eyes off my daughter. Separated, we cannot touch. I cannot feel the smooth skin of my daughter's hand, the roughness of Giovanna's. Maria is moaning now and shaking her head. Graziosa dribbles and curses, though her words are mostly unintelligible. Girolama and I keep our gaze steady. We look at each other, drawing strength perhaps, acknowledging our love for each other, and everything we have been to each other. Tears fall, and I do not stop them. I do not wipe them away from my dirt-smeared cheeks, the cuts from my scalp still weeping.

I barely notice the hangman arrive. He is cloaked in black. His face is covered. It is Graziosa who sees him first and she begins to scream. I cannot run to her to hold her. A jailer grips my arm and so I am forced to watch her distress. My daughter spits and throws a curse. With some ceremony, and a little effort, as the things he carries are weighty, he stands in front of each of us and prepares to slide a noose over our heads. Graziosa squirms but they hold her up. Maria embraces the rope as if it is a garland of flowers, a necklace from a lover. Giovanna accepts the heavy coil with her lovely eyes downcast, though she cries with pain when it drops onto her neck. Of all of us, she faces her death with the most dignity and peace. She is resigned to what is coming, to dying publicly. My love for her whom I have known for so many years wells up inside me and I fear I will choke on the power of it.

Then, it is my turn.

The hangman nods and I bow my head. My feet are bare and bloodied. My hands, still stained with tinctures, are roughened, my nails ragged and dirty. The rope is thick, rough, surprisingly heavy. I wonder how I will carry the burden of it. We are all famished, weak, and shaking.

We are led, carried, pushed outside and into the square that leads off from the jail. There, awaiting our entrance, are the carts and oxen that will be our fine carriages. Suddenly, I see Mamma's face, white and pinched as she arrived at the Piano della Marina for her execution so many years ago. She died to save my skin. She died because of me, and it is the secret I have carried since I was that pregnant child of fourteen. My mother would have guessed it was I who laced Francesco's wine that night. She went to the scaffold an innocent woman—of that crime, at least.

I was too frightened to tell the *Inquisitori*. My mother was too brave to tell them, her love for me too strong. She protected me, and briefly, we kept the darkest secret of all. But they say we sinners never escape punishment for our sins, though the crime may not fit the discipline. I have never regretted killing him. I have only ever regretted the loss of my mother. I watched her being strangled knowing it was I who killed Francesco. I have carried that moment through my life, and now, finally, I will be free of it.

I stumble toward the wooden cart and haul myself up. Here, in this cart, for my final journey, I will be cursed. I will be screamed at and condemned. I will know myself a woman hated, a woman feared, as we make our slow way through Rome's streets to the place of our death. The cart jolts forward. I clutch the side, but not before I feel the first globule of spittle land on my arm. The crowds gather. They are rowdy. They sound excited and outraged in equal measure. As we move off, the wheels of the carts lurching over the cobbled roads, we are pelted with clods of dung, with vegetable peelings that stink of rot. The sun beats down onto our newly blindfolded faces, our bare heads, as if it too is throwing its rays. Despite this, I realize I am smiling. *It won't be long now, Mamma. Soon, I'll join you and you'll meet my daughter, your grandchild. Soon, I'll tell you how sorry I am, how thankful that you gave me life by sacrificing yours, even though it has ended the same way.* Even this thought brings me comfort, brings me closer in my heart to my mother.

A large crucifix draped with black cloth sways as we progress. I saw it before the blindfolds were tied around our shorn heads. It is the banner of the confraternity accompanying us on this, our last journey. They chant the prayers that are said at these moments. At various points along the journey, the carts grind to an uncertain halt, and a trumpet sounds. Our crimes are proclaimed. We are the women who traded in poison that killed five hundred husbands, perhaps even a thousand! Or so they say. They have said so many things, I do not listen anymore. Time drags on. The heat intensifies. The noise of the swelling crowds builds. Finally, finally, we stop and there is a hush. I realize we have arrived at our destination, though I do not know where that is.

# 64

*Alessandro*

The heat is stifling but I barely notice it.

The crowds are filthy, reeking of sweat and animal ordure, but I find it does not alarm me. The burning sunshine is hot on the cloak I have wrapped around myself, but I am determined to see her, the woman whose death warrant I signed. I am pushed and shunted until I am almost at the foot of the gallows. There is anticipation and excitement. Nut sellers cry out their wares, the *avvisi* pamphleteers too.

This may be the first time in my life I have ever entered the arena of the common populace, and yet I find I do not care at all for my safety.

The sound of the drums begins to echo from the streets beyond. There is a rush of people and I stumble. Looking up, I see the large crucifix swaying over the heads of the crowd. It comes closer and closer, and I fight the sudden urge to run away back to the calm of the Vatican. I slipped out of a servants' entrance within the warren of rooms and corridors that make up my apartments. They will surely have noticed my absence by now and may be searching for me. Strangely, I find I do not care. I will return, but first I must watch what I have prayed for.

Now, the carts have stopped. There are shrieks and curses, prayers and invocations. I stay silent, waiting.

I see her shorn head, the sackcloth, the rope, her eyes covered with a blindfold. Tears stream down my face as she stands on the cart, ready to be escorted to the gallows. They fall silently and are unstoppable. I will carry this image until my last breath, knowing it was I who killed her.

When I write to Mamma tonight, it will be for the last time.

# 65

*Giulia*

My breath catches in my throat.

A male hand takes mine and I am helped down. I wonder if I will faint as someone screeches in my ear. The crowds cheer and heckle.

We make our way forward, through the throng of people. The blindfold covers my eyes but as I reach the step to the platform, the stage upon which my sisterhood and I will die, I look upward. As I do so, the black material of my blindfold slips. My stomach tightens, but I do not see the executioner. Instead, there is something shimmering in the skies. Breathless, I stare at the star that glimmers above me, above my beloved poisoners. Perhaps it is a trick of the mind, a shining delusion, but I can see it, I can see *her*. There is a woman with rippling hair, with deep green eyes, colored like the ocean after a storm. She is holding *La Stella*, the eight-pointed star.

Mamma is leading me home.

# EPILOGUE

*Ella esortando il popolo a pregare,*
*Dio per li falli suoi, Sali la scala.*
*Non sò se allor potesse astrologare,*
*Se havea sorte benigna, o Stella mala?*
*Arte o modo non ha d'indovinare.*

—·—

Exhorting the people to pray to the Lord,
For her sins, up she went to the top of the stair.
What of her predicting her heavenly reward,
Whether benign fate or a malignant star?
A soothsayer's arts us no longer affords.

—Francesco Ascione

# THE TALE OF THE
# MONSTROUS POISONER
# OF PALERMO,
## AND HER
# WICKED SISTERHOOD!

MDCLIX

This day, the sixth day of July in the year 1659, is printed a most Foul tale of Treachery, Witchcraft and Sorcery! Five women, accused and tried for Murder and Heresy, were found to be guilty and convicted of murdering in Cold Blood the men of the Eternal City of Rome through the work of their Cursed Water with no taste nor odor.

In this, the very heart of the Catholic Church, the most holy of cities, where His Holiness Pope Alessandro the Seventh resides, has sat a spider's web of Deceit and Magick whereby this Deadly Potion has been brewed and given to wives and concubines to kill and maim their spouses and those set above them by God. Roman sepulchers have been filled with victims of their Poisonous Beverage. They expired without fever, remaining ruddy and with all appearance of Good Health, as if they were still alive.

Hear this, that the Monstrous Witch whose name is Giulia Tofana, and whose mother was executed for the same crime in the year 1633 in Palermo by the grace of the Holy Office of the Inquisition, was not alone in her dealings with the Devil and his league of dark angels, spirits, and imps. For she had accomplices who shared the stage with her: the last act in a play that has seen the murder of many Righteous and upstanding gentlemen including a Duke. Those witches: Foul Sorceress Giovanna de Grandis, Treacherous Witch Graziosa Farina, Most Wicked Temptress Maria Spinola, and Devil's Whore

Girolama, *La Strologa*, who conjured many dark creatures, predicting the death of *Il Papa* himself. All five gave their necks to the noose as their despicable Circle of Poisoners received the Justice they deserved, and all of Italy is saved from the Terror they have struck into the hearts of God-fearing men.

*La Siciliana's* terrible crimes ended as they began: with the Scaffold. An antidote has been found; water of lemon and vinegar, and so this Poison has been vanquished, the trail of Murder, destroyed. Upon the order of His Holiness, *Il Papa*, her body was not buried with the other Satanic witches in the sepulcher but was taken to the convent where she had tried to flee holy justice.

Alessandro the Seventh instructed the guards to undertake Godly duties in the form of taking the most-afeared body of the Witch Tofana to the place where they were once pleased to offer Sanctuary. This Sorceress, wrapped in bloodied linens, and handled with grave seriousness by those who feared there may still be the Devil at work, was brought to the place. As proof of Witchcraft, the linens fell from her face and it was revealed to all that the Corpse was smiling.

This is the avowed word of those who witnessed this Great and Terrible event. May they writhe in Hell. Rome is saved and God's holy order restored.

# Author Note

This book is based on the legend of Giulia Tofana, a woman said to have poisoned a thousand men in seventeenth-century Palermo, Naples, and Rome. While some of the characters are based on actual historical figures, their portrayals are ficti-tious, as are many of the events that surround them. I have listed below the books that helped in my research. I owe a debt of gratitude to the authors who have painstakingly researched this period, and some of the events and people this book is based upon; in particular, the work of academic Craig A. Monson, who wrote *The Black Widows of the Eternal City*, which was an excellent resource uncovering trial documents from the infamous Spana prosecution, which forms the dark heart of this book. Cambridge academician and historian Mike Dash's essay "Aqua Tofana: Slow-Poisoning and Husband-Killing in 17th Century Italy" was central to the research I undertook, providing an overview of the Tofana legend and the undetectable poison that formed the basis of this most Italian myth. Palermo historian Giovanna Fiume's essay "Cursing, Poisoning and Femi-nine Morality. The Case of the 'Vinegar Hag' in Late Eighteenth-Century Palermo" inspired the character of Graziosa Farina, while Maria Pia Di Bella created a forensically detailed por-trait of the execution of murderers, poisoners, and criminals in her essay "Palermo's Past Public Executions and Their Lingering Memory," published in *The Hurt(ful) Body* (ed. Tomas Macso-tay, Cornelis van der Haven, and Karel Vanhaesebrouck).

I am indebted to Ketta Grazia in Palermo for her work translating obscure ancient texts and the staff at the Palermo State Archives and Communal Library.

Whether Giulia Tofana existed or not is still a matter for debate, but as with all good stories, her legend lives on. This is my retelling of Giulia, a woman who lived, loved, and died in an age when women were told what to do and how to be. She walked her own path, and, in this book, I offer a version of her story that celebrates her power and independence as much as it exposes her oppression and subjugation.

For a full bibliography of works referenced in the writing of this book, please visit unionsquareandco.com/9781454957461 /a-poisoners-tale-by-cathryn-kemp/.

# Glossary

**Aborto**: Abortion.

**Acqua**: Water—but in this context, it was used as the name of the poison (trial documents suggest it was also called *acquetta* or "little water" by the circle of poisoners and their clients). (Sicilian)

**Aflitto/a**: The afflicted or condemned one. The person (male/female) who had been sentenced to death.

**Alambicco**: An alembic. An alchemical still consisting of two vessels connected by a tube.

**Avvisi**: Gallows pamphlets. Newsletters, handwritten at first, then printed, produced with intrigue, gossip, and hearsay to sell at public executions.

**Baiocchi**: An ancient Italian currency denomination, value equivalent to a shilling.

**Bianchi**: Noblemen from the Company of the Santissimo Crocifisso, or Bianchi (the White Ones) whose task it was to comfort and prepare those sentenced to death from prison to scaffold. (Sicilian)

**Buttana**: Prostitute. (Sicilian)

**Camicia**: Linen undershirt worn by men and women. Women's was full-length and was worn under the heavier dresses. Also worn as a nightdress.

**Chopines**: Type of women's platform shoe, most notably worn in Venice by courtesans.

**Corna**: Horns. Making the sign of the *corna* to ward off bad luck or misfortune.

**Decollati**: Executed criminals.

**Falda:** Papal vestment that formed a long skirt with a train that extended beneath the hem of the alb.

**Fica:** Slang word for a woman's private parts (from the Italian word for *fig*).

**Figlia mia:** My daughter.

**Giuli:** Currency. The giulio was a papal coin with a value of 2 grossi or 10 baiocchi. Giuli (pl).

**Innamorati:** The lovers. Stock characters within commedia dell'arte. Despite many obstacles, the plays show the lovers always united in the end.

**Inquisitori:** Inquisitors from the Holy Office of the Inquisition (*Suprema Congregatio Sanctae Romanae et Universalis Inquisitionis*—the Supreme Sacred Congregation of the Roman and Universal Inquisition).

**Lazaretto:** Plague house or quarantine station for contagious illness.

**Lenza:** A jeweled band tied around the forehead.

**Malocchio:** Evil eye.

**Medico della peste:** Plague doctor.

**Peste:** Plague.

**Physick:** Practice of medicine.

**La Rota:** The Wheel of Fortune card in tarot.

**Saggia:** Cunning or shrewd woman.

**Santu diavuluni:** Sicilian expression meaning Holy Devil.

**Seminaria:** Plague seeds—it was believed they floated in the air as a miasma of tiny particles, causing plague (*seminaria contagionis*).

**Sfortuna:** Malchance or misfortune.

**Sibille**: Torture method where cord was tied around fingers and tightened. It was usually reserved for women and children.

**Strappado**—An implement of torture using ropes and a pulley. The victim is hung by their wrists, which are tied behind their back.

**Strega/streghe**: Witch/witches.

**Tarocchi**: Tarot cards, originally used as a game rather than for occult practices.

**Trinzale**: Net sheath or cap worn on the back of the head, held in place by the *lenza,* and often decorated with jewels.

**Vicolo**: Alley.

# Acknowledgments

This book is dedicated to every woman who knows how it feels when his key turns in the lock.

It is dedicated to female rage and resilience, to our strength and frailties. It is an ode to courage, to loss, and to freedom.

To my agent, Jane at Graham Maw Christie, who pushed me as a writer with a seed of an idea, to the unfolding of the story I wanted to tell, thank you.

To my editors Alice Rodgers, Olamide Olatunji-Bello, and Imogen Nelson at Transworld, Penguin Random House, for their dedication, inspiration, and for challenging me as a writer, and for knowing Giulia as a woman of our time as much as a shadow reaching through history.

To all the team at Transworld, including Publicity Manager Chloë Rose, Marketing Manager Melissa Kelly, Rights Director Catherine Wood, Rights Manager Beth Wood, Head of Translation Lucy Beresford-Knox, Senior Rights Manager Rachael Sharples, and cover designers Andrew Davis and Marianne Issa El-Khoury, thank you for bringing my story out into the world.

To the incredible team at Union Square & Co., I want to thank Executive Editor Barbara Berger, Managing Editor Christina Stambaugh, cover designers Elizabeth Mihaltse Lindy (front) and Jared Oriel (back), interior designer Rich Hazelton, and Production Manager Sandy Noman.

I owe a debt of gratitude to the Society of Authors, which was kind enough to support my research with an Authors' Foundation Award. For a single working parent with health issues this was transformational, enabling me to travel to the archives and libraries of Palermo and Rome.

To all those who helped with research, translation, and sourcing ancient texts—I can mention only a few people, but there were so many who supported the evolution of this book. I thank you all, and in particular Ketta Grazia and Pema Sanders; Dr. Andrew King, professor of English Literature and Literary Studies, University of Greenwich; Giovanna Fiume, historian and author, University of Palermo; Jayne Francis; Fanny at Sant'Agostino in Palermo; and the staff at the Palermo archives and communal library. To my Rome guide, Rob Miller, for his late-night storytelling, and to poisoner Michael Coby for his (so far, harmless) instruction. To Josie Humber of the Novelry, who read an early draft, thank you for casting a spotlight into the darkest areas of this novel.

To Sabrina Broadbent who taught me to "write in scenes" on the Writing a Novel course at Faber Academy. To Miriam Nevill, Emma Zacharia, and everyone on the course—your input, critique, and wisdom as writers continues to be inestimably helpful.

To Elena, for proper Italian-strength coffee, endless encouragement, and impromptu translation.

To my partner and son for everything.

# Book Club Questions for Discussion

1. What similarities can you draw between the characters of Giulia Tofana and her nemesis, Pope Alessandro?

2. What were Teofania's motives when teaching her own daughter to make poison? Do you believe she was condemning Giulia to a brutal death?

3. Why would Giulia choose to continue her mother's legacy after it led to her execution? What other options did Giulia have at the time, considering her traumatic childhood?

4. Motherhood is a recurring theme in the novel. In what ways did Giulia's and Teofania's experience of the Spanish court and their life in Palermo influence Giulia's relationship with her own daughter, Girolama?

5. What fascinated you the most about the circle of female poisoners? What did you make of their blind loyalty to Giulia?

6. The women in this book often made sacrifices that took them down the darkest and loneliest paths. Are there any common themes you can draw from their stories? And in what ways do their lives mirror or contrast with the average woman's experience in today's society?

7. Why did the Mother Superior attempt to shield Giulia from the mob? Can we draw comparisons between the two very different women's lives?

8. How do you feel about Girolama's behavior as a daughter, knowing the sacrifices Teofania and Giulia made?

9. How would you describe Pope Alessandro's fixation on Giulia? What were your expectations and how did they change at the end?

10. How did your perceptions of Stefano Bracchi evolve throughout the novel?

11. When Giulia reveals her final secret, does your opinion of her change at all? If you stepped into her shoes, would you make the same decisions that she did?